SELENIUM NIGHT

A SHADOWSHIFTER NOVEL

KHARMA KELLEY

WICKED BAYOU PRESS

Formatting: Wicked Bayou Press

Editor: Pinpoint Editing

Cover Design: Kharma Kelley

ISBN(s):

(Print) 978-0-9981573-4-4

(Ebook) 978-0-9981573-3-7

GLOSSARY

ShadowShifter - Human souls that were fused with the soul of a wolf. Their natural state is human form. However, they have the power to change in various metamorphoses of a wolf. They can go from human to wolf or half-man half-wolf (like a werewolf) There are two breeds of ShadowShifters: Aristans, which were created by one of the moon sisters, Arista. The other breed are Thesians, created as a retaliatory gesture by Arista's twin, Thesia.

Azanesti Order (Azans) - Aristan fighters/protectors of the pack. Chosen by the Alpha, young fighters are trained to protect the pack and the Alpha's family when away. Azans work as a unit and can be terrifying in full force.

Selenium Circle - A ritual where any Aristan can compete to become next Alpha of the pack.

Mamyn - "Mother" in Aristan.

Gravanos - "Hello" or "Greetings" in Aristan language.

Xerhmon - Aristan term of endearment. It means "My lovely".

Lukos - "Alpha" in Aristan language.

Courtesha - A derogatory term meaning "whore" or "courtesan". Aristans and Thesians alike use human men and women for casual sex, but they typically do not become anything more as they are an exposure risk.

Whisper - Ability to speak to other ShadowShifters through a telepathic method that humans cannot hear. This is typically done when some or all are in wolf's skin, when it's impossible to physically speak. Whispering is an ability of both breeds of ShadowShifters, as all still share a powerful mental connection.

Amplify - Like Whispering, it's the ability to widen the range of a ShadowShifter's telepathic connection. Whereas Whispering is a connection to those close to you, Amplifying significantly widens that range to call for assistance. Other ShadowShifters (even enemies) within range can also hear, which always makes using this a risk.

ACKNOWLEDGMENTS

TO MY READERS

Dear Readers,

I'm so excited to introduce you to my first book in my new ShadowShifters series. It stems from its own little legend that has been knocking around in my head for a few years. I've always been a lover of werewolves and shifters in general and wanted to weave a new world of them of my own. It's been an incredible journey writing this novel and have found such a strong appreciation for my characters, I know that you will fall in love with them just as much as I did. Expect more books from this series with your favorite characters taking the main stage for their own adventure.

I invite you to discover my fantasy world of the Shadow-Shifters; strong, sexy supernaturals with the power to shape shift into the cunning wolf. Whether you like your heroes dark and brooding or sensual and intelligent, prepare to read some sizzling pages of these badass creatures of the night!

Dream big, and love fierce my book-loving hellions.

With Light,
    Kharma Kelley

PROLOGUE

THE TWIN GODDESSES

A Thousand Years Ago...

The large, golden doors of the Selene Palace flew open as Thesia came charging to her sister's chambers, her eyes glowing orange with fury as she reached Arista's chamber doors and began to bang against the silver lunar wood until it started to splinter.

"Arista! Don't you dare ignore me! Come out this instant!" She continued to rap onto the door until it jerked open. Arista's hand-maiden stood at the entrance, frowning yet still bowing as Thesia charged past her. "Where is your mistress, you little brute?"

"I'm here."

Thesia turned to see her twin sister at the balcony. Standing calm, Arista's raven hair was twisted up into a bun, but her stray tendrils flew like banners in the wind. Thesia's frown intensified as she perceived the air of defiance in the room and the smug look of her sister. "Your creatures are an abomination! You lied to me!" She marched up closer to Arista, wanting to close the space between them.

Arista shook her head. "I did nothing of the sort - and how dare you call them an abomination!"

1

"They don't respect me. You told me that they would love us both! That they would praise us both! But at night I hear them call to you, Arista. They love only you, and it's repulsive." She folded her arms, making a barrier for her heaving, angered breaths. "I will not stand by and be forgotten and disrespected by these creatures. You must destroy them now!"

Arista stepped forward to Thesia with a fierceness so intense she instinctively stepped back, staring into the mirror image of her sister.

"You will not tell me what to do with my own people." Arista's voice was dark and stern. "It is not my fault they love me so fiercely. I made every effort for them to worship us both. This is not my doing."

When she molded the first of the ShadowShifters, it was done out of love. The communegers worshiped the moon and its gifts of the tides and harvest so deeply that she wanted to give them a reward for their honor. Her sister never really listened to them, but she did, and decided to transform them into beings who shared the essence of her and Thesia's beloved animal, the wolf. They were beautiful, loyal and cunning creatures who fought with valor, and she was proud of them. She only wished Thesia made more effort to love them too. She would never learn that love wasn't an obligation, and that the truest love was out of respect.

Thesia scoffed at the remark. "Then if they are disobedient, why won't you smite them? Or punish them?" Thesia's eyes stung with the pain of her humiliation.

When Arista told her she created the ShadowShifters, she was concerned about the wrath the other gods would put on them for tampering with nature. But when she observed them and remembered how they honored the moon, she agreed. The goddesses were to remain forever chaste and to never know a man's touch, so to Arista's point, she convinced Thesia that they would be her children. They would become the children that the goddesses could never have. But the ShadowShifters rarely acknowledged her. They were wayward, ungrateful children that only loved Arista.

"Do not ask me to hurt them, Thesia. Because I won't!"

"I see. You defend them because you condone their treatment of me." Thesia's eyes watered in spite of her fury. "They ignore your own sister. Your blood. And you accept this behavior."

"That's not true, Thesia." Arista tried to grab her sister's hand but Thesia moved away. A pit grew in her stomach even thinking about hurting them, scaring them into praising Thesia. Why? Because they loved her instead of Thesia? Because her sister was jealous? It wasn't right. "You may be a goddess who enjoys hurting the innocent, but I will not hurt them just because of your ego. I love you sister, with all of my heart, but you cannot ask me to force them to love you. You will have to prove to them that you are worthy of their love, just as I have done."

Blinking the tears away, Thesia rubbed her eyes and exhaled, releasing some of the mounting tension within her. She glared at her sister. She had some nerve to ask such a thing. "Prove to them?" Her voice escalated as the lunar winds picked up through the balcony. "You expect a goddess of Selene to grovel and prove to your little beasts that I am worthy of their love?" Thesia walked slowly towards Arista, her hair and red chiton dress flapping in the wind. The windows began to rattle and Arista's handmaiden screamed as vases began to break around the chambers.

Arista's eyes glowed, beaming with an orange hue akin to the fires of the underworld. "Thesia, I'm warning you to let this go." Her hands tightened into fists, anticipating her sister to strike her. *Just like her to throw a tantrum. But I'm not going to stand by and let her ruin this because her ego has gotten the better of her.*

Thesia charged to Arista and gripped her throat. "You dare defy me? Defy us? We are of the same blood and you'd let them humiliate me? You enjoy this. If our lives weren't bound together, I would break your neck!" Arista clawed at Thesia's hand. "Now you listen to me, sister. You will do as I say and punish those who do not pay me homage as their goddess, or I will reign down terror on them so furious all the fields of earth will be wet with the blood of your precious ShadowShifters! Do you understand?"

Arista growled and pushed her sister off her with such force she flew across the room and against the wall, sliding to the floor. Arista stood still, tears building in her eyes as she watched her sister slowly rise and reach to touch the back of her head. Pulling her hand back, she hissed at the blood on her fingers. Thesia cut her eyes to her sister, glaring in contempt. It was then, at that moment, that Arista felt her heart shatter. Never had they ever struck each other or intentionally hurt one another. The bond between them of kinship and love was now over. Only obligation held them together, and the pain of it hit Arista in the gut. "I'm sorry, sister. You left me no choice."

Thesia stood up firm and straightened her gown. "No, Arista. It is *you* who left me no choice. Havoc awaits your creatures, you'll see. They can stay your children, for I am not their mother." She began to walk towards the doors. "I will create my own children who will worship and adore me, and only me." She stopped and whipped her head around to meet her sister's eyes. "And you will know what it's like to be hated, and your children will never know peace! We are sisters only by blood, and I shall never forgive you for these creatures you have wrought. Never!"

With those damning words, Thesia stormed out of her twin sister's chambers, and out of her graces. Arista cried with the realization that her ShadowShifters were fated to carry the feud of the goddesses onto the realms of earth. She knew Thesia would make good on her vow and ensure her people would never know peace, just as she would never know her sister's love ever again.

ASHES

S moke hovered above the commune like ominous, celestial bodies sailing and contorting against the night wind. The roars of the fire that had ravaged their once beautiful and peaceful community finally stifled the howls and screams.

Aidan cradled the petite, limp body in his arms, his hand interlocking with one of her own. His body flinched as his fingers were no longer warm in hers. It hurt to look at her, as he couldn't have imagined a time there wasn't absolute warmth to her touch. Had he not known the truth, he'd think her asleep. About to wake up any moment and scorn him for pitying her when he should be out fighting.

Aidan stared at her, waiting.

But there was nothing. Just the crackling sound of flames nearby.

His mother was gone.

His eyes closed, envisioning her as she had always been to him. Stubborn. Beautiful. Alive.

Aidan tensed as he saw Cameron run towards him. As if Cameron's heart stopped cold, he skidded to a halt when he saw whom Aidan was cradling.

Her battered, crimson-clad body laid quietly in Aidan's careful grip. His heart sank.

"Arista's hand, Aidan," Cameron kneeled down, facing a very silent Aidan. "No, not her."

Gritting his teeth, Aidan stared down at his mother. Ninon, his foster mother who had stopped at nothing to take him in and give him a family, was dead.

Aidan's tongue tasted the metallic flavor of blood. His blood, as his fangs had grown. The wolf in him wanted to avenge, but the human heart needed to grieve.

Not now. I won't fall apart. No, not ever. Not when this must be put right. I'll greive later.

"Where are the others? Who all are injured or dead?" Aidan's somber tone reflected more of a military general than a heart-broken son. It could've fooled anyone.

If only Cameron could be fooled so easily.

Cameron stood up and ran his bloodied fingers through his white blond hair. His face was pale against the moon and the faint orange shadows of dying flames. " Jaks, Chase and Aaron are working to put the fire out with some other ShadowShifters. I just left Phillip and Jason, who are guarding the children east of the lake."

Aidan nodded. Who do we know in the local fire department? We need damage control on this. Is Jesse on duty?"

Cameron nodded. "Yeah. We called him as soon as the fires started. He's aware and coming, but we gotta collect and move the bodies first." Cameron was grateful the council agreed to some Aristan infiltration into the first-responder community. The days of isolating themselves from human interaction were long gone and when disaster struck, it was important to have one of their own positions to help sweep up incidents.

Aidan wasn't a fan of human society, but it had its uses. "We'll take care of that now." Aidan looked at his mother, then up at Cameron. "And Gage?"

Cameron looked away and sucked in an ominous breath. "We

found him behind Ninon's quarters. Looks like he fought a hell of a fight."

But not nearly enough. Or else Ninon would still be alive.

It's time to let her go, he thought, as he eased her to the grass. He gripped the medallion she gave him tight in his hand. When he released his grip and opened it, his hand was imprinted with the same elaborate and mystic prints from the Aristan compass he held. Ninon's blood stained the markings, a dismal symbol of the fate of their race. From the moment the Goddess Arista breathed life into the very first ShadowShifters, her twin sister Goddess Thesia vowed to destroy them all. After thousands of years watching their backs from humans and Thesians alike, only to have just a few clans survive—perhaps Thesia was making good on her vow.

Thesians.

His brother had help. The stench of it was unmistakable. With all that had happened, to even call Kieran a brother was enough to make Aidan retch. No 'brother' would betray and spit on his family the way he did. No son would ever hurt his mother.

Growling, Aidan looked at everyone. "Where is that piece of shit?" he muttered through clenched teeth to Cameron. For a brief moment his own outburst shocked him. That familiar sting of anger he tried to bury was starting to claw its way out.

Cameron didn't flinch or move. He was quite used to Aidan letting his anger lash out at his comrades. The other Azans respected Aidan, but kept their distance socially. No one understood his rough demeanor, except Cameron. He was one of the few who knew Aidan's feral past—and didn't judge him for it. In his eyes, Aidan had every reason to let himself go into the dark, and he had a lot of respect for the wolf. But even he could agree that Aidan wasn't the friendliest guy around. "Fled. The others tried to get a track on him, but he used the fire to distract everyone."

"What about the others who helped him?"

"Others?" Cameron's expression puzzled. "ShadowShifters?"

Aidan growled. "You don't catch that in the air? Thesians were here. I can't tell how many. Maybe one, maybe more, but one was definitely in this area."

"I agree," a voice came from behind them.

Aidan and Cameron both turned to the jet-black timber wolf approaching them. Its bright silver eyes were somber as the wolf focused on the dead older woman at their feet.

The wolf paused and bent its back as if to stretch. The beast howling, accepted the change, trading his fur for skin. Traded his lupine amber eyes for dark human eyes as his body became that of a man. His lithe body rose to its feet, walking meticulously towards them.

"I'm very sorry about Ninon, Lukos," Onyx said quietly. His eyes, now an unnaturally bright gray, still reflected sincerity. "She was a brave and beautiful Aristan."

Aidan didn't respond to the sympathetic gesture. Only Onyx and a few others called him Lukos, which meant 'Alpha' in their Aristan tongue. One of the oldest in the pack, he knew Tiberius Bloodlocke when they were young pups.

Onyx looked to Cameron. "Who is responsible for this?"

Cameron stepped forward. "The Thesians couldn't have done this alone."

"You're damn right they didn't." Aidan growled. "Kieran's scent is on Ninon's body."

Onyx shook his head. "Of course; she was his mother."

Aidan looked down at the cold, lifeless woman laid at his feet, and wanted to scream to the heavens.

She was my mother, too.

"Did you really think that mattered to Kieran? We have reprimanded him before about cavorting with Thesians."

"It's true, Onyx." Cameron interjected. "If anyone had access to bring Thesians into this, it would be Kieran."

"We have no proof, Azans. We can't just accuse our own without him speaking for himself. Where is he?" Onyx said with a frown.

"He fled."

A deep voice boomed behind them. They turned to see a slender, gray-haired man staring at Aidan. Aidan couldn't tell if the elder was smiling or squinting from the smoke in the air. It was always hard to tell anything concrete about Bastien.

"Some are tracking him now."

"I declare Kieran Bloodlocke solely responsible for the deaths and carnage involved here," Aidan said with his back to them. The three wolves went silent as Aidan spoke the ceremonial request for an order. "He is to face the Rite of Judgment."

"First, we have to apprehend him, Alpha. He's likely fled far from the only home he ever knew." Onyx looked out to the torn commune that was the pack's home. Here, they had lived in peace, many working and living quiet lives within the human world, with the children being safe from harm. After the loss of Tiberius, the pack just wanted to heal and grow, nested in the dark, rich forests of seclusion to own land away from humans' prying eyes until they were ready to mainstream again.

Aidan's face was stern with anger. "Well, let's do that."

Onyx sighed. He began to wish that someone other than Ninon was harmed. Why her? She was Tiberius' mate, and Kieran and Leigh's mother. Not to mention Aidan's foster mother. A wolf who wanted vengeance. Aidan was a born leader, sure, but his quick temper and stubbornness had been proven potent and lethal many times before. But that was a long time ago. Tiberius and Ninon tried to make sure of that.

"So be it. I will structure the meeting."

"Meeting?" Aidan scoffed. "You can't be serious, Onyx."

There was no humor in Onyx's expression. "I am. You know the rules, Aidan. You may be Alpha, but the council needs to sort this mess out. Bastien and I will structure the meeting with the others. We will get to the bottom of this and assign orders where need be."

"Not to worry, Aidan." Bastien patted Aidan on the back solemnly as he walked away. "You will have justice."

"And what of Ninon's justice?" Aidan glared bitterly.

Bastien froze and turned around. "Vengeance is ugly, Aidan."

"So is murder."

Bastien frowned at Aidan's cold retort and walked towards him. He eyed him thoroughly, a low growl in his throat. "You wish to quarrel with me, Aidan?"

Aidan looked levelly into his eyes, silent, his face stern as the orange color of the fires started to die down off the planes of his face. "Not yet."

"He's not quarreling, Bastian, " Onyx interjected as he moved between them. "Now let's go and prepare. Aidan, I presume the Azans will handle getting things in—"

"We'll handle everything. Including my mother's burial." Aidan did not take his eyes off Bastien even as he answered Onyx.

Though Bastien was his elder, he never cared much for the old wolf. Tiberius thought the world of him, but there was always something about the wolf that bothered Aidan. What drove him crazy was that he didn't know what it was. Nevertheless, he didn't dismiss his hunches. His past had taught him that nothing had more anger and treachery behind it than a smiling face. He recalled the last time he trusted a smiling, kind face...

All he could taste was dirt and blood as he kneeled naked before them.

"Why do you think he has no idea what he is?"

The other wolf looked down at him and smiled. Aidan looked up at the wolf's hands that were covered in blood. Aidan's blood. He appeared mammoth-sized from Aidan's kneeling angle. He feared he'd never forget the wolf's amber eyes that began to sneer at him. "Oh, he'll know once we're finally done with him. He'll be well informed of how filthy, weak Aristans are not welcomed in our territory..."

Oh yes. The past had taught him *very* well.

Bastien turned to join Onyx. They both ran until their bodies turned again to fur amongst the woods.

Cameron sighed as he caught a familiar scent. "Shit. Leigh's coming."

"I know." Aidan walked towards the opening of the brush. No

sooner than his movements quickened, a blond woman came running through.

"Mamyn!? Mamyn!" She sobbed as Aidan caught her, preventing her from going to her mother's body. She clawed and pushed, but Aidan held her still.

"No, Leigh! She's gone." He said to her, staring into her dark, obsidian eyes. "Ninon's gone."

With tears in her eyes, Leigh growled deep in her throat, baring her canines in anger. "No! She can't! Let me by!" She tried to keep her face strong in anger, but as she kept repeating her demand to Aidan, she felt her lips tremble. Finally, she stopped struggling and pushed herself from him. "Who did this? All of this?"

"We're going to find out." Cameron said, coming to her side.

She looked into Aidan's eyes and frowned. "I think you already know who did this, don't you?" Aidan found out a long time ago that he was a bad liar to his sister. Her face resembled that of Ninon and her tenacity more so. "Was it Kieran? Aidan, tell me."

"I have no proof, Leigh—"

"But is it what your gut tells you?" She looked in Aidan's eyes, searching. "The truth."

He answered with a solemn nod. "I have no doubt that Kieran is involved in this." An ominous air rose around them, and Aidan found himself ashamed to see Leigh lose all her family. And the salt in the wound: her own brother being the destroyer of it all.

She straightened herself up and swallowed the rest of her pain. "Then I have no doubt that you will avenge our mother."

"Kieran will pay for what he has done." Aidan said, his body already rigid with anger at what had transpired that night. Leigh walked away through the night filled with the unified howling of wolves. Their strong calling haunted the dark, but not giving way to the agony behind it. It was time for council. He only hoped that the old hounds of the council would leave him be to issue his own justice.

2

THICKER THAN BLOOD

Kieran slowed to a trot as he reached a creek. Two other wolves trailed close behind him as he stopped by a tree. His body exhausted, Kieran stretched until he appeared in his human form. He growled at the release of his body as he looked at the dark sky marred with the faint orange haze of his crime. The night filled with howling from the camp, the sound of mourning echoing through the woods. It nestled into his heart, where little remorse lived. His eyes closed, remembering the fight between him and his mother. Her eyes were so full of fury and disappointment as she scorned him.

"You are an embarrassment to us, Kieran! Never have I ever imagined my son would be such a disgrace that you seek friendship with our enemy! Because you didn't get your way? You blame Aidan for your failures, when it is you *that is the failure!"*

Gritting his teeth, he then remembered the final blow she had dealt him.

"It is fortunate your father is dead; he is spared from seeing how far you've fallen!"

All he could remember was red, and the sickening snap of his mother's neck. As the bungalows had burned around them, he had watched Ninon slump onto the ground, her vivid life suddenly extinguished. Kieran's nails ripped some bark from the tree behind him.

"She never *loved* me. I was never enough for her." This is what happens when a mother's love dies: she dies too. It was only righteous, and Arista only blessed the righteous. He could never go back there and he didn't plan to. If they wanted him to be an outcast, then he would graciously give them what they wanted. The Thesians weren't much for a family. Hell, they weren't even all that bright. But they were better than what he had been given. And the money that bought them lasts longer than loyalty.

He stretched his lean, nude body straight as he watched the two wolves also morph into their human form.

"Where the hell is Nornos?" The tall blond man looked out into the woods. His body was marred with strange tattoo markings in bands on his biceps, and he paid no attention to the bloody cut across his left thigh.

"Relax, he'll be here." The raven-haired man walked ahead to the edge of the hill in front of them. He stopped to hear the howling. "That was too easy. Why aren't they coming for us?"

Kieran scoffed. "Because they have to get permission to retrieve us now. They have the Azanesti Order's balls in a jar. This includes the Alpha. They can't take a piss without convening the council. Meanwhile, they are left beaten and exposed."

"That's pathetic." The blond scoffed.

"Why'd you think I left?" Kieran rolled his eyes. "Where's this friend of yours? I'm freezing my ass off."

"He'll be here." The blond retorted in annoyance. "And where's your end of the bargain, Aristan? You'd better keep your word to us."

"Brother," Kieran walked slowly to him. "Trust me, you'll get your just desserts for your help." He finally had his freedom now, and with this liberation all he could think of was how to build his own pack and take whatever was rightfully his. Despite what his mother believed, he deserved far more than he was given. His parents allowed his birthright to be stolen from a motherless wolf who had nothing of his own.

They all quieted as headlights reflected off the top of the hill. A moment later, their ears perked at the sound of a vehicle door slam shut.

"Nornos? Where the hell were you?" The dark-haired Thesian asked.

Nornos leisurely walked down the hill. A huge black duffel bag was hoisted on his shoulder, and a black skullcap shielded his face. "Traffic." He tossed the bag to the blonde. "I came bearing gifts. Now, please get dressed before I go blind. We need to move out."

The blond quickly unzipped the bag and started tossing out t-shirts, jeans and boots to Kieran and the other naked Thesian. Nornos walked up to Kieran, who was already putting on his boots.

"The rest of our brethren are up north in the southern parts of Maine. There are others out there without a pack. Loners."

"My favorite kind. Those without colors. Like me now." Kieran stood up to his full height and walked past Nornos. "Guess I'm going up north, then." He sniffed the air and slowly walked to a bed of rocks near the edge of the creek. Taking his foot, he kicked a rock over into the creek.

"What about—"

"Yeah, yeah. I said I was gonna keep my promise." Kieran turned around with a large bundle of money and a flask. "A deal's a deal." He tossed the money to Nornos, who stuffed it in his satchel at his side. The other two Thesians started to growl.

"Stand down, bastards! I plan to divvy up." Nornos' eyes flashed amber.

"Such manners."

"Manners are for pussies." Nornos replied. He eyed the flask. "What's that?"

Kieran grinned and tossed it to Nornos. "It's Nightshade."

Nornos cursed and tossed the flask back to Kieran. "Get that shit away from me!"

Kieran looked at the flask and laughed. The other Thesians stared at him as if he was nuts. "Relax, it's in a container, pussies."

The blond shook his head. "Are you crazy, messing around with concentrated forms of that?"

Kieran frowned. "I'll need it to treat some of my weapons. I'm taking up your practice, it would seem. Rather, efficient, though somewhat cowardly."

Nornos shook his head as he headed to the truck, "Yeah, but we hire humans to do that for us. We wouldn't risk ourselves or our own to procure them. That's meat rack work."

Kieran scowled as they all got in the truck. "Humans? Now who's nuts?"

The blond laughed. "We don't keep them, of course. But they are excellent labor for the cause. The meat racks do come in handy, you know?"

Kieran rolled his eyes in annoyance. "Yeah, so I'm told." Sometimes he wondered if he could actually get along with these idiots. Call it tribal superiority if you will, but for a man who had hundreds of "dead Thesian" jokes to entertain random members of the pack, it was hard for him to see them as anything but ridiculous, mindless meat machines. Building a pack with them wasn't going to be an easy task, obviously. In any case, they were right. He supposed 'meat machines' did come in handy as well.

He slammed the door shut as Nornos revved the engine. "Just let me worry about it, wolves," he tucked the flask in his boot. "Now, let's head out. I'd like to reach Maine by tomorrow night. I'm ready to move mainstream; I'm sick of the depressing shadows."

All of the Aristans stood about in a semicircle, their ever-traditional formation, waiting for the council to line up and begin. Within the shelter of night, they all stood anxiously as Aidan walked through the crowd. They silenced for a moment as he stood with the Azanesti Order, the expertly trained protectors of an Aristan pack. They were everywhere, and nowhere. The sleek, stealthy fighters that held no fear and risked their lives to protect the pack, including the Alpha. Each pack had Azans led by a general who usually served as the Alpha or Beta of the pack. Aidan served as general before Tiberius' death, and continued to serve after. The Azans looked to him, their leader, covered in soot and ash. As he walked past, they all slightly tilted their exposed necks to him in respect. He was bloody and covered with the remnants of the night's horrible events, including his mother's pyre. Cameron stood with him, forever admiring the courage in his old friend. Nothing was ever given to Aidan. Even now, he seemed to have to fight tooth and nail for anything, including peace.

"The council will now proceed to determine the fates of those involved with the mayhem that transpired here tonight. Including the deaths of two of our very own." Aidan's voice boomed strong and loud. He stood still as Onyx, Bastien and the others strode in and howled.

Onyx stepped forward. "Fires have ravaged our home. Most are saved, but the damaged must be repaired soon, lest we draw attention to ourselves. We have instructed Tamryn to begin reconstructing the destruction." He looked to Aidan. "Ninon and her guard were killed tonight." He quietened as the crowd of Aristans clamored. After it subsided, he continued. "The fires and the murders are tied; the same ones committed both. One of our own has been suspected in this incident, and we mean to seek him out and get the truth."

Bastien stepped forward and turned to Aidan. "By right of the

Selenium Circle, Aidan Bloodlocke is Alpha and has submitted a charge." With that, he nodded.

Aidan stepped forward, looking at all of his pack. His family. "I charge Kieran Bloodlocke with murder and mayhem by right of this pack."

More clamoring came from the groups. Some of their faces were laden with anger, some with disgust, and some with plain disbelief. He squeezed his fists tight at those who looked like they doubted at him, as if they expected him to have been the culprit. Pushing out a breath, he tried to ignore the feeling. Some would never let him forget his past and how they found him. Even when Onyx often looked at him, he could see the wolf's apprehension. As if he couldn't truly believe his recklessness was a thing of history.

It had been why he didn't want to fight in the Circle. Why he preferred to be left alone and be the invisible wolf he was meant to be. If only Ninon would have allowed it.

Leigh stood forward. She, too, was covered with black and soot, her bright eyes shining past the paleness of her skin. "The Azans have clear suspicions of Kieran's treachery. What information do you have?"

Aidan nodded. The group silenced. "Kieran has been reprimanded other times before for fraternizing with the Thesians. My father had caught him once before he'd died, and even since then he's been connected to them."

At the sound of their enemy's name, the clamoring reached its pinnacle.

"One of our own would be with Thesians? Impossible!" an Aristan from the crowd interjected.

Aidan looked to the crowd, then eyed Bastien, who stood center. "The council is well aware of the incidents I speak of. Thesian scent was all over my mother's—Ninon's chamber, and the area near the creeks. I don't know how many, but they are definitely involved as well. This couldn't be a coincidence."

Bastien cut his eyes to him. "Perhaps Kieran attacked the Thesians during this fray, and followed them out? Should we be so eager to pin this horrendous crime on one of our own?" His stern expression countered Aidan's challenge with equal bold-ness. He wasn't sure what Aidan was implying. Though Kieran did get caught trading with the Thesians, Bastien decided it was best to move past it as an indiscretion. The wolf had lost his father and failed to claim right of Alpha at the Selenium Circle. The rite was open to all eligible Aristans to compete to claim the pack as their own, and for what was once a sure thing of family succes-sion became a surprising twist of events when Aidan--the aban-doned and once feral ward of the Bloodlockes--became the champion. Defeat and shock clear on Kieran's face, Bastien feared it was the beginning of Kieran's decline into anger. Letting the pack write him off this way was a sign of trouble ahead.

Aidan eyed him levelly as he purposely issued advocacy over his charge. Damn him. He needed everyone in on this one. Kieran was not going to get any with this. Everyone there knew Kieran had become more and more reckless since Tiberius died. He had never cared much for Aidan, that was painfully clear, but at least there was some semblance of obedience within him to his father. Now, like a rabid dog, he bit at anyone that was in his way. And this time, it was Ninon.

"He is my brother!" Leigh shouted, and everyone silenced. "And I had lost my mother! Do you think we would purposely blame our own if we didn't think otherwise? In either case, guilty or innocent, Kieran must be found!"

Aidan wanted to smile at his sister's interference. And choke her at the same time. He decided to do neither. How could he? From the time Ninon gave birth to her, Leigh was a stubborn, tenacious one.

"She's right," Onyx looked to the rest of the council. "The Azans must track down and retrieve Kieran." He looked to Aidan. "You may assess your Order and send them out within a moon's cycle."

"Council," Aidan walked over to stand before them. "I request to retrieve Kieran alone."

Now it was the council's time to mumble. Frankly, Aidan was getting rather pissed at all the peanut gallery right now. A job needed to be done.

Bastien frowned at him. "Kieran is Azan."

Aidan gave a solemn nod. "Of course, he said begrudgingly. "I inducted him."

And what a mistake that was.

Tamryn shook his head. As the "silent" partner, the old white wolf rarely said much. "Retrieving a bounty alone is very risky, Aidan. Especially an Azanesti Guard. You would not be taken so easily with one guard."

"But Kieran is not me, Council. Far from it."

Bastien huffed. "I will not allow your arrogance to endanger us any further!"

"I will not—" Aidan interjected. How dare the wolf speak of arrogance, when he stood before them challenging everything in the pack? At least during Tiberius' leadership, everyone had their duties and did them freely. Now that the council was constructed, they had to okay every freaking thing, including the actions of their Alpha. He laughed to himself.

A leader who's only for show. I refuse to be a toy to anyone, heeling at their beck and call.

Still, he managed to rustle up some respect.

"I can bring him in...quietly. I am familiar with how Kieran thinks and I'm skilled at tracking. I can do this alone. The Azans need to stay and protect the pack while we're in disarray."

Onyx gave him a small smile of admiration. "I will oblige a grant of leave."

Bastien shot a look at Onyx in surprise. "But you must swear to bring him back alive."

Aidan scowled. "Council..."

"I know you, Aidan. We all do. Though you are rightfully Alpha, we are not foolish. We simply cannot allow you to make this some vigilante crusade." Bastien stepped closer to stare at Aidan, looking for any signs of weakness or protest. Aidan's face stoic, he did not give the old wolf what he wanted. "Kieran must stand before the council to receive judgment."

Leigh growled. She was getting tired of the council throwing their weight around. Who were they to challenge the will of their pack's Alpha wolf? "The Alpha should determine law."

Bastien narrowed his eyes at her. "What was that?"

Leigh stepped forward. "Leigh Bloodlocke, daughter of the Alpha Couple, Tiberius and Ninon." With that, she cast him a smug look.

Aidan groaned. How he wished Arista had gifted his beloved sister with an edit button—and given him the remote control.

She continued. "We all know that traitors are put down. There's no other place for them. In the time of Tiberius, there was no council. My father was the final word! He was judge and executioner. What has happened to us? Do we not trust our own Alpha leader to do right by all of us? The one who fought with blood and sweat to win the challenge of being our leader?"

Her statement sparked some agreements from the crowd, and Bastien folded his arms in annoyance. That bitch was constant trouble. And that mouth of hers needed to be bitten off. "Tiberius is dead, Leigh, and we have been without an Alpha to lead us for many moons. This council was assembled to maintain this Aristan clan until a new leader was ready."

"He's right, xerhmon," Onyx sighed, referring to Leigh with an old Aristan term of endearment. "Your father's last decree was for the council to form from the elders, and to postpone the Selenium Circle until his son was of age."

"You all know damn well which son my father meant! And he didn't tell you to continue after it!" Her blood was as unstable and hot. It was wrong, and she was beside herself with the injustice of it all. Her father never intended this to happen. Then again, none of them imagined Kieran would do such a thing.

She wanted to rip that council apart, save Onyx.

"Leigh," A calm voice brought her back to earth. She stopped talking and looked to her brother. His eyes were soft and tired. "Stop."

Normally, she would tell him to piss off and just continue claiming she knew what was good for him. But the look on Aidan's face, and the pain in it, quelled her very soul. She'd never understand why her brother let so much go when it concerned him. To offer so much to others and take nothing for himself. She wished to see Aidan happy and content for once, not let his duties take over his life.

"I will abide by the will of the council and bring Kieran back. *Alive*."

The council pulled their attention back to Aidan and stared at him.

Bastien smiled. "Good. You have one full moon cycle to bring him here for the Rites."

Just as Aidan started to walk to his Azans, he heard Bastien cough. "Aidan."

He simply turned to face him—impatience clear on his face.

"It is your duty as Alpha to protect your people. If you should fail in apprehending Kieran, you will be replaced as leader. Do you understand?"

"I will not fail."

Onyx nodded. "Of that, Lukos, I have no doubt."

Aidan grabbed Leigh by her arm and propelled her to the edge of the complex.

"Have you gone insane?"

"I was asking the same about you, big brother."

He raked his hair in frustration. "You don't!—" Aidan lowered his voice. "You don't call out the council like that! As if they're on trial!"

She folded her arms. "Why not? They certainly have no issues putting you up there. They are screwing you over!"

"Leigh, I know this, but I have no choice! Kieran needs to be brought back, and *I* have to bring him back. It's personal."

Shaking her head, she shouted, "What if you can't, Aidan? The cycle moves fast and he could be anywhere!" She walked past him and stared at the others a distance away, removing debris of the fire. "Aidan, if you fail, you'll be shunned. They are setting you up for failure. I won't have it!"

Leigh furiously wiped the tears from her eyes, angry that they had betrayed her. She turned to face Aidan, who stood quietly. "I lost my mother today. I just can't lose any more of my family, Aidan. You're all I have left."

Aidan started to remind her that Kieran was her brother—her flesh and blood. But he knew better, that Leigh would never again accept Kieran as her own. He closed the space between them and hugged her.

"Same here, little sister." He offered her a comforting smile, trying his best not to show his uneasiness over all the events. "But I have to go. You know I do, but I'll return as soon as I can—with Kieran. Now, would you at least try and hold your tongue and keep it from hanging us both until I return?"

Leigh looked up at her brother with laughter. This time she let her tears fall. "I'll try." She lightly touched their mother's amulet around his neck. "Mamyn thought the world of you, as do I. Please take care of yourself. If you need me..."

He nodded, thankful for having such a sister like Leigh. Aidan was barely getting used to being with the Bloodlocke family when she came along. Kieran never gave her the time of day when they were little, despising her for not being a boy. He wanted a 'real' brother, which defined his relationship with Kieran from the start. Leigh, being constantly pushed away, sought company with Aidan and wanted to play with him. He was far older than her but he remembered many times playing her ridiculous games, burying themselves in the autumn leaves and going for runs at night. Trying to find friendship within the pack, he was often mocked for hanging out with his little sister. She had always recognized Aidan as her brother, even when Kieran broke his promise to his parents and told her the sordid truth of him.

She bit his tail that day, boldly drawing blood from her brother twice her size. "Don't you ever speak that way about our brother ever again! Or next time you'll be wagging a nub!"

She was the only anchor he had left.

He cleared his throat. "I know." With that, he released her. "I'm leaving tonight before dawn, so I'd better pack up."

Leigh answered with a nod as Aidan walked away. She thought for a moment, and found herself even more angry than she was before.

Who did Kieran flee with? And why did the council feel so adamant about him being brought back alive, when in Aristan history, traitors were immediately executed?

She was glad Aidan was leaving, in a way. Hopefully, she'd have a chance to find out the truth about her brother's treachery.

Cameron strode up to Aidan, who was packing up his bike. He never went anywhere without his black Ducati Monster. Other Azans, especially on duty, rode bikes, partly due to Aidan's idea of them having his in the first place. Having a cool toy was indeed a good perk, thanks to the brooding wolf.

"Taking her with you, eh?"

Aidan didn't look up as he loaded his knives and packed them. "You know I'm not a 4-wheel person."

Cameron grunted.

"What's on your mind, wolf?" He cut his eyes to Cameron to find his face less than pleased.

"You shouldn't do this alone, Aidan. Not when you have that kind of time restraint and all of us here are able-bodied to hunt for you. To dismiss us..."

Aidan stopped and looked at him levelly. "I'm not dismissing you or anyone. You are all needed here, and I have to do this alone. I'm faster that way."

Cameron scowled. "Whatever happened to 'we'? There's no 'I' in team, you know." Cameron cringed as he realized that the comment was so child-like and trite, he feared Aidan wouldn't take him seriously.

"Yeah, well, there's no 'we' in team either." Aidan threw his satchel onto his bike and squatted down to load it up. "I'm sorry, but I need you here, Cam."

"There are enough of us here, Aidan. You don't need us with you, remember?"

Aidan stood up. "I understand your frustration, but I have to do this alone. And I need you here to look after my sister."

Cameron's eyes widened. "Leigh? Uh, I hate to break it to you, but Leigh can totally take care of herself."

"That's what I'm afraid of." Aidan sighed. "Her words may have put her in danger with the council,"

"You think our own council would hurt her?"

"Our own brother killed another of us. What is it you know about me more than anything?"

"That you're as cuddly as a porcupine—on speed."

Aidan did not look amused. "Cameron."

"Sorry, just trying to lighten this rather dramatic and depressing mood. Deaths, mayhem, an Alpha leaving; gotta admit, it's super depressing." He paused, and when Aidan eyed him, annoyed, he finally decided to answer Aidan's question. "That you leave nothing to chance."

"Exactly. I know she's strong, but she's also hurting, and may do something foolish without me here. Please, for me, just keep an eye on her."

Cameron sighed in defeat. He got along with Leigh well enough, but there was a sense of nervousness he got around her and couldn't understand why. It made him uneasy in an odd, non-threatening way.

"Consider it done." Cameron clasped Aidan's hand in agree-ment. "If you need me out there...I'm there, boss, you know that."

Aidan straddled his bike. "I know. Keep your eyes open here, Cameron." With that, he kicked his engine to life and rode off.

As he hit the road, he saw the ranch getting smaller and

smaller in his rearview, the damage of it apparent with spots of darkness on the tops of roofs.

Kieran, you bastard. Hope you like running, because I'm not stopping. And I guarantee the council won't save you. I doubt Goddess Arista herself can save you from what I have planned for you.

3

ONCE BITTEN

"**W**ell, she's not bringing that flea-bitten mutt back into my house!"

Maddie glared at the agitated man who refused to tone his voice down as he reamed her for something she had no control over. Folding her arms, she clicked her pen under her arm in increments similar to counting.

"Mister Grenier, the dog was in worse shape than you. I'm only doing my job." Her voice tried to be soothing as she pressed her glasses up on her nose. In truth, she was appalled that the man had the gall to come into her office and demand anything after what he had done. She stared at him as he frantically patted the bandages on his forearm and fingers.

Yep, the German Shepherd did a number on old Evan all right.

Good. I had to perform surgery on Comrade after you kicked him until he ruptured organs, you shithead.

She had seen such cruelty and stupidity in that man's eyes it took all the power she could conjure not to geld him on her surgery table where Comrade laid.

He waved several papers in his hand. "I want that psycho-mutt put down! He endangers me and my family!"

Not phased by his urgency, Maddie turned to look at his

wife, who leaned quietly in tears against the wall. Linda's tall, frail body faced the edge of the window. She was probably a beautiful woman when she wasn't in tears. Unfortunately, Maddie never had the pleasure of really seeing her when she wasn't crying.

She wasn't an idiot; she knew Evan Grenier wasn't the greatest to Linda—and it seemed the only one who had guts to stand up to the jerk was Comrade, the 80 pound German Shepherd who fought for his life in her back room. "Linda, did Comrade attack you or your daughter?"

Linda looked up at Maddie, her eyes trailed with black tears from her makeup. She timidly shook her head. "N-no, Comrade wouldn't hurt us. He loves Sandra."

Evan Grenier turned his head at Linda, who slightly recoiled at his gaze. "What the hell do you call this!?" He showed off his bandage stained with seeping blood. "She may be partial to the dog, but I don't care! I'm not paying to keep that damn dog alive!"

Linda pushed herself off the wall. "Evan, you can't! I had Comrade since I was a teenager!"

"Well you can go on and stay with the dumb mutt if you want."

Maddie threw her pen on the floor. "I've heard enough! Mr. Grenier, seeing how this animal is not registered under your name, you do not have the right to command to have the dog put down."

"Now just hold on a sec—"

"*And* granted I have a full report of the damage done to the animal, I will have you know I am obligated by the state of Maine under Title 17 to turn this report to the authorities for alleged cruelty."

Evan's eyes widened at her threat then turned into a sneer. "You can't prove anything except that dog attacked me and it was merely self-defense."

Maddie had no choice but to call his bluff. "Perhaps...perhaps not." She turned to her assistant, who had rather auspiciously witnessed the whole ordeal. "Greta," she said with a cold, stern voice.

"Yes, Maddie?" Greta's voice was eager and attentive. She was barely used to her assistant, who seemed to come with the vet office in a package deal from the previous owner. Greta was quite passionate to the causes around her.

"Can you get those lab reports ready for sending by way of Sheriff McTiernan, please? I'll ask him to send the report to the Ag Commissioner."

Greta gave Evan a sinister smirk. "Most certainly, Doc," She rose from her chair when Evan put his hands up.

"Wait!", he sighed. "Fine, let the dog live, alright!" He turned to look at Linda who appeared to have relief in her eyes. "But he is not allowed at my home, are we clear?"

Linda's eyes began to water again, "What?! No!"

Realizing that was where he could hurt her, he smiled a sinister grin of his own. "I'm not joking, Linda. I won't have you put it down, but you cannot keep him with us. He's not welcome, you understand? Give him away to someone else who wouldn't mind having a rabid mutt to gnaw their hands off!"

Maddie frowned. *If only Comrade was successful in doing that along with your tongue and your d-*

Her evil thoughts were cut off as Linda started to bawl.

"That's not fair, Evan! He's a good dog! He's been with me forever!"

Maddie wanted to reach out to the tortured woman. Evan knew exactly how to continue hurting Linda. And it worked.

He glared at Maddie. "Send me the bill for him, but consider him an abandoned pet."He snapped his look to his crying wife. "Say goodbye to it and let's go, Linda. It's late and we need to pick up Sandra." With that, he walked away, letting the bell ring him out.

Greta passed Linda her box of tissues and let her snatch several out to dry her red eyes. "I'm so sorry, Linda."

"What do I tell Sandra?" she asked, punctuating her question with a sniff. "She loves Comrade just as much as I do."

Maddie motioned to Linda to follow her to her operating room. "You should at least see him, Linda."

Linda nodded, her tissue close to her nose, sniffling. She proceeded to follow her in.

Upon entering through the double doors, Linda saw Comrade lying on his side with tubes stuck in him. Part of his stomach's fur was shaved off and bits of him were bandaged up. Still, Linda could see the steady rise and fall of her beloved dog's body. He was still alive.

Linda sighed. "Oh, Comrade." She looked to Maddie. "Is it okay if I touch him?"

Maddie smiled and nodded. "Of course. He's just heavily sedated post-surgery. It was really close, Linda."

Linda softly rubbed Comrade between his ears. "Hi there, sweetie. How are you?" She rubbed her fingers against his ear. Scratching his head, she looked up at Maddie. "He likes his ears rubbed." Maddie walked over to her as she looked at the bandages and started to sob. "I'm so sorry, Comrade. I'm sorry. You did nothing wrong, and this shouldn't have happened. Ever. I'm sorry." Linda backed away to the wall and wiped her eyes.

Maddie ached for the woman. Linda was a sweet person, one of the first to welcome her to Bridgepoint, Maine. She and her daughter came to the dusty office to deliver cookies and dog biscuits to the town's new veterinarian. It was the first time she saw their big, friendly dog Comrade, who went everywhere with them. She had hoped that bringing Linda back here to see the family member who fought so courageously for her would help Linda get the strength she needed to return the favor.

Linda dried her tears and looked at Maddie. "Do I need to sign anything to let him go?"

Maddie shook her head. Her heart sank in disappointment, but she refused to show it to Linda, who had enough demons at her feet. "I'll take care of Comrade, Linda. He'll go to a loving home. I promise."

Linda gave a quick nod. "Thank you so much for saving his life, Maddie. I'm in your debt, honestly."

You can repay me by standing up for him. She shook the thought away. It wasn't fair to Linda to feel that way; she had no right to pass judgment on her. She knew how much Linda loved the dog. But to her, it just wasn't enough. Yet, she just shrugged. "The surgery bill is all that's owed, and I'll handle Comrade's well-being personally and pro bono."

"I appreciate that, Maddie." Linda gave a small smile and rubbed Comrade one last time. Her voice was shaky, holding back her sadness. "Goodbye, friend...and thank you." She kissed his muzzle and walked out as Evan's horn blowing came to the fore-front of sounds. "I'd better go."

Maddie didn't see her out. Instead, she stayed with Comrade and checked his vitals. He was a strong dog and with some loving care would be back to his old self in a month or two. "I'm sorry too, Comrade." She said quietly. "You deserve so much better than what you've been given for your help."

A banged up body from a maniac owner, and abandonment from the family you protected.

Greta peeped in on her as she circled around the table. "You okay in here?"

Maddie gave her a timid smile. "Yeah, I guess. Just checking up on him before I leave tonight. I'm coming in a little late tomorrow morning."

"Oh yeah?," Greta asked with budding curiousity. "Got a hot date, Doc?"

Maddie looked up to see Greta grinning in anticipation. "Ha, I wish."

Greta blew a raspberry. "Booo."

Ever since they started working, Greta was absolutely obsessed with her love life. Or in this case, lack thereof. She often made jokes of hoping to find a note from her boss claiming to have met a dashing male, endowed with greatness unlike any other, to whisk her away from Bridgepoint. Maddie often shook her head and would reply that she had just got to Bridgepoint and wasn't done paying the lease on the business yet.

Greta leaned against the counter and looked at Comrade, sighing. "Poor guy. This was an intense call. You did a helluva job with him."

"Yeah. Thanks for coming to help me so late." She smiled at Greta, who was as free flowing as a river. She either rarely got upset or was just way better than Maddie at hiding it. When the Greniers called frantically about the animal, she knew she'd need some help with the surgery. She paged Greta, who surprisingly rushed over without a single complaint.

"Eh, no worries. Cassie is with her grandma tonight, so all is well." She walked over to pat Comrade on the head. "What are you gonna do about him? Want me to call the humane society in the morning?"

Maddie scratched his head. Time and time again she saw the downside of taking a chance and helping others, this animal being her latest example. Animals will always appreciate your kindness; people, not so much. "No," she said, looking up at Greta. "We have to hold him for a few days anyway. Abandonment period."

"He's a great, well-trained dog. I'm sure someone would take him and love him."

Maddie sighed and adjusted the temperature in the room. Someone definitely would. Even if that someone would be her.

"Great job handling Evan, by the way." Greta adjusted the clipboard on the rack next to her. "He's a bully."

"He's a big asshole is what he is. I'm still considering reporting him despite his agreement to 'allow' Comrade to live. Could you believe that? " Maddie frowned, recalling the way Evan treated everyone around him. Part of her saw nothing but a deranged bully, and another saw something scary and unstable about him. Her fear always manifested into anger and at the time of trying to save Comrade's life, she wanted a bat and five minutes alone with the man who did it.

"I don't blame you, Maddie. You're right, he's an asshole. But more attention to him will just make things worse for poor Linda."

Maddie nodded solemnly. She'll take her word for it. Still new to the environment, it was best for her not to meddle too much until she got used to everything. Including the locals.

Greta waved to her. "I'm going back home. Call me if you need anything."

Maddie tried her best to give her a reassuring smile. The look on Greta's face told her she'd failed miserably. "Thanks." And she *was* thankful to her assistant. Greta was bright and silly, but had helped her tremendously in and out of the office. The emotional roller coaster made her sigh with exasperation. She had barely been in this town for a month and already she was bombarded with the people of this town and their dramatic issues. Though she was lucky to take up the practice in such a beautiful town, part of her was worried about the people here. Many of the men seemed voracious and crude. She didn't want to go back to her old 'sweetheart' days where she made excuses for everyone and wanted to save the world; but then again, she didn't want to be a man-basher. Not all of them were controlling like Evan Grenier. Hopefully. She had been so busy lately moving in and setting up the vet practice, that it took her a while to notice that no one hung out much after dark. It totally sucked because she'd been a night owl since she could remember. It was definitely going to be a new lifestyle change that she promised herself she'd make the best of.

The place wasn't all that bad. It was a new start, and with every new start, things are a little shaky.

Her Nana assured her that this move would be very good for her. Adventurous and eventful, she said.

Hmph. Though everyone brushed off her grandmother's optimistic talk, Maddie had appreciated it very much in these times of doubt. Now, for some reason, she hoped her Nana was right and that she wouldn't die of boredom in this strange town.

4

BROTHERHOOD

"**W**here the hell are we?" Kieran twisted his neck as daybreak started to shine in his face. He had had enough of being cramped up with the Thesians, who were much thicker and weighed more than his kind. No one knew exactly why. Rumor has it that the Goddess Thesia wanted to give her people the upper hand on brute strength and power. Some of their elders believed that they just evolved that way. However, the size of them still didn't hold a candle to his kind's agility and swift power. But there was an old saying that Aristans were built for speed, Thesians were built for comfort. There was nothing underdog about the Aristans.

He laughed to himself at his own pun. "I need to go for a run."

Nornos glanced at him through the rearview mirror. "Iris, Maine. This is where the majority of us are holed up. There's a string of towns around us to help us stay under the radar, and Riko's got a Haviscasi in Bridgepoint, about 40 miles away."

Kieran looked through the window and steadied his eyes on the abyss of trees and laughed. Strange, he figured the Thesians would infiltrate a more modern, urban area. Since they were only able to change once a month, choosing a place of excessive flora seemed unnecessary. Perhaps they did have sense to realize that such a rare treasure to change should be cherished.

"How many of you are living here?"

Dante took a swig of water. "Lone wolves come and go, but about fifty, give or take."

"And still growing," Nornos interjected. "Not to mention the other towns around us."

Kieran sat back and gave Dante a smirk. "What's the matter? Can't any of you play fair in the sandbox?"

Nornos glared defensively at Kieran through the mirror. "I was banished for killing humans to protect my pack, Aristan. I was betrayed by my own people, as many of us. Play fair in the sandbox we do not."

Kieran shook his head. "Fair enough."

He wanted to tell Nornos that he left out how he killed those 11 humans. He had heard that not all of the pieces were found. But then, why judge? His own mother was killed by his hands.

No, not killed. Exacted justice more like it. She betrayed her own blood by turning her back on him.

She contributed to his downfall and disgrace. Coddling some bastard Aristan over her own son. He should have been Alpha leader, and everyone knew it. He was cheated out of his birthright thanks to his mother and that conniving elder, Onyx. It was all justice well served for his own people to turn their backs on him. They had more justice coming their way and they just don't know it. If he can't govern it, he'll destroy it. Simple as that.

"We'll have you talk to Riko. He has his bar as a haven in a nearby town called Bridgepoint. From there, he can give us information on getting you settled, and start recruiting."

Kieran nodded. "Good."

As they pulled into the town, Kieran breathed in the air and sighed. There definitely was a healthy presence of Shadow-Shifters. How nice to live in the open instead of being in seclusion like the council and his father believed in. It was why they were behind in everything. Had he been Alpha, that would have been his first change: to enter the human world mainstream and take what belonged to them. Now his former pack's ignorance would be their downfall. He looked out the window to see the old-fashioned buildings of brick and classic wood. Bridgepoint held a historic look with a brickstone main street. He could tell it was a bit too small to lay low. If anyone was going to come looking for him, he needed to blend into a bigger spot...and keep moving away from prying eyes. Which reminded him... "What of human law enforcement?"

Dante shrugged. "Riko is better off answering that for you out here. As far as I know, we clean up after ourselves in Iris and do not alert the police."

When they finally approached the bar, Nornos led them to the office entrance from the back. He performed a patterned knock which signaled to the owner to open the door. Riko stood at six-foot-six, easy. His dark hair pulled back into a ponytail, with a streak of gray. To even get gray hair the wolf had to at least be well over 100 years old.

Riko scowled at Kieran. "Why is he here?"

Kieran didn't flinch as he walked in. Confidence in full bloom, he sat in his chair, relaxed, staring into Riko's eyes.

Dante stood between them. "He's clan-less, Reek. No colors." He called the alarmed Thesian by his nickname that so many gave him. "He's with us and we need your help."

Riko cursed under his breath, watching Kieran smoke his cigarette. "I can't have him here, clan or no clan. You three know that; this is for Thesians to socialize in peace."

"And I have come here in peace as well, Riko." Kieran put his cigarette out on the counter ashtray. "I'm not stupid,. No self-respecting Thesian who belonged to any pack would come here. This is for the abandoned only. Even yourself has been cast away."

Riko's face softened.

Kieran eyed him rather flippant. "Am I right?"

"What do you want, Aristan?"

"I want what you and all the others want, Riko." Kieran sipped his drink. "We were thrown out, cast out of our respected places. Thesian or Aristan alike, we deserve respect and a pack of our own. We are all just as strong and formidable alone; imagine if we all were together."

Riko laughed in their faces. If he ever heard of something so ridiculous...

Kieran's stoic face didn't condone the laughter on his expense.

Riko slowly sobered. "Wolf, you are insane to think that you can wrangle all of these animals to work together for anything. And you're thinking of mixing both ShadowShifters for your 'pack'?" He shook his head. "The Goddesses will rather see this world burn than to see that happen. You know that." Riko took Kieran's empty glass. "Hope you enjoyed your drink. Goodbye, and save your 'We are the world' idea for someone else."

Dante turned to Riko. "Give him a chance. He's proven himself very valuable. He's a great fighter and he knows his people."

Riko slammed the glass on the counter. "Good! Then he can go back to them! We are Thesians, Dante! What do we need from an Aristan?"

Dante scowled. "Nothing from an Aristan, Riko. That's the point. We will only have allegiance to ourselves. We belong to no one now! Kieran's right. No Thesian who is loyal will even come here. They do not even consider us Thesians anymore. We're nothing to them. Aren't you tired of relying on yourself and humans to keep your business alive when our own people refuse to help any of us?"

Riko looked away.

When he was exiled and left for dead, they made his son watch, telling him that's what happened to traitors. Years passed until he laid eyes on his son. And when he did, Berwyn looked at him with such disgust it took everything in his power not to hurt him. Even in his own son's eyes, he was nothing. He was *tired* of being nothing.

"What do you want from me?"

Kieran nodded. Nothing like abandonment to ignite anger.

And he should know--that was most of his life. "From what I hear, many will listen to you. That will make you quite useful. We'll start with your people first. After the Thesian loners are reigned in, I will seek out any lone Aristans, who indeed have a lot more animosity for what I have planned. Where do they gather?"

Riko motioned to the window. "They often hang on the outskirts of town. Close to the wooded areas, so I've heard. A couple of bars and such out there. Just know that Greenwoods is strictly off limits. We don't bother them and they don't bother us, so it would be wise not to recruit from Devin's group."

"A truce? Seriously?" Kieran asked.

Riko shrugged. "A sensitive one. In either case...off-limits."

"Figures," Kieran said, rising from his seat. "What of the law enforcement? Are they in pocket?"

Riko looked at him as if he spoke a foreign language of some sort.

"Do we *own* them, Riko? We can't have the police meddling in our affairs...That is, of course, unless you want to infiltrate them too?"

Riko shook his head. "We don't own them. We are just very careful. I don't know of any of us in the force out here. I highly doubt it, but maybe some loyals are."

"Screw them." Kieran scoffed. "We don't need their help. Point me to the highest voice and I'll silence it. Sheriff?"

"McTiernan." Dante replied. "He's easy to find. He's been poking his nose around too much anyway. Riko here is running out of lies."

"All in good time, then." He motioned to Dante. "I have something for you, brother."

Riko stood behind the counter as Dante tossed an envelope in front of him. Opening it, he exposed several hundreds and looked at Kieran.

"Before you try to be noble and refuse it," Kieran said as Riko started to open his mouth, "Understand that money never was a thing of either of our people. However, to survive in these demanding times, it's vital. This is for your business, Riko. We take care of our own."

Riko thumbed through the money and placed it in his pocket. "Thanks."

Kieran leaned across the count and patted Riko on the shoulder. "You're welcome. You see, I'm not that bad a guy."

"That remains to be seen, *brother*." Riko replied solemnly.

Kieran grinned. "Seeing is believing, indeed. We'll be in touch."

With that, all three of them walked out. Riko glanced at his pocket. A pack of their own. Sounded too good to be true. Aristan or not, he wasn't sure if they had found a savior, or made a pact with the devil.

5

BARK AND GROWL

"You know what, Maddie?" Greta asked while straightening up the chairs in the lobby. "All I see you do is work and—well, work."

Maddie set her coffee on her desk and looked towards the office door. The sun had a beautiful way of making a little rainbow right at the entrance. "That's simply not true, Greta. Just the other day I went to have lunch with the board."

"Oh, well I bet that was just too dandy for words there, Maddie." Greta pushed a chair back. "Did you write Nana about that?"

Maddie groaned. "I'm fine, Greta. I'm still new, remember? Besides, my lack of adventure and love life should not affect you. It's not like I'm contagious."

Greta looked up at her and smiled. She loved her new boss, but often she found the woman a glutton for punishment. "I didn't say that. What I am saying is that you'll never find someone worth meeting if you hang under the geriatric committee. You're young and vibrant. It's time to shake that thang!"

Maddie shook her head at Greta's comment.

"Please don't start, Greta. This *thang*, as you so call it, needs to hit the gym before I can even think about shaking it. And as far as the geriatric committee goes, it's not by choice. My landlord never fails to invite me."

Maddie walked over to the door, careful not to step in the rainbow, and turned the sign to 'Open'. She didn't care to be holed up with the oldest people in town, constantly grilling her about her life. As if there was something to talk about! She remembered two weeks ago when she had one Long Island iced tea too many and politely summarized her life for one of them.

"Let's see...I'm one-eighth Pawnee, never so much as received a parking ticket (so much for being bold, right?), my ex-boyfriend nearly destroyed my life—which brought me way out here to care for your sick and mistreated animals. Oh, and I have the worst tolerance for alcohol. Can't you tell?"

She was hoping that outburst would permanently ban her from any more obligation to the lunches. Unfortunately, it made her a hit at the lunch and now her landlord, Miss Brady, was much more diligent in getting her to come.

Greta plopped down in her seat, thumbing through a magazine on her desk. "I know you don't care for those lunches. Why not check out a bar or movie or something? Just get out and meet others like you for a change?"

"And what about you, Miss Pot-Calling-the-Kettle?" Maddie said, as she opened the blinds more.

Greta blew a raspberry. "I need a break, that's all. Besides, you gotta be careful about the guys here."

"Yeah, I know. I had the pleasure of meeting Evan last night."

"Ah, don't let too many Evans spoil it. There's a lot of guys here who are super cute and super available."

"What's the catch?" She walked past her to check on Comrade. "Isn't there always one?"

Greta followed her. "Well, they are not in the safety of the town hall, that's for damn sure." Her face softened as she saw Comrade wagging his tail slowly in his large kennel. "Look at him!"

Maddie turned to look at her. "Don't get him too excited. I don't want him struggling to move too much. It's good to see him up, though." She rubbed his ears through the kennel and stood up. "Now, what were you seducing me into?"

"I know it may not be your style, but there are tons of hangouts, bars and pool halls where there are men to rev some engines."

Maddie frowned. "Bars? No thank you." She leaned against the wall. "Doesn't everyone tell people that bars are the worst place to meet someone?"

"Well, those people don't live here. It's not like doctors and lawyers don't frequent bars as well, Madeline. At least be open to it; you never know." Tugging her lab coat, Greta winked at her.

The entrance bell rang and Greta peered out the double-door window.

"Here comes Bill and his neurotic tabby. I'll get them set up." She glanced at Maddie. "I won't hassle you any more for today. Promise." With that, she burst through the double doors as if she were awaiting the paparazzi. The woman always knew how to make her exits and entrances larger than life.

As the last hour was coming to a close, Maddie sat in Greta's desk for a moment. She had let her go early to pick up her son and was pretty sure that the last little bit of time would be uneventful. Often she liked to look at the town from her office. The buildings were so neat, yet old-fashioned and antique. It was one thing she loved about the eastern seaboard and this town: the beauty in the classic.

Very little of the town went with modern architecture and she couldn't have been more grateful. She walked over to the door where she saw people on the sidewalks passing by and saw the bar across the street from her. It was still part of the antique buildings but had a much different aura, it seemed. Riko's, as the bar was named, didn't look like a dive from the outside, and she saw many men and a few women enter the bar, which gave her the impression it was popular.

Maybe Greta was right. Perhaps she should go venturing out of the safety of people she had nothing in common with. She was lonely, she'd admit, but despite that she was leery of jumping into anything. Her last relationship was less than stellar and she had no intention of repeating that failure in her life. Ever.

Maddie bit her lip indecisively and then smiled. "A little drink in a new environment may be good for me." She flipped the sign to 'CLOSED' and slowly turned her blinds as Riko's Bar was the last thing she focused on.

Maddie found herself frozen at the entrance of the bar, trying to give her feet courage to step inside. No one really paid attention to her. The bar was as typical as anything could be, right down to the scantily clad waitresses leaning over, passing their orders to boisterous men. Nothing seemed out of the ordinary. What was it that felt so eerie about the place?

She hadn't realized she was still blocking the entrance until she heard a voice so close in her ear, she felt the heat of his breath, "Excuse me."

Maddie jumped at the sensation and moved to the side as she caught an eye of the incredibly tall and thick figure of a man pass her by. She was barely level with his throat! He was looking at her then, so she could in turn see him. His body was bulky and muscular, incredibly proportioned, as was his strongly chiseled face. His long black hair was pulled into a ponytail with a streak of silver near his left temple. It was the only thing on him that told her he was perhaps older than he looked.

But he still looked twenty.

"You are leaving us so soon, are you?" He eyed her with a charming smile.

"Actually, I'm ..."

"Still deciding?," he cut her off, watching her intently. His smile seemed more of a hidden agenda as she noticed his eyes lingering on her breasts just a tad too long.

What the hell, Maddie? He's a man and you have breasts. Frankly, the mathematics is done on this issue.

She returned his smile and stepped inside.

"Nice. You'll be fine here. I won't let anything hurt you." He followed her as she headed to the barstools.

"Oh?," she said inquisitively. He pulled back the stool for her so she could sit. Maddie was flattered by his chivalrous action. "Are you the bouncer here?"

Before he could help himself he scowled at her. "Honey, do I look like I'm a bouncer?"

Maddie was confused at his question. He looked insulted. She was going to honestly say 'yes' until she saw him burst in laughter. *Great. The butt of a joke so soon.*

He pushed himself off the bar and started to walk towards the counter entrance. "I'm only kidding, honey. But you were close," he flipped the counter section up and stepped in, "I own the place."

Maddie returned the smile he gave her. "Hmmm. Then you must be..."

"Riko Otarian, at your service." He gave a mimicking bow of a civilized gentlemen.

She couldn't help but laugh. It was an odd visual indeed. Though he sounded respectable, the man looked like an overgrown rock star. The irony was amazing. "Nice to meet you. My name is Madeline."

Watching her, he flung his towel over his shoulder. "Pleasure's all mine. What can I get you to drink?" He continued to pull up shot glasses, then grabbed the bottle next to him.

Maddie never knew what to get at bars to drink. She hated beer, but it was the most laid back choice. "Can I have a pint of your darkest lager?"

Riko had a surprised look, lifting his brows. "I'm impressed. You're a brave one."

She shrugged. "It's all I ever really drink."

Between his waitresses and him serving, he broke away and poured her a draught pint and set it before her with a grin. "Here you go, darlin'."

"Thanks," She took a sip and pulled back to reach into her purse. Riko shook his head.

"This one's on the house."

"I can't do that. You have a business to run." Shaking her head, she continued to through her purse.

"Sure you can. Just lift your hands off the purse slowly and put them where I can see them."

Amused, she found herself doing as he asked, placing her hands flat on the counter. She could learn to take a kind gesture, she supposed. "Yes Sir." Maddie pulled the glass back to her and took a sip, smiling. "Thank you."

Riko tucked his towel in his back pocket. "You're welcome. Business is doing fine, darlin', but thanks for the small business support."

Maddie looked around the bar, trying to glance briefly but not stare. The only women there were the waitresses, who seemed to be built to perfection. Both wore tight t-shirts with the bar's name scrawled across the chest, and wore different variations of a jean skirt. The blonde waitress kept winking at Riko when they didn't think Maddie noticed. She used to remember being cheeky and flirty with Eric once upon a time. Although he didn't get into it as much as she, the effort at least made her feel wanted and happy. She sighed and went back to sipping her beer. There's a reason he was an ex and she rather be alone than deal with any more relationship crap.

"You good on drinks for now?" Riko asked as he poured some whiskey into a glass. "I have to step out and run an errand."

Maddie stared at her glass, in which she had barely put a dent in the lager. Since college, she had the annoying ability to nurse a beer forever. She shook her head. "Nope. I'm good. Thanks."

He nodded, then whistled at the blonde waitress who had played eye ping-pong with him earlier. She looked up, smiling, and strode towards the counter.

"Yes Reeks, what's up?" The blonde asked, with an unmistakable deep Southern accent. Her hair was pulled into a neat bun with two stray tendrils curled against her tanned face. She smiled ear to ear, her breasts riding up against the counter as she leaned. Riko definitely had his hands full.

He tossed her the keys. "Dana, hold down the fort while I check up on something. I shouldn't be too long, and these knuck-leheads are all supplied with fresh drinks so everything should be good for now."

Dana jammed the keys into her pocket. "Okay. Will do."

Maddie watched Riko pop out to the back and disappear while Dana prepared some drinks and proceeded to take them to her customers. As her eyes followed the woman out to the house area full of loud, chuckling bikers, she caught sight of someone observing her. He sat near the front, closest to the door, leaning in his seat casually. Smiling at her. Maddie cut her eyes from him, thinking perhaps he was looking at some poster or something. Clearly he wasn't looking at her. Was he?

Sipping her beer, she thought to turn around again, just to be sure. Indeed, the handsome blonde was looking at her. He was dressed in leather pants and a black tee, which hugged his torso slightly. His muscular arms were covered with tattoos. If he wasn't smiling at her, she would think him quite menacing. Despite her awkwardness, she smiled back.

What the hell? Be open, Greta says. So here I am. Open.

Maddie was concerned as the mysterious guy's smile suddenly faded.

"Hi, there." A thick voice rumbled in her ear behind her.

Maddie turned around to find a tall cherry blond man with a goatee grinning at her. Slightly startled by his sneak attack, she scooted to her left. Whoa, was something in the beer?

The redhead with gorgeous grey eyes looked her over. "I'm sorry, honey. Did I scare you?

A nervous laugh shook out of her. "Sorry, you just surprised me. Hi." She extended her hand and he shook it gently.

"Hi yourself. What's your name, love?"

"Madeleine. Everyone calls me Maddie."

"Beautiful name. I'm Axel. Would you like a drink, Maddie?"

Her answer was cut off by a ruckus behind her. Turning around, she saw the blonde man glaring at them, his chair and table knocked over onto the floor. He looked wild and feral, not charming as he was before. The blond came up to her, and in reaction she slid off the barstool, only to become sandwiched between both men. As Maddie looked to the redhead, her body went rigid as he was fuming just as much as the blonde.

"You son of a bitch!" The blonde hissed past her to his rival. "You should back down and walk away now!"

The redhead gave a sinister grin. "Like hell I will. Let's not get juvenile, okay? It's obvious the lady isn't interested. Take your ass back to your seat."

Both continued to growl obscenities at each other, snarling like mindless beasts. It was like they suddenly devolved into animals in five seconds flat.

Great, just what I need. A tug of war between two giants that can tear me in two.

Maddie stretched her arms out in attempt to distance them further, yet it was barely any use. Their voices were so loud, she could barely hear herself trying to speak to them in efforts to calm them down. She didn't know either of the men and had no clue what either was capable of.

6

BRAWLERS

Exhaustion in Aidan's body manifested in not only ache in his bones, but a fog in his mind. He rarely took a break, other than a short rest before he entered town. The woodsy atmosphere was a goddess-send, but he had no time to bask in it. Kieran did a pretty good job covering his tracks, but there were areas where he did runs and failed to backtrack. The rains in between didn't help, but at least Aidan was able to pin down an area within three towns that were possible places for him. Breckinridge was one of those places. A seascape town with lush forests seemed unlikely for Kieran to visit. He preferred bigger cities and often complained about Tiberius' choice to melt into smaller communities rather than larger ones. In any event, he couldn't put anything past his brother, who was basically on the run from the law. Their law. He didn't care about the colluding with the Thesians; Aidan wanted him to answer for the murder of his own, including the only mother he had ever known. The thought of her funeral pyre hit him in the gut and was the final blow to make him take a break.

Pulling in through the main street, he assessed the area around him. There weren't many people about, and considering that the town was much bigger than he anticipated, he found that a little strange. A town this big should have a nightlife. Aidan parked his bike near a shop and took his riding jacket off. Locking it up in his compartment, he inhaled the night air around him. He always preferred to hunt on his feet, and with a town this big and unfamiliar, it was best he took his time.

As the last bit of dusk faded, Aidan walked the strip of businesses, microbreweries and shops until he picked up a faint scent of Kieran downwind of him. Looking around where he stood, he lifted his nose to the air, but as soon as he recognized it, he was barely able to pick it up again. *Shit.* He was here. Maybe several days ago, but he was here. Aidan saw a bar a ways from him. Dive bars were to wolves as caves were to bears. They swarmed there, mingling with humans, where they chalked up Shadow-Shifters' rude and boisterous behavior as machismo or toxic masculinity.

Someone in this place had probably seen his brother. Kieran didn't know how to stay incognito for very long. He made a beeline for the bar. *Don't think. Just get there.* Reaching the doors, he paused as a realization paralyzed him.

Aidan hissed a curse at his overzealousness. This bar wasn't just some dive on the edge of town.

This was a Thesian Haven.

A haviscasi, in the Aristan old world language. How distracted had he been not to pick up the scent sooner? Kieran's scent lead him right here and Aidan didn't think of anything else. His eyes shifted from left to right. Luckily, no one had noticed him yet. It would only take a second for them to catch his scent. Then all hell would break lose.

However, everyone appeared to be deeply distracted, and their eyes focused on two bickering Thesians near the counter.

As the big blond Thesian shifted to his right, Aidan observed the real reason for the distraction. He watched quietly as the beautiful, brown-eyed brunette stood between the two, frantically trying to calm them down.

Upon seeing that, he didn't even have to hone her scent to

know she was human. A she-wolf would be cheering on the possible bloodbath in her honor from the sidelines—not trying to hinder it. Watching her hopelessly raise her voice above the growling and swearing, he realized the sidelines would have been a much better position for her.

Right now, she was in danger.

When a Thesian wanted a female, often he would challenge— sometimes to the death—to win her affection. Neither looked as if they were backing down anytime soon. With her in the middle like that, she was likely to be seriously hurt—or even killed with those two mongrels.

In fact, had this bar been loaded with Aristans, this incident would never be. Aristans seldom claimed human females. Though they were incredibly feminine and beautiful, it was a waste of time, since it could only be quick and casual—never anything more. They could never be real mates. And even with casual sex, it was risky to do. It was often difficult to keep yourself in one form when in the throes of sex. You were at the mercy of your own passion. To do that was to endanger your pack and everyone else.

He should leave. Aidan's interfering could cause an all out brawl in here. The animosity level was unmistakable, and with this many wolves under one roof—any unwarranted move would trip this bar like a powder keg. He was better off walking into a nuclear missile barn. *Just get the hell outta here, Aidan. This isn't your fight, or your business.* His eyes lingered on the brunette in the middle. There was something compelling about her. Something bright and truthful. Her arms were outstretched like some gracious captive bird, her wide eyes lit with confusion. She was definitely above this place. He released a distressed sigh.

If only he would listen to himself...

With a fierce growl, the redheaded Thesian pulled back his fist to swing, now oblivious to Maddie between them. Upon seeing his force move forward, Maddie screeched and covered her head in defense, still sandwiched between the two. Aidan moved so quickly he was sure he appeared to have teleported himself to them. He only had time to react; no politeness or pleasantries.

Not that it was his forte anyway.

He connected a fierce jab to the redhead before his punch made contact, and the wolf was knocked backwards, skidding across the floor. The blonde Thesian advanced towards him, his body rigid and ready to strike. Without time to waste, Aidan grabbed Maddie, hastily whipping her behind him, taking care not to dislocate her shoulder.

"Stay back!" he growled at her as the blonde swung at Aidan, hitting nothing but air with a blow that could have taken his head off. Maddie did exactly what he asked, leaning against the juke-box, stunned.

Next to her, the redhead pulled to his feet.

"This isn't your fight, Aristos!" the blonde declared through clenched teeth as he swung again in rage.

Aidan used the miss to his advantage to grab the blonde and slam his face into the bar counter and knock him back against the tables. The onlookers backed up in time before he crashed into them.

Aidan's pulse escalated, and his forehead beaded with sweat.

"Well, looks like it's my business now."

The alchemic reactions in his body threatened to will his change, but he swallowed it back down, whipping his head back to see the brunette pressed against the wall, her eyes shifting back and forth to all three of them. The other wolves were all out of their seats, some glaring at them, some glaring at each other. Thesians preferred to keep out of fights between other Thesians. It was their way of respect in trusting their brethren to handle things on their own. However, if it was between a Thesian and an Aristan...

He heard snarling from the spectators.

It was open season.

If he changed now, he could take them all on. In wolf form, he was always able to tolerate more pain, and he was stronger when he fought in his other skin.

But then the woman would see what they really were. She may not survive.

Thesians didn't like being exposed outside of their own terms, which for once, Aidan could respect. He was certain that once he changed, so would everyone else in defense. She would see everything, and whether she believed what she saw or not didn't matter. If she witnessed it, she would die. That was the code. Primal and definite. Breaking that code in his world was punishable by death.

No jury. No negotiations.

He didn't know her, but she didn't deserve that. Not for being at the wrong place and wrong time. When his eyes met hers, he was determined for both of them to make it out alive.

Unable to move, she stared into his bright green eyes and her breath caught in her throat. Maddie forced herself to look away to keep from gawking at him. She didn't remember him being in the bar when she was sitting, so where had he come from? Not that she was complaining. She was certain she would've been knocked senseless if he hadn't intervened - or worse. He stood his ground, silently, now eyeing both men. She was so confused. Was all this fighting because of her? Her stomach filled with dread as she realized. *I only wanted to relax and have a little adventure.* Like watching some chicks throw themselves at drunk hot men, or maybe meeting a nice guy who had just moved to Bridgepoint like her, eager to make a friend, or something more.

But not this.

The redhead barred his teeth at Aidan. "You're outnumbered, asshole."

Aidan looked around the bar for his eyes to meet the grins of wolves responding to the comment. It seemed that the spectating wolves desperately wanted in on the action.

Dammit. *You either step in it, or leave it, huh Aidan? Shit forever finds you.*

There was no use chiding himself. Life had given him more than enough evidence that he was indeed some sort of shit magnet. In the end, he only did what needed to be done.

He bit down his will to change, forcing it down until a dangerous calm began to hum around him.

So be it. Who needed fur flying in such a nice bar anyway?

Aidan's mouth curved slowly into a meticulous, sardonic grin. His flesh tingled as his adrenaline coursed through his body, feeling the familiar heat enveloped him with sweet, incredible strength. He almost forgot the moon was waxing. Fuck it. Let it be their mistake.

Aidan shrugged as his eyes flashed amber for a split second. "I kinda dig the odds, if you ask me."

7

BONE TO PICK

The gang of wolves bared their teeth in anger and moved to advance on him. Aidan slinked back to give himself ample room to maneuver. *This was gonna be a long...*

A blast of a shotgun interrupted his thinking, and suddenly everyone was frozen in their stance, including Aidan.

"Now just what the hell is going on in here? I turn my back for one minute and you shitheads are tearing my place up?!" Riko still had his sawed-off shotgun aimed at the ceiling, his large hands bracing it for firing. His dark eyes stared out at the now quiet troop of brawlers.

The blond wiped the blood from his lips and turned to Riko. "We were protecting your place, Reeks—"

Aidan frowned. "Like hell you were."

The blond curled his lips. "You son of a..." His voice trailed off as Riko shifted the gun to aim at him.

Aidan stifled a laugh as the blond noticeably flinched. Funny how a wolf rearing a gun could keep most of them in check.

Unless you were a gambling man.

Had it been any other bar or bar-owner, the gun blast would have triggered a brawl instead of stopping it. Gunshots were a pain in the ass to take, but unless it was a fatal hit to the head,

Aristans and Thesians alike would regenerate and live. Regular slugs would do nothing but piss a wolf off.

With that being said, wolves know better than to carry a gun with ordinary rounds. With everyone being dead stiff, Aidan was positive that Riko's 'bartender's special' held nightshade rounds—bullets laced with concentrated nectar of the poisonous nightshade plant. It was devastating for nightshade, even in its smallest quantities, to mix with wolf blood. It was the only natural thing known to kill them without uncertainty. Its poison was swift and wreaked havoc on their kind's nervous system, bleeding them internally. Out of all the history of their kind, even the strongest wolves had succumbed to the poison. It was certain death.

As Aidan slowly turned his head to look Riko in the eyes, Riko hissed a curse. "Who the fuck let him in here?"

"I let myself in."

Maddie flinched as she saw Riko aim the gun at Aidan. And cocked it.

"Stop! Please!" Maddie ran up to the counter, facing Riko. "He didn't do anything wrong! He was trying to help—"

Maddie's heart leapt into her throat as Riko cut his dark eyes at her, his handsome face now crinkled into a sneer. All of the kindness he showed her when she first arrived was gone. He looked more of a feral animal than the nice bar-owner who tried to hit on her. Everyone here proved to be nothing as they seemed. "I should have figured you'd bring trouble here." His voice was raw, accusing. It stung her...and she wasn't one to be stung.

"How dare you accuse me! You don't know what—"

Riko turned back to look at ahead, no longer at her. "I don't care what happened." He glared at Aidan, whose expression was stoic. "I want you out of here. You and your kind have no place here, so you are not to enter my establishment ever again. Are we clear?"

Aidan raised a brow. "I'm not the only Aristan who's been here, aren't I?"

Riko's expression tightened to stone at the mention of Kieran's faint, but unmistakable scent in his supposedly Aristan-free haven. No doubt he knew exactly what Aidan was talking about. Kieran was here, of all places. Why?

Riko mimicked the same stoicism Aidan bestowed him. "Get the hell out of here."

"I'll see you soon. I'm not done yet." Aidan turned away, with fury in his veins. It was enough he yielded to Riko, who was desperate to re-establish dominance in his place. Despite it, he did respect the wolf. He maintained his haven, and sought to keep peace. Part of him suspected the incident wouldn't have escalated had Riko been at his post. Aidan cast a look at the flustered brunette, whose full angelic face was disturbed by her scowl. She was in one piece, at least. A surge of relief went through him that he didn't quite understand.

She met his eyes, her frown softening for only a moment, until it resurfaced so fast he figured she was possessed.

He sighed to himself. It appeared he had overstayed his welcome. He started for the door, when he heard a feminine voice mutter a curse.

Maddie flung her purse over her shoulder and stormed out the corner to the exit, her face hot, her movements brisk. *Bastards!*

Riko lowered his weapon. "And take your courtesha with you!"

Aidan frowned. "She isn't mine."

"You damn right I'm not!" Maddie hissed as she stopped at the threshold. She glared at all of them. She had enough of them treating her like she was some toy that didn't needed to be addressed. Like some bobble-headed bimbo who enjoyed being tossed around. "Or anyone else's!" She jerked the door open and marched out. Tears welled in her eyes, but she blinked them back. How could she be so dense to go there in the first place?

Aidan walked out, stunned at her snappy remark. For some reason he couldn't fathom, it stung him that the thought of her being his was unimaginable to her. That's what he got for helping, no doubt. As she walked through the darkness of the street, Aidan tensed. The air wasn't right.

Tension was still rampant even in the open outdoors. "Hey, are you alright?" Aidan caught up to her, all the while looking through the patches of darkness the street lamps and moonlight missed.

Maddie stopped dead in her tracks and whipped around so fast, Aidan was sure she was going to hit him. Her face still held that contemptuous scowl at him, but it somehow made her no less beguiling as the shadows of the night played across the planes of her face. She looked up at him, holding her purse tightly.

"Ya know, I'm just perfect! One moment I was minding my own business having a drink, then the next I have two apes trying to kill each other! Then to top it off, I get blamed for it all?" She took a deep breath. "Oh, yeah, I'm fine. Thanks for asking!"

Aidan frowned back at her sarcasm. "Hey, look, I was only trying to help you. I didn't put you in that bar." His accent flared from his annoyance.

Maddie stepped back, her anger flaring her nostrils. "Oh, so I was asking for it?"

He rubbed his head. "That came out wrong."

"Yeah, well I wasn't smacking people around looking to egg on a dozen men!" She pressed her finger to her chest. "Ooh, look at me tossing dudes around," she mocked.

Aidan couldn't believe this woman. Now she was blaming him for protecting her? No good deed goes unpunished.

"Listen, I'm sorry, but sometimes a punch across the face gets the point across a lot more clearly and efficiently than pleasant babble and poetry. I don't know what planet you're from!"

Maddie's mouth gaped open at his comment. Just because she didn't approve of barbaric behavior, didn't make her naïve. She didn't deserve to get booted from a bar because dudes rather have a pissing contest.

"I'm from earth! And with about several million years of evolution under my belt, I might add! What about you and your friends, huh? Neanderthal Nation? Maddie crossed her arms in addition to the snide remark. She wanted to lash out again but she bit it back as his green eyes captivated her. *And that strong jawline.* She shook the thought away, realizing they belonged to a man she was busy chastising.

To Aidan, this all was a mistake. Perhaps he did cause more harm than good. She was free from the love-hungry Alphas, but what if he made it more dangerous for her being linked to an Aristan?

Aidan raked his fingers through his hair as he oddly took her scolding. In truth he found her contempt strangely amusing to him now, but he dared not laugh. She was still glaring at him. If looks could kill, Aidan would be in Éoncé by now. *To hell with this. Just leave her be.*

He moved a step closer to her, feeling her tense ever so slightly. She stared up at him, silent now, her scowl softening. Aidan felt her body heat, and with him staring down at the soft fullness of her lips, it was hard for him to not think of pulling her in to possess her mouth, tasting all the fire that was hers right now. Or pressing those amazing curves of her hips and rise of her breasts flush with his body. His groin jerked at the fantasy in his head.

His body froze as he heard a car coming. He muttered a curse seeing it was a police car. *Great.* Sinking back between the shadows of the brick building they were next to, he pulled Maddie with him. He looped his arm across her waist, pressing her back against him.

"What the—" Maddie breathed.

"Shhh. The cops were called in."

"Good." She started to wiggle from him. "I have a bone to pick with that owner."

He pulled her back into the shadows against him. "No you don't. Chances are we're the bad guys, not him."

"I didn't do anything!" Maddie lowered her voice.

"Shh—" Aidan warned as they watched the lone cop ease out

of his cruiser and paused to look around suspiciously, spotting his light in different patches of darkness. When he shined his light inches from Maddie, she scooted a step back in haste. Aidan quietly hissed as her nails scratched his swollen knuckles. She sucked in a breath as if it pained her more than it pained him.

Maddie looked up and mouthed "sorry" as the cop continued to walk into the bar. Embarrassed, she glanced down at Aidan's well toned arm encircling her like the most exquisite belt. He was holding her so close, his grip loose but firm enough to feel the fierce, sinewy body he possessed. His heart was beating against her back. The steady pace reflected the calm and patience that seem to resonate from her unorthodox rescuer. How could he be so reserved hiding from police, or taking on a bunch of steroid freaks at Riko's?

So this is how is felt to break rules and get into trouble. For as long as she could remember, Maddie was a very self-disciplined girl. When her friends were out partying and flirting with all the hot guys, she stayed home and studied for her next assignment. She was too scared to sneak out of the house as a teenager and sneak alcohol with her girlfriends. Even in college, where everyone was free from their parent's wrath, Maddie rarely went out. Of course, she wasn't without a few mild youthful transgressions, but mostly she lived vicariously through her reckless friends. Her philosophy of bad luck also kept her out of a lot: she firmly believed was that if anyone's luck would run out doing something bad, it would be her. It even seemed to be the case now: Any other girl could've walked into that bar and been okay...

She, on the other hand, triggered a fight and got herself kicked out.

Maddie briefly looked up at the man holding her in the darkness, his eyes fixed on the bar across the street.

Well, at least I'm not alone in this crazy luck.

She didn't know why she didn't pay attention before, but his face was an oddly enchanting blend of boyish features and rugged good looks. As if there were two men at war with each other in his body.

He was so compelling she lightly smacked her hand to keep herself for reaching out and caressing that gorgeous face of his to see if he was real. And when he inadvertently locked eyes with her, she had a feeling that maybe her long-awaited rebel days were maybe upon her.

8

TAME ME

They both tensed as the cop came back out. He didn't bother to look around this time, just got in and drove off. Maddie took a breath as Aidan slowly loosened his grip. Aghast, she snatched the arm back as she noticed the unmistakable gashes on his knuckles. They looked excruciating. Aidan stood still as she inspected his battered hand. He had figured her to curl her lips at it, scorning him about the consequences of violence. To his surprise, she instead held a concerned expression as she dutifully ran her fingers around the bone.

"It's not like they're broken. It's nothing."

A pang of guilt pulsed through her like fever. Those gashes were there because he protected her. And he was the only one willing to do anything in that whole bar. He fought, and was ready to fight again until Riko showed up. He deserved kindness, and what did she give him instead? She lashed out at him when he was the only one who didn't deserve it.

Aidan was uneasy with her small hands cradling his. The soft pads of her fingertips roamed over his flesh so carefully, he forgot that it ached. No one touched him this way. Delicately, like a lover. He watched her intently as she fretted over him. Yeah, he needed to leave. At least get her out of the shadows before he was tempted to do a few discoveries with her of his own and they didn't have a damn thing to do with pain.

"Are we fugitives now?" Maddie cast a look towards the bar.

Aidan shook his head. "Trust me, the last thing old Riko wants is to make a spectacle out of his bar with cops. I think you're safe from the long arm of the law." His face was stern with warning. "I wouldn't ever go into that bar again, though."

Her jaw slacked. "I've been banned?"

Aidan pulled his hand away. "Best thing that ever happened to you, really."

"From a bar? But I didn't do anything!"

He tried to move from her, but she caught his hand again. "I know, but it's Riko's place and he can ban who he chooses." She was back examining his hand with that feather touch again. "Uh, could I have my hand back, please?"

"No."

Aidan was taken aback by her response. "No?"

"I mean," she squeezed her eyes, as if putting her thoughts in order pained her, "Uh, look, these are pretty nasty gashes. They could get infected. You need to get them patched up—"

Aidan frowned. "No hospital."

Maddie blew out an exasperated sigh. "I know, I know. You can handle a little scratch, Macho Man!"

His mouth gaped open at her comment. "Macho Man?"

"You know, testosterone packing, punch throwing, karate kicking men who don't cry? Like Superman and uh...a *younger* Arnold Schwarzenegger?"

"Now you're insulting me again." He attempted to pull his hand, but she resisted.

"You're right," she sighed and bit her lip. "I don't mean to be a shrew. I'm asking you to let me patch you up. It's honestly the least I can do."

It wasn't hard to hear the sincerity in her voice nor the see the tender warmth in her eyes. That was plain to pick up. What he couldn't was why she even gave a damn. "No hospitals. It's not a big deal, honest."

She smiled. "What about a clinic?"

Aidan frowned, puzzled.

She turned her head in direction of the nearby brick building. "That's my clinic over there. I can patch you up without the unbearable stress of an emergency room." She began to walk towards the building, Aidan's hand gently in hers.

He shook away his temptation to smile. Sarcasm appeared to be this woman's drug of choice. Moreover, he couldn't stop himself from following her. He didn't say yes, but his curiosity of her kept him from refusing the gesture. His trust was scarce for nearly everyone, however, he wasn't ignorant to the fact that she was trusting him too. A woman alone helping a stranger at night had more to risk than him.

Aidan looked at the building's sign as he approached, sniffed the air and scowled. "A pet clinic?"

"Yes. I do have med supplies for humans, you know? Humans work in my place of business." Maddie turned loose his hand to grab her keys in her purse. As she fumbled through her little bag, Aidan briefly considered making a break for it before he got her into more trouble. He figured it absurd as the thought presented itself, and couldn't level with himself why he was so worried of this woman.

As the door's locked snapped, Maddie pushed open the door and turned the lights on in one effortless move. Aidan's sight adjusted at the vision of the obnoxiously bright lemon yellow office. Oddly enough, the vivid color was the only out of the contemporary look of the place, and he suspected her as the culprit who had modified it.

"Nice...color." Aidan stepped in, looking around. "Sucks I left my shades."

Maddie stopped walking to cast him a quelling look. "Don't go there."

Aidan threw his hands in surrender. "Wouldn't dare."

Maddie's faced blossomed into a soft smile. "Good. Cause I happen to like it. It's cheery." She threw her purse on the receptionist desk and walked behind it. "Now have a seat over here. Greta has my kit locked here up front."

Rather obediently, he came up to the desk and sat in the chair behind it. Maddie looked through a cabinet across from him. Watching her bent over, rummaging through another cabinet, Aidan couldn't stop himself from staring at that gorgeous backside of hers. The woman had the sexist ass he'd ever seen. There was no way he could shake all the thoughts in his head now of all the things he could do with—and to—a body like hers. Never mind that she was considered off limits to his kind.

What the hell is wrong with you?! Leave her be!

He whipped his head back as she turned around with a container in her hand.

"Found it," Maddie shook it gently as she strode over to the desk. Sitting beside Aidan, she turned to pull her stool up to him and sat. It took her a moment to realize Aidan was staring at her.

Not looking at him, Maddie opened the kit and started taking items out. "You're not scared, are you?"

"Should I be?"

"Well, do you trust a vet doctoring on you?"

Aidan could hear the underlying bitterness in her voice as she rolled up his sleeve to examine him. In fact, the irony was enough to make him roll in his seat. What medical assistance could be more apropos?

"Veterinarians are doctors," he said looking down at her hands touching him, "I'm sure you know basic human medical as well as many other species."

Maddie paused and looked up at him in amazement.

"I may actually be in better hands here than an M.D., I suppose." He looked up and met her light brown eyes, realizing his compliment based on his theory was correct.

At that moment, Maddie could've kissed him. He didn't have any idea that simple affirmation meant so much to her. So often was she ridiculed for being a vet. Many assumed she was some sort of 'med school reject' and had 'settled' for veterinary medicine. In fact, Erick gave her that same low blow just before they broke up. Her mother and grandmother told her a long time ago it was her calling, and that Maddie's 'healing hands' would benefit more caring for animals—those who would be grateful for it. It was weird, but she agreed with them. Her family was nothing if not a little creepy.

"Thank you for that." She said quietly. Her tone was heartfelt and tugging; he barely recognized her voice. Aidan was satisfied she welcomed the compliment. He meant every word. Vets were very much admired by his kind, so much that Aristans were often influenced to become veterinarians themselves. The value of one was indispensable, especially to Aristans who refused to fight in human skin, or were damaged to where they were too weak to change back to human form. He knew enough of them to know the stigma that often came with the profession, could see the past anger in her eyes of those who had belittled her. It made him angry for her.

"For trusting you?"

"Yes." She paused, dabbing peroxide on his cut. "For everything." She blew on his cut across his arm and tensed as it sent chills throughout his body. Though it likely wasn't intentional, the sensation of her cool breath on his skin was flirty and seductive. "We started off on the wrong foot, didn't we?"

"Perhaps."

"I'm sorry for yelling at you, for being a royal bitch." She said, while placing gauze on one cut on his forearm. "Thank you for helping me out of that mess. It sucks you're banned from that place too. I know you were only trying to help me."

Aidan grunted. It did suck. He was bound to be banished from that bar given being Aristan, but he needed some answers first. Now the Thesians would be on guard for him, and perhaps warn Kieran before he could get his hands on him. However, there wasn't any regret in doing what he did for her. "That bar sucked anyway."

"You're right, it did. Stupid bar. Stupid...Neanderthals with their shitty beer." She pouted her soft, oval face, pretending to be angry.

Then Aidan did something he hadn't done in forever.

The corner of his lips curved into a breathtaking smile, his features brightened and turned so incredibly sexy, Maddie's heart fluttered at the sight of it.

Goodness, the man was beguiling! He definitely needed to smile more often!

She beamed. "Was that a smile?"

He looked back at her hands tending to him, letting his smile fade. "Perhaps."

"That was a smile." Her face was triumphant as if she'd won some great battle. She dabbed alcohol on his other hand. "What's your name?"

"Aidan."

She blew on his cut and pulled his hand onto her lap. "I like that name. Aidan." She met his eyes levelly as she pronounced his name. "I'm Madeline. My friends call me Maddie. Where are you from?"

Aidan cocked his head as she dutifully tended to him. She didn't fear him, nor hate him. A stranger to her, her heart reached out to assist him. Her altruism was blowing him away just as much as her feather touch that seemed to heat his blood.

"South Maine," he finally answered. "Near White Mountain."

"Never been there, but I've heard the scenery is awesome. That's a long haul. You out visiting?"

"Interrogating me, doctor?" He quipped.

"No," she smiled. "I wouldn't be small town if I didn't mettle. Besides, I will be sending you a bill, so I'd like to know where to send it."

"Ah. Here I thought you were showing a gesture?" He smiled.

"Well, one good turn deserves another, but business is business." She said, smiling back at him as she closed the bandage on his arm. She ran her hand around his bicep to make sure the bandage was smoothed. Maddie actually enjoyed tending to his wounds. It was a great excuse to grope around on his delicious physique. To feel the hardness of his honed, lean body. Let's face it, he was definitely the best looking patient she'd had thus far.

Aidan looked into her eyes, a little overwhelmed that he'd managed to find himself with this woman who sought to be kind. Looking around, he found himself worried for her well being. This wasn't a town to help strangers. "Do you make a habit of tending to strangers all alone?"

Maddie shrugged. "I hate to blow your ego up, but in truth, no. It appears you're a special case." She was amazed herself at her trusting kindness rising to the surface again with him. For such a long time, she reserved her hospitality to animals, which had proven to be more accepting of help. After Eric, she realized that all her kindness would do was get her used and hurt. Now, Aidan showed up and she practically rolled out the red carpet for him. "My Nana says that all friends were strangers once."

"That's a dangerous sentiment. Taking in strays."

"I appreciate the concern, but that's kinda my territory." Applying the liquid sealant on one gash, she glances at him. "Besides, it's dangerous to take on a whole bar as well."

"That's... different."

Maddie nodded. "Umm hmm." Her voice was playfully unconvinced. "What if I was to tell you that I happen to know that you aren't going to hurt me? That I could tell if you would?"

"Is that so?" Aidan leaned back, curious of her explanation. "I would ask you how."

"Well, I, being a vet, can read a lot of body language and such since I deal with patients that cannot speak. I know mannerisms that are threatening."

"Go on."

"Well," She cleared her throat, and tried not to stare at him. He was unbelievably easy on the eyes. "For starters, you haven't challenged me yet. Many animals stand their ground and stare me down, intimidating me to back off, especially since they're injured. It's vulnerability most animals can't stand, and won't let you near them."

"Is that it?"

"Yeah, and you haven't initiated closing in space enough to attack me.

"Hmm. Am I that transparent?"

"Let's just say I'm not an idiot. I trust you, but I do have a shotgun in close proximity to me as well."

He wanted to smile in disbelief, but he honestly wasn't sure if she was joking or not.

"You don't trust your instincts?"

Maddie's spunk got knocked down a few notches as she thought of Eric. "I don't give them too much clout anymore." She rebounded with a little smirk, but not fast enough to keep Aidan from seeing the pain on her face a moment ago.

"Thank you." Aidan inspected the bandage. His other hand was still on her lap, resting against the dip of her thighs. Her skirt was of such thin, silky material, it felt as if his hand rested on water. As he stared down at her bare legs between them, he wondered if her skin felt the same way—or better.

He shook the thought away, annoyed with himself for being so taken by the interest of her. Of Maddie the human. But something about her kept him wanting to explore who she was.

"You're welcome, Aidan. I don't mind helping you at all." She placed the extra bandages back in the case and snapped it. "You were an excellent patient. Not a single whine." She gifted him a kind-hearted smile. "I'd give you a lollipop if I had one, but most of my patients enjoy doggy biscuits instead."

Before Aidan could stop himself, the hand on her lap hooked around her waist and pulled her in the stool even closer to him. Their eyes locked, and though her face was shocked by the quick gesture, he sensed no fear from her. How was it she was comfortable with him? A lot of times, he just gave people the creeps, but she looked at him with fascination, not fear.

Maddie swallowed hard as the faint scent of him and sandalwood surrounded her. There was something very demanding and predatorily sexy about the man before her. Possessing a raw, masculine power about him that was tempting, frightening and deadly. The air around him seemed to hold a thickness between them, as if he was more than he appeared. It drew her to taste that power, and the thought of it nearly left her speechless.

"You just... closed the space between us..." she trailed off as she stared at his lips. Heaven be merciful and let me sample those please?

"So it would seem." He leaned closer to her, as if his body wanted to gravitate to her. He couldn't remember the last time a woman ever riled him up to a point it disoriented him.

"Are you planning to attack me?" Maddie leaned into him, feeling his body heat.

"Not...exactly." His voice became distracted and slow as he concentrated on the idea of claiming a taste of her. Feeling the softness of those heart-shaped lips and sate his curiosity if they tasted as sweet as they looked.

The spell was broken as Maddie jumped at the sound of loud knocking on her front office door.

Aidan shot up, glaring at the door. Maddie stood up as well, her body tense from the sudden intrusion.

"Who is it?" She asked shakily as she cut her eyes to Aidan, who hadn't taken his eyes off the door and the shadow behind the blinds.

"It's Sheriff McTiernan. I saw your light on and just wanted to check in?"

She cringed. She couldn't let him in with Aidan there all bandaged up. The sheriff would place him at the bar and ask questions she didn't have answers for.

Aidan still stared at the door, his look unyielding and deadly. "You better go greet him so he'll know you're okay."

"And that I'm not harboring a suspect?" She whispered to him. He nodded. "That too."

"What about you? If Sheriff—"

"Answer the door, Maddie. As for me, I don't exist."

She wrung her clammy hands. "I'm a terrible liar, Aidan."

"It'll be in both our best interests for you to rise to the occasion then."

The Sheriff knocked again. "You okay in there?"

"Okay, I got this," she whispered. "Coming!" She ran to the door and, midway, she stopped to check on Aidan. Her mouth gaped open to find him gone. Without a trace.

Okay, like that's not creepy.

She shook her body loose and opened the blinds. Sure enough, a tall, pudgy man all in tan stood in front of her door. She offered him a smile, unlocked the door and opened it to see him.

"Sheriff McTiernan."

"Good evening Doc," he gave her a curt smile. "Sorry to disturb you, but I noticed your lights were on at such a late hour and thought maybe someone had broken in or something."

"Oh," looked around. "Thank you. But I just decided to stay and finish some lab work and what not. I had a busy day today." She backed away from the door as the Sheriff walked in looking around. He took his hat off and scanned the office. "You do lab work in the dark, Doc?"

She scowled in confusion as she saw that the back lights were off.

Shit!

"Actually, I was getting ready to leave when you knocked. I still have to open this place back up again at seven in the morning, and I'm beat."

He nodded. "Ah, I hear that." He strolled past her and turned the lights on in the lab.

She held her breath as she thought he'd find Aidan hiding in there. But there was nothing. Just a few samples on the table. She scowled at the Sheriff, for it seemed to have peeved her that he didn't believe her.

"Sheriff, is something wrong?" She turned the lights back off, her face struggling to appear polite.

"There was a disturbance across the street a while ago. You know, over at Riko's Bar?"

"Really?" Her feigned surprise didn't alarm McTiernan.

"Yeah, some guy started a brawl in there and ran out. No one got a good look at him, but he busted the place up pretty good."

Maddie tensed as she realized Riko completely put the blame on Aidan. She quelled her need to plead his innocence and simply folded her arms. "Those biker bars, what do you expect?"

"You haven't seen anyone strange around here, any noises or new people bothering you?"

Maddie shook her head. "Nope, it's been peaceful here."

McTiernan gave her a little smile. "That's good. At least you're safe. When you're working late, make sure all your doors are locked, alright?"

"Thanks Sheriff, I'll remember that." She lead him out of the office. "You have a nice night."

He placed his hat back on. "You too, Doc. Don't work too hard."

"I'll try not to." She nodded as she closed and locked the door on him. Maddie then turned her attention to the silent, empty office, looking around. "Aidan? Are you still here?" She turned the light on back in the lab and saw nothing. She knew he couldn't have been in the kennels, because the animals would have given him away. Walking back to the front desk, she plopped down on the stool and sighed.

"What a day." She twirled in the stool and stopped abruptly as a gold reflection on the floor caught her eye. Moving the other chair to the side, Maddie picked up the small medallion that she remembered to be around Aidan's neck. She sat on the floor and examined the beautiful, intricate markings on the edges. It looked antique and held a mild shine on the gold. Two silver crescent moons formed an "X" in the center and it was smooth to the touch. The latch that held it on a chain was worn off and broken. It was intriguing and mysterious. Like Aidan.

She clasped it in her hands as she stood up taking another glance around her office, making sure no one was there.

"I could use some sleep." She prepared to close up and smiled to herself. Despite their unconventional introduction, Maddie couldn't help but hope this wouldn't be the last she saw of Aidan.

"It's a nice night out tonight."

McTiernan turned to the thick voice interrupting the silence of the dark. He turned to see Kieran leaned against the cruiser, a cigarette lit in his mouth.

McTiernan shined his flashlight on Kieran's face, his demeanor tense and on alert. "You're on my car, son." He stood in front of him, but far enough to safely get away from any impending danger.

Kieran turned and looked at the car he leaned against as if he was surprised he was on it. "And so I am. Tell me, Sheriff, how goes it here in Bridgepoint? Nice town?"

"Do I know you?"

"Not yet." Kieran grinned. "Heard about that fight tonight. Bridgepoint can be a pretty crazy place."

"I'll ask you one more time to get off my vehicle, son."

"I'm not your son." Kieran glared at him. "You'll do well to listen to me. I have a favor to ask."

McTiernan glared at him, his hand hovering over his sidearm. "Who are you?"

"Eh," Kieran smiled. "Just a concerned citizen of Bridgepoint. Riko's Bar is now off limits to law enforcement going forward. I'd turn a blind eye to any goings on around there if I were you. You and your deputies. It doesn't even have a blip on your GPS. We clear?"

McTiernan stared at him as if he'd just lost his mind. He proceeded to aim his gun at Kieran as he stepped forward. "I am the Sheriff of Bridgepoint. Who are hell are you to tell me what to do?"

Kieran shook his head, his tone turned ominous. "That wouldn't be smart, McTiernan. Not smart at all, considering I'm ready to pay you for your silence. It's either that or you wind up part of Bridgepoint's missing. And a town needs their sheriff."

"Go to hell!" He pressed the gun up to Kieran's face. "I ought to run you in for harassment and extortion. You playing games with me? Who the hell you think you are, son?"

Kieran grabbed the gun and in one fluid movement elbowed McTiernan in the throat, knocking the wind outta him. "One, I'm not your fucking son." He put deeper pressure against McTiernan's head. "And two, I tried the polite angle. It just never seems to work with you humans." He snatched him up and tossed him against the car with a thud. Kieran looked at the gun, then threw it so far it disappeared into the darkness. "That was only gonna piss me off even more, trying to shoot me."

When McTiernan managed to get his focus back from the blow, he went pale as he found himself staring into two bright yellow eyes. Kieran's face was twisted in anger, growling at him.

"Jesus, what the fuck are you?!" his voice cracked, revealing a fear that matched his eyes.

"I'm what makes you check your back seats and closets. I am horror. Guess I'll put this to you in a way even a small town prick like you can comprehend. You may not understand what I am, but rest assured we are many. If you interfere or tell anyone about the things going on here..."

He paused to smile and expose his canines. "I'll rip up your family and maim you so you can watch—are we clear?"

McTiernan nodded quickly as his stomach felt sick from the confusion and fear that plagued him. "I understand," he sighed in defeat. "I understand. I don't want any trouble."

Kieran blinked his eyes to his natural blues, still smiling.

"Good. As long as we understand each other." He released McTiernan who leaned against the door. "You should run along now, Sheriff. It's late. You have no idea what's running around here in the dark."

The Sheriff scurried into his car and, with a quick glance to Kieran, pinned the petal to back out, screeching the tires. In the midst of his terror, he began to drive away.

Dante came up to him as he watched McTiernan's tail lights fade into the distance. "Want me to tail him or nah?"

"Nah. He reeked of shit and fear. He's not going to do anything brave. What did you find out about that fight at Riko's?"

"Some Aristan and some Thesians got into a pissing contest over some mangy courtesha. It's nothing."

Kieran paused glaring at Dante. "Aristan? Did he have a pack?"

Dante shook his head. "Nope. Dumb bastard was alone and didn't identify himself as Aristan. Probably making trouble. Why, what's up?"

Kieran began to ponder if his relentless foe had managed to find him. But Aidan didn't travel without the Azans, and he was sure the council would have made him anyway. Aidan only cared about the missions, so it would be a different tune if he rebel-roused at a bar.

It seemed unlikely. And yet still...

"Messing with humans. When will our kind ever learn not to tamper with the weak? They are only good for a handful of tasks. In any case, find out who she was. I'm curious who she came in contact with."

"Why the girl?"

Kieran rolled his eyes. "Because humans are constant. They don't change routine and places frequently, but we do. Find her and you'll find the wolf."

Dante nodded. "I'll check up with some guys tomorrow."

"Good. I'll head back to Iris. If you or anyone else sees an Aristan ShadowShifter packing with anyone here, I want to know about it. I won't have any damn Aristans especially trying to play hero. I have a little surprise coming for old Tiberius' pack, understand?"

Dante smiled, exposing his canines. "Absolutely."

Kieran grinned. "I love having an understanding with my new brethren. No council..." he trailed off. "I *am* the fucking council!" His maniacal laughter echoed as he tipped his head to the moon. "Arista or Thesia—what does it matter, Dante? We all know the simple primal rules that our creators instilled in both of our kind."

Dante stretched his body. "And what's that?"

"Survival of the fittest, Dante." Kieran's eyes glowed as he grinned at Dante. "Survival of the fittest."

9

BEHIND THAT FANGED SMILE

Aidan whipped his head in the direction of the howling far in the distance. A part of him hated the idea of housing at the edge of town, but he didn't want to risk the wolves picking up on him before he hunted on them. It had managed to work so far, but it worried him how the distance enabled the loners to do as they pleased.

The whole town reeked of Thesians and a few Aristans alike, running amuck. They walked and dwelled among the humans in that town—but not in harmony as one would think. He did a little research on Bridgepoint and found that there were four times as many reports of violence in the last three years and even as he walked along the marketplaces, he frowned at seeing so many people on 'Missing' flyers in town. No wonder people cleared the streets like they did. It seemed that the haven didn't just stop at Riko's bar: this *town* was a Haviscasi.

Aidan almost laughed at his displaced humor even as he thought of it. *This place has totally gone to the dogs.*

Of course, Kieran, being the sick freak he was, would pick this area. Where madness seemed to run free. And the council had the gall to think him dangerous? That was a laugh. Kieran had just as much a sordid, violent past as Aidan did. At least he grew out of his recklessness. Kieran was always the resentful child of an Alpha family that tried to love him. His life was so much easier than Aidan's, yet he insisted on whining at the injustice of him being second. The irony of it was that Aidan hated the attention Ninon doted on him, and at one point begged her to forget about him. It only continued to brew bad blood between him and Kieran, who insisted he came to destroy the pack with his "lunacy". Ninon, of course would have none of that. Thinking of that moment, he closed his eyes to his mother's voice.

"Where the hell do you think you're going? You will come back here and be a son to me, or so help me, by Arista's hands, I will have Tiberius ring your throat!"

Granted, he had been a stubborn, willful youth, and sometimes regretted being so cold and harsh to Ninon when she and Tiberius took him in. She never held any of his animosity against him, as if she could see into his heart and knew the pain he faced as a lost youth who woke up to find himself naked, cold and alone in the woods many years ago in Romania. Aidan looked out the window and found the memories of his youth tormenting him.

He winced as his body remembered the hunger pangs and aches that tormented him while going weeks without food. That dark time when he started to become the woods: haunting, cold and primal. He stole from transients who traveled through his territory, sneaking away food until he was caught one day. Naked and bleeding from exposure, a dark-haired woman in a caravan pitied him as he only looked like a little boy. She fed and clothed him. Even gave him a name, much to her own chagrin. In truth, Valenka was afraid of him, like all the others who traveled with her. Closing his eyes tight, he remembered her face screaming in horror as Aidan changed before her very eyes in face of the full moon. He knew nothing of willing the change; his body did it whenever it felt compelled to. And it cost him Valenka's trust. Aidan's heart ached as he remembered her crying, pleading for her life when he only wanted to lay at her feet. He trusted and loved her, only wanting to be safe. Now she had looked at him with fear and disgust. As he had completely changed, he saw her sweet, but frightened face turn scornful.

"They were right! You are an evil, cursed child, and sent here to lure me into damnation. Get out of my sight!"

Her father and the others drove him out, cursing his existence as he ran far off into the shadowed woods. He had no place in the human world given what he was. No one would want him if they knew the beast within him. Fearing another heartbreaking incident, he only stole when things were scarce, but taught himself to hunt instead. It wasn't as easy as he thought. Though his body was growing, he still didn't know how to change when he needed it, as he found himself stronger and more suitable to hunt when he was in wolf skin. Things often came clearer then, his feelings more focused instead of maudlin emotions speaking gibberish in his head.

It was then that fate saw fit to teach him even more harsh lessons of the world and his kind. A night he could never forget.

In the cold, unyielding woods of Romania, a pack stumbled across him in the winter woods. Only half-changed, Aidan stood there motionless as two wolves stretched their bodies into beautiful human beings before him. Both the man and woman looked ethereal and warrior-like as they smiled at him. The man stepped forward and scowled at his half-morphed appearance.

"Having a little trouble now, are you boy?"

Aidan backed away ashamed, "Who are you?"

His frown deepened. "I'll ask the questions, you little Ar—"

The woman next to him placed her hand against his arm, silencing him before he could finish. Tall with long auburn hair, she had a soft face that remained stoic as she cut her eyes to the man-wolf beside her. Aidan watched quietly as it seemed the man and woman was communicating to each other without uttering a single sound. It gave him an eerie feeling, until her yellow eyes looked down at him and smiled the most beautiful smile he ever seen. It was comforting and welcoming.

"I'm sorry." She said maintaining that gracious smile. "My mate and I have not run into many good surprises in these woods. With so many humans we've spotted, it seems we are rather still on our guard. My name is Elestat and this my mate, Callorii."

"Where's your family, boy?" Callori asked. His face softened but only slighty, still appearing on guard. "You're here alone?"

Aidan was afraid to speak. Would they chide him for being alone? Mustering up bravery, he stepped forward and straightened himself. "I am Aidan. I've been hunting alone since I could remember."

Elestat gasped ever so slightly. "No family? It's not safe for ShadowShifters to pack alone, especially as young as you."

Aidan shook his head. He wanted them to know he was strong, that he was worthy to be among them. "I can manage." He scowled at the term she used. "ShadowShifters? Is that what I am?"

Both Elestat and Callori looked at each other. Callori folded his arms. "Of course that's what you are. Have you no idea the powerful creature you are, boy?"

Aidan shook his head, ashamed of his ignorance. "No. I had no one to tell me what I am. Even the humans I stayed with hated me."

Elestat stepped back as if his confession appalled her. "Humans? You stayed with humans?" She sighed. "Humans will always hate you...and fear you. That's their job. To hate and to fear —and to spread that fear all over like a disease. You are lucky they did not poison or burn you, which they are known to do to us when we're exposed. You must be careful of whom you show your true form."

Aidan's heart sank as he remembered Valenka and the others throwing anything they could at him and chasing him off. Running as fast as he could from the flames that threatened him. He never would have imagined Valenka, who had such a capacity to love, to hate him so much. Elestat was right. Valenka, though noble and taught him much, in the end had feared and hated him.

Elestat squatted down and touched his face. The first kind

touch he experienced since Valenka. "Not to worry. Come with us, Aidan, and we will show you what you are and how to channel your strength. As a ShadowShifter, you have much to learn." She held out her hand. "Come with us."

Aidan looked at the rest of the pack, still in wolf form, quiet yet staring at him. He was nervous but couldn't deny the happiness that began to swell as he found someone who could tell him what he was. People who wouldn't hate him for being the creature he honestly had no control over. He was one of them and surely they would love him here.

"Will you show me what I am?" He took her hand and saw a smile creep onto her face.

Elestat shared a knowing smile with Callori. "Of course, Aidan. We will definitely show you what it's like to truly be what you are. Definitely."

Aidan didn't know he would once again be betrayed until it was too late. He was beaten and tortured for days. His body healed, only to be beaten again by anyone in the pack who was interested in showing the Aristan just how unlucky he was running into the Thesians. None of them had the decency to just kill him. They found it so funny to have an Aristan just march himself up to the lion's den. Right into those smiling faces and open arms. And when they bound him naked in the biting snow, his blood staining where he lay, Elestat spat on him and gave him that same cunning smile she lured him with in the woods.

Up until that point, he wanted to die and was grateful the beatings were over so the cold would finally take him. When he saw her eyes, he knew that she imagined him in that position when she first laid eyes on him. Wanted him dead. They all did. And for some reason, perhaps for spite, he didn't want to give them that satisfaction. Given his experiences, he thought himself stupid—but he was not weak.

He gathered up his courage that night and tore himself free. His anger was so aching and fierce, he finally changed. But something else changed in him that night. He was truly a beast now, inside and out. Swearing he'd kill whomever and whatever came into his territory, in the years before Ninon and Tiberius found him, he did just that. No one was safe from his wrath. Mercy was only a dream to him—and so it should be to everything else.

He looked at the dressing on his arm and sighed. He had to have been the biggest fool on the planet lately. Wandering into places, putting humans at risk. He had to get back his control. Sticking his nose into Riko's to save Maddie probably wasn't the smartest move, but one he couldn't bear to regret. Thinking of her name, he envisioned her sweet face and sighed. For a reason he couldn't define, her kindness amazed him. She stood up for him at Riko's. Though part of him believed that Riko may not have pulled the trigger in front of her, the fact that a human had defended him bewildered him. She didn't even hand him over to the Sheriff tonight.

She had no choice, Aidan. Don't go jumping to conclusions. Trusting her is unwise.

He should know better. Life had taught him many things...

But her compassion felt so genuine and warm, he couldn't shake it. It was a warmth he associated with acceptance, as he felt when taken in by the Bloodlockes. And that was what worried him. *The Goddess giveth, and she takes away.* Never could he enjoy anything for long before it was ripped away from him. Now Kieran ran about wreaking havoc, playing spoiled boy and consorting with the enemy. He had everything, yet pissed it all away on jealousy.

The thought of it plowed through him as he kicked a chair away from him. "Don't understand why peace and I are never bedfellows." Aidan stretched his neck in exhaustion and noticed Ninon's necklace was missing. Hissing a curse, he looked around the room and pulled away the cushions. But no sign of the pendant nor the necklace was in the room. It was all he had of Ninon. Thinking about the events of the night before, he swore again. What if he left it at Riko's or in the street? His scent would be all over it and would be a tell-tale sign he was there. He couldn't let Kieran get wind of him; all he had was the element of surprise.

Pacing, he suddenly thought of Maddie and her pet clinic. The likelihood of finding the pendant there made sense and he decided that perhaps he owed the little veterinarian a quick visit in the morning.

10

THE MYSTERIOUS MR. D

Maddie had a nagging headache and prayed that the day would move along a lot faster than usual. Greta seemed to have a curious grin that she sported every time Maddie looked at her. She was surprised Greta kept quiet this long. The woman couldn't hold water, let alone her thoughts.

"Just spit it out, Greta."

"Heard there was a little ruckus at Riko's the other night," Greta turned in her chair to face Maddie, a broad smile on her face. "Quite a big one."

Maddie didn't turn her attention to her. "So? What else is new? It's a bar full of morons."

She began to straighten the vials of specimens on the counter, taking a pause to scribble on her notepad.

Morons indeed.

It would be great to just push the whole crazy incident out of her head. If only a certain green-eyed guy didn't make the situation bearable. She could close her eyes and see that incredible face and jet black hair. Those full, perfect lips that tempted the hell outta her. The guy was definitely sex on a stick and painfully hard to ignore.

"Uh huh." Greta's voice droned with doubt.

Maddie rolled her eyes as she heard Greta take a huge breath, as if to declare some great prophecy. "What is it?"

"Well, I heard from a very reliable source that it was a brawl over some quiet vixen in there. Apparently a couple of guys got the hell kicked into them by some very tall, very lean stranger after the guys harassed her. Then, like Cinderella, she up and walked out."

Maddie shook her head at Greta's odd comparison.

"Cinderella?"

Greta just waved the comment away. "Oh, come off it Maddie. I know it was you. What possessed you to ever go there?"

"No clue. I just wanted to relax and hopefully meet someone interesting. I should have had my head examined."

Greta tsked and twirled around in her seat.

"I could've told you. That bar is full of trouble. I won't lie though, they have some hotties in there, but they're rough. Probably come with a ton of baggage."

Maddie cocked a brow at Greta's ill-timed advice. "Thanks for the warning. A little late, but thanks." New chick in a new town and what did she get? Pounced on by a couple of muscle-bound idiots. And to have the news paraded around the tiny town in which she resided. Looks like she'd reached a new level of shame.

Greta took another deep breath.

Maddie rubbed her forehead. Ugh, did it ever end?

"So, do you know the guy?"

Maddie whipped her head to find Greta staring at her with the same annoying grin.

She sighed. "Shouldn't your 'reliable source' supply you with that tidbit of information?" Greta needed to find a new job. *I think the FBI is hiring now.*

Greta twirled off the chair and leaned on the shelf across from Maddie. "Well, you wanna know what I found out?"

"I doubt you will keep me in suspense for long, Greta."

"Well...my source told me the stranger ran off before anyone could ask him anything."

Maddie scowled before she could help herself. For some unknown reason, she didn't like Greta's misperception of Aidan running off like some coward. Not that it should matter, really. She knew it took a lot from Aidan to leave the situation alone and apologize to her.

If that's you call what he did an apology.

She scoffed to herself as she remembered his charming parade of heroism.

"Lady, it's not even my forte to do the damsel in distress bit. Do you see a cape anywhere?! I'd rather save my own ass."

And yet, something told her that his altruistic behavior was more innate than he let on. That look in his eyes when she first saw him told her there wasn't a moment hesitated before he stepped in.

Maddie faced Greta, leaning against the counter.

"Okay! I give! Some guy kept trying to get in my pants, and then another and then this super hottie guy came in and kicked their butts. Now me, totally embarrassed, tries to haul ass, only to find Mr. Delectable coming out to apologize. Now he's gone. And I'm working, what you should be doing. The end."

Greta squealed with delight and clapped. "I knew it! I knew it!"

Maddie walked towards the kennels when Greta hopped in front of her, purposely blocking the entrance. "Greta, please."

"So how hot was he?"

"I don't know. Leave me alone, I gotta work." Maddie tried to move past her only for Greta to dart in her way again, bouncing eagerly back and forth.

"C'mon, you called him delectable. So?"

Honestly, Maddie felt she couldn't answer without being a schoolgirl about it herself. What could she say about her unorthodox hero that hadn't already been said about UFO's? He was downright alluring and magnetically mysterious. He also possessed what had to be the most poised, sexiest body she'd ever seen. His movements were controlled and methodical, like a predator hunting. Just imagining his deadly swagger made her body hot.

Oh, how a part of her wished she was the one being hunted.

Maddie looked back at Greta and smiled. "On a scale from one to ten? ...Fifteen."

Greta's jaw dropped so low, Maddie feared she might have to help the woman pick it up off the ground. "Wow, wow, wee!" She shook her hand as if she'd touched something hot.

Only then Maddie was able to move past her. Her back to Greta, her lips quirked up into a smile for her actions. She had always been a free-spirited, boy-crazy woman. She had no doubt Greta's bedroom wall was plastered with sexy men everywhere. Like a teenybopper, but more Rated R than PG-13, probably.

"Oh my God yasssss! Tell me you've got some digits?"

Maddie was silent.

Greta crinkled her face at her silence. "Or at least copped a feel?"

Still no answer. Maddie moved to pick up a kitten from the kennel above her. The kitten's gentle mews broke the silence.

Greta folded her arms in annoyance, her face scowling. "Maddie!" She sounded more like a scolding mother than a friend all of a sudden.

"What now?" Maddie swabbed the kitten gently on the paw with a topical cream and stroked it as it continued with its mewing. It always amazed her to be able to let her actions and her emotions be completely separate. Most women would have imagined Greta was the kitten and choke it to death. Yeah, that would be bad for business.

"I didn't even know the guy! He helped, I patched him up and sent him on his way. You said it yourself. The men there are trouble. Last thing I need is a meathead with a short fuse."

She had enough history of that in her life.

Greta started to inspect her nails nonchalantly as if her statement was trivial at best. "Didn't seem like a meathead to me. Helping some chick he didn't know, not asking for anything in return. Sounds like a pretty decent guy." She looked up at Maddie and sighed. "And here in Bridgepoint, Maddie, that's a rarity."

And Greta would know. She had lived in this town all her life. Her ex-boyfriend was a womanizer who spread himself all over town. And, of course, with all the whispers and snickering of a small town—Greta was the last to know.

Angry and bitter she sent him packing, refusing to fall for the trap of keeping him because she was pregnant. That was three years ago, and despite Greta's faulty relationships, Maddie praised her for having such an amazing resolve and to find romance her daily childlike obsession.

"Just forget it, Greta. I just had a little adventure and it's all over and done with. Back to reality." She petted Comrade. "And back to work."

Greta sighs. "You and work. Comrade's not at risk from dying of boredom. But you are."

"Scolding will get you nowhere." Maddie gave her a hopeless sigh. "Now back up front and let me know who's up next after I give Comrade his antibiotics."

Greta snapped a mocking salute and marched out the double doors.

Maddie couldn't help but laugh at her assistant's hilarious actions. Sometimes she wasn't sure if she came out on top with this office and assistant "package deal."

The seaside town of Bridgepoint was quite a classic Norman Rockwell during the day. Aiden was beginning to like the lush, saccharin scenery, very much to his own chagrin. He had also forgotten how much he'd missed living by the water. Before leaving for the States, Tiberius had set the pack near the Black Sea. Though they only stayed there three years, before things in Romania turned horribly ugly, he had fond memories of being so close to the sea then. Bridgepoint had a quaint, serene feel during the day, even though there were people everywhere. But there was something bubbling under the surface of this small town.

There was no doubt the people here were a little leery of something. And with him following a trail to Kieran to this place, he had a pretty good idea of what. The wolves at the bar were loners, and those were the worst. They believed in nothing and wanted nothing except revenge of some sort. So why were they lying about Kieran? He spent most of the day trying to track him, but the scent had gone cold and so did any clues. He needed to branch out to the other nearby towns, hoping someone knew something.

He zipped up his jacket and sped up after he cleared the intersection. As his eyes glanced to each side of the street, he saw the pet clinic to his right.

You can always get Ninon's necklace back. You know where she is.

Regardless, Aidan found himself slowing down and making a U-turn as something in him didn't want to listen to reason. If she did have it, it was probably in a safe place. However, he didn't stay to find out if the Sheriff truly bought her story, so peeking in on her to make sure she was okay couldn't hurt.

Turning into a parking space, he turned off his engine and sat back on his bike for a moment. Inhaling the area around him, he was bombarded with animal scents, people and food. Nothing of Kieran, but he also picked up that there were more Thesians in this town than he thought. As he sobered, he got off his bike and walked towards the pet clinic. He shouldn't be attempting to see her. In fact, he needed to stalk and hunt Kieran down before anyone got hurt or even knew what was going on, not visit the intriguing veterinarian.

Aristans tried to shield their lives away from humans. Coexisting, but never exposing their true selves to them. They hid in plain sight, but couldn't help but stay close to their own kind. The less they drew humans into their lives, the less the chances of being exposed. Thesians, however, thrived on humans and used them whenever possible. But if they learned too much, or served their purpose, they were killed. Aristans couldn't dismiss human life so casually, so they just preferred to steer clear.

He had no intention of getting Maddie involved with any of this. It was dangerous and his burden to bear. He had to keep telling himself that he was only here to retrieve Ninon's necklace, and that was it. But the sudden nervousness as he stood at the entrance wanted to betray him. Eagerness tempted him to move faster inside. What the hell was the matter with him?

Aidan walked in, sweeping the area. The chairs were lined up against the lemon-colored wall. The bright color made the entire office insanely bright - so bright Aidan debated whether he should take his shades off. There were no tables, just the receptionist desk that sat directly up front. There were a few patrons seated—namely, a very petite elderly woman sat to the left of him. Her face was crinkled into a frown as she held her dog on the leash. And as he took two additional steps, he was greeted with the huge Rottweiler growling at him at the end of the leash. It was a surreal image at best. The woman had to weigh around a buck twenty, and didn't even budge from her chair as the dog there eyed Aidan as a feast.

"Hush up, Hercules! Heel!" She looked up at Aidan with a sheepish grin. "I'm so sorry. He's not gonna bother you. He's all bark."

Aidan stopped within a foot of the dog and took off his shades, staring into the canine's eyes as it growled at him. His stance unwavering, the dog whimpered and rolled on his back to expose his belly. The older woman's jaw dropped at the sight of her huge mutt under submission. Aidan's lips quirked up to a smile as he folded his shades and slid them on his shirt.

"All bark, indeed."

Aidan walked up to the counter where the assistant sat there gawking at him. He paused for a second, slightly unsure of himself as he approached. Her jaw slacked as her gaze dropped from his face down to the entire length of him. *Did she know him or something?* Her pheromones enveloped her like an aura and were going berserk. Uneasy, he took a cautious step back.

"I'm looking for Maddie...Madeline. Is she here today?"

Greta pushed the words out as she stared at him. "Ahh..." She motioned to the back. "Ahh...hold on one moment. I'll go get her!" She barely finished the sentence when she slid out of the chair and loped down the hall as if a fire broke out, sprinting like an all-American champ until her shoes squeaked as she skidded to a halt at the other entrance.

Maddie turned to Greta who stood between the double doors, gasping for breath.

She frowned at the sudden intrusion. "What's the matter?"

"Someone's here to see you."

Maddie fanned her away. "Well, tell them to wait outside for an appointment. You know this works, what's the matter with you?"

Greta smacked her lips. "Not a customer...Mr. D."

Maddie blinked and scowled deeper. "What? Who?"

Greta looked back towards the hallway as if to check if anyone was behind her listening. "D as in Mr. Delectable!"

As the nickname registered, Maddie's face dropped. "Crap," she breathed. "You're kidding, right?"

Greta, reflecting the same shock, just shook her head. "Dark hair, bright green eyes. Built like a hot tower of lust?"

Yep. That sounded like him all right.

Maddie hurried over to the door with Greta and they both peeped at him standing there facing the entrance waiting.She stared at his form and her mouth went dry as she recognized that long, lean body anywhere. "That's him. That's Aidan."

Greta sucked in a breath, admiring. "Holy moley, Maddie. You were rescued by that over there?"

Maddie whispered. "Yeah."

"And you didn't do anything?"

Maddie nudged her in scorn. "Greta!"

"I'm just saying. You could've borrowed my desk. I'd totally forgive you."

Maddie rolled her eyes at Greta's giddiness. But in fact, her stomach fluttered and her nerves stood on end as she realized he was there for her. She backed away from the door fearing he'd see her. "What the hell is he doing here? What do I do?"

Greta pursed her lips and nodded. "You lure him back here and wear him out. It's time to take it back to the animal kingdom, doll. You're a vet, how could you not know this?"

"This isn't one of your cheesy romance novels, Greta. It doesn't work that way. Besides, I barely know him. Didn't you say all the guys here are off their rocker? He could be a serial killer or something. That would totally be my luck."

Greta peeped at him again and grinned. "Looking like that, he could slay me any day."

Maddie chewed her lip with angst. She wanted to talk more with him, but a familiar part of her was hesitant of even getting to know him. They kinda just crashed into each other's orbits last night when she got into some trouble, and if she was a hopeless romantic like the old days, she may have considered it fate. But then again, she felt that same way about her ex-boyfriend; and look where that got her. No. There's no such thing as fate. "Eh, I don't know."

"You make things far too complicated, Maddie. Why don't you just talk with him and see what he wants first, huh?" Greta gave her a playful push, grinning.

Maddie sighed. "I hate you so much."

Greta winked. "Shut up. You love me." She pushed her again. "Now go. Don't keep fine customers waiting."

Maddie straightened her jacket as she was pushed through the door. Aidan turned around to meet her eyes as she walked over to him. She swallowed to drown the butterflies in her stomach. That man stuck out like a rock star at a bible study. His thick, dark hair hung loosely around his handsome face complete with his leather jacket and boots. He wasn't clean-shaven like the other night, but the stubble gave him just enough ruggedness to give any mortal woman palpitations. She offered him a smile, her charm threatening to come back to her just being in his presence again. But the man had a poker face that was truly intimidating which made her awkwardness kick her charm square in the chops the moment she opened her mouth. "Howdy do, buster." She cringed. "I mean, hey there."

There was a soft curve to Aidan's lips. "Hey yourself, Doc. Are you busy?"

Maddie looked around her chaotic office. She should be. Everyone decided to bring the most problematic dogs and cats here today. Then again thinking about it, she owed herself a small break. "I have a few minutes. We can talk in the back if you want."

As if on cue, Greta bursted through the double doors and patted Maddie on the back. "I checked on Comrade and the dog's fine. The kittens need those shots and prepped for you. I'll handle the front so you two could...um...*talk*." She gave Maddie a knowing smile.

Ignoring the poorly coded suggestion, Maddie talked through her smile. "Thank you. Aidan, please follow me."

Carefully moving past Greta who still surveyed him like a side of beef, Aidan followed behind Maddie past the double doors to the lab to safety.

Maddie put on a fresh pair of gloves and reached for a kitten in the kennel. It mewed softly in her arms as she brought it to the exam table. "Surprised to see you here again after last night. I'm talking to you, not the kitty. You sure know how to do a disappearing act."

He walked closer to her, observing her tend to the kitten with gentle care. The same care she had for him the other night before the sheriff came knocking. And when he left, he couldn't get the desire to kiss her out of his mind. Even now, in such close quarters, his wolf half clawed at his composure to taste her. Lucky for him, both halves was used to wanting something they couldn't have. He gave her some space. "Well, I figured it would be best for the both of us. And you're right what you said. You're a terrible liar."

Maddie shrugged. "I warned you."

"That you did. Doesn't matter. Hopefully, the good Sheriff won't pay you anymore visits."

Her eyes narrowed."Why would he?"

Aidan looked around the kennels, but not at her. "I'm not sure."

She eyed him with scrutiny. "Are you a fugitive from the law?"

"No, actually..." He paused, being very careful with what truth he shared next. How much ugliness was she ready to know? "I'm *after* a fugitive."

Maddie stepped back, her face puzzled. "So, you're like a bounty hunter?"

Aidan nodded. *Not a total lie,* he thought. *At least it was plausable.* "Pretty much."

"Hmm." It seemed to make some sense to her. The guy obviously could take care of himself, and seemed incredibly calm under pressure. But she never met a real bounty hunter before. The ones on TV always looked so punk, so rough, so dangerous. They seemed like thrill seekers anxious with plans and guns. However, Aidan had a much different vibe to him. And considering how he handled himself at Riko's Bar the other night, she didn't doubt he was every bit as deadly.

"You don't think Sheriff McTiernan will help you?"

Aidan shook his head. Either the Sheriff was as clueless as hell in his own town, or he was in someone's pocket. "Definitely not. Cops don't normally approve of skip tracers honing in on their territory, stealing their thunder. And in truth, his help will only cause more trouble for me."

Maddie froze as he came closer to her. She set the kitten in its crate. His light sandalwood scent had the chemistry equivalent to a magnet to her. "You don't strike me as a bounty hunter."

"Do you know many bounty hunters?" he asked.

She shook her head. "No, not really. Guess the ones on TV don't count?"

"Probably not." He looked around before settling back on her bright, warm eyes."Have you seen anything strange going on here in town?"

"This is a strange town, Aidan." She said, while rearranging some samples. "I'm pretty much new here. I've only been here about two months. But to be honest, you're the only strange occurrence I've been involved in."

"Glad I've managed to reach the top of the charts."

"Well, what do you expect when you clobber men into submission and have me hiding from the cops?"

He frowned. "It was either that or let two meatheads play keep-away with you."

Maddie sighed. "Touché." She removed her lab coat, hanging it on the rack. "Do you have a picture of who you're looking for? Maybe I can help."

"I'd rather you didn't." His voice was quite matter-of-fact and curt.

Maddie grimaced at his resistance. "Rather I didn't see the picture, or rather I not help you?"

Aidan didn't look her in the eyes. "Both. It's best I handle this quietly with no interferences, Maddie. The less you know, the better. The man I'm after is very dangerous."

"Well," Maddie walked up to him. She didn't want to care that he didn't need her, but in truth it peeved her that he cut her off so easily. "If you didn't want my help, why are you here?"Aidan sucked in a breath. He knew exactly why he was here. Why he couldn't get her out of his mind ever since he met her. She was quite a beautiful distraction for his search for Kieran, and it was a distraction that, though he couldn't afford to appease, was difficult to shy away from. But he couldn't say those things. He made a mistake coming here. Before he could think of a lie to tell her, she answered for him. She made a big "O" with her mouth. "To make sure I didn't blab to McTiernan about you, right?" Aidan tried to think of a rebuttal, but he couldn't. Perhaps it was best to let her believe that after all, than to risk telling her the truth.

11

SECOND CHANCES

Maddie couldn't believe what he was implying. Why would she blab to the Sheriff? She would have been better off if he'd slapped her. She wouldn't do such a thing. Not after he helped her. Despite his rough, dry demeanor, she knew he had some good intentions. She folded her arms mockingly. "Don't worry, your secret's safe with me. You can mosey about under the nose of the law freely beating people up without fear I'll turn you in, alright?"

He felt the sting in her voice. "Are you starting the chain of insults again?"

"It's purely reactionary when I'm feeling dumped on." She walked over toward Comrade.

Aidan sighed. "I wasn't concerned with your silence, if that's what you're thinking."

She didn't respond, instead continuing to tend to the German Shepherd in the kennel.

Aidan frowned. He didn't know what was worse - the cold shoulder or her string of sarcastic insults. He found it awkward at the turn of attitudes. He didn't like the idea of her thinking he was only using her, trying to cover his own ass. That wasn't who he was.

Aidan sighed. "Look, I'm not the nicest guy, Maddie. But I am thankful for your help to me."

Maddie turned around and leaned her ear out. "I'm sorry, is that your way of apologizing?"

Aidan grounded his teeth. He couldn't even remember the last time he openly apologized to someone. It was a piece of submission that even his mother barely got out of him. Now here he was, ready to apologize to the little brunette on the floor.

"I just want you to understand that I'd rather keep you out of trouble. My job is dangerous and I always work alone. I'd like to handle this without any incidents. I'm sorry if I came out sounding..."

"Ungrateful?" She turned to look at him. Her face wasn't angry, just merely inquisitive.

He scoffed. "Are you going to rub this in my face?"

Maddie gave him a confident smirk. "Maybe. Since now I saw that look on your face that said you'd rather be gutted than say you're sorry. The win of this is more tempting to wallow in."

He started to walk towards the crate where Maddie stroked the fur of the German Shepherd as he whimpered in pain. The dog looked like it was in a fight with a cougar. Patches of his fur were thin and Aidan could still see the line of stitches.

"What happened to him?"

Maddie stopped petting Comrade and leaned back. "His owner was in some type of trouble, and like a great protector, Comrade here came to her aid."

Aidan looked into her mournful eyes that told so many stories. He felt the need to look away. "Is his owner...?"

"She's okay," Maddie interjected. "But look at what Comrade had to go through for her. All this, for him to be signed away."

Aidan's face crinkled into an appalled frown. "What?"

"He's abandoned. I know that she didn't really have a choice, but I was really hoping she would risk it anyway. This dog is worth it." She took a deep breath to calm herself. "Any living being is worth it."

Aidan stilled at her words. Looking into her soft brown eyes, a pang of admiration hit his heart. Her kind heart seemed to know no boundaries. The skeptic in him almost wanted to reject her hopeful philosophy and how it bothered her to see others in pain. However, looking into those eyes he knew she was genuine. It was a rarity, to meet someone who valued life and was passionate to help.

"So what are you going to do?"

Maddie, at first, didn't know either. She had stayed up some nights thinking it over. But last night she had made her decision. "I'm going to give Linda one last chance to give Comrade the home he deserves, despite her jerk of a boyfriend."

Aidan found himself intrigued by Maddie's determination, which didn't seem to give up on either the owner or the dog. "Do you think she's even worthy of a second chance? Hasn't she made her foolish choice?"

Maddie smiled at him. "Everyone is worthy of redeeming themselves, Aidan. Everyone and anyone. That's what I believe, anyway." She looked into his eyes and began to see sadness in her rescuer's pools of green. Concerned, she lightly touched his hand that rested against the crate. "What's the matter?"

Aidan shook the emotions away. "Nothing." He stood up, pulling away from the comforting warmth of her hand. Maddie's touches were dangerous to him, her words finding their way into that stubborn heart of his, and it made him feel uneasy. What also scared him was that Maddie seemed to be a magnet for trouble, and her determination to help this woman gave him a bad feeling. "When are you going to take him to her?"

She stood up after giving Comrade one last stroke. "Later on this evening. I'm thinking Evan will be out doing who knows what then, long enough to get through to Linda and convince her that keeping Comrade is the right thing to do."

"Do you need me to accompany you? Make sure everything's okay?" Aidan's voice was devoid of all amusement.

Maddie felt her cheeks flood with heat. The man was quite

fickle. He confused her with his guarded yet chivalrous personality trait. What a strange combination. As much as she'd enjoy having him with her, she didn't need a bodyguard. And she definitely didn't want him to feel obligated to do so. Shrugging, she brushed her tendrils back. "Nah, I'm good. She's not far from here and Comrade and I will be fine. But thanks."

Aidan blew out a breath. If he had any sense, he'd bully her into taking him with her, not even giving her an option. However, he respected her need to handle things on her own. If only he could shake the dreaded feelings from his head. "You sure?"

"Yes, Superman, I'm sure." She gave him a playful wink.

Aidan winced at the name she teased him with. "Must you call me that?

"Why not? You don't like it?"

He groaned in dismay. "It could very well be the last thing called to me before I jump off a bridge, plummeting to my death."

Maddie rolled her eyes. "Sheesh. You're a cuddly one, aren't you?"

Aidan smiled. "That coming from a woman who called me a 'mindless Neanderthal', warning me she housed a shotgun?"

Maddie lifted her head defiantly and grinned. "Well, I never said I was cuddly either." She laughed until her memory struck her. "Oh! I almost forgot. I have something for you! Something you're gonna love having back."

Aidan raised a curious brow. Sounded tempting. He had quite a few things in mind about what he'd love having, as far as she was concerned. And as she bounced to her desk, her hips swaying and her pinned up hair falling loose, he found it hard for his mind to focus on anything else. He was beginning to understand why those Thesians were ready to kill each other over her. And perhaps her modesty to the reasons why made her even more charming. A she-wolf would have basked in the attention, whereas Maddie wanted nothing to do with the incident.

Maddie grabbed the small medallion from her desk and hurried back to him. "I don't want you to leave without this." She pulled the pendant from her hand onto a new chain. "I had the attachment repaired and put it on a chain in case you lost the chain, too."

Aidan was surprised it so well taken care of. He gave a small smile, thankful it was indeed in her care. "Thank you."

Maddie closed the space between them and unhooked the chain. Tiptoeing, she tried to place the chain around his neck, her arms reaching, cradling his face. "Geez, you're a skyscraper compared to me." He leaned down to accommodate her, his face so close to hers he could feel his own breath against her skin. There, he smelled the strawberry scent on her skin, the cream soap on her face. His mouth watered for a taste of her. His wolf half demanded it. And by the escalating heartbeat from her chest, he became curious if she wanted it too.

"Why do you keep saying you're not a good guy?" Maddie whispered as she had her arms around him, trying to fasten the necklace.

His face brushed against hers as he turned. "Because I'm not. I'm surly and very unpleasant."

"I think you're just a glutton for punishment."

His breath fanned her tendrils as he lingered dangerously over her skin. His voice thick and deliciously haunting in her ear. "Is that your analysis, doc?"

She coyly bit her lip and smiled. "Just merely observing the facts. I'll believe bad when I see it. So far, I have no complaints. Surly? Yeah, a little. Unpleasant? Not at all."

Before Maddie could turn her face to be brave enough to face him, Aidan caught her arms.

"Perhaps." Aidan's lips unintentionally brushed her face, but made him painfully aware of how badly he wanted to kiss her. "You should hold this for me."

The feel of him so near threatened to turn her mind to mush. All she had to do was turn her head to his and she would've been kissing him now.

Pushing her arms back, he grabbed the necklace and placed it in her hand.

She looked at him, puzzled. "But this is yours."

"I know. But I may get into some skirmishes and I don't want to lose it again." He closed her hand around the necklace. "It means a lot to me."

Maddie nodded. His standoffish behavior reminded her of herself when she started to trust. Though she understood it, and knew Aidan had no obligation to trust her, she still wanted him to try. "Sure, I'll hold it for you while you beat the hell outta people."

Before he could open his mouth, she put her hand to his lips. "I know. You're not a good guy. Duly noted." She smiled at his silence, almost tickled at his shocked expression that she dared quell him. Winning victories with this man was akin to slowly taming a very wild, very stubborn animal.

"Hey, Maddie." Greta then popped her head through the double doors. "Hate to interrupt, but I don't think I can hold off the mob of crazies out here for you any longer."

Maddie turned to Greta, timidly taking her hand away from Aidan's mouth, who also turned to face Greta. "The pets aren't that bad, are they?"

Greta scoffed. "I was referring to the owners." She popped back out into the main area. Maddie could hear Greta's muffled voice behind the double doors, yelling at pets and their owners. Maddie sighed as she saw Aidan straightening up, realizing it was time he left.

"I better get going. I have some places to check out." Aidan moved past her.

"Doors to kick down? Criminals to chase?" Maddie shrugged her lab coat back on giving him a playful smirk.

"Something like that." He said, stopping short of going through the doors. "You're gonna be okay?" He immediately wanted to kick himself at his concerned tone. Though he'd hope she didn't notice it, when he saw her grin, Aidan knew she did.

"I may have been a little outside my element at Riko's, but I can totally handle myself. However, I really appreciate the concern, considering it's supposed to be somewhat a rarity."

"Your sarcasm knows no bounds, it seems." He folded his arms. "If it was a soap, you'd reek of it."

"Just like you with your testosterone. I think we're even." Maddie playfully brushed past him and out through the double doors. Aidan followed behind and nodded to Greta as he left. Her eager wave, though friendly, amused him.

Aidan watched her work the office, meeting her patients and greeting the owners. Make no mistake, there was something quite magnetic about the woman. Perhaps it was her charm and good-will, or the fact the woman managed to get a rise outta him, in more ways than one. In either case, he had a feeling she may be in a little over her head. There was something lingering in that kennel that didn't smell right.

After the biggest chunk of patients were visited, Greta sat back in her chair as Maddie took off her lab coat. "So, how was Mr. D?"

Maddie sighed. "More and more strange. Perhaps more mysterious than strange."

"Mysterious is good." Greta smiled, raising her eyebrows in a racy fashion. "No one likes an open book, even if it is a sexy one."

"You're strange, too." Maddie went to the back and approached Comrade's kennel. Eagerly, he patted his paws against the wire as she unhinged the door. "Come, Comrade, let's go." Upon releasing him from the kennel, Comrade shook himself off and with a stop and go pace, trotted behind Maddie as she walked out. "I'm going to try and make a miracle, Greta. Keep your fingers crossed." She stopped at Greta's desk as Comrade made a tiny detour and came to Greta, who patted his face and rubbed his ears.

"Linda will see the light, but if she doesn't, Comrade is totally welcome at home with me."

"Thanks." Maddie grabbed her keys, headed out with Comrade close behind her. Time to see if Linda is ready for that second chance.

DEATH HOWL

A s Maddie drove down Main Street, she realized there was a league of bikes parked at Devin's – another bar on the far end of town near Linda's house. Most were without riders, but a few men were leaning back on their bikes talking. Something about that immediately reminded her of Aidan. They all looked young, beautiful and surprisingly intimidating. As she took advantage of the stoplight and looked on, she noticed the bar seemed quiet and oddly...civilized.

Perhaps I should've tried here first instead of Riko's.

Pulling up at Linda's house, Maddie blew her horn before she hopped out and got Comrade out the truck. Linda opened the door and froze at the doorway. Comrade paced and wagged his tail as Linda shrieked in happiness and started running down the sidewalk. Careful of his wounds, Maddie walked over to meet her, Comrade excited to the point of whining and growling on the lead.

"Oh, I missed him so much!" Linda sobbed as Comrade ran over to her. "Sandy will be so happy to have him back home."

"What the hell?"

Linda went stiff at Evan's voice from behind them. She turned to see him standing by the doorway. His face was dark and brooding, watching them both. Comrade growled at Evan, standing his ground.

"I thought I made it clear that dog is off this property, or didn't you listen?"

Linda held on to Comrade, who didn't take his eyes off of Evan. "He's mine, Evan. Sandra and I miss him. He's been in our family forever, long before you."

"I don't give a shit!" He yelled.

Linda jumped at his tone, which triggered Comrade to growl and bark.

Evan pointed to the dog, still frowning. "You see what I mean? He's dangerous, Linda! You want him around Sandra like this? What if he flips out and bites her?"

Maddie stood next to Linda, who finally rose to her feet. Linda's face held a stern expression, yet Maddie knew that behind it was a woman who was scared to death. It in turn gave her an extra boost of courage to help Linda reclaim her life.

"He's not dangerous, Evan. You are! He attacked you only because..." Linda's fragile, trembling voice trailed off. She shook her head, refusing to voice all his sins. "He stays and that's final. I should have never gave him up. I should have...I should have let *you* go!"

Evan saw red. "What the fuck did you just say to me?"

As he lunged forward, Linda moved back, still restraining Comrade. Maddie stood between them, her body shaking intuitively at the large man before her. Evan had to be at least six foot four. His arms were like hunks of ham, thick and muscular, easily shadowing her. Despite her apprehension, she glared at him in warning, being Linda's only shield.

"You should cool down, Evan, before you do something you'll regret."

Evan's eyes darkened. "Move."

The air between them was palpable and warm, echoing their tension. Maddie stood exposed, realizing that Evan could very well strike her and it would be lights out. *If I don't stand for her, who will?* "No." Maddie stood her ground between them, her face void of kindness. "Back off or I'll call the Sheriff over here. I have him on speed dial." She swallowed, looking back at Linda, then to him. "You don't want another arrest now, Evan."

"You're threatening me?" Watching the shock on both their faces, he laughed maniacally at her threat, so much that it made Maddie's skin crawl. "He'll never make it here in time. Now move!"

He pushed her aside onto the ground, then Maddie saw Evan rushed to the ground in front of her so fast she couldn't make out what exactly happened.

Flabbergasted, Maddie watched as the man who appeared out of nowhere grabbed Evan by his clothes and forced him back. She recognized that face, though it was twisted with anger. It was Aidan. Maddie cringed as fury lit his jade eyes. Part of her wanted to run for cover upon seeing this fierce demeanor of her gentle rescuer.

Evan tried to swing, but hit only air; Aidan's punch connected, forcing Evan hard onto the lawn. His breath heaving and his black-clad body tense, he looked down at the bleeding Evan. Wanting to establish a mental connection with the Thesian, away from the ears of their human audience, Aidan realized his only option was to do what the Aristans called whispering. It was typically used to speak to each other when one of them was in wolf form. A telepathic connection that was deaf to humans. He placed his boot on Evan's throat, and at that moment, Evan's eyes met Aidan's with horror as he heard Aidan's firm, accented voice creep into his head.

"You made a fatal mistake, laying hands on the females. You're lucky I have an audience, Thesian, or else you'd be doing your death howl right now you, meathead bastard. You fucking coward."

Evan's dark eyes narrowed to thin slits. *"Filthy Aristan. You keep sticking your damn nose where it don't belong and you'll find that us merciful Thesians will bite it the hell off!"*

Aidan pressed harder on his throat and Evan grunted in pain, gasping for breath.

"Aidan, don't!" Maddie pleaded.

Aidan had no acknowledgement of Maddie, but glared down at the arrogant Thesian and shook his head. Thesians, mindless meat. No wonder Kieran found a connection with them. He kicked over stones with a higher IQ than most of the Thesians he'd met.

"*If you challenge me*", Aidan warned, continuing to whisper. "*Trust me, you will lose. And whether I have witnesses or not, I won't give a shit. I doubt anyone would miss you. Choose!*"

Linda ran up to Aidan, her face white with shock while Comrade sat completely still, sitting, watching Aidan. "Please, don't hurt him," she pleaded. "He isn't worth it."

Maddie nodded in agreement as she watched him. There was a heartfelt calmness to her eyes that Aidan determined was the Thesian's saving grace. "She's right. Let him be."

Evan interrupted them with his choking and Aidan sneered. "*Look at those women. They have more sympathy for your life than you're worth. It's because of them I'm allowing you to live. But your residency in this town is null. Understand?*"

Aidan eased his foot off his throat, and Evan rubbed it stiffly. "I'll leave. You'll never see me here again."

Aidan glared. "Not enough. What of the woman and her daughter? And Comrade? You will never be responsible for any harm to them, ever?"

Evan shook his head. "You have my word."

Aidan accepted his submission, despite the rather colorful choice words the Thesian shouted at him in his mind. "I'll accept your agreement, Evan." He stepped back to allow Evan to stand up, looking around suspiciously. He didn't even make eye contact with Linda as he slowly walked towards his truck. It wasn't until he revved his engine and sped off that Linda took a breath of relief.

Aidan turned to look at Maddie, who still had her hands

around his arms. He was surprised to see her bright brown eyes gazing into his rather admiringly. What was even more surprising was that the look didn't make him as uncomfortable as he thought.

"You okay?" He stepped back, taking a once over to check her.

"I'm okay. Nothing a little soak in a tub won't cure."

His adrenaline coming down, he managed to soften his features a bit as he walked over to Linda, still holding a calmer Comrade. "I doubt he will bother any of you ever again. Are you okay?"

Comrade whimpered and laid down in submission, exposing his line of stitches across his belly. Aidan squatted down and stroked his coat gently. Comrade groaned and licked his hand. Aidan flashed his eyes at Linda, whose cheeks were streaked with black from her makeup. Maddie said everyone deserved a second chance. He hoped to Goddess, Linda would make good with her new found opportunity.

"He's a remarkable animal. Take care of each other."

Linda nodded frantically. "We will." She rubbed Comrade's ears. "Promise." Before Aidan could blink, Linda leaped over and hugged Aidan so forcefully, she knocked him back against the ground. "Thank you so much!"

His body frozen to the sudden rush, Aidan helplessly casted his eyes to a giggling Maddie. "Um...no problem."

Maddie had to cover her mouth to keep herself from laughing so loud. It had to be the cutest thing she had ever seen. Aidan looked so lost at the gesture of gratitude, he appeared quite thankful Maddie was there to help Linda up.

Linda rose to her feet and gave Maddie a hug. "Thank you. I owe you."

"You don't owe me anything."

As Aidan got to his feet, everyone froze as sirens blared and a sheriff's department cruiser pulled against the curb. He cursed under his breath as he recognized who got out of the vehicle.

Maddie swallowed hard at Sheriff McTiernan walked up to the

sidewalk. She shouldn't have seemed so surprised as they had caused quite a ruckus outside, but it worried her about Aidan. Explaining himself would just get him in trouble, or at least blow his cover.

"Hi Sheriff," Linda waved nervously.

Maddie scooted closer and whispered to her. "Linda, just...follow my lead, okay?"

Linda simply nodded as Sheriff McTiernan approached her. "I got a call that there was a disturbance. Is everything alright?"

Aidan stood still, looking at the Sheriff, while Linda smiled at everyone.

"Yeah, everything's okay." Linda motioned to Comrade. "Comrade came home and Evan didn't like it, so he went to air out."

Sheriff McTiernan nodded in acceptance until he turned and noticed Aidan standing there. Aidan tried not to glare back at the cop, as he knew they both shared a certain feeling of suspicion between each other. He had to settle down as the cop started walking towards him. "Haven't seen you around here, sir. May I ask who you are?"

Not if you want to keep your arm, Aidan thought to himself.

Maddie walked over to Aidan and hooked her arm around his affectionately. "This is my old flame from back home, Aidan, uh… Addington," She stated gleefully. "Aidan, this is Sheriff McTiernan."

Aidan nodded and outstretched his hand awkwardly, and McTiernan shook it briefly. "Nice town."

"Thanks Mr. Addington. The people here are what make it, really. Good, wholesome people in this town.

Maddie briefly frowned at the suspicious tone McTiernan took on. What was up with him?

"How long have you been here, sir?"

"Just rode in this afternoon."

"Yeah, while I was showing Aidan around, I decided to kill two birds with one stone and drop Comrade off to Linda." Maddie expected her nose to poke McTiernan in the eye, it felt so long. She dared not look into Aidan's eyes or deviate from the façade she was weaving. "Linda missed him so much."

As if on cue, Linda nodded eagerly. "Oh, yeah! I did, but Sandra will be the one even more excited."

McTiernan slowly shifted his eyes back to Linda. "So, every-thing's okay then?"

"Absolutely, now that Comrade's home." Linda smiled. "Sorry if we caused the homecoming to be such a ruckus."

"No, no. I'm sure it's fine. I'm glad he's all better. He nodded at Aidan curtly. "Nice to meet you, sir. Enjoy your time here and be safe."

Aidan simply nodded at the wired Sheriff. If he didn't know any better, he would have sworn McTiernan meant to threaten him. Something stunk.

As McTiernan turned and headed to his car, Aidan turned and looked over to Maddie, who was still wrapped around arm. "Addington?"

"Shhh." Maddie said. "Whaddya expect? I told you I was a horrible liar."

"I sound like a children's book character, or an asshole--take your pick."

"Well, we both know you're quite far from either of those, so let's not kid ourselves." She replied through clenched teeth. Waving, they watched Sheriff McTiernan drive off.

With a sigh, Maddie smiled at Linda. "Thanks Linda for cover-ing. We've gotta go. Let me know if you need anything, okay?"

"No worries, Maddie. You have a sweet and amazing guy there. Thanks for helping, you two."

Before Aidan could interject about Linda's misperception of their relationship, Maddie stepped in front and gave Linda a hug. "No problem."

Maddie grabbed his hands and inspected them. "Are you okay? No more gashes?"

Aidan pulled his hands away. What was it with her and his hands? "I'm fine, Nurse Nan."

Maddie folded her arms at his defensive attitude. "Fine, be bitchy about it. What were you doing here anyway? Are you stalking me?" *Cause I just might be into that if it's you.*

Aidan didn't answer right away. Was it ridiculous to let her know he was worried about her when had smelled a trace of Thesian scent on Comrade? Probably so. "Why is it you attract so much trouble, Maddie?"

"Why is it you dodge my questions by asking a question?" she asked, leaning against the car. She smiled at him knowingly and nudged him. "Thank you. I'm glad you were here."

Aidan shrugged it off, giving a curt grunt. "I did nothing spectacular. He had no right to touch any of you. Don't worry, he won't be around again."

"I'm sorry. I honestly didn't expect it to come to that, Aidan."

"Which, unfortunately, is the reason why I'm here." Aidan walked past her and looked around before meeting her eyes again. "I *always* expect such a thing to happen. You don't expect it because you're good-natured and kind."

Maddie smiled as she realized he gave her a rather sweet compliment in the process of explaining himself. But even then, he sounded as if her kindness was unwarranted. It sounded like an accusation. "So you were worried about me?"

Aidan did a double take at Maddie as she came to her own conclusions. "What?" Before he knew it, his face started to heat.

"Umm hmm," She replied upon seeing his cheeks darken.

Aidan cleared his throat. "You're totally capable of handling yourself, so I have no idea what you're implying."

"And I can," she reiterated to him, walking up to his drastic height. A normal woman would be intimidated at such a man, full of fire and strength. His aura was dangerous, calculating, but he kept giving her glimpses of his softer side. "Lemme give you a lift and Nurse Nan can take care of that hand. I got lollipops this time." She gave him a playful wink.

Aidan shook his head. "It doesn't hurt. And I can't expect you to patch me up every time I get in a scrap. I have work to do tonight, so I'm afraid I have to be on foot."

He opened the car door and let her in. Aidan tried to ignore the worry in her eyes, but it was no use. "Maddie, it's best I disappear tonight. That Sheriff knows something. And whether it's about me or who I'm after, I can't get you involved. "

Though Maddie wanted to protest, she respected his need to keep her out of danger. He shouldn't have to be alone all the time, being a single-handed hero. Though so far their relationship, was one consisted of him clobbering jerks and her patching him up, she was already getting quite attached to him. "Okay. I'll let it go this time. Be careful."

Aidan's lips quirked into a smile. "Worried about me?"

Maddie's mouth gaped open at his question. If she didn't know any better, she would have thought he was flirting. "Of course not! Why would I? You practically go looking for trouble."

Aidan merely answered with a grunt. "It's late, Maddie. Please tell me you're heading home. I really need you to be safe."

She answered with a start of the engine and smiled. "Yes sir!" She snapped a salute and made him smile. This time it was a brilliant smile that nearly stopped her breath. "See, I knew you had teeth, Aidan...what's your real last name?"

Aidan was silent.

"Hey, you can trust me, I promise." She crossed her heart. "I won't tell a soul unless you want me to."

He sighed in defeat. She was right. She was indeed trustworthy... and brave. She really deserved that much, if not a lot more. "Bloodlocke."

Maddie smiled. "Aidan Bloodlocke." She let his name roll off her tongue. "It suits you. Kinda gothic last name, but I like it. Belongs in a vampire movie or something."

13

BLOODHOUNDS

Cameron kept working on his bike, greatly distracted, however, watching Leigh's bungalow. He gave her as much space as he could, especially after the funerals, but Bastien was behaving a bit detached from the rest of the council and he worried it had something to do with Aidan being gone. Sighing, he stopped tweaking a gear and checked his phone for a message from Aidan, but scoffed when he looked to find nothing. It had been at least two days since he'd heard anything more other than the Alpha making it to Maine. The clan was getting restless and the reconstruction had been emotional. Everyone was on high alert, cautious of another attack. Fronting a commune was easy when there was peace and there was lots of money to keep things silent. But with the attack, it had taken all the elders and their connections, massive effort to help clean up the issue from curious humans. It was a bit easier to do in the old days, but now, technology had leaped forward and made it easier for people to record, post and dig into your life. ShadowShifters from both sides had to learn that in order to survive, they had to infiltrate.

It was a long, necessary undertaking and with Aristans against the rival Thesians, getting sloppy in your clean up made it easy for your enemy to find you. Cameron had seen what happened when the enemy knew where you slept. He'd burned enough of his brothers to know. Everything was a little too close to call for his tastes.

He looked up at Leigh's door opening, and saw her quickly step out and head for the bushes. Quietly, he went to follow her, staying in stealth as she moved through the thicket. *Aidan owes me seriously for making me go from zero to creepy like this. And towards his sister, no less.* Moving through to an opening, distracted, Cameron lost sight of her, though her scent told him she was near.

Suddenly, Leigh caught his attention by clearing her throat behind him. "Came out here to take a piss, or are you stalking me?"

Cameron frowned. "What are you doing out here?"

Leigh scoffed as she walked past him. "I'm not an idiot, Cam. I know you're here to spy on me for big brother. Doesn't make you any less of a creeper."

"He's worried about you, Leigh. Have you heard from him?" He grasped her hand.

"Well, I don't need a babysitter, regardless of what Aidan thinks." She jerked her hand back in defense, but Cameron still held on. "And he texted me yesterday that he was in a town called Bridgepoint. He hasn't found Kieran, but has a hunch he's close. Now can I have my hand back?" No sooner than she tried to jerk her hand free again, Cameron pulled her forward, whipped her back into his arms and covered her mouth with his hands before she could get her bearings. She was strong, but Cameron had some years on her. And the Celt was just as stubborn as her. His piercing blue eyes were dark with warning as she listened to the scuffling and rustling of someone coming through the trees opposite them. They both froze as they saw Bastien and Onyx walk through in human skin. Unable to whisper to each other without exposing themselves, Cameron and Leigh kept silent. Cameron quickly morphed into wolf form and Leigh followed, both finding it easier to stay in stealth as they eavesdropped. Crouching low to the ground with their bellies to the dirt, staying downwind, they laid quietly, scoping the two council members.

"Why did you bring me out here? You know that either all of us, or none of the council members are allowed to discuss business, Bastien."

Bastien looked around, confirming no one was near. "Sorry, but I have a bad feeling about Aidan hunting down Kieran."

"And why's that? Afraid he'll succeed and show you out?"

Bastien scoffed at the comment. "Pfft! Don't be ridiculous, Onyx. That wolf is a menace. He's short-sighted and full of piss and vinegar. I won't see this clan lose any more people because of all this."

Onyx rubbed his chin. "Are you referring to Aidan or Kieran? Why do you have it out for that boy? I've known Aidan for a long time and yes, he had some rough times and a strange past. But the boy has paid in full, Bastien. He's earned his place in this clan and beat out Kieran for Alpha. Let him be."

"All he does is undermine us. He has no respect for authority."

Onyx shook his head. Bastien, just like the others, sometimes couldn't see the forest for the trees, or the irony in the choices they made. "Do you realize that this is us undermining him? Leigh was right, Tiberius had no intention on having the council continue on after a new Alpha had been named. We were supposed to be stewards until some children reached necessary age to fight for Alpha in the Selenium Circle. Aidan had met that requirement."

Bastien glared at his friend. Onyx was a fool if he believed that the council was not needed just because that balls-before-brains wolf made it out the Selenium Circle. "Yeah, and look at how his rivalry with Kieran was wrought over that challenge? We are hanging by a thread. Our *people* are hanging by a thread. They need us more than ever, especially since he ran off like a one man army to track one of our own. No, Onyx, the council cannot dissolve."

Onyx sighed. "Well, we aren't planning on doing it now, of course, because our Alpha is gone and we are in the midst of rebuilding our resources. But be aware, we'll need to address this when Aidan returns. Right now, we're stuck in status quo."

Bastien's expression told Onyx the wolf was not satisfied with his response, but moments later, Bastien shook his head. "We have to leave here."

Onyx frowned, folding his arms. "How do you suppose we do that? I've checked the savings and we are broke. We are depleted in funds for some reason--more than what any of us anticipated."

Bastien whipped his head around in shock. "What?!"

"That is what I wanted to call you in yesterday about. I checked the logs and it seems all the pack funds have dissipated. I have no idea how to tell our people we are stuck here, regardless of when Aidan returns Kieran to justice."

"We had a lot of loss here, friend." Bastien reassured. "Look at all we had to rebuild and handle. It was bound to eat some money. Perhaps this was the case."

Onyx shook off Bastien's theory. "But all of it? Something isn't right, Bastien. We need to go through all the ledgers and see what went where. We still need to eat and live. The families are working and paying their taxes, but we can't turn around and say we have no money."

"You are going to worry your pack with money problems Onyx? Don't be ridiculous. We will worry with this when it proves as a problem. It's enough we are dealing with the aftermath of a brutal attack that left us less than whole."

As they left, Cameron stretched back into his human form, as did Leigh, who looked in their direction with a low growl. "I should have known Bastien was up to something. You saw how he flinched at telling the pack about the money? Like he didn't want to open that particular can of worms? He's hiding something."

Cameron pulled his jeans back on and inadvertently let his

eyes trail to the curve of Leigh's hip as she bent down to pull up her own jeans. He must have seen her naked a thousand times, but it seemed every time he did, it was the first time he ever saw the curve of her beautiful body. She was lithe and strong and full of fire. Leigh was far younger than him, but wise beyond her years. Though she never showed her softer side around Cameron, he knew she had one. He knew she was soft underneath that tough shell she liked to show the world.

"Yeah, something is up. I told you that Bastien was a douche. Aidan never liked him." Leigh pulled on her t-shirt. "I'm gonna tail him to see what the hell he's hiding."

Cameron ran in front of her, blocking. "Wait a damn minute, Leigh! We need to think about this and watch ourselves."

Leigh, frowning, gritted her teeth in growing frustration. "You can watch yourself; I have to make sure our clan doesn't get rolled over on by these authoritarians." Her eyes glowed amber, thinking about all the problems that had befallen her large, proud clan. Her mother, brutally cut down like she didn't even matter, from that sick bastard of a brother, Kieran. Friends injured and dead from Thesians attacking in the dead of night. It was too much. "Something's peeling away at our pack, and I don't like it."

The glossy bud of water pooling under her eyes threatened to betray her resolve, and Cameron saw the pain in them. It gripped him so hard to see her bordering on grief that he foolishly tried to grab her shoulders to pull her close. "Leigh, come here."

Leigh quickly stepped back, avoiding him, but looked at him perplexed. "What the hell are you doing, Cam? I don't want to be consoled! I'm not one of those prissy she-wolves that need to cry on your shoulder! I don't want hugs! I'm fucking pissed!" She pushed him out the way, only for Cameron to growl and snatch her back, pulling her hard. His strength pushed her back against a tree as he forced her to look into his now glowing blue eyes. Cameron's lean body pressed against her, sandwiching her between his rock hard mass and the tree. Her face so close to his, their angered pants mingled into one as they both struggled to calm down. Cameron found himself staring at her lips a couple of seconds too long before darting back to her eyes.

"You don't want to be coddled? Fine with me. But you *are* gonna to listen and hear me out, because I vowed to Aidan that I would protect you, so whether you like it or not, I'm not gonna give a shit, because Aidan's my brother, my Alpha and I answer to him, not you! Alright?"

She looked at him, sincere, still panting. "Fine. But don't tell me we're aren't doing anything, Cam. Because I can't sit around and let this all happen. I just can't."

"I don't intend us to, Leigh. But we have to be organized if we're gonna dig into this. If the Council, or anyone on the Council is suspected in anything, we better come with the proof or we'll be guilty of treason. Aidan will come back to a firestorm of problems and finding you in danger." He eased his grip on her allowing some space between them. "I'm well aware you don't need a babysitter, Leigh. But you're all Aidan's got for family and it would absolutely break him if something happened to you. Let's partner on this."

Leigh sighed. She knew he was right. And she absolutely *hated* when the Celt was right.

The day seemed to drag on and on, despite the steady flow of appointments. A check up here, a vaccine there, Maddie made a promise not to look at the clock if it promised to move quicker. Every so often, her eyes would move to the door and hope to see the tall frame of Aidan coming into her clinic to say hello or something smart. She hadn't seen him since he came to Linda's rescue and wondered if he was still in town. She couldn't even begin to think about how much she was kicking herself for not asking for his number before he made her drive off at Linda's. She probably would've chickened out, but at least the thought should've crossed her mind.

Hell, he could have asked for my number, but he didn't. Maybe, he wasn't interested after all. She shook the thought away as the sound of Greta's voice invaded her thoughts.

She looked up to see her assistant standing in the doorway with her purse and lunch bag. "What?"

Greta rolled her eyes. "I *said* have a good evening, and don't forget that you're closed tomorrow. I moved all your appointments."

Maddie smiled. "Oh! Yeah, thanks. I'll see you Thursday." She waved, watching Greta walk out, closing the door behind her.

Finally alone, Maddie sighed and looked at the clock. It was six o'clock and her last appointment was over an hour ago. Most would've called it a day and packed up early, but it felt useless to Maddie. Where the hell was she gonna pack up early to go? Greta sometimes went to happy hour with a couple of her friends, but they ran in different circles and she only really liked Greta. She had no pets to play with and no boyfriend to entertain.

She laid her head on the desk at her own frustration. "Ugh, I'm the most boring person in Bridgepoint. Guess I'm going to my landlord's dinner group...again." She stayed there for a few moments and heard the door entry bell ring. Not lifting her head, she spoke against the wood, muffling her voice. "Sorry, the clinic is closed unless this is an emergency."

"Well, that sounds like a real shame." A familiar deep voice replied. "I'm all outta fresh cuts today."

Maddie immediately raised her head to see Aidan standing in the entrance in a black leather jacket and jeans. His gray heather shirt was fitted against his abs, almost able to see the smooth ripples. He still wore his shades and Maddie was a bit thankful for that, because all that man standing there threatened to over-stimulate her to the point of hollering like a "woo" girl at a club.

"Wh-what are you doing here?" She sat up, unsure about how she should react.

Aidan took off his shades and smiled. She looked surprised to see him. In fact, he was surprised to find himself there. He should be out looking for Kieran. He still had other areas to search. But when his search came up empty and no leads came from the Sheriff, he figured he could look again tonight. Though he hadn't spoken to her, he did check her clinic when she was there after hours. He often found himself sleeping less and worrying about Maddie more. Seeing her in the flesh was part of an attempt to quell those gnawing bouts of protectiveness he was getting. The other part was that, Arista help him, he just really wanted to see her.

He strode over to her desk, his boots clomping against her hardwood floor the air around him intimidating as he closed in on her like prey. "I came to check on you."

Maddie smiled, maybe a bit bigger than she wanted to. "You assume that I'm in some sort of trouble, is that it?"

He looked around. "Well, given the several incidents we shared, that seems to be the theme. I came by to make sure you didn't disappoint."

Maddie rolled her eyes. "Well, hate to break it to you, but I'm not in any distress...unless your definition of distress is absolute boredom." She pushed herself away from the desk so she could stand up. "I was just about to head out."

Aidan shook his head. "Boredom, huh? Well, I'm sure you have a whole mess of books to catch up on."

Maddie gasped. "Did you just insinuate that I was a nerd?" Maddie grabbed her bag and shut off the back lab's lighting. "You did, did you?" She playfully pushed him, but he was a wall. Nothing budged. *Oh my.*

"Aidan threw his hands up. "I was just saying that you look like a reader. A well-read individual who would enjoy the company of books. That's all."

"Yeah, well I'm not a nerd, okay?"

He nodded, his expression amused. "Okay."

"Just so you know. I'm hella cool, alright? All the old people and kids in my neighborhood think so," she mused, almost immediately laughing at herself.

Aidan shared in her smile, looking into her bright brown eyes. Staring at them almost made him forget what he came there to do. Almost. "I have an idea that would chase away that boredom of yours."

Maddie smiled as her thoughts begin to turn naughty. *Oh? I bet yours is not half as good as my idea.*

"I'm listening."

"It's gorgeous out. Let's take a ride. Seriously, when was the last time you got out? Not counting that catastrophe at Riko's Bar?" Aidan stood quiet as she nodded.

"It's been a while." She looked up at him and smiled. He did have a point and one thing was for certain; hanging with Aidan was bound to be some sort of adventure."Alright. Let me get my things." She grabbed her red hoodie and hoisted her bag to her shoulder. She locked her clinic's door as Aidan walked out ahead of her, past the sidewalk.

Maddie stood still as he gracefully straddled the bike and slipped his shades on, still looking at her. Have mercy, he had moves that reminded her of liquid. He was slow and fluid. Dangerously sensual. She could watch the man all day, making the most mundane actions sexy as hell. However, her thoughts hit the brake when it dawned on her what they would be traveling on.

She looked at his bike as it was some alien spaceship.

Confused at her hesitation, Aidan grimaced. "What's the matter?"

Her expression deflated. "You ride a motorcycle?"

Aidan looked down where he was seated as if he was confirming her observation. "It would appear so."

She scowled at his sarcasm and took a step back. "For some

reason I thought you had a car." Most likely a muscle car, but a car nonetheless. "I'm not getting on that thing."

"What's the matter? Bad experience?"

More like no experience. She had friends in college who rode them and though they fascinated her, she couldn't bring herself to ride with them. And mostly her friends were young and stupid, eager to be the next daredevil. Wanting to keep her head intact, she had declined every single time. She had regretted it, of course, because she hated to be afraid of anything.

"I've never ridden on one before." She confessed, half embarrassed at her honesty. She had expected Aidan to laugh at her. But to her surprise, he didn't.

"Then it's an experience you should have. It's just a short drive, and I'm very careful. I won't let anything happen to you."

His concerned, reassuring tone didn't surprise her. She's watched him too many times doing simple tasks. Every move he'd ever made was calculated. Precise. He seemed to be a cautious man by habit. When he walked her to the office that night, she noticed how tense he was, watching the darkness. As if he was ready for something to pounce and attack them.

He leaned back on his bike and smirked. "C'mon. You don't strike me as woman who'd give in to her fears and ignorance. A well-read woman like you?"

She frowned at his comment, "Are you trying to provoke me?"

"A little bit," his smile broadened, "How else will I get you to trust me on this?"

Keep looking at me that way...Maddie shook the thought away. The man had a nasty habit of bringing out the horniness in her. Being around Greta did not help either. She was glad her thoughts were private. She didn't know who would me more embarrassed - she or him?

Giving an exasperated sigh, she looked at him."Just a short drive?"

Aidan slipped on his gloves and crossed his heart. "I promise."

Maddie looked at the seat and her heart sank. It was too

narrow for the both of them. She was cursed with full hips and there was no way there was room for her on the seat. *Damn my mother's genes.*

Aidan sensed more hesitance in her. "What's the matter now?"

"I'm too...round to sit on your bike." Her face flooded with heat from embarrassment. That was another reason she had declined her friends' many offers to ride. Who would want a big-hipped woman riding on the back of them?

Aidan couldn't have been more shocked if she said she owned a unicorn. Despite it, he managed to keep his expression impassive. Was she insane? He rather enjoyed looking at her body. It was a woman's body-- curvy, soft and lush. Even now, he wanted to mold that tempting body into his until she came in his arms. A man would have to be blind not to want her. In fact, he thought best to remind her.

Maddie couldn't breathe as Aidan raked her with his heated gaze from top to bottom. His shades still on, but no less powerful a stare. A shiver ran through her.

"I don't see a problem from where I'm sitting."

When her cheeks once again mottled red, he offered a roguish smile in spite of himself.

Funny, he never struck her as the blushing type. It made his body burn for her. She looked so ethereal and inviting, even more so this way. It was all he could do not to grab her and pin her against the fuel tank, kissing her senseless. She really knew how to bring out the beast in him.

He scooted up. He no longer wanted to hear such craziness from her lips again. "There's plenty of room for you, Maddie. Ride with me."

His voice was deep and tender and she was totally unprepared for it. How could she turn him down? Zipping up her hoodie, she walked up to him. He extended his hand out to her to give her leverage to straddle the bike, and her touch seared him. She was so warm, her hand soft and delicate. Her closeness made it hard for him to focus. What was it about this woman that forced some alien part of him to be so tamed? Maddie settled herself behind him and smiled. She was comfortable, to her amazement, but tensed as he revved the engine, her hands wrapping around his abdomen. Her fingers wanted to play across the hardness of his stomach, but she pulled back as nerves deterred her. This felt so intimate to her, her body so close to his. The heat of him was enticing, the feel of his body just as much so.

Aidan felt her begin to pull back and he grabbed her hands gently to pull her closer. "No *xerhmon*, hold onto me tight. I don't have a sissy bar so you'll have to hold on to me."

She nodded in agreement. *What did he call me?*

He leaned back towards her so he could speak to her above the engine. "Whenever I take a corner, just sit straight, leaning into me. I'll balance for the both of us."

"Okay!" She shouted above the engine. *That I can definitely do,* she thought.

Wrapping her arms around his waist, she cuddled up to him as he took off. She looked around the street as they pulled out, squeezing him has he switched gears. When she finally found it in herself to stop squinting and look around, she realized it was absolutely beautiful along the streets. The farmer's market was open, with people everywhere walking along the sidewalk. Children were playing around the antique candy shop on the corner and of course some on the sidelines staring at their phones. Hearing the engine roar, some stopped playing and waved at them.

"Hi Miss Ardelle!," they said in unison. Their giggles threatened to mortify her. It didn't occur to her that this small town will be buzzing about their one and only veterinarian cruising around with some yummy guy. *Screw it. I deserve a little fun in my humdrum life.*

As they stopped at a red light, she saw the driver next to them roll down their window.

"Doctor Ardelle?"

Maddie leaned in to see her landlord gawking at her. The

woman should had been a reporter—her entire life revolved around the goings on of others. What a treat for her.

"Hi, Miss Brady, how are you?" Maddie couldn't help but grin as her curious landlord shifted her eyes from Maddie to Aidan, who took his shades off to greet her.

"Uh, I'm fine. Thank you," she shouted back, staring atAidan. "And how are you, sir?"

Aidan gave the woman a devious smile. "Perfect."

Maddie never seen her so flabbergasted. She feared they may have to resuscitate her in a minute.

"Um, will you joining our dinner group tonight?!"

Yeah, right.

"Sorry, Miss Brady, but I seriously doubt it." She shouted above the run of the engine. "My friend and I are taking a little outing." *Where I plan to ravish him under a tree somewhere until we both pass out from sheer exhaustion.*

Miss Brady gave them both a sheepish grin. "Okay, well...um, have fun."

"Don't worry. We will!" Aidan growled, putting his shades back on just in time for the light to change to green. Maddie was able to see Miss Brady's jaws drop just before he sped off towards the highway. Her body racked with laughter. If only Greta was there to see that. She would die!

"That was absolutely awesome!" she yelled to Aidan, hoping he could hear her.

He slightly turned his head. She felt his abdomen jerk with laughter as well. "My pleasure. Did you see her face?"

Maddie guffawed at the thought of it. "I thought we would have to call the paramedics."

Aidan laughed, thankful she found it equally amusing. His breath caught in his throat as he felt Maddie lean her body against him, her cheek resting on his back. She snuggled him tightly, intimately. No one had ever ridden with him. As an Azanesti General, his job was pretty lone and militant. Throughout Aristan history, they were the protectors who guarded the pack at all costs, maintaining a flank when they traveled. Funny how times changed. The Azanesti went from guarding on foot, to horses, now cars and motorbikes. Though the Azanesti fighters were allowed to have mates, they were never allowed to travel together. Aidan treasured his bike, which he had before he was chosen, more than anything. It was tied to a certain freedom he adored. It was as close to flying as he could get. Nothing was better than burning up the pavement with his Ducati Monster.

Nothing except the little minx riding with him.

His body roared as loud as his engine at the feel of her with him. He didn't feel so alone with her here and was quite enjoying her giggles and squeals of delight as he jet down the highway. Loved hearing her laughter in his ear. Loved her small hands gripping his body.

Arista's hands, why didn't I leave her where she was? He shouldn't be out with her, but he wanted to. If only for today to get a feeling of what it's like to be in her company. Then he would go back to hunting Kieran down. Back to the memories of his mother he took away from him. He ground his teeth as he took a corner. *I don't know what's going on, but I'd bet my ass Kieran is up to something big here.*

The wind was chilly, but Maddie didn't mind. She was amazingly warm inside and out. And she knew exactly why. She couldn't distance herself from this man, the graceful one with her. Who stood up for her at the most fantastic moments and didn't ask anything in return from her. She wasn't quite sure what to make of her unorthodox hero indeed. One moment he infuriated her, the next he was making her melt. It was enough to make a woman nuts.

Calm down, Maddie. He's just a friend. Men like this don't date women like you.

It sucked, but it was true. She wasn't the type of woman that hot, self-assured men like Aidan sought out.

Yet, he was with her. And he helped when he did not have to. Saved her and even protected her and Linda. To say he was supposedly cold and unyielding, there was an awful bit of him with quite a hero complex. He wanted to be a bad guy, but it just wasn't working.

That warmed her even more, wanting to squeeze the life outta him for being so sweet. She never felt so safe and looked after. Even as they sped down the highway, there was no other place she wanted to be right then. None.

14

RED RIDING HOOD

As they rode down the causeway, she spotted the lighthouse they were approaching. She was in complete awe. The picturesque view of the seascape below the clear autumn sky threatened to take her breath away. Had she known this existed, it would definitely be her getaway. He was right, she needed to get out more. Aidan pulled in and turned the engine off.

"After you, riding hood." He offered her his hand once again as she hopped off.

Maddie gave him a playfully peeved stare. "You had that just sitting in your arsenal waiting, didn't you?"

Aidan set the kickstand and in one sleek move, got up from the bike. Taking his shades off, he met her eyes and smiled. "I couldn't resist."

"Nice. Real nice." She looked up at the lighthouse in front of them. Its white painted brick maintained a rough but timeless texture. The sheer height was monstrous compared to them, and she felt so small being in the presence of so much nature and beauty. "How did you know about this place? It's gorgeous."

Aidan looked out to the sea. "I came about it coming into town somehow. I like to look around the shore. There were a lot of these being destroyed. But with the government's preservation act, it's being transferred to some private owners. I think this one is up for auction soon." He began to head towards the lighthouse. "C'mon, wanna take a look around?"

She followed close behind him as he looked around heading for the entrance. "Aren't these normally locked?"

He grunted. "You're quite the rule follower, aren't you?"

Maddie looked around, suspicious as well, wondering if they would be greeted by the lovely Sheriff. "Well, breaking and entering doesn't necessarily look good on paper. And I look horrible in orange." Her arms folded defiantly.

Aidan reached for the door. "Maybe you could get them to give you red to wear instead. It's very becoming."

She gasped. "Aidan..."

The door opened effortlessly. "Relax. Some kids had opened this up already last week when I was here." He stepped in, but paused as he saw Maddie follow him. "Wait here while I check it out."

"Do you think the kids are armed and dangerous?"

He should be annoyed at her sarcasm, like Cam's or his sister's, but instead it really amused him. "Well, I did steal their stash of Skittles last time I was here. They may be out for blood."

Her face lit up in laughter, unprepared for his witty comeback.

He looked up at the stairs then at her and she sobered. "That was a week ago, Maddie. I just want to check to make sure it's safe for you to go in. Wait here."

Before she could comment, Aidan went inside. She tightened her hoodie and stood at the opening. Aidan did that a lot. She didn't consider him jumpy, but he was very...observant. It was a force of habit for this man to check everything, it seemed. Maybe it was the bounty hunter in him. It was strangely endearing to her for him to be so concerned with her safety. Part of her hoped he wasn't like that for everyone, but that was a selfish thought.

It's in his nature to be this way.

"Maddie," Aidan called out from inside.

She opened the door and stepped inside to find him at the edge of the swirling stairs, his handsome features exposed against the rays of sunlight peeking in and out the window of the lighthouse. Yes, this man was gorgeous. "Is it safe, Sarge?"

"As much as it'll ever be," he motioned his head towards the direction of the stairs, "Come on up."

She followed him up, taking her time with the steep steps. Thank God she didn't wear dainty shoes, or else Aidan would be nursing her sprained ankle—or broken leg. Reaching the top of the swirling stairs, Aidan opened the door to the top and stepped out, holding it open to let her through.

Maddie gasped at the exquisite scenery that was the seascape. She looked past the glass to get to the outer deck to get a better look. The air was slightly cooler, the wind more fierce as she stood leaning against the rail peering out into that beautiful oblivion. She turned around as she heard Aidan come through the glass door.

"This is...wow. That's all I can say." Her face glowing with childlike wonder as Aidan approached her. She grinned at his silence. "What? No smart-assed comments?"

His gaze was soft as he met her eyes then looked out to the waters. "Not right now."

She turned around to continue looking out. "When my mother and I moved away from our family in Oklahoma when I was seven, Nana promised me it was for the best. She told me stories of how beautiful the eastern seaboard was. Ghost stories and lost ships. Beautiful lighthouses and seascapes." She took a deep breath. "And boy, was she was right."

"Where's your Nana? Still in Oklahoma?" he asked.

She smiled thinking of her beautiful maternal grandmother. "Yep. She's actually coming to visit. I haven't seen her in a year, so I'm excited to see her. She would absolutely love this view."

"So you're not from Bridgepoint? What brought you here?"

She sighed. "The truth?"

He met her eyes. "Only if you're up for it, Maddie."

"I was running. Looking for a fresh start." She cut her eyes away, a bit ashamed to admit she was running. "I met a disaster of a guy and he tried to destroy everything I had. So I finished my degree and internship, packed all my shit up and found this town that had a practice for sale. Every cent I have is in that clinic. I learned some hard lessons."

Aidan could hear the trembling in her voice as she broke. The pain in her words. He wanted to reach out to her, but he didn't quite know what human women needed at moments like this. An Aristan woman would lash out if he coddled her, held her. They saw it as pity and got infuriated. But, looking at Maddie, he found it hard to believe she would behave that way.

Her eyes stung, but she bit them back. Thinking about the past always made her emotional. She couldn't pack up everything. Some things, she had to abandon or sacrifice. She felt Aidan's body heat as he moved closer to her side. So close it felt as if he was embracing her even now. She wasn't alone up here at all. She had someone here with her, and his kindness was astounding to her.

"I'm sorry, Maddie." His voice was a deep whisper. He, too, had known what it was like to be alone. To have people who loved him ripped away from him, only to be alone once more. His pain, he could bear—but it was Maddie's that bothered him. "There's nothing wrong with running, Maddie. As long as you rebuild." He gave her a soft smile. "Looks like you built something pretty great here, doc. Nothing to be ashamed of."

Maddie sighed at his voice. He was so sincere. "Thank you." She turned to face the sea. "Nana always said that as long as we're breathing, we will know loss. But perseverance keeps us going. It's just sometimes you get pissed off at the injustice of it all. She turned around, pressing her back against the rail, when she met Aidan's eyes.

The sadness in his face was unmistakable. She had to catch her hand as she wanted to touch him and let her fingers trail over the remarkable planes of his face.

She finally gathered the nerve to say what was clearly written on his face. "Who have you lost, Aidan?" she whispered to him.

Everyone.

He thought of Ninon. The only mother he'd ever known. Tiberius, as close to a father as he could have. Aristans who had been his friends and fought alongside him. They were gone, and now he was left to bear the brunt of it all. There wasn't a moment that hadn't gone by that he wished he had lost the Selenium Circle so there would be peace. But it was too late. Kieran made his strike and with a blink of an eye, changed his life forever. Now he had to face fate, which, before stumbling across his clan so many years ago, had been complete and utter shit.

"My foster parents died. I don't know where I would have been without them."

Aidan froze as he realized he willingly shared that part of him so easily.

Maddie was stunned at his answer. "Foster? I'm so sorry, Aidan. What happened to your biological parents?"

"I never knew them." He said, reigning in his emotions. His voice was back to its calm, relaxed tone. Aidan didn't mean to come off nonchalant about his past, but he couldn't afford letting the anger creep up in him. "I barely remember my childhood. I was abandoned. When Ninon and her husband discovered me, they took me in and I'd like to think my life began then."

He had his poker face, but it didn't take a genius to know he still held some anger and sadness beneath it. How awful to be abandoned so young? And to lose the only people who wanted you? For someone so kind, it just wasn't fair.

"Ninon is a beautiful name. What was your father's name?"

Aidan shook his head. "Why is it important?"

"Because I care." She stared into his eyes. "I wouldn't have asked if it didn't matter to me. I'm allowed to care, you know."

But Maddie was right. There are times you feel utterly help-less, and it enrages you of the injustice of it all. In the end, we must do what's within our power to do. And to live.

Maddie, unable to help herself, gently touched his whiskered cheek. He closed his eyes to her soothing touch. "You don't have to talk about it, Aidan. I'm sorry for bringing it all up."

She offered him a soft smile before she turned around, facing the water, rather sheepishly.

Maddie, you are a blabbermouth, indeed. Do yourself a favor and stop trying to be charming.

"His name was Tiberius." Aidan finally said, quietly. He admired her strength. She didn't hurt or take her pain out on anyone, she handled it wholeheartedly. How beautiful it must be to see life in all its unfairness and still manage to find wisdom and acceptance in it all?

He wanted to hold her. Just once, in hopes she would be able to transfer that wonderful gift of hers to calm him. She was so close now. Inviting. Aidan ached to feel her against him, to taste her, feel her writhing beneath him as he buried himself inside her over and over until they were too weak to move. The thought was driving him mad.

Maddie felt him even closer to her. Good grief, if she didn't move away from him, she was going to explode. He hadn't touched her yet, but her body couldn't take much more of his presence and not do anything.

Down, girl. He's leaving soon. Isn't he?

"How long are you going to be in Bridgepoint?" She still looked out towards the sea.

Her question sobered him. "I don't know. It depends on how soon my business here is done."

"Just passing through, huh?" Her voice took an odd tone, so much she didn't even recognize it.

Aidan looked out. "Something like that."

Maddie turned around to face him. "Oh."

He saw her face darken with disappointment. Never had he

seen anyone so upset about him leaving. Most people couldn't wait until he disappeared. He saw the light go out of her. Why would she even care?

"Why are you going to miss me?" he quipped, fishing for some truth.

"Perhaps I think I'll miss annoying you, and playing doctor at inopportune times most of all." Maddie gave a confident, yet flirty smile. "I was just getting in the habit of giving you a lollipop when we're done."

Before he could think it through, his hands braced the rail on each side of her, trapping her with his feral gaze. He began to lean in slowly, staring longingly at her lips. He could think of something far sweeter than a lollipop she could give him. Its temptation wanted to get the better of him.

Maddie's eyes widened at his unexpected gaze. *He's going for it...*

Her breathing escalated and she thought her heart was going to beat out of her chest. What was the use? He was leaving. There was no room for a relationship. *I don't want to be heartbroken. Not now.*

She began to panic. *I can't even remember the last time I kissed a guy!* Her body tensed, and Aidan stopped cold as he picked up that scent he knew all too well.

He pulled back with a curse, his face tender and apologetic, refusing to meet her eyes. He should have known better. "I'm sorry. I'm not very good with people." He pulled completely away and released his hands from the rail. Maddie missed his warmth and closeness almost immediately. A pang of guilt tore through her. She wanted to kiss him, she did. Why was it so hard for her to give in? Before she could say anything Aidan began to walk towards the glass doors. "It's getting late, let's get you home."

Trying her best not to feel awkward, she followed him down the stairs to the doorway. Aidan did not say a word as they walked down. He was too busy kicking himself for his behavior.

He knew this was for the best. Aristans don't typically get involved with humans. Definitely not long term. It was best to stick with your own kind. He remembered all too well that humans did not accept anything different. She would never accept him if she knew what he really was. Would anyone? Would she think him disgusting and push him away?

He had never wanted a mate before. The council had urged him as Alpha to choose, but he refused. He didn't want anyone tied to him again. Everyone tied to him died, one way or another. They all left him. And he was tired of losing loved ones. Distance was smart, but Maddie was different. She cherished every little thing he'd done for her. It always wanted to make him do more for her. She was strong, caring, and floored him with her welcoming touch. No one dared touch him before. Not even Ninon. Yet, Maddie's nurturing had gotten the better of him. Eager to believe that he was capable of having a future where someone loved him and not tossed him to the wolves, so to speak.

But she was not for him. He had to leave her alone.

The ride home was quiet, the only sound the roar of the engine. It was so dark on the highway with only their headlight to brighten their way. She had no idea how Aidan managed to see the curves in the road in such darkness. She held on to him tight, her face resting on his back. He was so comfortable with her there as she tried to focus on the stars in the eastern sky.

Maddie, you are an idiot. Why couldn't you just let the man play tonsil hockey with you? It's not like you don't want it!

There was no doubt she would enjoy it, she admitted. But she had rejected him, she saw it in those beautiful green eyes of his, when she tensed. She was beginning to believe Greta when she told her that she'd probably not see a good thing if it was staring her in the face. She groaned in annoyance. But who was she kidding? Her luck with men had summed itself up when she had to move here to escape the parasitic nature of her last boyfriend, Eric, who barely found her suitable for sex.

He had started off charming and helpful, until his selfish nature got the better of him. When the smoke cleared, she walked out and she thought she had won. But soon she noticed the barrier that existed between her and the men she tried to date. Eric clearly left scars she feared would never heal. She deserved to be happy, didn't she? Why did it come with such a high price?

Tears welled up and were soon blown away by the speed of the bike. *I wish I could be the one for you, Aidan. I wish I could give all of my trust to you. I'm just scared.* In truth, her heart shattered as she met his sad eyes at the lighthouse. He allowed her to open up, and she sensed a certain empathy and sincerity with him. And she wanted to bawl as she refused herself to sink into his arms and let go. She never met anyone that made it so hard for her to control herself.

He stopped at her office first, so she could check on the locks. Sure as the sun sets, Aidan monitored the area as she locked up, looking towards the alleyways and patches of darkness. He did not say a word, nor did his politeness towards her change. Despite his nonchalance, she couldn't help but think she'd somehow hurt him. The idea sounded crazy to her. Aidan didn't strike her as a guy who lamented over things like that. She was sure there were women lined up somewhere ready to make him forget all about her.

Moments later, the bike revved through the neighborhood as he pulled in her driveway. When he turned the engine off, she filled with dread and her feet felt anchored in cement. And worse yet, she didn't want to leave his side. The night had turned chilly and she had grown to like her new friend very much. She liked herself when she was with him. She was able to be herself and speak her mind without him thinking she was odd. Able to joke and banter with him and him not take it so seriously. And when she was near him, her body grew hot and giddy with a need she couldn't yet describe.

Aidan extended his hand to help her off the motorcycle. She sighed as she took it and hopped off the bike, straightening her clothes. When she met his eyes, she expected to see her confusion mirrored in him.

There wasn't. He had the poker face that he patented.

"Aidan, I had a wonderful time. Thank you for taking me for a ride. And for leaving me in one piece, no doubt."

His lips curved into another smile. She tended to do that to him. "Next time I'll aim for two, Little Red."

She smiled as he pulled the hood off her head, releasing her soft curls that were tucked underneath. He was pleased that she was tickled at his little pun. With her living on the edge of the woods, and him desperately wanting to follow her home, she had no idea how well it really fit.

"Thanks a lot," her voice feigned annoyance.

His hand reached out and picked up the compass around her neck. It would be safe with her. His heart hammered as his fingers brushed her neck, and he released the medallion, letting it fall against her gently.

"Try to stay outta trouble for me."

He looked at the moon, then down at her, and how beautifully fitting it was for her naked face to be under the moonlight. He found himself staring at those full soft lips that seemed to beg for his kisses. Her almond shaped brown eyes burned into him, dug into him, finding a heart that he swore was torn to pieces ages ago.

You have to leave her.

"I'll wait here until you've made it inside. Have a good night, Maddie." He offered her a tender smile. It was one of the most charming ones yet. It turned her to absolute putty. She nodded in agreement, afraid the uncertainty in her voice would betray her. She started for the stairs to her front door, and found herself walking slower than she should. Maddie was bombarded with a bevy of crazy emotions.

If she let him go, would she regret it? She feared she'd be heartbroken from this night, regardless of what happened. Maddie couldn't focus as she thought of him with every step to the door she took. That gorgeous smile, how his protective side got the better of him with her, how he made her laugh. As she reached the top of the stairs, just a foot from the door, she heard Aidan's bike roar to life.

It was now or never.

SURRENDER

A idan was about to put his bike into gear when he saw Maddie turn around and run down the stairs as if hell-hounds nipped at her heels. His guard up, he turned the engine off. "Maddie?" As she continued to run toward him, Aidan leapt off the bike, his face puzzled and riddled with concern. "Maddie, what's wrong?"

Maddie couldn't breathe as she reached for him and brought her lips to his, needful and seductive. She held him tight, throwing her arms around his neck, crushing herself to him. Her senses reeled as she thoroughly tasted him. His lips were so soft, his tongue sweeping the cavern of her mouth with a skill that made her tingle all the way to her toes.

She would have missed this? She was crazy.

And she had no idea what tomorrow morning would bring. If he would disappear upon her waking. If it turned out like a bad cliché with him gone in the morning with money or a flower on the dresser. She didn't care now. There was something about this man she needed. Something that called her to him. It was fierce and primal and downright scary. And tonight, she'd willingly surrender to it.

Aidan molded her hips closer to him, pressing her even closer.

His groin tightened as she skillfully ravaged his lips. And when she nipped and sucked his bottom lip, it took everything he had not to throw her on the ground and take her with the savage need he had for her right then and there. Burying his hand deep in her mahogany curls, he tore away from her lips, only to run his tongue along the hypnotic pulse of her throat.

Tonight, she belongs to me.

Despite the million reasons against it, he couldn't deny himself. So long had he tucked those emotions inside and fought and clawed his way through his violent life, shielding himself from the pain of it all.

With Maddie, he was naked.

She allowed him to be human again. To feel alive; and as much as he knew best to push her away and leave, he couldn't. He wanted to feel her bare skin against his, hear her moans as he slid himself inside her over and over again. Aidan couldn't think of anything else more exquisite.

In one swift move, he dipped down to scoop her up against his chest, his hands splayed against her buttocks. He lifted her so effortlessly, Maddie's breath caught in her throat as she wrapped her legs around him. Her core pressed against his. Feeling the fullness of his bulge, she moaned in anticipation, then captured his lips again.

As much as she savored the feel of him, she wanted to at least make it into the house. No doubt Miss Brady would be on patrol, inquiring why she was basically dry-humping Aidan in the front yard.

Aidan held her tight and nuzzled her neck, inhaling her. Maddie was such sweetness to him, so soft and delicate. Her body was absolutely bewitching. His cock grew achingly hard as his whirlwind thoughts of what he wanted to do to her took over.

"Aidan," she swallowed, "My landlord may be watching us." Her voice was overwhelmed by breathlessness. Even then, she could barely stop her lips from touching him.

Aidan spoke in between his kiss. "I haven't heard a thud or a scream of shock yet, so we're fine. I'm really hoping for that thud, though." He felt her lips curve into a smile on his neck as she buried herself there. The man was incorrigible.

Aidan hated it, but Maddie had a point. He didn't want an audience any more than she did, but it was hard to turn her loose in fear she'd come to her senses and run from him. With a sigh, he lowered her down from him. Breaking from his kiss, Maddie groaned in protest. As soon as she was able to get her knees to work, she took his hand, leading him upstairs to the front door.

If she thought it was hard finding her keys in the dark, it was damn near impossible trying to find them in the dark with the six foot-something biker hottie behind her nibbling on her neck, his hands roaming over her backside and her breasts, cupping her through her clothes.

The door finally opened. Yeah, she deserved a medal.

Thank God she had sense to leave her book light on in the living room, or they would have bumped into every single thing by the door as he pulled her against the wall, giving her a deep, hot kiss. His tongue darted against hers, sending spikes of pleasure down to the center of her body. She pulled off his jacket, letting it fall to her hardwood floor. Taking her hands, she ran them up underneath his shirt, wanting to feel his hard, bare flesh under her fingers. Aidan unzipped her hoodie and helped her shake it off her to the floor, then buried his face against her neck, nipping her flesh. He inhaled the sweetness of jasmine in her hair, the salty ocean air on her skin. He gently took her hand and led it to the bulge in his pants so she could cup him, feeling the hardness he had for her. The sensation of her hands on him was starting to drive him to madness.

"Tell me to make love to you, Maddie," he whispered, before he swirled his tongue in her ear, sending chills up her spine. "Tell me to ravish you like I've wanted to since the moment I saw you in that bar, trying to stave off two men who were as enthralled by you as I am."

Maddie couldn't think with his hands all over her like this, let alone respond with more than an enraptured moan. She couldn't stop her body from grinding against his. The sounds that came out of her were unlike any sounds a man has ever drove out of her. She wanted to be his, to make love to him like nothing else ever existed. To wrap herself around all that sinew and power, until they both screamed from the ecstasy of it.

Aidan grabbed the hem of her shirt and pulled it over her head, and drank in the vision of her. Her dark hair was swept to the side, exposing the beautiful curve of her neck, her lips glossy and swollen from his kisses. He never saw anyone so gorgeous. Maddie locked eyes with him as she ran her hands over her breasts. She could have sworn she heard Aidan whimper at the sight of her touching what he so desperately wanted. His feral gaze alone made her body hot, moisture pooling between her thighs. Maddie unhooked the clasp between her breasts and let it fall to the floor. Aidan sucked in a breath at those soft, honeyed breasts that begged to be tasted. As he moved closer, she gripped his shirt and helped him strip it off him. As soon as he was free, he dipped down to take one into his mouth, flicking it gently with his tongue. The warm, wet stroking danced across her hardened tips.

Maddie hissed as he suckled her, pressing her body back to the wall. Her fingers raked through his hair as he kissed and nipped slowly down her stomach. Sinking to his knees, he ran his tongue around her navel, as he skillfully undid her fly and slid her panties and jeans down to her feet. She gingerly stepped out of them. Her breasts tightened as she met Aidan's eyes, hungry for her. He ran his hand between her thighs and tore a moan from Maddie's lips as his fingers probed and gently parted her slick flesh. Aidan groaned at the feel of her ripe, naked folds against his fingers. He couldn't believe how wet she was for him already. What she offered him was too miraculous for words. For her to give herself and trust him so freely truly floored him. Looking up at her, he realized that he was totally at her mercy. He wondered if she had any idea how easily she could shatter him now. How she alone had made him tame when the world forced him to be wild.

Maddie felt his warm breath against her inner thigh, teasing her. There was something so erotic about a man so poised and powerful so driven to desire this way. In one fluid movement, Aidan slipped her leg over his shoulder, opening her body to him, and took her into his mouth. She yelped in pleasure as he licked and delved into her moist center. Fearing her knees would give from it all, she braced herself on his shoulders, arching her back to his hungry quest.

Aidan groaned at the taste of her. There were no comparisons made between her and any other feeling in this world. This was what he wanted. She was the soft, liquid pleasure that he could've only imagined having.

Maddie's grip on him tightened as his tongue lapped, teased and swirled her folds. She never remembered feeling this wanted, this desirable. Her moans escalated until the mounting pleasure inside begged for splendid release.

"Aidan," she breathed as her body contracted in a wicked climax. She barely caught her breath as her center began to rack with promise as Aidan refused to stop his conquest and licked even more intensely. Losing control, she lowered her hips to him and ran her fingers frantically through his hair. He watched her intently as her back arched with another orgasm, close on the heels of one before. Her breath panting, she rocked her head back and forth. "Please...no more. I can't take any more."

He gave one last lick and eyed her deviously. "Are you sure you want me to stop?"

The desire on her face drove his need to fill her to bewitching. What was it about her that made him want her so obsessively?

She managed a smile through her panting. "No. But unless you want to call me a paramedic instead of Miss Brady..."

His posture slowly straightened as he stood back up to his full height, his eyes raking over her. Her face was flushed, her lovely brown eyes dilated as she met his.

"Well, we certainly can't have that, now can we?"

He swept her up in his arms, growling deep in his throat as her lips found the hollow of his neck. No one ever handled her like this. It made her feel so feminine and petite.

Standing at the edge of the bed, he slid her off onto it, his hands squeezing her hips. Maddie worked to unbutton his fly as she kneeled on the bed facing him. He hissed as her hands worked to free him. Wrapping her fingers around him, she softly stroked the rich thickness of him, and felt him shiver as her thumb rubbed the slick wetness at the tip.

"I love your hands on me, Maddie," he groaned, climbing onto the bed on top of her like some stealthy, sleek animal. He leaned over her, his heated green eyes scanned the entire length of her naked body. His look was not one of lust, but pure admiration. As if he couldn't believe she was real, lying there with him. "You're enchanting. I don't think you truly understand that."

A lump caught in her throat as his sincere and heartfelt words seared her. No one ever made her feel so beautiful and alive as Aidan. Never had she dreamed any man could desire her so deeply. She pulled him closer as he shifted his weight, nudging her legs apart. She moaned against the pillows as he ran his fingers along the cleft and sank two inside her, his hands quivering at the tight wetness of her. Lost to desire, he withdrew his fingers and drove himself deep inside her. Maddie gasped at Aidan's incredible thickness sliding in and out of her body. A moan ripped from him as she met him stroke for stroke, her moist walls contracting around him as he rocked against her hips. Her hands trailed down his back to grip his buttocks, urging him on, as wave after wave of unfathomable pleasure crested over her.

It had been so long since a man had touched or held her. She had closed herself off, afraid to be hurt again. But her body welcomed his touch. The fluid beauty of this man made her want to fly every time he touched her. And as they made love she couldn't help but feel a sort of freedom, a change in her as she allowed this man into her body and into her life.

"Oh Aidan..." Maddie wrapped her legs around his waist as he rode her hard and steady.

Aidan watched her writhe beneath him, her body melting into his, gripping him beautifully. He let one hand sink down between them to bury his fingers between her wet, throbbing folds. "Come for me, xerhmon...*Ciele gre ni*... I want to feel it."

Burying himself deep within her, she cried out fiercely as she came for him. The intensity forced a primal growl from his throat, hearing her come for him. Her sweet purrs and moans gripped him with such emotion he felt blinded by it. Her arms now bracing against his, she looked up into his eyes, wanting to mirror the same tenderness he gave her. Maddie reached up and caressed his handsome face, feeling the prickly texture of a day's growth on his cheeks. His eyes seemed a brighter, deeper shade now.

"What gorgeous eyes you have."

He turned into her touch, kissed her hand and smiled. "The better to see you with, my dear."

And that he did. He looked at her as nothing else mattered, with admiration and respect. How lovely for this man to feel so comfortable in her arms.

Aidan groaned as he felt her exquisite body contract around him again...and again. He reveled in her moans in his ears as he released himself inside her, growling at the ferocity of it. Catching his breath, he rolled off and gathered her into his arms. She tucked her head under his chin and sighed. Aidan smelled her hair, inhaling the faint jasmine in her feathery curls, then kissed her hand tenderly, playfully nipping her fingers.

His scent was all over her body, like a mate. She was his, according to Aristan Law. She chose him, and he claimed her.

But she wasn't Aristan—she wasn't even Thesian. She was human and not bound by his laws or him whatsoever. The sting of it all wasn't half as painful as realizing how much he wanted her with him. *She simply wanted a normal life—the only life I could never give her, no matter how much I wanted to. Never.*

In the silence, he felt her heartbeat against his body as she slept. It was a soft drumming he cherished and realized that all he wanted was to protect her. To make certain no one hurt her like Ninon, his father and his people. She deserved his protection. This was getting more complicated now. He had to find out what Kieran was up to, and fast. Time was running out. He looked at Maddie's serene oval face as she stirred. If Kieran or a Thesian found her, they'd kill her.

He wrapped his arms around her at the horrifying thought, hugging her so tight, she slightly winced at the pressure. Immediately, Aidan loosened up his grip, as he realized something else. Even if somehow Maddie was able to be with him, she would never be able to survive in his world. Her human body was so frail in comparison to a ShadowShifter, her years much shorter than his own. How could he ever make a life with her?

Aidan felt a lump in his throat as he tried to shake the thoughts away. He didn't know what was worse: being plagued by nightmares as he slept, or being tormented by the unfairness of his life while he was awake? Maddie cuddled up to him sleepily and he laid his head down above hers. Her body was warm and comforting, and he found that his body relaxed quicker than he anticipated. Aidan closed his eyes and drifted off with the woman he wanted so badly as a mate.

LOVELY DISTRACTIONS

M addie rolled to her side and rained little kisses on Aidan's sleepy, stumbled face. Her hand slid across his abdomen, letting her fingers surf across the taut plains of his stomach. He gave an acknowledging groan. "Morning."

Maddie's fingers circled around the mysterious tattoo over his heart. It was a black paw print with the same markings around it as his necklace. It looked more of a seal of some sort. "Were you in the military?"

"Hmm. More of a private sector form of military." He yawned. "What brought on that question?"

"Your tattoo." She traced her finger around the paw print, feeling the slight pucker of his skin filled with ink. "And you seem like you would have military background, I guess you can say."

He raised a brow. "Should I be insulted?"

"No, not at all. I just find it an intriguing part of your character." She smiled at him. "I can totally see you in the military. So stubborn, probably commanding people twice your age."

She actually wasn't that far off. "Seems like you have me figured out." Aidan pushed her hair back. "But stubbornness and the military doesn't mix. All the men, including me, were respectful of that. But that's not to say I followed every protocol to the letter. Some rules can be broken."

"Do you miss it?" Maddie asked sincerely, her face inquisitive.

He sighed. "I don't know yet. To be honest, I never completely left it. It's always a part of me. The camaraderie of the men to fulfill duty and make sure we can all go home in one piece - it's invaluable."

"I see."

She kissed the rippled plains of his stomach and pouted. "Are you ever gonna leave this bed?," she asked. "It's 9am."

Aidan smiled, his eyes still shut. "Not if you keep that up." He captured her lips as she leaned closer and Maddie burned with the heated promise of it.

She gifted him an impish grin. "Well, this magazine Greta gave me did say sex is statistically better in the mornings."

He opened one eye at the enticing comment, his expression filled with wicked temptation. Aidan gently took the hand she had sprawled on him and swiftly pulled her across him, rolling her underneath him with his body pressing against her. She couldn't resist moaning as she felt his erection hot against her inner thigh. The man had unrivaled agility.

"Ready to test that theory?" He flashed those gorgeous green eyes; the look was playful with an intensity she read as pure sexual desire.

Before she could answer, he lowered himself to run his lips along her throat, his body rubbing against her breasts. As tempting as he made it, she'd be on her back all day if she'd let him. And even in coming to that realization, she was still trying to decide if that was a bad thing or not.

"Let me make some breakfast for you."

When he rose up to look into her eyes with a predatory gaze, her breath caught in her throat. He looked at her as if *she* was breakfast.

She smiled at him, almost nervous. *How can I ever get used to this man looking at me as if I was constantly naked?* "That wasn't a request, Superman. Go shower and I'll whip up something before I go to work."

Maddie wanted to laugh as Aidan groaned in protest and rose up enough for her to ease from under him. He playfully nipped her thigh as she slid away from him.

"You're not going to join me?" He asked, lying on his side, propped on his elbow, in all his amazing morning glory.

How in the hell is a red-blooded woman supposed to walk away from that? Maddie cast him an impish smile to his somewhat innocent question.

But she knew better. This would not be a quick shower. In fact, the way Aidan looked at her kind of gave her an inkling that he may change the whole definition of "shower" to her, forever. Again, she needed to decide if that was a bad thing or not. She did need to go to work...at some point.

Maddie grabbed her panties and tank top from the dresser and pressed them to her body as a sudden shyness prompted her. Funny, she never used to be so open with her body before, but this time she barely thought of it, until Aidan's heated stare.

"I'll shower after I do breakfast. Now stop stalling and go." As she walked past him she swatted his butt playfully.

He smiled at her as she scampered off. She was so cavalier with his body and didn't behave skittish or frightened of him. She entertained no regrets of laying with him, of giving herself to him.

He picked up the sheet and inhaled her scent, imbedding it to memory along with the images of her face as he made love to her.

Maddie trusted him.

And despite the nature of him, he desperately wanted to trust her too. Though he hadn't flat-out lied to her yet, he didn't tell her the whole truth of himself. Knowing it was quite impossible, and could very well endanger her more, he couldn't help but want to be free with her. Would she still let him touch her if she knew what he really was? He rose from the bed and headed to the bathroom to shower. It took more energy than he imagined to control himself with her last night. Intense pleasure almost always inadvertently triggered a change for his kind. Both essences of their being wanted to be free with their mate, but it was only acceptable when both were ShadowShifters. He didn't even do so much as change his eye color when he was with her. It was a risk he couldn't take with Maddie's safety.

His feelings for her were confusing the hell outta him. If he could only stay away from her - but from the moment Aidan met her, it was an impossible feat. He'd been more successful in blood battles than he had trying to stay clear of this woman.

Aidan paused at the kitchen threshold to finally discover what all the commotion came from.

Maddie, still dressed in her black boy shorts, the scant one with the word *LOVE* scrawled across the backside. Her blue tank top clung to her exquisite body as she swayed her hips back and forth to the music in her iPod, tucked between her skin and the shorts. He cocked his head and grinned as he watched her backside.

If this wasn't subliminal messaging, he didn't know what was. Maddie's voice was pleasant, with sudden changes in the key that were less than perfect. He choked down his laughter as Maddie scampered about the kitchen, making what would appear to be breakfast to him. He didn't know why, but seeing her so domesticated and jolly was beguiling. He couldn't take his eyes off her. The woman had more energy than a toddler. Her glasses set on the table and it somehow tickled him that she braved the kitchen without them. Without them or her contacts, she could barely see three feet away from her. Entertained by the alluring minx romping across the linoleum, he propped himself against the kitchen's threshold. The aroma in the kitchen she conjured was simply amazing.

He squinted as she hit another off note. Then couldn't stop himself from smiling as he watched her.

And so was she, he thought.

He scanned every bit of her with adoration. Soft, ample thighs, the soft curve of her breasts...those swaying hips. He began to think of the night before, her body straddling his. He knew exactly what those hips of hers could do. His mouth watered, and it wasn't from the breakfast. At that moment, Maddie caught sight of Aidan and damn near jumped out of her skin.

"Shit, Aidan!"

Her silver mixing bowl popped out of her hand and fell full force on her foot.

"Ow!" Her voice was almost a whine. "I need these toes!"

Aidan, snickering under his breath, hurried over to her side. He picked up the bowl of split batter, placing it in the sink. The floor wasn't as huge a mess as he would have anticipated. The batter was too thick to really go anywhere. "Sorry about that, dancing queen."

Maddie plopped down on the chair adjacent from him, pulled her earplugs out, and inspected her foot. Part of it was splattered with pancake batter.

She cut her eyes at him "You scared the crap out of me!" She stopped to look at the mess on the floor and sighed, "My Nana's recipe."

Aidan turned off the burner with the empty skillet and turned his attention back to her. He squatted down beside her with one of his ever-growing collection of smiles.

"Sorry, I'll clean up the mess. I didn't mean to scare you." He took the kitchen towel off the rack and gently wiped the batter off her foot.

Maddie's cheeks mottled pink as she realized she was performing for an audience this time. She was so used to entertaining herself alone at home. Singing, dancing and reciting made it seem that she wasn't so alone. It filled the space in her empty home. Now she really wasn't. Leaning over, she watched as Aidan took her foot gently in his hands softly bending each toe. "Does that hurt?"

Maddie shook her head. "No." Then she smiled inquisitively. "Were you spying on me?"

"Do you always gyrate while you cook?" He looked up with a charming, sexy smile of his own.

She sat back in her chair, folding her arms as his hands rubbed her foot. "I asked you first."

"And so you did. No, just admiring the um...view." Aidan leaned in and ran his lips up her calf, "Did that hurt?"

Maddie shook her head. "You trying to seduce me?"

Aidan grinned. "God, I hope so. Is it working?"

She tipped one hand side to side. "Ehhh. A little. I was going to make pancakes for you."

Aidan felt instantly warmed at her confession. It'd take him a lifetime to fully understand her kindness to him. It was the simple things she did that tugged at him. "I'm sorry about that."

Aidan got up and turned the burners back on under the bacon and the eggs. He grabbed the spatula and flipped the bacon, and turned to Maddie, who was grinning at him.

He scowled. "What?"

She folded her arms, smiling. "Don't tell me you know how to cook?"

Aidan shrugged. "I can hold my own, I guess. One has to cook in order to survive, right? How do you like your eggs?"

"Hard scrambled." Maddie tried to get up.

"I've got it, Maddie. Just rest your foot." He moved over to the bread box and grabbed a few slices of bread to put into the toaster and set it.

"Well at least let me get the juice or something." She threw her hands up in submission. "I'm feeling like a freeloader in my own kitchen."

"I'm already up." He grabbed the orange juice out the fridge and poured it into the glass she set on the table and set it down. He grabbed a plate from the rack, scraped the eggs onto the plate and grabbed the toast just as it was done.

Maddie grew hot as she watched Aidan make her breakfast. Wearing nothing but jeans and a smile, he made the simplest of tasks of cooking absolute eye candy. Nothing was sexier than this man and his enigmatic surprises in his personality. She'd imagined never getting bored with Aidan, as he had so many layers to him. Her mouth went dry as she stared down the length of him from his lean, toned torso, down to his hips where his vintage jeans rode on half-buttoned. Her eyes followed down to that sexy "V" muscle below his abdomen as he worked around the kitchen. Biting her lip was all she could do to not to pull him into the bedroom for round two.

Oh, I could definitely get used to seeing him like this.

Aidan wasn't blind to her looks, nor the fact that she was getting pretty excited and wanted to play. He wanted to play too, but he had to get back into work mode again. Aidan prepared her plate and handed it to her, trying his damnedest to ignore the fact that they both wanted each other. He needed to concentrate now. Time to focus on Kieran and what was going on in this town.

"Thank you." She accepted it with great ceremony, then set it down in front of her. She watched him turn everything off and sit down with his toast and bacon. Maddie laughed as Aidan eyed her eggs. "Why are you flirting with my eggs? Where are yours?"

Biting his bacon, he swallowed. "I honestly didn't think they'd come out so well. You aren't gonna share?"

Maddie continued to eat nonchalantly as if she paid no attention to him. "Nope."

Aidan sat back folding his arms. "But I made those."

She waved her fork in his face. "Yup. And that you did. I thank you, as they are perfect eggs. You could be quite useful around here, after all." She took a bite and teasingly moaned at the taste, totally going over the top.

Aidan shook his head. "What a cruel thing to do. I feel I should retaliate."

"Oh yeah?"

Aidan grinned. "Yeah." *Fuck it*, he thought, as his resolve disappeared. She was a beautiful distraction.

Before she could realize he was getting up, Aidan leaped up

and grabbed her, hoisting her over his shoulders. Giggling, she smacked his butt. "Put me down, or you'll be sorry!"

Aidan walked out of the kitchen with Maddie over his shoulders, her feet kicking. "I'm already sorry. How could I have met such a shameless and selfish woman? Discipline is in order." She wiggled her legs about to no avail. All her struggling to get free just threatened to burn her out. Aidan appeared totally unaffected by carrying her around like a caveman. "Now say you're sorry."

Maddie giggled. "Never! Those eggs were mine. Get over it, dude."

"Fine. You asked for it." Aidan plopped her on the sofa playfully. He couldn't stop himself from laughing at her hair wild from being tossed around. Maddie leapt up and toppled over the sofa, landing on him and knocking him to the floor.

"You're making this hard on yourself!" She yelled as she wrestled with him on the floor. There they taunted each other and tussled about playfully in the living room. Finally, she thought she had him pinned, until Aidan simply shifted his weight and pinned her beneath him, holding her arms above her head. She tried to struggle away, but Aidan had clearly won.

"Jeez. You couldn't even just let me win, could you? Just so you know, you're not winning any points with me, and you're a sore loser over those eggs. I hope they're cold as ice right now."

Aidan raised a brow arrogantly. "You would, wouldn't you? The whole 'if I can't have it, no one can' mentality?"

"Damn right. Now you're just trying to bully me over it. I tell you, Aidan, it's pathetic."

"I'll let you up if you say you're sorry for eating my share."

Maddie scoffed. "Pfft! Well, if that's the case, we'll just be here all morning.

Aidan shrugged. "Fine by me." He gave her a cocky smirk. Loosening his grip on her wrists, he dipped down and kissed her neck. "Guess you better call in today."

Maddie purred at the sensations of his teeth playing on the sensitive flesh. It was a tempting suggestion she would admit; she loved being with him. Aidan had a way of making fun out of anything, which surprised her since when she met him he was quite guarded. It warmed her heart how he managed to open up to her.

"You drive a hard bargain." Maddie quipped, casting a glance below her. "You see what I did there?"

Aidan smiled at her and nodded. "Yeah, real nice. I take it you're here all week?"

She slipped her hands from him and poked his stomach. Aidan stifled a small laugh and Maddie gasped at the revelation.

"Superman's ticklish?" She poked him again before he tried to restrain her again. Finding it a charming vulnerability to a man who seemed like steel, she smiled at his controlled laugh. "Now I've found your Kryptonite, buster! You will submit!" Maddie rolled him over, catching him off guard. Aidan looked into her fun, bright eyes filled with peace, and he wanted to fall into her.

She was his Kryptonite.

He shook his head. "That was a win by technicality. The lamest of all wins."

Maddie blew a raspberry at him. "Whatever. I beat you fair and square. Beaten by a girl, no less." She gave him a quick kiss and got up.

He propped himself on his elbows, confused. "Where are you going?"

Maddie reached into her purse and grabbed her phone. "I'm taking your advice and calling in late. Greta wouldn't mind." Dialing the office number, she waited for Greta to pick up. But no one did - it went to the answering service.

"That's weird. Greta isn't there." She hung up and dialed Greta's personal number. A couple of rings and then she heard her assistant's voice with her daughter in the background.

"Yes ma'am? How are things?" Greta answered cheerfully.

"Hi there, Greta. Why aren't you in the office? I was calling to tell you that I'm going to be a bit late coming in this morning, but I'm on my way."

"What?" Greta paused. "We closed the office today, remember?"

Maddie frowned to Greta's response. "Huh?"

"Yeah, you have all day blocked off. Don't you remember?"

Maddie scowled on the other end. "Are you sure? What's my calendar say?"

"Hold on," Greta began to hum to fill the time it took to pull it up. "Here it is. It says November 2nd Hanging with Nana. Close office. She's flying in to visit you, remember?"

Maddie nearly tripped over the chair. "What!? You've got to be kidding me!" Her heart jumped into her throat with shock. *You freaking forgot Nana was coming in today?! WTF?*

"Nope, not kidding." Greta continued, obviously taking Maddie's remark literally. "It says so right here in your hand-writing on my personal calendar. You were pretty anal about it a couple months ago. You put it everywhere. How could you forget? What time is she coming in?"

No sooner than Greta spoke those words, she heard the doorbell.

THE LOVELY ARDELLES

"Shit!" Maddie leapt up from the floor with such agility, Aidan wondered if she was perhaps Aristan after all.

"Greta, gotta go!" As she hung up she saw Aidan standing at her side, still with only his jeans on.

Great, what a picture.

She could see the introduction already. *"Nana, I'd like you to meet my half-naked lover Aidan. No, I don't know much about him except he saved my life and he's absolutely incredible in bed. Yes, your grandaughter sleeps with hot, strange men. It's all the rage in Maine, haven't you heard?"*

Aidan saw the panic in her eyes and frowned. "Who's that?" His muscles tensed as he looked towards the door.

A muffled female voice yelled through the front door. "Madeline!? Honey, are you home?"

Maddie bit her lip and looked up at him with embarrassment. "It's my Nana." She began to push him into the bedroom. "Put on a shirt, please! I'll die if she catches us post-coitus like this!"

He stood there beyond the bedroom threshold with a bemused smirk. She said the strangest things when she panicked around him. "Do you want me to leave?"

"Yes!" she shook her head. "No! I mean, let me think!"

"Madeline?" Nana called through the door. "Is everything alright in there? Are you home?"

"I'm coming, Nana!" she replied back through the door, hastily putting on her sweatpants. "Just a second! I'm not decent!"

"Oh, love!" Nana scoffed. "I've seen you without your clothes, dear. It's alright."

Not like this, you haven't!

She stared up at him and gave him a quick kiss. "Aidan, I'm not embarrassed by you," She looked to the doorway. "It's just, she's Nana. You know?"

Aidan smiled and nodded. "I understand, xerhmon. No sense in complicating things." He stretched his shirt over his muscular body and for once she wished Nana had come just a little bit later. "I'll go, you need to spend time with her. Didn't you say yesterday it was her birthday?"

Maddie nodded. "Yes." She found herself pouting as he leaned over and kissed her forehead tenderly. She didn't want him sneaking out of her window like some criminal. Maybe she should stop being a baby and own up to it. She was a grown woman, after all.

She placed her hand on his lips. "Wait here, okay? Please?"

She loped out past the kitchen to open the door.

"Nana!" she embraced the daylights out of the short, white-haired woman. Despite her family's oddities, Maddie always felt at ease and calm around the mere presence of her Zen-like maternal grandmother. She wore red-rimmed glasses on her soft, mature face, and pushed them up in the same manner as Maddie. She wore a badass black leather jacket, not the same as Maddie. Having a Nana that was hipper than most people half her age was the bane of her existence.

Nana laughed heartily as Maddie hugged her. "I was about to bake in the sunlight you left me out there so long, sweetie. You okay? I told you, I've seen that little rump of yours more times than I can count. It's no big deal."

Maddie cut her eyes to the bedroom door, which was closed,

then let Nana in. Walking into the kitchen, Nana set her purse and jacket down in one chair and plopped down in the other chair.

"So how have you been?" Nana asked, almost grinning. " You look so beautiful, sweetie. Almost glowing."

Maddie smiled and pushed her hair back. No matter how crappy she felt or looked, Nana always saw her as a beautiful woman. But in turn, she always admired her grandmother's beauty, which seemed to know no bounds. At 71 years old, she was a still a curvy, grinning firecracker, who wasn't ever ashamed of her age. She always kept her platinum hair cut short and loved to wear her plum lipstick.

"Wow, you too, Nana. I've been great." Maddie grabbed a glass from the cabinet and filled it with water from the pitcher in the fridge. Setting it down in front of Nana, she continued. "The clinic is going very well and business is picking up because, so far, I don't have any competition except the clinics in the nearby towns." She plopped down in a seat. "So, what shall we do for your birthday?"

Nana didn't answer, just scanned the breakfast on the table— and the two plates. "Breakfast already, love? I thought we were gonna do brunch together or something? At least, that's what you said on the text."

Maddie swallowed as, in her panic, she totally forgot to remove all traces of Aidan.

He was right. I am a horrible liar.

She prayed then that she could get Nana out of the house before she exposed Aidan. She didn't want to introduce him that way, lest they both be mortified at the context.

Maddie nervously rambled on something that would quell the curiosity in her precocious grandmother. "Oh, I uh, had a friend of mine stop by for breakfast this morning, that's all."

Nana took a sip of her water, then shrugged. "Oh. Well if you've just eaten, we can just hang out here and catch up if you want."

Maddie jumped. "No!"

Nana jumped as well, scowling at her outburst. "What's the matter with you?"

Feeling panic in the worst way, Maddie finally sobered and lowered her voice. *God, Maddie get a grip!* "Nothing. I mean, I need to get dressed, Nana. I'm sorry."

Nana stared at Maddie's beet red face and began chewing on her bottom lip, letting gears turn. Her grandaughter was the most bashful thing she ever met. A gorgeous little bookworm who was so easy to tease. It's no wonder that she called her many times, complaining she hadn't made many acquaintances. Well, apparently, she'd made one recently. "No worries, hun. But tell me, is your friend of the male persuasion?"

Maddie gasped, feeling like her head was going to explode. "Nana!"

"Just asking." She put up her hands defensively. "Not that there's anything wrong with that. You're a grown woman, Madeline. I expect you to meet significant others...enjoy your youth with fancy." Nana pushed her hair back, smiling. "Besides, I saw the motorbike out front."

Maddie went cold at the revelation. It was time to come clean. She felt like the biggest idiot to keep Aidan in her bedroom, hiding out like some creeper. She wasn't ashamed of him. In fact, she was sure Nana would love him.

He's gonna hate me for embarrassing him this way.

"Nana," Maddie stood up. "I have someone for you to meet."

"Ooh, now we're talking." she clasped her hands together. "Who is it?"

Maddie slowly walked to her bedroom door and cracked it open. "Aidan," She whispered.

When she heard no response, she opened the door to find no sign of him, only an open window. "Aidan?"

Suddenly, she heard a knock. When Nana yelled at someone to come in, she ran to the kitchen. Maddie froze as she saw Aidan standing in the doorway, fully dressed and holding a bunch of wildflowers in his hand. Aidan's small smile was safe but dashing. The six foot three man who stood before her and Nana looked good enough to eat.

However, she couldn't help the shock of the surprise any more than her Nana could, who was all smiles now. She stood up to get a better look.

"And who's this, Maddie?"

Before she could open her mouth, which didn't seem to work fast enough, Aidan spoke. "I'm Maddie's friend, Aidan. I live not too far from here."

"Oh, friends?" It sounded more Nana convincing herself of the definition than her asking.

Maddie groaned, embarrassment heating her face. "Yes, Nana. He had breakfast with me earlier."

Aidan wanted to laugh at Maddie's angst, but instead he decided to choose the high road and focus on her Nana. It was clear that both of them shared some deep resemblances such as the big, bright eyes and cheekbones. It gave Aidan an inkling of how maybe Maddie would look when she got older. He was glad he decided to act fast and sneak out when he had the chance. He pretty much broke a new record on how fast he could dress and race out the window. "When she mentioned it was your birthday, I went to gather a little something for you in the wooded area out back." With that, Aidan presented the beautiful array of wildflowers with great ceremony. "I hope this is okay on such short notice."

Nana's eyes lit up. "Thank you so much! Oh, I love wildflowers! Some of these have great healing powers too! That was so sweet of you, Aidan." Seeing how happy she was, Aidan smiled at Maddie, and she melted. Sincerity was all over his face, and it seemed all of his hard, guarded demeanor faded away.

"I better head off so you two can catch up."

Nana scoffed with shock. "But you just got here!" She pouted a bit and turned herself towards Maddie. "Maddie, ask him to stay. I never get to meet any of your friends anymore. And this one actually knows the difference between a run-of-the-mill bouquet and one that took real physical effort."

Maddie grinned, looking up at him, tickled her Nana was eager to play wingman. "Aidan. It'd be great if you spent some time with my Nana and me. In fact, I'd like it very much."

Despite his apprehension, he found himself nodding yes. "Sure."

"Great!" Nana clasped her hands in excitement. She stood in awe at Aidan, who pulled out a chair for her to sit. "My heavens, Maddie, this one is like a mountain." She winked. "Hope you know how to climb, dear."

"Nana!" Maddie's face mottled red at her family's never-ending need to shame her. Even Aidan managed to look a little pink at the remark. "You're going to scare him off."

Nana placed the flowers in the empty carafe and filled it with water. "Oh, somehow I doubt that. He's a brave one. I can tell." She smiled at Aidan, who tried to sit comfortable, but didn't exactly know how at the moment. Before, he never cared. He was where he was. But now, with Maddie and her grandmother, he felt awkward and eager to make a good impression.

What the hell was this?

"You aren't frightened of a little old lady like me are you, Aidan?"

Aidan looked into her eyes in earnest. For a moment, he thought he was looking at Ninon. "I think it's wise for me not to underestimate you."

Her pleasant, hearty laugh resonated through the kitchen. "A very wise one indeed. Where did you find this smart, handsome man?"

Aidan tenderly cut his eyes toward Maddie who sipped her juice.

"Well, Nana." She gave him a heartfelt gaze. "He kinda found me."

Nana nonchalantly shined her glasses. "Well, I am certainly

glad you did, Aidan. Because Maddie Bear can be quite scattered sometimes. She's a true Ardelle."

Nana and Aidan shared a laugh, but he sobered quickly when Maddie frowned at him.

"Hey!"

He laughed. "I like your Nana, Maddie Bear."

She rolled her eyes. "Yeah. You would. Like two peas in a freakin pod." She cast Nana a quelling look.

Nana tapped Aidan's arm playfully. "Okay. I think I've embarrassed my darling grandchild enough. Let me freshen up and let's check out this town of yours." When Nana went to the bathroom, Aidan looked uneasy at Maddie, who eyed him.

"Do you want me to go?" He asked, before Maddie leaned over and stole a hot, promising kiss from him. Aidan's groin tightened as her soft lips probing his, before pulling away.

He smiled. "Soooo. Was that a no?"

"You're damn right that's a no." She breathed. "That is, of course, if you're not afraid my Nana and I will cramp your style. I really don't want you feeling awkward or obligated."

She gave him an out-clause that he didn't actually care to exercise. He wanted to be with her. Not just to protect them; it went much deeper than that, and he knew it. Maddie's companionship became his unicorn. She was unique, beautiful and a very elusive personality to his kind. When would he ever learn?

Aidan gently touched her chin. "Now, how can I turn down a date with such gorgeous women? I'd be honored."

Maddie was all aglow when Nana came out and smiled at them both. Nana threw on her black leather jacket and grinned. "Well, let's see what kinda trouble we can get into in this town of Bridgepoint."

Maddie always had a great time with Nana, but listening to her joke and talk with Aidan was an absolute blast. As they walked through the marketplace, picking up antiques and talking about Nana's adventures, Maddie was intrigued how Aidan knew so much about historical events. He helped Nana up and down steps and obediently laughed at her grandmother's quips. Every time he smiled or laughed, it warmed Maddie's, heart. Aidan was so incredibly charming when he let his guard down. As much as it was, she still noticed him patrolling along with them, observing people as they wandered along the strip of merchants. Ever the protector, she squeezed his hand when it seemed he got too tense.

When Nana asked for ice cream, they gathered outside to Ripley's Creamery.

Maddie stopped at the entrance. "I'll go in and grab us some cones. You want anything, Aidan?"

He politely shook his head. "Just bottled water, you two go ahead. I'm actually gonna check out the motorcycle shop across the street and will meet up with you ladies later."

Maddie shrugged. "Boooo. You're missing out, bud. C'mon Nana, let's see what flavors they have this time."

Nana grinned. "Ooh, if they have Bohemian Coconut, I'm all over it!" There were crowds of people on the warm day, and as they disappeared inside, Aidan made his way to the shop, hoping to pick up anything that might lead to Kieran. There was bound to be a ShadowShifter who knew something.

Inside the creamery, as kids oohed over the flavors, Maddie stood in line with Nana. As they each got their cones, two kids ran past Nana, causing her to drop her purse. Before Maddie could bend down to retrieve it, someone with leather gloves picked it up and dusted it off. Following the hands up, they were greeted with a tall, dark haired man. He had a gorgeous smile, almost charming. But Maddie's first thought was how odd it was for someone to wear driving gloves when they weren't driving.

Dressed in a dark blue button shirt and jeans, he stood there grinning, handing Nana her purse. "Kids can get a little crazy around here. I believed you dropped this." Nana took the purse and gave a polite smile to the kind stranger.

"Thank you, thank you very much, Sir."

His bright blue eyes flashed past his shaggy cut. He stared at Maddie as if he were waiting for something. Or looking. "You are very welcome." Maddie began to feel a little odd as she noticed him cutting his eyes at them, then beyond them outdoors. What was he watching for? "It's no trouble really. Just doing my job as a gentleman." Kieran inhaled deeply and sighed at Maddie as if she was a breath of fresh air. "You have an intoxicating scent. It smells so familiar."

Maddie gave a nervous smile. "Called Obsession." She wanted to distance herself from him but wasn't quite sure why. He seemed nice enough, but her gut felt otherwise. It was uneasy, and by the looks of her Nana's body language, she was in a weird place with him too.

Sensing their mood change, Kieran figured he'd better exit. It was safe with so many people there masking his scent, but people clearing out made it risky. He just wanted to get a little up close and personal with Aidan's distraction. And she was a distraction indeed. The ward had good taste. It was stupid of Aidan to get attached to some humans. Everyone knew they were worthless and growing a weakness for them was dangerous.

He snapped his fingers like something triggered his memory. "Yep. That must be it. You ladies take care now."

"Thank you." Maddie replied as she gently propelled Nana towards the door.

As they left the shop, Brody came up behind him, looking out the window with Kieran. Both of them watched as the two Ardelle women sat outside talking. About a minute or so passed when Aidan ran across the street to meet them. "That's him, isn't it?"

"Yep. It appears I may have underestimated my little brother. Riko told me an Aristan was looking for me here. I suspected

Aidan, but didn't imagine he'd come alone. And I thought I was so careful dodging in and out of other places in Maine."

Brody growled and clenched his fists. "What about the plan?"

Kieran pat his Thesian comrade on the back. "No plan is perfect, Brody boy. We just have to watch our steps until everything's in place. Besides, he obviously has a little distraction going. Let him play." At least humans were good for something.

Brody crossed his arms, turning to look at Kieran. "And in the meantime?"

"Keep an eye on them, especially the courtesha. We can use some leverage. He's smart and will catch on quick. When the time is right, I want to clip him before he gets me."

18

ENSNARED

Aidan gaped as both women sat down with ice cream cones towering past their faces. Maddie kept begging him to try some, yet Aidan was quite content with his water. But sitting there became a much harder task for him, as the innocent licks Maddie gave her ice cream turned into something much more enticing in his mind. The gleam in her eye every now and then told him she was aware. As they sat at the ice cream parlor, Nana touched Aidan's pendant around Maddie's neck in astonishment.

"My word, that is absolutely beautiful. Where did that come from?"

Aidan set his water bottle down. "It belonged to my mother. She always wore it as a symbol of her family."

Nana pulled back from the necklace, as if she feared it.

Maddie frowned in concern. "It's okay, Nana. He doesn't mind you touching it."

"Oh," Nana settled in her seat, trying to relax. "I didn't want to damage it. It feels like a very sentimental piece of jewelry - not just for your mother, but you as well."

He nodded, watching her rub the pendant again in admiration. Ninon wore it every day. She even wore it when she was in wolf's skin. "It does mean a lot. It's all I have of her."

Nana patted his hand. "I'm sorry to hear that. She must have been an incredible woman to raise such a great young gentleman like yourself. I'd imagine her very proud of you."

Aidan looked away, and Maddie graciously changed the subject.

"So, Nana," Maddie bit into her cone. "Have you decided what you want for your birthday this year?"

Nana shook her head. "I don't know, sweetie. Surprise me. I'm old so not too much of a surprise!" She smiled at Aidan. "However, he did give me a great gift. Perhaps you should ask him for pointers."

Maddie looked to Aidan, who shrugged innocently. "What?"

She fanned him away. "Oh, whatever. I'm gonna break you two up."

"Why?," her grandmother asked.

"Lets just say, what a life I have where I'm ganged up on by my Nana and boyfriend?"

As they headed back to Maddie's home, Nana stopped at Aidan's bike. "This is your bike, right, Aidan?"

He walked over to her. "Yes, ma'am. I've had her for a while."

Maddie stayed back with her arms folded. She knew that look in her Nana's eyes. And with a chiding tone, she thought to warn her. "Nana..."

She turned to Maddie, her eyes wide and innocent. "What?! I'm just curious. I'm just asking your friend about his motorcycle. That's all."

Maddie's tone flipped to a more maternal tone. "No way, Nana. Forget it."

Aidan stood in front of Nana, a bit confused about the situation. For some reason, Maddie had the 'mom' look. He'd seen it on Ninon a million times. "What's going on?"

Maddie sighed and slowly walked toward her grandmother. "I'm not going to ask him, Nana. He's your new friend now, you ask him."

Nana looked up at him. "I haven't ridden on a bike since

before I was married. Could you indulge an old woman on her birthday?" Aidan's eyes widened in apprehension as he saw Maddie's worried look on her face. He knew perhaps Maddie wanted him to tell her no, but as he looked at Nana, he saw so much of Ninon in her. The impending joy on her face was too much to turn away. No matter what answer he gave her, he feared he'd upset one of them, which he had no intention of doing.

"I, uh..." He stumbled, raking his fingers through his hair. He couldn't take the puppy dog stare Nana was giving him. He was caving in like a salt pillar, piece by pathetic piece. Desperately, he looked over to Maddie and mouthed to her. "You wanna help me out here?"

Maddie began to smile, seeing that she was apparently the only one who had any objections. Nana had a way of getting what she wanted. She was clearly a spoiled woman, but she loved her nonetheless. A piece of her melted, watching both of their faces. "You guys be careful."

Nana squealed with delight as she looked to Aidan. "Yasssssss!"

He laughed at Nana's contagious excitement, then nodded to Maddie. His face was serious as he spoke to her. "I'll take very good care of her, xerhmon." He guided Nana closer to the bike. "Come on, Nana. Let's take a cruise."

He gave her his helmet, helping her fasten it securely. Finally, Aidan straddled the bike and helped Nana on. Revving the engine, she wrapped her arms around him.

Though a natural worry ran through Maddie, she knew deep down that Aidan would rather hurt himself before anyone else. And seeing the two of them on the bike was hilarious in its own right. A saucy mature lady with better style than Heidi Klum and a sexy, biker bounty hunter. She laughed to herself. Boy, whatever would the locals think of the Ardelle women and the strange, alluring man who rode around with them? Miss Brady should see this, too.

Though Aidan pulled off very slow, Nana still jeered and laughed at the shock of it. They drove out to the street and disappeared. Maddie sat on the swing while they rode and smiled to herself. Aidan was truly a person worth adoring. Her old ex, Eric, wanted nothing to do with Maddie's family and often refused to do anything involving them. One of their biggest fights was when he would rather go party with his buddies, then drop by for one hour to meet Nana. He was such a selfish prick who cared of nothing but his own gain. She wished she had seen it before, and listened to her mother and Nana when they both told her that Eric was no good for her.

She was so stubborn, claiming that she could change him and make him a better person. Instead, Eric changed her. Made her afraid to trust anyone. Made her afraid to be kind and offer anything of herself to them. He made her want to be alone, even when she dreaded it. With Aidan, she found it so easy to be kind and loving to him. He didn't demand it or ask for it - he was just simply shocked at her capacity to give it. It shocked her as well, but somehow she didn't regret it. She melted at every smile, every touch he gave her, and it left her alive and hopeful that being alone wouldn't be her curse forever.

Ten or so minutes passed, then Aidan and Nana pulled back into the yard. He gently let Nana off the bike, as she was still laughing at the exhilaration of it.

"That was great!" She removed her helmet and looked to Maddie grinning. "Did you see me, love? Did you?"

She got off the swing and walked up to her. "I did, Nana. Are you okay?"

"Okay? That was amazing!" Before Aidan could blink, Nana pulled him down and hugged his neck. She was a lot stronger than she looked. "Thank you! You are an amazing man. Zipping around those corners. Wow wee! Talk about thrilling!"

Aidan laughed at how giddy the old woman was, as if she tasted vitality for the first time in ages. He gazed into Maddie's eyes, which were lit up with happiness. Looking at her, he could relate to what Nana felt. He felt that same vitality when Maddie smiled at him, as if he mattered.

"I'm glad you enjoyed your birthday present." He engaged the kickstand and slid off his bike.

"Now I'm going to make cupcakes for you guys!" Nana followed them up the stairs.

Aidan couldn't remember laughing so much at Nana's stories of Maddie growing up. Both of their laughter was warm and infectious, full of joy. It reminded him of family. Being accepted and loved. Besides Ninon and Leigh, he'd been alone. Now with Maddie, he was floored at how she let him into her life.

They all laughed and talked until Nana was ready to leave. As the cab came to take her back, she gave Maddie a big hug and whispered in her ear. Aidan couldn't hear what was said, for some reason, but he saw the huge smile on Maddie's face. Nana walked up to Aidan and hugged him tightly. He tensed a bit, stunned at her actions. "It was so pleasant to meet you, Aidan. I can tell you're a great person and very good for my Maddie. She's combative and willful, but she's an Ardelle. We're built that way. Please look after her for me."

Aidan didn't have time to react to her words as she tore away from him and settled into the cab. Maddie came up beside him, waving to her. As the cab pulled out of the driveway, Aidan smiled as he went over what Nana said to him.

Maddie looped her arm under his and smiled. "My Nana is absolutely taken with you."

He shook his head. "I doubt it."

Maddie scoffed. "I don't. She had a great time with you. Thank you." Maddie stood on her tiptoes and kissed him.

"For what?" His eyes searched hers intently.

"Everything. The flowers, the bike." She ran her finger down his jawline. "You're incredibly sweet when you think no one's looking." She took his hand and started to guide him to the door. "I'm starving, let's go inside." She lead him inside, closing the door behind them. Then, she kicked off her shoes and piled up on the sofa, patting the cushion next to her. "First, tell me a story. You said that you would."

Aidan hesitated when he saw her on the couch smiling at him. He wanted this life. He wanted to be with her, and yet he couldn't allow himself to become obsessed with a life he could never have. "Maybe another time. Maddie, I should go."

"No, you don't!" She gasped.

When Aidan tried to open the door, he found it locked--from the inside. He jerked the knob several times, but the one lock that wouldn't budge was the key lock. He turned to find Maddie with her body propped against the sofa, grinning. She looked like the cat that swallowed the canary.

"I figured you'd try and leave." She jingled the key in her hand. "You are all mine tonight." She opened her shirt and let the key fall down.

Aidan turned around fully and eyed her in bewilderment. He didn't know how to react to her playfulness and tenacity. It amazed him how she challenged everything he'd ever battled within himself as far as she was concerned. It made it so hard for him to leave and forget her, despite that it was best for them both. Any Aristan in their right mind would run away for fear of the inevitable.

Yet here he was, staring at the dark-haired beauty that was everything a wolf could ever hope for. And wanting every inch of her to want every inch of him.

Maddie swallowed as Aidan came towards her in that deadly swagger he possessed. His determined strides always seemed to make her weak in the knees. His raw, hungry gaze fell over her. *Heavens, this man was totally and undeniably sexy. I don't think I can take it.* From his walk to his dark gaze, to that body that was complete male perfection, Maddie often thought she was simply in over her head--or definitely head over heels.

"You know," Aidan continued to close in on her, sporting a sexy smirk. "I could get that key from you if I really wanted it."

She grinned to her own chagrin. Indeed he could. And oh, what fun that would be. "I suppose, but not until you keep your promise to me, buster." Maddie folded her arms defiantly, and

Aidan couldn't help but smile at her determination. She should have been a she-wolf. Stubborn and impetuous to the bone. Though he had no doubt he would make that key treasure hunt a very pleasurable one for the both of them, Aidan was even more warmed by how much she bartered just for his company alone.

He raked her with an odd stare.

Maddie grimaced. "What is it?"

"I just don't understand why you want me around." He stepped closer to her. "I've been nothing but trouble to you since I met you. Don't you ever get tired of taking in strays?"

Maddie leaned forward and grabbed his hand. Looking up into his eyes, she saw the confusion and pain that tugged at his heart. He spoke as if he never deserved such attention and kindness. In her eyes, he couldn't be more mistaken.

"I don't take in strays. In fact, had you met me years ago, perhaps I never would have given in to you. Everyone I've ever let in didn't deserve it. But you, Aidan, I never met anyone who was so unsure of his own kindness. Sometimes I think you're just as standoffish as I am. It annoys me, but ironically enough I really adore it about you. I enjoy being with you and you deserve kindness in spades. That's why I want you around." She kissed his hand gently. "Now, will you stay with me?"

Her confession shook him to his very soul. His resolve blown away, he sat next to her. "I'm yours for tonight, xerhmon." He pressed his back against the cushions and felt his body roar to life when Maddie snuggled up against him, her head resting on his side. Her lush body was so close to him, her sweet scent of peppermint hair and rosemary reminding him of all the beauties of nature. An impish lover in spirit she was. She possessed powers over him he dared not proclaim.

"Now, will you tell me what that means?" Maddie asked.

Aidan smiled softly. How funny. He didn't realize he'd called her that till just then. An old Aristan term of endearment was often heard throughout the Bloodlocke household, but only among Tiberius and Ninon, as the term was meant solely in the context of lovers. "In my mother's tongue, it means 'my lovely.'

She grinned. "It's sweet. I love the way you say it." Maddie listened attentively as Aidan went on and told the most amazing tales of half-wolf warriors, goddesses, and warring love. He kept her spellbound, with his deep, relaxed voice lilting in her ear. It touched her how patient he was answering her questions and laughing at her side comments. She often caught him smelling her hair as he told his story, his hand softly stroking her shoulder. And when he was done, he kissed her forehead.

"How many times have you told that story?"

"A handful of times, but I've heard it many times." He looked down at her. "Did you like it?"

She smiled up at him, toying with his shirt. "I did. It was a little sad, but I liked the hero. He was so proud of his people. I hope that goddess realized what she had done."

Aidan tensed. "Gods and goddesses don't have any regrets, Maddie. They wouldn't do the horrible things they do if they did."

She heard the dark undertones in his voice and wondered what regrets and sadness he harbored along with his childhood abandonment.

"Hopefully a heart will negate regret."

He could help but smirk. "I wish I had your optimism."

"I try. Truth is, I hadn't always had it." She looked towards the kitchen. "I need a sugar fix!" Scampering to the kitchen, she reached into the fridge and hurried back with one of Nana's cupcakes. Scooting back next to him, she grinned and scooped the cream onto her finger and shoved it in her mouth, moaning at the taste. "You should try it, they're awesome."

Aidan shook his head. Not because he wasn't a fan of pastries, but if he saw Maddie lick anything else tonight that wasn't him, he swore he'd go insane.

"Come on," she urged, taking a piece and waving it in his face. "Just a little bit."

Before he could protest again, she shoved the small piece of cupcake into his mouth and licked the remaining cream from her fingers. She shifted against him, gifting him with a devious grin, having fed him. "Good, huh?"

Aidan tasted the sweet vanilla on his tongue before he swallowed. He never really thought twice about sweets, pastry and the like. However, when Maddie presented it...

It made him burn. His blood running hot, he eyed her with a deep intensity that ran a shiver up her spine. "You know, that's a good way to get bit."

Maddie ran her finger playfully under his chin. Her voice husky with temptation. "Oh, now you wouldn't bite the hand that feeds you, would you?"

"Oh, I think you'll enjoy my bite." Aidan leaned in and claimed her lips. The sweetness on her lips enticed him as he explored the secrets of her mouth. Maddie pulled herself up against him as he urged her to straddle his lap. Meeting her dark brown eyes, he cupped her face gently and claimed her lips again. Dazed, it took Maddie a second to collect some sort of focus, especially when his skilled tongue darted into her mouth. She moaned deep in her throat at the sensations and taste of Aidan.

He began stroking her back, conjuring chills throughout her body. And when she wantonly pressed her hips down to his, he met hers instinctively. Maddie writhed against him as her body grew shamelessly wet with desire for him to fill her again. She peeled the shirt off him, damn near tearing it from his chest.

She glanced at it with hooded eyes and giggled. "Whoops, sorry about that."

His hands rode up her t-shirt and unhooked her bra. "I didn't like that shirt, anyway." As the bra loosened, the key fell into his hand. He smiled to himself and held it as he lifted it all off her. He cupped her breasts, teasing her nipples with his thumbs. Between his kisses, he mumbled against her skin in a sensual mixture of broken English and another language Maddie couldn't place. It sounded wonderful to her ears, the sweet lilting of his voice as he delicately touched her was enough to make any mortal woman cry out in ecstasy.

With broken English, Aidan recited the poetry of his life to her. She was angelic, tempting and seductive, her dark brown hair cascading down her bare back, her lips swollen from his kisses. Dear Goddess, how he wanted her, all of her, until she begged for mercy in his arms. Shifting her onto her back, he quickly stripped the denim skirt from her, tossing it to the floor. A shiver ran over her as Aidan raked his eyes over her body. He lowered himself to her, letting his hands knead and explore her entire body. There wasn't an inch of her he wanted to leave untouched. His lips lowered achingly to her hipbone, where she moaned his name. Pushing her panties aside, his fingers rubbed and teased her slick flesh, letting his fingertips ever so lightly glide against her hardened nub in the very center of her. Maddie bit down on her index finger as the tortuous pleasure threatened to make her come. As if he sensed she was on the verge, he withdrew his fingers.

Maddie writhed and gasped. "Aidan, please," she begged. "I'm gonna die if you stop." Enthralled and completely lost to passion, he ripped the little black thong from her hips and buried his face against her core as his tongue teased her. He hooked his arms across her thighs, wanting to taste and consume everything she was.

Maddie squirmed beneath him, grasping the arm of the sofa above her head. "I need you, Aidan." She arched herself to him brazenly, panting as she felt her body on the edge of a furious climax. And when his fingers entered her, surging hot, she screamed his name an octave too high.

Aidan pulled away with a hiss, stripping off his pants to free his erection. Eager, she hooked her ankles around him and drew him to her.

"What is it about you that makes me insane with wanting you?" he whispered, his voice hoarse.

Licking her lips, she wrapped her fingers around the thick, hard length of him and guided him home. Maddie sharply sucked in a breath as she arched her back to take him in. Nibbling her shoulder, he drew himself up, thrusting himself deeper into her. He was powerless as their bodies joined in splendor. Every promise he made to himself about her, he'd broken. He'd allowed her in to know him and now, realizing how great it was not to hunt or be hunted, to be admired and treated with compassion, he feared he would never be able to go back to his own life. Away from her smile, her touch that never once failed to awaken some alien part of him that wanted to be cared for. That wanted to see himself as more than the savage Ninon and Tiberius found in the woods--the one that killed out of anger and rage. Maddie made him want to forget.

He held on to her tight, as they both reached climax hard and heavy, leaving both of them spent and breathless, almost laughing at the exhilaration shared between them. He briefly rested his head against her breast, before shifting his weight toward the back of the sofa.

"Heavens, that was amazing!" Maddie cooed as she wiped the sweat from his brow.

"You can say that again, love." Aidan smiled as he pulled her closer to him, watching her small fingers play on his chest. He hated to leave her. The idea was almost unheard of now, but he couldn't stay. The sooner he picked up what was going on, the better everyone would be. The safer Maddie and the town would be.

"Maddie, I'm sorry. I wish I could stay tonight, but I can't. I have to go."

Maddie sighed against him. "More bounty hunter stuff?"

"Yes."

Maddie sat up to face him. "Aidan, I know you want to protect me, but will you ever trust me enough to really tell me what you are doing here?"

Aidan sighed. "It's not that I don't trust you, Maddie. That's not the issue at all."

"Then what is it? Are you in some sort of trouble? If you are, I can help you." Maddie looked at him with concern. He was so mysterious and aloof, and though he maybe didn't mean it, she was shut out from him. She wished she could say she was done with secrets, but that was not how the world worked. Maddie wanted more of him, but maybe more than he was willing to offer her.

Right then, he wished he could tell her everything. Who he was, what he was and who he was really after. And, most importantly, why. She deserved the truth. But there was no way to explain everything without losing her. *I'm not ready to let her go.*

Aidan sat up and kissed her hand. "I'm not in any trouble, Maddie. I promise to tell you when it is safe for you. For now, the less you know, the better."

Maddie silently nodded her head, reluctantly, "Alright." She stood up from the sofa and kissed his cheek. "You better get going, then. Good night."

Aidan heard the pain in her voice behind her strained smile. He didn't want to hurt her, but he was at a loss with what to do. "Maddie..."

"You can let yourself out." Maddie closed the door to her room and sighed. What was she doing? She was supposed to be protective of her heart, to guard it from being hurt. But now, Aidan owned it. He possessed so easily from her it scared her to death. She wanted to trust him, but she was vulnerable with him, not fully knowing if he wanted to be with her. *I have to protect myself, don't I?* She started to feel lost, that no matter what she did, she would fall for someone who would break her heart. Please, *Aidan, don't break my heart.*

19

BIRD DOG

A idan stood in front of Riko's Bar as the lights went out. He was tired of the running around, and everything that was wrong with that town seemed to stem from this shitty bar. Something needed to bend and it damn sure wasn't going to be him. Time was running out to bring Kieran to justice, and someone was gonna give him some answers.

Riko went to the alley to toss some trash when he felt Aidan come out of the shadows and smash him against the door of the bar. His arms pinned against him, he spat out a cure in Thesian that was definitely meant for Aidan. "What the hell do you want, asshole?!"

Aidan felt prickles all over his body as his anger threatened to change him. "Another Aristan ShadowShifter was here the other day, wasn't he? Maybe a few others hiding from the law? You better start talking, or we're gonna have some massive problems tonight, you understand me?"

Riko struggled against him, but the more he squirmed, the more pressure the arm bar gave him. "Screw you, man. Why the hell would Aristans hole up at my haven? I was about to blast you outta mine just the other day. You think I welcome you bastards here?" He pushed up against him, but couldn't move.

"I don't know. Perhaps you tell me. From what I've learned about your kind, money talks, right Riko? It's why we Aristans call your kind a fucking joke. All this honor, all this pride...and for what? Greed? You may as well be a human." Aidan slammed him viciously against the wall, with a sickening thud. "Now, you're gonna tell me what I need to know, or I'm gonna to go to work on you right here, right now. You get me? I'll have you howling for your goddess before you can blink!"

Through gritted teeth, Riko responded. "Look, Aristan. The guy and two others contacted me and said they needed asylum. I didn't know the other guy was Aristan until he got here!"

"Okay, so what did he want?" Aidan eyed him suspiciously. When Riko remained silent, Aidan used his force and hurled him into an adjacent wall, watching him smash against it and fall with a thud. Before Riko could recover, Aidan was on him, grabbing him and pushing him back up with a solid hook to the face and a low growl. "Perhaps you didn't hear me, Riko. I'm not fucking around. This asshole killed other ShadowShifters! Those that were supposed to be his pack. His family!"

Riko spit blood at him and scoffed. "He killed Aristans. Who the hell cares what happens to your kind?"

Aidan slammed him again. "He killed his own mother! Say what you will about my people, but you know as well as I that a ShadowShifter who murders his own blood without cause is a mongrel--Aristan or Thesian." He watched as Riko's face briefly stilled. "You don't need to protect him, Riko. I'm not here to bother the Thesians, I just want to get him! He's dangerous to both our races. He's a fucking twist!"

"Alright!" Riko yelled in distress. "Just spare me the guilt, alright? About three weeks ago, my buddy Nornos called me and said we could come into some cash. All we had to do is help some pissed off Aristan burn down his commune and get him out of there. We didn't hurt anyone, Nornos said they just torched some places, that's all!"

"Why did he choose you guys?!"

"I don't know, I just know he specifically asked for Thesians without colors. No one with loyalties to a pack."

Aidan sneered. "He wanted your allegiance? Is that the smoke he was blowing up your ass? Seriously?" It made perfect sense. Thesians that belonged to clans didn't behave like this. They couldn't make an unsanctioned hit on an Aristan pack without their Alpha giving the say. With Thesians without a pack, they were one step from hired mercenaries. They didn't have the support of the clan to keep their businesses afloat and their bellies fed, so for them, money talked. Money...where the hell did Kieran get that kinda cash? "How much were you all paid?"

Riko shook his head. "Hey man, I don't know. I just know my cut."

Aidan frowned. "Well?"

"Five grand. I don't know about the others, but I overheard Nornos bragging about at least ten grand coming his way."

Aidan felt a pang in his stomach as his gears started to turn. There's no way Kieran had that kinda cash on his own. He barely worked and contributed nothing to the pack. If he funded a strike with Thesians, it wasn't by his means. A sickening feeling washed over him. Someone had to have a hand in this...a lot closer to home.

Riko glared at Aidan. "What the hell else do you want from me? I've told you everything I know!"

Aidan sneered. "Where is he?"

"He's in a nearby town called Iris. Most of the guys he's recruited are there."

Aidan eyed him back. Anger mounted within him, slowly manifesting in his eyes, turning amber. "Does he know I'm here?"

Riko nodded violently. "Nornos was there when you visited my bar. He's known all along."

Kieran was in the area indeed, and well aware of Aidan's presence too. *Good, that means all bets are off.* "If Kieran makes contact with you, tell him I'm coming. And that hiding behind Thesians won't help him when I'm fucking crushing his windpipe during judgment!" With that, he slammed Riko and released him with a growl. Sauntering away, Aidan pulled out his phone and hit a number on speed dial.

He waited in tension until he heard Cameron's voice. "Yo, Aidan?"

"Yeah, listen. Are you alone?"

Cameron looked around where he sat, his back leaning against a wooden chair, while club dance music played. He smiled as the flexible thong-clad vixen in front swayed her hips and blew him a kiss.

He gave her a wink. "Umh...not... really?" Cameron winced at the phone but felt all his blood flow south as Sapphire flipped her body up high on the pole. Then with her long, caramel legs in a split, seductively and slowly slid down the silver pole. "Just a little...um, company. What's up?"

Aidan scowled. "I need you to be alone. It's important."

Cameron didn't hesitate. "You got it, hold on." Cameron stood up and smiled at Sapphire once more as she whirled around, waving at him. He sighed. So much for a night out to get his rocks off. *Another duty calls.* He rushed to the side exit, still holding his phone. "Okay, what's going on. Any sign of Kieran?"

"And then some," Aidan replied, still walking. "Kieran did hire Thesians to do the raid. They had no colors, and he paid them handsomely."

Cameron frowned. "How handsomely?"

"Very handsomely, Some walking away with as much as ten G's. How the hell would Kieran get hold of that much money to grease the palms of Thesians?"

Cameron sighed and leaned against the club wall. "Shit." He rubbed his head. "Something's not right, Aidan. Leigh and I over-heard some talking between Onyx and Bastien. Our coffers are empty."

Aidan froze. "What?"

"We're broke. Onyx told Bastien, and for some reason, Bastien seemed to brush it off and stop Onyx from telling the others. I can't prove anything, but something tells me Kieran having all that money to lather up the Thesians and us being broke is not a coincidence."

Aidan sighed. "Which leads us to an even more interesting question. Like what the hell does Bastien know about it? If this trails back to our pack, and it does, that means something foul is going on in the council there, and the pack is in more danger."

Cameron shook his head. "What do you need me to do? I can call Bastien to question--"

"No, don't," Aidan warned. "We don't want to spook him, and we don't have anything concrete to tie him to Kieran and the money. I need you there to do some more sleuthing. Lay low, but tail Bastien for me. I need to know what he's doing, who's he seeing. Anything suspicious, I want you to call me."

"You got it. I'll start tracking him tonight." Cameron felt his body already tense and ready to change as he stared up at the moon. "What about Kieran?"

"I haven't seen him, but he's here. He also knows I'm here. He's holed up in another town not too far from Bridgepoint. Likely laying low, hoping I didn't get wind he was here. Either he's crazy, or he's bold. Either way, I'm gonna pull the rug right from under him. How's Leigh?"

Cameron scoffed. "Same. Still pissy. She misses you, though."

Aidan smiled briefly to himself. "Yeah, I bet. She's staying out of trouble?"

"Well, within reason." Cameron began walking to his bike. "I hate that you're out there on your own, Alpha. With the Thesians out there on Kieran's side, you don't have any allies there. What if something pops off?"

Aidan continued to walk until he saw a structure up ahead. Then froze. "I think I may have a plan to acquire some reinforcements. Listen, I'll talk to you later and watch your back, Cam."

"Same to you, Aidan," Cameron said in farewell. He hung up and hopped on his bike. It was time to get back to the pack and get back to work. No sooner than he got on his bike, Leigh's face and number popped on his cell. Groaning, he slid his finger across to answer. "Wow, your little pup ears must've been burning. What do you want?"

Leigh scoffed. "Well, I'm hoping I didn't disturb you. Playing around at the titty bar, no doubt."

Cameron frowned to the phone. "I'm sensing judgment."

Leigh rubbed her forehead. "Did you talk to my brother lately?"

"Yep, I did. I'm leaving the quote, unquote 'titty bar' as you said, and heading back. Something's rotten in the pack, and we've gotta find it, kitty cat. I'll come by with details." With that, Cameron hung up, kicked on his engine and sped off.

Meanwhile, Aidan eyed the tiny bar in the distance. He didn't know why he didn't pick it up before. Perhaps because it was so obscure, for good reason. Aristans liked to be invisible. But as he put his nose up to the night air and inhaled the familiar scent of his own people, he continued to approach the little bar called Greenwood's and decided it was time to make some new friends.

20

REBEL YELL

Very slowly through the night, Aidan continued walking towards the small bar called Greenwood's. The little neon lights flickered on and off, almost seeming like a beacon in the dark. Since his time in Bridgepoint, he had not encountered any Aristans. It wasn't like he was looking for them, or even expected them to have residence in this town, but his people liked to lay low and inconspicuous, and the outskirts of a little town like Bridgepoint probably was a perfect place. He hadn't been out this far and was glad the goddess blew the air downwind to pick up such a faint scent. In his contacts, he didn't know of an Aristan Haviscasi being set up here. So either it was done without sanction, or he was severely behind on news. Either way, it didn't matter. If they weren't on Kieran's side, then they would be on his, and he needed more feet on the ground if Bastien and Kieran were up to something.

He wanted to curb judgment or accusation on Bastien until he met the old wolf face to face, but he trusted Cam and Leigh and, despite it being a hunch, it all seemed pretty damning and plausible.

Aidan approached the steps, seeing a line of motorcycles of various styles parked outside. Walking to the door, the scent of

Aristan got stronger, so he slowly walked into the bar. Though the outside was weathered and worn, it also was terribly deceptive, as the inside of the bar was very different. The hardwood floors and bar stools had a gloss to the wood. The mahogany bar was long, curving out into a semi-circle, and behind it were aisles of bottles with various liquors. A semi-modern jukebox was in the corner, playing a bluesy rock anthem while scattered patrons drank and shot pool.

A few Aristans stopped to turn and look at him, but briefly nodded and continued carrying on about their business.

As he walked towards the bar, he noticed a tall, curly haired Aristan male behind the bar, serving drinks to those sitting there. Quietly, Aidan walked up and made eye contact with the bartender.

Snow offered him a curt smile as Aidan sat to the bar. "Gravanos," he greeted Aidan in his native Aristan tongue.

Aidan gave a nod. "Gravanos, brother. What's your name?"

"Snow."

"Snow, I'm looking for the owner of this Haviscasi. Greenwood?"

Snow set a liquor bottle back on the shelf behind him. "Yeah. You mean Devin," he replied. "She's in the back by the loading dock." He pointed at an exit towards the back.

Aidan walked back until the clinking of glass got louder. On the loading dock, two Aristans were unloading alcohol onto the dollies. As the guy wheeled one dolly away, he noticed Aidan and smiled. "Devin, you've got company."

Her back still facing him, she lifted another crate and set it on the other dolly. "Yeah, yeah, just a second."

Aidan came closer to where the dock and the truck met. "You need a hand?"

Devin turned around, carrying another crate of whiskey and, with a grunt, settled the crate onto the others on the dolly. She pushed her dark hair back, slid a rubber band from her wrist and fashioned a bun out of her asymmetrical haircut. With a pant, her reflective eyes met Aidan. "Nope, I can manage." She rubbed her hands on her jeans and extended her right hand to shake his. "Haven't seen you around before. You looking for a pack or something?"

Aidan firmly shook her hand and saw her arms adorned with various tattoos. "Or something." He smiled, as he noticed her sizing him up before offering her hand. It was brief but spoke volumes, because it wasn't a size up like a woman would do for ogling or interest. It was more along the lines of Devin gauging her tactic to subdue him should she need to. He knew that look, and it wasn't something every Aristan or she-wolf did when meeting someone. Devin must've had some training. "My name's Aidan Bloodlocke. My pack is in Terrytown, actually, but I'm here tracking down a threat."

Devin grimaced at his comment. "I'm Devin Greenwood, owner of this establishment. What kinda threat are we talking about here?" Her hands found her hips and rested there, inadvertently tightening the cloth on her white tank top. It sculpted to her toned torso, clinging to the curves of her breasts. "Are we talking about Thesians?"

Aidan shook his head. "Not really. A rogue from my pack. He may have came here seeking asylum, but right now he's been seen with lone Thesians. His name's Kieran Bloodlocke. Sound familiar?" He pulled up an older picture of Kieran on his phone and showed it to her.

Devin curled her lips, shook her head and pushed the dolly onto the dock. "No, but that might explain some strange Thesian activity lately."

"What kind of activity?"

"Well. There's been a lot of talk. Some Aristans came in here recently---drunk off their ass, of course, saying Thesians without colors have been laying waste to Iris and even Bridgepoint. Packing up together, saying they hate other Thesians and Aristans alike, that the new world for ShadowShifters is brotherhood, yada, yada, yada."

Aidan frowned. "And what did you do?"

"What I typically do." She picked up a crate and set it on top of the others. "Kick their drunk asses out of my bar so they can sleep some of that nonsense off. There ain't no mixed brotherhood of Aristans and Thesians out here. And if there was, I guarantee you they would be at each other's throats faster than a rabbit gets fucked. Our kind and theirs just don't mix."

Aidan sighed. She didn't believe them. If this was going on under her nose, who knows how big this was getting. "Are lone Aristans welcomed here, Devin?"

"As long as they don't start any shit, any Aristan is welcomed here. But I haven't seen this Kieran, though. So who is this threat? Family?"

"Brother."

She nodded. "Ah, I see. Still, has got to hurt, right? Tracking your own blood is a lot like chasing your own tail."

"He's not my blood, he's a cold hearted shit starter who paid Thesians to attack our complex, and killed his mother. I'm itching to bring him to justice, Devin. Please help me find him."

Devin looked at the Alpha and sighed. Riko and her had a strict pact. Don't mess with mine and I won't mess with yours. She understood the pain of losing someone so close. The devastation that it did to one's life, and she ached for him. But helping him would muddy that pact, and all she had in this world was her word. "Look, I wish I could help you, Aidan, but I don't cross into Bridgepoint. Neither me nor mine. We stay out, and the Thesians stay in. That is how it is here. I have others to think of."

Aidan frowned. "You can't just turn your back here, Devin. People are getting hurt out there."

Devin scoffed. "*Humans* are getting hurt, Aidan. Don't get it confused. And they can handle their own. That Sheriff out there in Bridgepoint is a trip. Besides, the guys would have told me if Thesians were attacking us. Yet here we are. "

"I wish you were right, but something is brewing, Devin. I talked to Riko and Kieran has been purposely working with lone

Thesians to do his dirty work. It may not be a full brotherhood, but it was enough to nearly destroy our pack." Aidan walked up to her. He was right about her, it seemed. Devin was more than just a Haviscasi owner. She oversaw the safety of the Aristans there, and that was all she cared about...very much like him.

Devin was Azan, most likely a general like him. "I understand your responsibility to your brothers, and I don't want you to jeopardize any peace you've created around here. All I ask is that you let me know if you or yours cross paths with Kieran. He knows I'm here, but he's slithery. He won't challenge me outright, which is telling me he's up to something big. Do not trust him. He doesn't care about anyone but himself, and those Thesians are just pawns to him. Please, Devin."

Devin crossed her arms. The wolf was sincere, she'd give him that. She was really hoping that talk around the bar was just that, talk. But seeing an Alpha from another pack standing before her talking about the same thing had her concerned. What if shit was going down right on Bridgepoint's doorstep? If Kieran was anything like Aidan said, he would most likely see her little ragtag pack a threat. Had he been here and she not known? Her pack was small and took great care to lay low, not even registering her Haviscasi with the others to be found. Those who needed to find her place for refuge often found it on their own. They long ago stopped spying on the Thesians in the area, which meant they were a bit more blind to the environment than they should've been.

"Of course, Alpha wolf. I'll tell my crew to keep a nose out. If anything turns up rotten or that name turns up on anyone's lips, we'll know about it. He'll also have no sanctuary here, you have my word. Any wolf that betrays his people and takes his own blood is beyond redemption in my eyes. He'll have no sympathy from me or mine." She extended her hand again, and Aidan shook her hand.

"Thank you."

Devin stretched her body upwards and smiled as the moonlight washed over her. She cast Aidan a smile. "Wanna go for a run?"

Aidan was taken aback at Devin's invitation. He hadn't heard an offer like that in forever, and it usually came from either Cameron or his sister, Leigh. *Awkward,* he shook his head. "I better not, but thanks."

A smirk grew on Devin's face. Then she rolled her eyes. "Arista's hands, I'm not asking for your hand in marriage, Alpha. I'm not even asking for you to wear me out against these crates, though I would be lying if I said the thought didn't cross my mind. I'm just asking you to go for a run, that's all." She stepped back and leaned against the wall, slowly shaking her head at him. "Besides, any fool can tell you're in love with another. I wouldn't dare waste my womanly wiles on the likes of you."

Aidan frowned. "How did you know that?"

"What? Besides that wounded pup face you're trying to hide from the world?" She tapped her nose. "I smell female on you, Alpha. Oh, but she's not Aristan. She's a little human of the female persuasion, am I right? No doubt, probably the reason you even care about the good people of Bridgepoint."

Aidan didn't know what to say next. He'd completely forgotten that Maddie's scent was all over him, a tell-tale sign he'd been fraternizing with a human. A forbidden gesture for any Aristan if she wasn't just some courtesha. He tensed as he realized the foolish mistake perhaps put him and Maddie in danger, especially if Devin was part of the Azanesti Order. A low growl started in Aidan instinctively, as his body felt a challenge.

Devin smiled. "Relax, Lukos," she cooed, sensing his uneasiness. "I don't judge. And I definitely would never harm her. We've all pissed on the laws a time or two." *Or three, or four...,* she thought to herself. "Rules exist because no one ever found a decent reason to break them. And I've learned a long time ago not to ever come between a ShadowShifter and its mate. Your secret's safe with me."

Aidan, still suspicious, nodded quietly. "Thanks." It was her duty to reprimand him for such behavior, yet she simply brushed it off. He took it as Devin Greenwood having a bit of rebel in her. She didn't behave like other generals.

"Has she accepted you?" she asked, curiosity getting the better of her.

Aidan sighed. "I don't know. She doesn't know the truth, and I have to keep it that way."

Devin shook her head disapprovingly. "Then she'll never accept you."

Aidan grimaced at her declaration. The idea of it stung his heart. "That doesn't make any sense."

"Of course it does." Devin shrugged. "How can we love someone who lives their life behind a mask? It's like loving them behind a sheet of tin, never knowing them fully. How can you expect anyone to make a choice?" She met his eyes and walked closer to him. "It's not just because your mate is human, Alpha. It's like that for all of us. Acceptance is about letting them in at your most vulnerable time, letting them see all of you and who you are. Only then can your mate truly decide if they love you or not."

Aidan let Devin's words seep in. But it was no use. "If I tell her, I'll lose her. But even if I don't tell her, I'll still have to let her go because she's human. Either way, I'm fucked."

Devin sighed at Aidan's frustration. "Then, what do you have to lose?"

Aidan eyed her. "Do you have a mate, Devin?"

Devin's face softened for a moment. "No."

All Aidan could see was the disappointment in Maddie's face when he'd left her tonight. He could only imagine the fear and horror she would get if he came clean. See her face filled with hate, lashing out at him in terror and disbelief.

It would be his childhood all over again.

He wouldn't be able to take that. He would probably spare some dignity if he just left her alone, but a rejection after telling her everything would crack him. "I wish it was that easy, Devin. Truly." Realizing he was sharing far too much of himself and his plight, he straightened up and felt the tension creep into in face again. "I'm sorry. I didn't mean to go into my problem. It's not your concern."

Devin opened a crate and pulled out a bottle of whiskey. Cracking open the top, she raised it and brought it to her lips, taking a couple of swigs. "Nope, it isn't my concern, Aidan. But that doesn't mean I can't care, now does it? I wouldn't have asked if I didn't care. Trust me, I'm not one for small talk. Small talk is for humans. Real talk is for family." She passed him the bottle. "Loosen up a bit."

With a sigh, Aidan took a swig of the rich, amber alcohol, letting the sweet burn tingle his throat. Devin may be right, but he couldn't go back to Maddie's. He knew she was still pissed at him, and with every reason to be. He couldn't continue to shut her out, but he still had a duty to his people. It was the most painful tug of war he'd ever imagined. Perhaps it was why Aristans didn't get close to humans, and like a fool, he was falling for one. Maddie's face was worth any pain he had to endure to keep her, and he prayed to Arista that she would want him.

He took another deep swig of whiskey.

Devin grabbed the bottle from him and set it down on the dock. He needed to be sober if he was going to protect his mate. It was clear the wolf had a lot on his mind. He was, after all, being attacked on all fronts of his life. A lost parent. The weight of leadership. A forbidden mate. She knew better to say it out loud, but it kinda sucked to be him right now. She understood two out of three of his hardships, but she definitely wouldn't trade places with him.

Who knew how long he'd been without connecting with himself in his wolf skin? Her father always told her that bonds between their people and themselves were made in their wolf skin. Bonds to others of their kind, even a deeper bond with one's self. They were, after all, a creation wrought from a human heart and wolf spirit. Both creatures were all about building deeper connections. She was intrigued by the high strung Alpha. He had honor, and she could tell he was a fighter. If rogue Aristans and Thesians were at her doorstep making trouble, and chaos was at hand, she needed to know who she was swearing allegiance with.

Devin kicked over the whiskey bottle, looked at the moonlit sky, then to Aidan. "Now, how 'bout that run?"

YOU DIRTY DOG

Leigh frowned as she watched Bastien's silhouette in the window of his bungalow. Her breathing was forced but steady, trying to concentrate on being calm. It wasn't easy considering the news Aidan gave Cameron, who, in turn, brought her up to speed. Kieran had gotten funds from somewhere in order to grease the paws of the Thesians in his company. They had just recently heard from Onyx's own lips that the pack funds were nearly empty. It all was connected. And she hated Bastien for it.

In the deep, silent dark of the forest, the only true light was the moon shining down on her. Her mother always said that their race was magical. They were the first ShadowShifters created, and the Moon Goddess Arista herself molded the first of their kind with her bare hands. From the first Alpha couple, they were given strict instructions to be fruitful and multiply and that their existence depended on harmony amongst their race.

Ninon used to say that from that day on, every Alpha was responsible of keeping that harmony, and to punish anyone who proved a threat to it. Communeins of the pack were disposed of quickly to restore faith and peace within the pack. She knew it was true. Leigh had seen with her own eyes her father, Tiberius, restoring order from traitors. Leigh was no Alpha, but she was her father's daughter.

Tonight, she sought out a traitor. She held the transmitter in her hand and listened quietly downwind of Bastien's bungalow to mask her scent. Cam was able to bug his place after visiting him, regarding the Azans going up to check on a new place for the pack. Staying behind as part of the community security, Cameron asked her to tail him while he organized the Azans to leave.

The Celt made it painfully clear to Leigh that her job was just to tail him, and eavesdrop, in hopes he would slip up and expose himself. But as she hid there in the shadows all she could think of was her mother, Ninon. She was beautiful and strong and died horribly because of all this. If that wolf in there had a hand responsible for her death and those of others that night, he better pray to the Goddess Arista for a quick death.

Bastien peered out his window staring out into the night, his phone clutched in his hand as if it was part of his body. It was nearly a week since he heard from Kieran and he couldn't risk making any moves until he knew Kieran wasn't going to shit all over his plan.

Things were getting way outta hand, and Onyx was starting to get suspicious. He could feel it. The old wolf was already sniffing around the financial records. It was only a matter of time before either Onyx or the Council will discover that he moved the money. Kieran was supposed to just take the money and run. But when he offered to shake things up to build distrust and ensure the Council would remain, he foolishly agreed. The pack depended on the function of the Council more than ever since Tiberius' untimely death. He only wanted a little scare. But instead, the shitty little brat took it upon himself to try and destroy the community. Now he was implicated in the entire ordeal, realizing that Kieran used the money to fund the attack. Using Thesians as mercenaries to hide his ulterior motive...revenge.

But he was sloppy. Instead of getting the Thesians to kill Ninon and Aidan, he killed Ninon himself, tracing everything back to him. The stupid wolf was always more balls than brains, and now he didn't know what the rogue Aristan was up to now. If Aidan gets his hands on him, he'll make him talk, but he couldn't allow the Alpha to outright murder him. After all, he still had a reputation to uphold and the Council should always been seen as the voice of reason. Onyx may think their time at the head of the table was only temporary, but he was an old fool. This pack would never survive just listening to the hot-headed Alpha, who is also bent on revenge for the loss at Kieran's hand. He needed to either reason with Kieran or eliminate him in order to save his own skin.

His thoughts were interrupted by the vibrations running through his hand as his cell phone rang. Turning away from the window, Bastien accepted the call after seeing the "unknown" number pop up on the screen.

"Where are you?"

Kieran began laughing on the other end. Bastien cringed. Something about that wolf's laugh always gave him the creeps.

Anger began to creep up into his expression as he decided to ask Kieran once more. "I said, where the hell are you? Did Aidan locate you?"

"I didn't call to check in with you, old man." Kieran's voice was dark and annoyed. "I'm minding my own business away from the pack, just like we agreed. And as for your meddling joke of an Alpha, yes, he's well aware by now that I am here in this town."

Bastien started to pace back and forth in his kitchenette. "W-What are you going to do? He cannot be allowed to capture you, Kieran!"

He scoffed. "Of course he won't capture me, you idiot. I have my Thesians here, and he's greatly outnumbered. I'm surprised you sent him up here without reinforcements, Bastien. Very bad form." Kieran shifted the cell to his other ear. "How's the pack? Did you send them my love?" Kieran gave a light chuckle.

Bastien shook his head at his ill-placed humor. "Many died from your half-assed execution, wolf! No one authorized you to practically destroy the fucking pack! I told you a small scare to get everyone's attention!"

"Did I not get their attention, old man?" Kieran replied. "And you're right. No one authorized me to destroy the pack because I need no authorization." He sighed at Bastien's haughtiness. It was cute, really. The old wolf thinking he had some sort of reign over him. "Let's not forget, Bastien, you came to me about that coup. You were open for anything to keep your dirty little secret from getting out to the pack. Especially Aidan, who would've ripped your fucking throat out from stealing from your own people. You know what a crusader he is."

Bastien didn't trust Kieran at all. The only reason he entertained any of the spoiled wolf's ideas was that he caught him with his pants down. He was pulling money away to build his future and what he thought would ensure the future of the pack. But it was all a lie. Deep down, he wanted to ensure the pack would need him. If he had a chance in hell, he had to cut ties with Kieran and everything he's done.

But the idea Kieran had over fifty thousand dollars, a group of disgruntled Thesians and pure malice in his heart didn't sit well with him. "What are you doing up there with the Thesians, Kieran?"

Kieran smiled to the phone. "Wouldn't you like to know."

"Yes, I would. Rumors are flying that you are offering them brotherhood. That can't be true."

Kieran sighed. "And what if it is?" He walked around in the office where the moonlight washed in through the window. "What the fuck can you or anyone do about it? We're talking Shadow-Shifters that were cast out and abandoned. No home, no allegiance. They just want a family and a leader, and I'm gonna give it to them." It was his dream. He was born to lead, and now all his enemies that prevented that were gone, he had a chance to make his own destiny.

Bastien did not share the same sentiment. In fact, the thought disturbed him. "You're insane. The Thesians will never allow some Aristan to be their Alpha. Least of all a ragtag, fleabitten group of rogues and loners."

"Well, I'm sure when you remember your community in a fiery shambles and Ninon dead, you won't think so lowly of this supposed ragtag fleabitten group. It's a new day, Bastien. I don't need my kind, I just need the like-minded. It's my destiny to be Alpha. My fucking birthright, until you let Aidan steal it from me!"

"You got what you wanted, Kieran. The pack is in shambles; you're rich. Now disappear, and I never want to know you exist again. Never contact me or my pack, again."

"It's not your pack. It's Aidan's pack, remember? And if I let him live, he's just as a threat to you as he is to me. How much is his death worth?"

Bastien frowned. "I've already paid for Aidan's death, and you left that contract empty. Instead, you killed your mother, who had no political clout or gain to secure the future of this pack. I'm not biting this one. He's your headache, and if you don't kill him, he'll kill you soon enough. I've had enough of this discussion. Take your ridiculous social experiments, the money I gave you, and disappear."

Kieran shook his head. Annoyance began to escalate his voice. He was growing impatient for these games. "I'm afraid it's not that easy, friend."

"What do you mean, 'It's not that easy'?" Bastien stopped his pacing, scowling at the cell phone. "I told you to disappear!" Bastien began pacing again. Fury sharpening his movements.

"Well, first of all, I'm broke. It's taken twice as much cash to pull that attack and support the brothers without colors." Kieran leaned against the desk in his office. "Soooo, I'm gonna need a bit more cash if you really want me to stay away."

Bastien growled at Kieran's insolence. "Have you gone fucking rabid? I'm not giving you any more money. Whatever you do now, you're on your own, you goddamn nut! I've had enough of this! The fates were right to deny you the victory of the Selenium Circle. You're insane and destructive! We never would have allowed you to become Alpha. No more, you little shit!"

Kieran's eyes changed as they cut to the phone. Beads of sweat formed at his temples as he struggled to keep himself from hitting the change. *Not yet,* he thought. Not now. But soon. He'd had enough of Bastien, Aidan, and that whole fucking pack. It was time for retribution. They thought he was hell before...

"You have insulted me for the last time, Bastien. I guess you haven't learned that those who cross me don't live to brag about it. I was merciful when I cut tail and ran from the first strike. But now, I will make sure that every man, woman, and child in that pack dies. If not ripped apart by teeth, then executed with nightshade!"

Bastien froze at his words. "You're lying! You don't have access to that." Aristans didn't deal in Nightshade. It was expensive, and the risks far outweighed the benefits. It was lethal when it entered the bloodstream of a ShadowShifter. Thesians used it to exterminate Aristans, not caring for the risk of contamination. Tainted ammunition was devastating; a ShadowShifter could dig out a bullet and heal, but if the bullet is tainted with nightshade, it meant death. Putting that kinda weapon in the hands of someone as crazy as Kieran was bad news.

Kieran smiled deviously out his window. He watched Nornos carry in two crates of guns and ammo. There was a biohazard symbol on the ammunition box, warning the carrier of potent nightshade extract on the cartridges. Nodding at Nornos as he walked it, Kieran gave a chuckle. "I think you forgot all about my new friends. They're all pretty rad, and they made sure I had access to the coolest stuff. Including tainted ammunition."

Bastien went cold at the revelation. "You can't do that, Kieran."

"You know, I've had enough as well, Bastien. I've had enough of you and that poor excuse for a pack telling me what I can and can't do. If I have no money, than I will have to bleed you all dry."

Bastien felt panic rise in his stomach. "You'll be outnumbered, Kieran. The Azans will make sure you never get that close."

I guess that you think I'm not aware of the operations there, old Bastien. We left that place pretty charred. By now, the Azans would be deployed to find a new place - am I right? Maybe just a skeleton group to protect the 'whittle wones,' right?"

Bastien closed his eyes to rein in his anger. "How much money do you need?"

Kieran sneered. "I've changed my mind. I don't need more money to incentivize what I've wanted to do ever since I lost the Selenium Circle to a lone, rampaging bastard. I will come and burn down every home, every single breathing Aristan in that pack. And when I'm finish toying with Aidan up here, I will bring him along for the ride for you and him to watch every singe, and listen to every scream until all that is left of the pack is the two idiots who watched them fall!"

Kieran hung up and, with a roar, threw the phone against the wall with such force it shattered against it, some pieces making its way to his feet. His eyes a bright amber, he smoothed his hair back in frustration. Did they think he was playing around? They had news coming.

Nornos rushed in from the racket. "Hey man, you alright?" He looked at the decimated phone on the linoleum. "Bad news?"

Kieran took a deep breath. "No, we've got everything running one hundred percent, Nornos. But tell the new recruits' money is going to be a bit tight until we take care of some unfinished business!"

"What business is that, boss?" Nornos asked.

"We're going to stomp out my old pack."

Nornos scoffed. *This old song again?* "We've already done that, Kieran. The guys are ready to move forward. Are you?"

Anger hitting a fever pitch, Kieran grabbed him and pulled him to his face. "I'm not ready to move on until they are fucking annihilated! Do you understand?" He released Nornos and smoothed his sweaty hair back again. "And the guys want to get paid, right? Right?"

Nornos shrugged. "Right."

"Well, bully for them! The rest of our money is tied to that fucking pack, so unless they want to be reduced to hunting in the forest, eating dead carcasses in wolf's skin, I suggest we pack up and get ready to show the world of ShadowShifters what a pack forged from true brotherhood can do." Kieran began panting, his emotions triggering changes in him until he bit it back down again. "Call a meeting, and we'll bring them up to speed. First, I'm gonna take care of Aidan; then, we're gonna turn that pack to ash."

"Sounds like a plan." Nornos liked the idea of getting rid of Aidan. The wolf was too close to them, and if he was seeking justice from the first attack, he wasn't going to just judge Kieran. All of them were a part of it. It just made sense to finish all of it, so they could finally move forward. Perhaps Kieran made sense after all. "I'll get a line on that courtesha of his. He won't be too far behind."

Kieran crossed his large arms and grinned. "Excellent. Let me know. I want to be sure to meet her again."

FINE LINES

After hearing the dial tone of Kieran hanging up, Bastien threw the phone down. "Shit!"

A curt knock on his door sobered him. "Go away! I'm busy!"

There was silence for a moment, then, there was a deeper, more determined knock. Frustrated, Bastien jerked open the door. "For fuck's sake! What?"

He barely had time to register who it was as he was met with bright yellow eyes and fangs as a snarling Leigh reached in, pulled him and flung him several feet from the steps of his bungalow with such force, the impact flung dust high in the air. His face skidded across the gravel upon landing.

Bastien rebounded, yet dazed from the blindsided attack. He shook it off, feeling his bones pop at the will of a change. His teeth bared and eyes laser bright, he hunched down on all fours, ready to strike back.

Leigh, fuming and shaking from anger, charged towards him. He caught her in a bear hug, constricting her breathing, lifting her several feet off the ground until she head-butted him, forcing him to release her. Leigh grunted as she kicked him squarely in the chin, then caught him in a head-scissors takedown - clutching his head between her legs and flipping him, drilling him down onto the ground.

"You son of a bitch!" she yelled through gritted teeth, tears in her eyes. Just as she was about to change, strong arms grabbed her and pulled her back. Kicking, she growled at the stranger until he flipped her around to face him.

"Leigh, calm down!" Cameron looked into her watery, angry yellow eyes. She was wild and pure fury in his arms as he struggled to keep her from trying to kill Bastien. "Stop it."

Leigh's hair was longer; her nails dug into Cameron's arms has he held her tightly. Panting, she couldn't keep control. "He's a fucking traitor! I heard him! I fucking heard him, Cam! Let me go!"

Bastien changed back, trying to sit up from the dirt. Wiping the blood from his mouth, he frowned at Leigh being restrained like a wild animal. "I don't know what the hell she's talking about! She came to my door and started attacking me for no reason! That bitch is crazy!"

Leigh, hearing his words, roared and pushed herself free from Cameron, charging towards him until Onyx appeared out of nowhere and grabbed her. He stared her down with his pale eyes. "Don't."

Confused, she pulled against him. "Onyx, you don't understand!"

"Yes, he does," Cameron said softly.

Bastien stood up and dusted himself off. "What the hell is this!" He looked to Onyx. "She attacked me, which is grounds for punishment!"

Cameron, growling low in his throat, strode over to Bastien and connected a jab to his face that knocked him back to the dirt. Circling around behind him, he pulled Bastien up and pinned his arms behind him to restrain. "It would be wise to be silent now before I decide to fed you to her." He looked at Leigh as Onyx finally released her.

His stubbled face was solemn as he stared at her. "We need to be calm, Leigh. Cameron brought me here for answers, and I know you want the same. Please trust that I'm not on anyone's side. I just want the truth, same as you."

Leigh braced her hands on her knees and took in a breath, quelling the anger and will to change along with it. Standing to full height, she met Onyx's eyes and nodded. Onyx was old school and grew up with her father. She wanted to trust him, especially since Cameron convinced him to come. Without a word, she stepped aside.

Onyx proceeded to walk up to Bastien, whose face was contorted in silent anger. He sighed, looking at his friend covered with dirt and guilt. When Cameron approached him after organizing the scout duty of the Azans, he didn't go into detail. Only told him that Aidan found Kieran and that the Thesians he worked with were paid a lot of money for the attack. As soon as Onyx heard that, he came to his own suspicions that something wasn't right because the pack's money disappeared. Part of him was afraid of the truth, but he needed it nonetheless.

"Where is the money, Bastien?"

Bastien shook his head. "What the hell are you talking about? It was you who told me we were broke! I didn't even know until you said something."

Onyx sighed. His voice deepened to a colder register. "Bastien. This is one of those rare moments in life where you have a chance to come clean without the shame of being found out as a liar. Did you have anything to do with the money disappearing? Or the attack on our pack?"

Bastien's knot in his stomach grew bigger. "I don't know what you're talking about."

Leigh slowly walked up to him and pulled out her transmitter, and plugging it into her phone. "Well, maybe this will refresh your memory." She pressed play and the night echoed with the recording of Bastien's phone conversation with Kieran. Even just hearing the one-sided dialogue of the event was horribly damning. Cameron and Onyx listened as he made references to paying

Kieran, his idea to "scare" the pack, and when the part came up about paying to kill Aidan, Onyx asked her to shut it off.

Bastien's face sunk and fear crept into his eyes. He was found out, and he knew it. There was no way to save his own skin, but he had to try. "Listen, I didn't mean for it to go this far. He caught me skimming money from the pack and blackmailed me into giving him a chunk of it. I had no idea he was going to do the damage he did! I swear!" He looked into Leigh's eyes and only saw fury. "I didn't mean for Ninon to get hurt."

Leigh stood tense, staring into his eyes with contempt. "No, you only wanted it to be my brother instead," she replied. Her voice was dark and cold as her eyes trained on him. "With Aidan out of the way, you could do anything you wanted, right?"

"Why?" Onyx felt compelled to ask. But in the end, it didn't matter why. It mattered that Bastien assisted in the destruction of his own people. It was dirtier than the most neglected sow, more foul than a week's old carcass in the summer. Something like this could crush the morale of the pack. Finding out that one of their own, a trusted elder member of the council and lifelong pack member, stole from them and funded an attack against its own people; it would throw everyone's faith in the pack into a fiery tailspin. It has been a long while since Onyx felt heartbreak.

But this was heartbreak.

Bastien spit out the blood from his mouth. "I needed to secure our future as council to this pack, Onyx." He pulled against Cameron but was aptly pulled back with harshness, feeling his arm jerk back. "Look around you! We are attacked on all sides! Thesians have been systematically closing in on Aristan packs all over the place! We have an Alpha running down a personal vendetta when he should be here taking care of his own people. When Tiberius died, everyone was ready to tear each other apart to take his place! If it wasn't for our council of elders to restore order, we would have imploded, and you know it! Do you really think putting our future in the hands of crazed Aristans like Kieran and Aidan would be the smartest choice?"

"It was not for you to decide, Bastien," Onyx replied. "Just like we followed Tiberius, we always chose the strongest and loyal leader to follow. That leader is now Aidan. Not you. Not me, or anyone else in the council. Tiberius requested the Council as a short term leader, nothing more. I understood this going in. Why couldn't you?"

Bastien gritted his teeth but remained silent. He only wanted what was best for the pack, or so he thought. Yes, he wanted money and needed the security, but it would have been nothing if the pack didn't survive. But they wouldn't understand. He could see Onyx's eyes swirling with doubt and anger. And Leigh was probably already thinking of how to kill him. It was over.

Cameron shook him. "Aidan said Kieran's with Thesians, trying to build a pack. Is that true? What do you know about it?"

Taking a deep breath, Bastien felt washed over with shame. One way or another, he was going to die. It was their law. But he had to do something to make this right. "Kieran wants to lead a pack of lone ShadowShifters, Aristan and Thesian alike. All the outcasts, murderers and traitors, assembled into a ruthless pack...and armed with nightshade tainted weapons.

Cameron hissed a curse at the thought. This was bad, and one didn't need to guess as to how as to how Kieran had the money and the access to get such weapons. "Where's he taking them?! Huh, you son of a bitch! Answer me!" He violently shook him again.

"He needs more money. Without it, he'll lose the support of the rogues because they couldn't build without the funds. He's gonna convince them to prove their force by attacking our pack. This time, he wants total annihilation. It's the only way he'll gain more support and solidify his place as their Alpha."

Cameron sighed and looked up to the heavens. He had just sent the Azans away. They could be spread all over by now. Their pack was now leaderless and without the Azanesti Order to protect them. As Beta, he knew he had to start planning now. "How big is his following?"

"I don't know. But with money and recruiting, he could have over a hundred men. He probably was planning to do this all along. I just gave him the means to do it faster."

Erupting with fury, Leigh backhanded him across the face, snarling down at him as the force of it sank him to his knees. "You stupid bastard! You did this to us! You gave him everything to ultimately destroy us, don't you see that?!" Leigh's long blond hair waved violently in the wind as she shook her head. "He would have been nothing without that money you gave him! Nothing! And now he's got weapons and a kill squad of basically mercenaries! My mother would still be alive!" She grabbed his face and forced him to look at her raging yellow eyes. "What good is your need to fight the enemy when our own is fucking us over!" Her body was rigid, but the pain in her heart gripped Leigh so violently she gripped her chest. "You don't have any idea what you've done just to secure a seat for yourself."

"Was it worth it, Bastien?" Onyx asked quietly. The reality of the situation was swirling in his head. Their pack was small, and even if Kieran only had half of what Bastien was guessing, they would still be horribly outnumbered. And with poisonous night-shade to add to the situation, so one would come out alive. It would be absolute slaughter. Leigh was right, with funding Kieran, Bastien had signed their death warrants.

Shame took over the hardness in his face as Bastien answered. "I'm sorry. I've told you all I know, old friend." He looked down briefly, then finally met Onyx's eyes with surprising sincerity. "What happens now?"

"You die," Leigh replied. "Death will only have you now for what you've done."

Cameron frowned. "She's right. You are a traitor to this pack. The judgment is death."

Bastien gave a quiet nod, content with the judgment made. He always told himself that no matter what happened, he would always accept death bravely and on his feet. "I have only one request."

Leigh shook her head. "Fuck off!"

Onyx raised his hand to silence her. "Let him speak, Leigh. What is your request?"

Bastien swallowed, his eyes showed a hint of mist before he blinked it away. " I know what this could do to the pack. I don't want to face them at a trial, and you and I know that a trial will waste valuable time when you could be preparing the pack for a fight."

Onyx nodded. "What do you want?"

"I rather be judged right here, right now. Let's get this over with." The look in his eyes held defeat, but his stance was confident and clear as if he had come to terms with his fate. He didn't want to cause the pack any more grief, and Bastien would not be able to deal with looking into the faces of all he'd betrayed. This way, they could move on quickly.

Cameron looked to Onyx. "I don't want us to hide anything from the pack. That is what got us into this situation, to begin with. Besides, what kinda precedent would we be setting if we started judging without a trial? I don't like it."

Onyx folded his arms. "I don't like it either, but Bastien is right. What good would pulling a trial together right now when we need to be pulling together to save ourselves? We have recorded proof of his misdeeds, and once we tell them and Bastien is gone, then we can rebuild. We won't be hiding anything."

Onyx's eyes softened and placed his hand on Cameron's shoulder. "Letting the pack dwell on this will only break us further apart, Cameron, and you know it. We need to heal and unify. It's our only hope."

Cameron slowly released his grip on Bastien's hands and nodded in agreement. Onyx was right. They needed to move on. Even now, anxiety was piling inside him on what his next steps were to protect the pack and bring Aidan back to fight.

"Okay." Cameron moved to the front of Bastien to meet his eyes. " Bastien, for your crimes against the pack and crimes against the race of Aristans with contributing to murder, treason, and mayhem, I now sentence to a quick and immediate death. May Arista's hands guide and accept you into her halls."

"A quick death is too good for him!" she spat at the decision. "A more harsh punishment is needed for what he's done to us, Cameron! This isn't right! He must suffer! The vengeance in my heart demands it!"

Cameron shook his head. "No. This is not about vengeance, Leigh. This is about justice. That is what we owe to our pack, and that is all I can offer you."

"Cameron, as Beta, it is up to you to commence judgment." Onyx stepped back.

Cameron took a deep breath and looked at Leigh. Vengeance had consumed her. It was frightening and soul-wrenching, but it also meant it needed to be fed. But it had to be fed the right way. The way Aidan would have approved and the way Aidan taught him. There was a fine line between justice and revenge, and it is that line they were treading on right now. Leigh had a loss in her that needed closure, and there was nothing more he wanted for her than that. Stepping aside, he nodded at Leigh. "I elect Leigh Bloodlocke to carry out sentence."

Leigh's heart turned inside out at what Cameron was suggesting. She looked at Bastien and must've thought of a million ways to torture and kill him. His treachery was too awful to describe. She loved her pack. Every single soul that dwelled among them was strong, loyal and beautiful. The pride of Arista, every one of them. But her mother felt the same way and look where it got her. Despite it all, Leigh, just like Ninon, would die for them, and here was this elder Aristan, who should have felt that same commitment, but didn't. It didn't make any sense, and it was that confusion that fueled her mill of hatred for him.

Now, Cameron offered her justice by her own hands.

Bastien saw the conflict in her eyes and nodded at Cameron with a small smile. "Wise choice, Beta."

Leigh walked up slowly to Bastien, who stood erect and quiet, without restraint. He met her yellow eyes that appeared like a sad sunset against an ocean of tears. It was at that moment, he felt the guilt and pain of being responsible for Ninon's death. She didn't deserve that, and now Leigh had to live with that hole in her heart the rest of her life. Staring at Leigh, for a moment, her strong features to her mother confused him. As if Ninon's ghost was coming to seek justice for her death. When he blinked, his eyes adjusted to see Leigh standing a breath away from him. If his death would fill even a little of her heartbreak, at least he did something to make it right.

With a shaky breath, Leigh stared at him. This was supposed to be a good moment for her, but as her hands started to tremble, she couldn't understand the turmoil rumbling inside her. Reaching inside herself, all she could think about is the smile of her mother. The laughter of Gage, Ninon's protector and all the other Aristans who died from this treachery. It was no longer about her. It was no longer about her mother. It was about justice for all of them. Those of whose smiles she'll never see again.

Bastien quietly whispered. "Do it, Leigh. Do it for your mother."

Leigh took in a deep breath and blew it out her nose. She looked at Cameron, Onyx and then finally Bastien, her face finally calm for the task at hand. "No. This is for the pack."

With lightning speed, Leigh reached up and quickly snapped Bastien's neck. The sickening crack echoed through the forest, and she stepped back as his lifeless body crumpled to the ground, his grey eyes open, looking out to dark abyss of unknown.

Onyx bent down to place his fingers on Bastien's throat. When he confirmed his pulse was no more, he stood up and looked to Cameron. "It is done."

Leigh's body gasped for breath as she panted, trying to keep her whirlwind emotions bottled in until she couldn't anymore. She looked up at the moon and roared out to Arista, looking down at them from her gold palace. It was loud, bellowing and heartbroken. Cameron pulled her close into an embrace, and this time she couldn't find it in herself to push him away. She needed that connection. She sobbed against his chest as he crushed her to him, hearing his fierce heartbeat against her ear. Her fingers gripped the fabric of his t-shirt at his muscular back held onto him, not ready yet to pull away and face the rest of her life. "Thank you," she quietly whispered.

Cameron breathed in the scent from Leigh's blond hair and sighed. He knew the turmoil in her heart, but couldn't deny the pride he felt in her doing the right thing. She realized the need for justice and carried it out for the good of the pack. As self-serving as it may have seemed to her at first, the weight of executing him wouldn't crush her like an act of vengeance would. As always, Leigh never ceased to amaze him. Cameron savored the moment of her allowing him to see into her soul, because it wouldn't be long until she closed it back, getting back to duty as they all should right now. He would hold her as long as she wanted it.

A moment passed, and Leigh finally pulled away. She wiped her eyes and sniffled, trying to sober up for the next move. She looked at Cameron with blue eyes. "We need to inform the pack."

Cameron nodded. "I'll call a circle tonight." He cut his eyes to Onyx. "Onyx, bring his body to the circle. We burn him tonight." His eyes turned amber and began to walk away. There was much to be done and not a minute to waste. Aidan needed to know the whole story, and they needed him here.

Leigh turned to follow him. "Where are you going?"

Without looking back from his predatory and determined swagger, he replied.

"To prepare."

23

SPRING-RELEASE

Aidan finally opened his eyes to the faint vibration of his phone on the bed. His body was tired, his muscles sore after the run from last night. Devin took him all over the wooded area, and it wasn't without consequence, running all night in wolf's skin. Groaning as his arm reached for the phone, Aidan finally grabbed it and saw it was Cam.

"Yeah, what's going on, Cam?"

"What the hell is going on, Aidan?" Cameron yelled into the phone. His deep, loud voice against Aidan's groggy head forced him to pull back from the phone. He winced at the pain in his head. "I've been calling and texting you for almost an hour!"

Aidan rubbed his temple. "I'm sorry. I went for a run last night, and it must've been a while because it took a bit outta me. What's going on?"

Cameron sighed. "You're not gonna like this..." He warned, apologetically, which Aidan always hated.

"Tell me now," Aidan commanded.

"You were right, Aidan. Kieran was getting money from within the pack. Bastien was the one to give Kieran the dough. They made some sort of fucked up partnership that went bad."

Aidan shot upright at Cameron's statement sobered him from the grogginess. "Shit."

"Yup, but that's not the half of it." Cameron paced by his bike. "Kieran is building a brotherhood there, just like you suspected, but they are coming for the pack."

Aidan moved from the bed. "What?" He forced himself upright, trying to process what that meant. "He's going to attack the pack...again? Why?"

"Who knows why the screwed up mutt does anything," Cameron sighed. "Bastien told us that Kieran needed more money, that he was running out from taking care of the Thesians. When Bastien said no, Kieran went berserk. Now he's planning on pulling off a coup, with nightshade tainted weapons."

Aidan went cold against the window as he heard Cameron's words. ShadowShifters and nightshade did not mix. "Are you sure?"

"Yes. Aidan, this is bad. Our pack isn't prepared for something like this." Cameron ran his fingers through his hair, a million things running through his head. He struggled with his response because it sounded needy, but in the end, it was the truth. "Aidan, we need you. The pack needs their Alpha."

Aidan nodded. "Look, the Thesians haven't mobilized yet with Kieran, and that gives me an idea. I have a better chance to fight this if we can cut the legs off from under the son of a bitch." Aidan thought about how fickle the Thesians were for strangers and money--and that Kieran was running out of money.

"What's your plan?"

"We fucking hit him before he mobilizes. We take away his crew, his weapons, until he's nothing but an Aristan with fancy words. By then, the Thesians will be turned off and no longer interested in him trying to be their Alpha. Thesians, like us, only choose the strongest, and Kieran will no longer look as such." Aidan looked out the window. He couldn't afford Kieran getting his house in order. Couldn't risk his pack facing nightshade poisoning. It was the most sensible tactic to protect everyone. "Where are the Azans?"

"They were sent out to scout a new place for us," Cameron replied begrudgingly. "After Bastien's confession, we had them called back, but some already covered some serious grounds. I'm sorry, Aidan, I just did what you would've done."

"There's nothing to be sorry about, Cam. You did the right thing. I'm glad you called them back so they can look after the pack." He paused for a minute. "Where's that shit Bastien?"

Cameron looked to Leigh, who quietly leaned against a tree. "He's been judged properly and executed for his crimes. The pack is going to be brought up to speed as soon as I'm done talking to you." He wasn't ready to tell Aidan that Leigh carried out the sentence; perhaps it was just enough to know that the traitor was out of the picture.

Aidan felt satisfaction in knowing that Bastien was no longer going to cause the pack any more pain, but the pang in his chest felt sympathy for putting that burden on Cameron. Besides, even with Bastien gone, he had already done enough damage to the pack. How could he be so blind not to see that Bastien was a snake in the grass? "I'm sorry this all fell on you, brother." Aidan knocked his head against the window pane in angst. " I wish I could have picked up on his involvement sooner."

Cameron shook his head. "You and me both. But he hid well, and we trusted the Elder Council. There wasn't anything you could've done differently, Aidan. Now, what do you need from me to help?"

"I need you to stay with the pack. Keep them armed, keep them safe. I'll look into Kieran's plans and where he's keeping the weapons. I have allies here that can help me."

Cameron frowned. "Who?"

Aidan gave a small laugh. "Someone just as insubordinate as you are. Can't wait for you to meet her. How's Leigh? Is she okay?"

Cameron eyed her scowl as he talked to Aidan. She hadn't said much, and it kinda scared the shit outta him. The she-wolf normally didn't know how to shut up. "Um, she's fine--Look, are you sure you don't need my help up there? Even if you find Kieran's stash, do you have the manpower to pull it off?"

Aidan cracked his neck, his bones finally beginning to heal from the run. In all honesty, he didn't have a full confirmation from Devin on her alliance. She did confess that she admired him, respected him, even wanted to screw him, but none of those things meant she was serious in lending her pack and her men into a fray that didn't concern her. She was a tough nut to crack, and despite the run they had, he just didn't have that 100% confidence he could convince her. Aristan women were crafty and believed in minimizing risk to their loved ones at all cost. Would Devin willingly sacrifice herself and her pack to try to save his?

He couldn't bullshit his Beta. "Devin hasn't completely signed on, but I probably could convince her."

"So that means no, you don't have the manpower," Cam frowned at the phone, almost as fiercely as Leigh was frowning at him.

"What would you have me do, Cam? I need you to look after the pack there in case something up here goes wrong. You said it yourself, the Azans aren't there, and there's no one there I trust to lead but you. If Kieran is looking for me, which I'm told he is, it's only a matter of time I find out more details. If I can even just destroy the tainted weapons, and disorganize the Thesians, it'll make the battle a fair fight. I have to do what I can to tip the odds in our pack's favor while I'm here, Cam. Do you understand?"

Cameron growled at the frustration in this throat. Aidan was right, but it seemed destined to fail. He loved Aidan, but he was only one Aristan Shadowshifter. One in a whole sea of colorless Thesians--ones that their own clan or society wouldn't even accept. He knew his Alpha friend too well. If it turned out he had no allies to do this, Aidan would just try and go it alone. His throat constricted as he thought of Aidan being captured or tortured at the hands of Thesians and Kieran. It made his skin crawl. Defeated, he rubbed his face. "I don't like it, Aidan. But I understand."

He smiled softly to the phone. Cameron always was the sensitive one, always watching Aidan's back whether he wanted it or not. It was that and his ability to pick up leadership like he was born for it that made him his Beta. "I know you don't, but it's the way it has to be, brother," Aidan said putting on his boots. "Look, I'll do some recon here and let you know when I find the weapons. Whatever happens, if I don't contact you in the next eight hours, mobilize the pack to a new place. I don't care where, you understand? You're stronger on the run, and the Thesians hate to chase food."

Cameron nodded to the phone. "I promise."

Aidan grabbed his silver-lined, serrated edge Ka-Bar and sheath to fasten onto his belt. "Cameron, if anything happens to me, I want you to keep moving and take care of my sister." He spoke in earnest. "You will replace me as Alpha and keep the pack safe at all cost, alright?"

"At even the cost of my life, Aidan." Cameron looked up to the moon. "Arista's my witness."

Aidan shifted the phone to his other ear as he slipped on his jacket. "Good. You be careful and tell Leigh I miss her yapping obscenities at me." He smiled at the thought of Leigh's scowl, and disapproving head shakes when she wanted to chide him. She was his only tie to a simpler life with a family. The only family he had left.

Cameron scoffed at the request as Leigh began to walk towards him. "And have her chew my ass out instead? No thank you." he cleared his throat. "I hope to talk to you soon, Aidan. If you need me, call me. Understand?"

"Understood. Bye." Aidan hung up the phone and put it in his pocket.

Cameron hung up the phone and looked to Leigh. "Your brother is stubborn, kittycat."

Leigh scoffed. "Tell me something I don't know. Is he coming or what? What's going on?"

Cameron shook his head. "He told me to stay with the pack. He's going to try the disrupt the weapons on that end."

Leigh crossed her arms as Cameron straddled his bike. "What? By himself? And you're gonna listen to him?"

Cameron frowned at her accusation. "Of course I'm not, but I need Onyx to know the score and act in my stead. Go tell him, and I'm going to help Aidan. If you don't hear from either of us in the next eight hours, pack up and ship out, no questions, understand?"

Leigh shook her head. "I'm coming with you."

Cameron scoffed. "Leigh--no, I--"

Leigh frowned, lifting her chin defiantly. "I'm coming with you, or you can tell Onyx your damn self."

Cameron blew out a frustrated sigh at her impertinence. He really regretted teaching her how to ride. " You know, I remember a time when you were super duper nice to me. You used to follow me around, go for runs until midnight...little love taps," he grinned at her arrogantly.

That is, until she punched him in the shoulder. Hard. "You mean *those* love taps?" Leigh glared at him, annoyance all over her mannerisms. She was often fascinated on how Cameron could provoke her so easily. He always seemed to have that gift. And no matter how hard she'd push him away, the cheeky, Celtic wolf always managed to come back for seconds. He and Aidan were like night and day, she totally didn't understand their friendship, nor how Cameron never ceased to give in to her in some form or fashion. "Would you like another?"

"Ow! No!" Cameron rubbed his shoulder, shocked that he found himself in pain. "Fine! Just get on the damn bike, and we'll both go tell Onyx, alright?"

"Then we'll go help my brother?" she eyed him. This time, she was just enjoying seeing him flustered.

Cameron revved up his bike, filling the night with its roar. "Yes , we're going. Now get on the bike before I leave you!"

Leigh gave a victorious smirk as she straddled the bike behind him, locking her arms around the firm and rippled abs of Cameron Flanagan. "You know, something tells me you wouldn't speak that way to Sapphire." She quipped.

Cameron shook his head. "Well, that's because she uses her mouth a bit more creatively than spouting obscenities at me, and her hands for jobs other than punching."

Aidan didn't have time to waste. Riko was probably a good source to rough up for more information, and if he could locate the weapons, he could destroy them. However, that would take something that he didn't have...explosives. Either he had to get a little creative or find some resources. And if anyone had access to black market items, it would be Devin.

Before his thought could barely complete, he caught a whiff of danger right as his apartment door ruptured and he was thrown on his back as a huge, muscular Thesian literally broke through the door and onto Aidan. His red hair was long, shaggy and meeting his bright yellow eyes. Aidan recognized him from Riko's bar when he first arrived. With fangs exposed, the Thesian's massive weight sat on top of him, as he connected a solid hook to Aidan's jaw, forcing his head all the way to the left. Biting back the metallic taste of blood in his mouth, Aidan shook off the punch and connected a crucial hook of his own. And another. And another until he could pull his legs up to his chest and with a hard thrust, kicked the Thesian flying against the wall. The force cracked and dented the drywall until the studs were exposed. Hopping to his feet, Aidan charged at the Thesian and, with brute force, punched him in the gut, forcing the Thesian to lunge his torso forward, where his chin was met with Aidan's knee.

Panting, Aidan kicked him in the ribs. "Where's your weapon stash? Huh? Where's Kieran?"

At the mention of Kieran's name, the redhead grunted with a twisted smile. "Fuck off, Aristan!" The Thesian charged forward and swung at Aidan, but missed, giving Aidan the opportunity to leap onto the giant Thesian's back, squeezing his muscular arms around his neck. As the Thesian's air supply was cutting off, he struggled to the desk, but soon dropped to his knees.

"Now, I asked you a question! Tell me, or I'll end you right here!" Aidan struggled to breathe himself as he put all his strength into subduing the Thesian ShadowShifter. "Where are the weapons? Tell me!" Aidan's low growl rumbled through the tiny apartment, still holding until the Thesian sunk down. He coughed, bracing himself on one arm, while the other tried to pull at Aidan's deadlocked arms around his neck.

He sputtered. "Riko has a warehouse...outskirts" He tried to pull up, gasping for breath. "Th-that's all...I know!" The Thesian slowly wrapped his hand around the leg of the chair. "Just...let me go!" Quickly, the red headed Thesian flung the chair behind him and across Aidan's face. The wood shattered and knocked him back in a daze.

The giant Thesian stood up. "You'll never get there anyway. You'll be lucky if you see that little courtesha alive - or your pack!" He kicked the remnants of the chair away to get to Aidan on the ground. He clutched him by the throat and pushed him against the wall. The Thesian offered him a sinister smile as he watched Aidan struggle to breathe, anger in his reddened, sweaty face. "Don't you worry about that little courtesha of yours, alright? Me and the boys will make sure we take turns comforting her over and over again!" He chuckled, showing his bloodied fangs until he suddenly heaved and choked. His eyes widened and continued to meet Aidan's cold ones as he sunk his silver-edged Ka-Bar blade into the Thesian's chest. Aidan felt the warm blood spill onto his hand as he pushed the blade further in at the thought of them violating Maddie. The Thesian's hands dropped from Aidan's neck, and he staggered back, gasping and bloody with the blade still in him.

"You won't get near her enough to smell her, let alone touch her." Aidan stretched his neck, feeling the relieving crack of his bones, then walked up to him as he dropped to the floor. He leaned over his body and pulled out the blade with a harshness that made the Thesian wail. Aidan wiped the blade against his jeans and sheathed the blade, before walking through the hollow where his door used to be. "You wait here and slowly die. I'm going to make sure your brothers soon join you."

Maddie stared at the clock, listening to the tick-tock go by as the day moved horribly slow. It was almost three o'clock and she was already done with her appointments. After that, the day was sprinkled with a few walk-ins and vaccinations.

Usually, she would crave a light day like this, being as over-worked as she typically felt, but without the work to keep her busy, she couldn't help but dwell on thoughts of Aidan. She sat at her desk, pushing around the lettuce in her salad, replaying last night in her head. Was she being too harsh on him? He was mysterious when she first met him, and all she knew was that even knowing what she did now, he was still just as mysterious. It was the secrets that was killing her. Did he have someone else? Was he really a bounty hunter? Was he a criminal?

She scoffed at herself, realizing that in her head out of all those questions, the thought of Aidan having someone else made her feel the worst. She pushed the salad away. Her heart would break to pieces if that was true, but she wasn't sure. Maddie just didn't get that vibe from him as a two-timer. If anything, she sensed a dangerous side to him, which would explain him being a bounty hunter.

But what if he wasn't? What if *he* was the bounty? she thought to herself. She wanted to laugh it off, but it may not have been the craziest thought. Aidan wasn't a fan of the law, and he knew how to handle himself. He was a fighter, she could tell. What if he was in trouble and couldn't bring herself to tell her? Maddie sighed and looked up at the ceiling.

Could she deal with an outlaw? The thought of it was kinda sexy, and to wit, Aidan would probably be the sexiest outlaw she'd ever seen. But what outlaw would stick his neck out to protect her and take her Nana for a motorcycle ride?

The most amazing anti-hero outlaw ever.

Her feelings for him frightened her. Even now, she craved him to be near her. What the hell happened to the control freak in her that kept people at arm's length?

Maddie loved to see him laugh, to feel his eyes on her. Loved watching his walls break down and become playful and mischievous with her. With him, she was able to totally be herself, dorkiness and all. And when he wrapped his arms around her body and kissed her with those lips of his, she felt like melting to the floor.

Impulsively, her body gave a wicked shudder as she dwelled a little too long on the thought. It would have been easy to say Aidan worked magic on her body. Hell, the man was a smoldering pot of sex. But in reality, he had really done something magical to her heart. As much as she tried, she couldn't shake out what her Nana whispered in her ear yesterday. It made her think all last night, even after Aidan left. She couldn't sleep, tossing and turning, wondering if it was true and her Nana wasn't a complete nutcase like the family seemed to think.

Flustered, Maddie pushed herself from the desk and stood up. "That's it, I need to talk to him or see him, or I'm going to burst out of my skin!" Finally getting out loud, she blew out a breath, nerves striking at her confidence.

Am I really ready to do this?

Maddie tossed her salad in the trash and began gathering her things to close out early. She didn't know where he was staying, but she had his number to text and ask him to meet her. She turned to start putting things on the shelf when the door opened with a ring of the old-fashioned entrance bell.

"I'm about to close my clinic early today. How can I help you?" Maddie didn't bother to turn around as she continued to put the treats and other items away.

"Yes, ma'am. I've seemed to have lost...a dog."

"Sorry, this isn't the pet shelter, Mister. You'll have to check downtown within business hours. Maybe they--" Maddie turned to take a look at her customer, and her voice trailed off. "...can help you."

A shiver ran cold down her spine, nearly freezing her where she stood.

Kieran stood at the entrance, brimming. "Oh..." He grinned, then looked back as if to check the door once more before taking two more steps in. "I have a feeling he wandered in here not too long ago." His bright eyes stared at her, waiting as his whole body blocked the door.

She recognized him as the handsome, polite man from Ripley's Creamery the other day. Nearly the same height and build as Aidan.

But he wasn't Aidan.

No, there was something dark and empty in his eyes, and it chilled her to the bone. An eerie calmness that warned her of impending danger with him. His hair hung wet in his face, his muscular body strained against the white t-shirt he wore. Intimidating wasn't a strong enough word for what came to Maddie's mind, looking at him. Aidan said he was looking for someone. What if that someone was this man before her?

"I'm...not sure what you're talking about." She pulled off her gloves quite cavalier, thanking herself for not letting her hands tremble and betray her seeming nonchalance. If he was looking for Aidan, he was likely dangerous, and she wasn't looking to share any information. It was clear this man wasn't searching for a dog.

One corner of his lips curved into a smirk. "I'm sure you do. You took him in not too long ago." As he moved closer to her, her anxiety heightened. His smile was a lie. "He seems harmless enough, I suppose. Have you seen him, Madeline?" This time his voice was terse, demanding.

Madeline's eyes wondered around the area. There wasn't much to defend herself with at the desk, and he was blocking the entrance. Something about him terrified her. He looked like a normal man.

But his eyes. His movements.

They reminded her of some form of sleek, horrible beast. Ready to pounce and rip her to pieces. Maddie shot her eyes to her bag with her phone that was too far away. Even then, she could hear the faint buzz of her phone ringing for her. Maddie eyed him back, mustering bravery. "We. Are. Closed. Kindly leave before you're escorted out by the Sheriff."

Kieran ran his hands tauntingly across the wood of the desk as he closed in on her. His voice deep and ominous, he gave her a warning. "You have no idea what you're dealing with."

Maddie backed away slowly. If she could get to the back exit, she'd have a fighting chance in making it out. She knew the hiking trail back there and could lose him out there. She blew a breath through her nose, ponying up courage to not let this asshole see her sweat.

"Suppose you tell me." She lifted her chin defiantly.

Kieran bared his teeth, his body tense with anger. "Suppose I show you instead!"

24

THE HUNT

Maddie barely saw Kieran leap over the desk as she ran toward the back of her lab where the emergency exit was located.

Kieran quickly cleared the desk and, with unnatural speed, caught Maddie by her lab coat and pulled her back against the wall near the table. The impact of it threatened to take her breath away. Before Maddie could even think of moving, Kieran pinned her against the wall.

Gritting her teeth, Maddie sneered at him, holding onto the hope that she could get away. "Get your hands off me, or I'll scream!"

"I'd like the sound of that." He smiled deviously, counteracting her struggles. He leaned in and smelled her hair. "C'mon now, courtesha. I can smell his stench all over you. You reek of him. And you know who I'm talking about and you know where he is."

Maddie screamed, but Kieran covered her mouth. The fury in his dark blue eyes made her silence immediately.

"Madeline, if you anger me, I'll have no control over what I do to you. And I can be quite uncontrolled, you know. Things could get completely out of hand." His tone was subdued and brooding as if horror bubbled under the surface. He meant what he said. The darkness in him was too much to ignore. It sickened her to her bones, and she silently wished Aidan were here. She wanted to look around to find something to defend herself, but Kieran was watching her, noting every move she made. She tried to suck in a breath.

Kieran eyed her. "Now, are you gonna be a good girl?"

Maddie nodded quietly, tears in her eyes.

With that, he slowly slid his hand off her face, letting his fingers lightly touch her full lips. His bright eyes raked over her, getting a full look at this beautiful distraction that had somehow managed to twist up Aidan.

"So, you're the one helping Aidan. His fingers caught her chin. "You're fucking beautiful. Look at you—so frightened." He brushed the hair back from her trembling face. "No wonder he fought for you, human or not. Aidan is nothing if not a chivalrist."

"I don't know anything." Maddie struggled against him.

He smiled. "Oh, you must know plenty."

She shook her head, tears welling in her eyes."I just patched him up, and he disappeared. That's it!"

Kieran wiped a stray tear from her eye with his thumb and tasted it. "I wish I could believe you. But I bet if I stripped you down, I'd find him all over you, wouldn't I?"

She squeezed her eyes shut as his hand roamed down her hip, and disgust distorting her face. "Don't."

He cut his eyes to the swing doors of the lab as a tall, blond man walked into the back room. His jeans were torn and dirty, with a long wallet chain across him.

"Am I interrupting, Kieran?"

Maddie looked at the blond and gasped as she suddenly recognized that all too familiar thick voice and blond hair.

Kieran smiled. "Not at all, Brody. In fact, Doctor Ardelle was just about to tell us where we can find her little wolf. Isn't that right, Madeline?"

"Go to hell! I told you everything I know!" Maddie's eyes welled with tears. She fought to blink them away, determined not to let this maniac know he was getting to her.

Brody laughed deep in his throat. The blond from the bar eyed her crudely, his eyes lingering on her body, and her stomach churned at the horrific acts he probably was thinking about. "She tends to be non-compliant, boss. Perhaps I can be of some assistance. She may even like it."

Maddie cringed in horror at his lewd suggestion. She'd die before she'd let them touch her. Still, she maintained a frown. "I doubt it, half-inch."

Kieran roared in laughter, looking back at Maddie, genuinely amused at her insult.

Brody gritted his teeth. "You little worthless—"

"Brody, relax." Kieran smiled. "I'll take care of her. You get back on detail in the front. If we keep her here long enough, he'll come looking for her. I want to be ready."

Brody hesitated a moment, still growling at Maddie, then walked away.

"Brody's a good Thesian soldier, but he's a little slow. I assume you've met before?"

Maddie shook her head. "Why are you doing this?"

"Because Aidan means to bring me back. I know him; he won't stop until he finds me. Eager to appease the elders. I'd much prefer to see him suffer again, and I can't follow my destiny if he's looming about. I won't lie, he's a good tracker. One of the best. But he has no idea what he's up against here. Just like you." Kieran's taunting smile faded. "Now, one last time, Madeline. Tell me where to find him."

"I told you! He left! Now let me go!"

"I wish I could believe you." Kieran picked up the medallion around her neck. "But he practically gave you his dog collar. He inspected the gold etchings on the disc of silver. "You see this? This belonged to my mother, you know. She gave it to him I assume, before she choked to death on her blood. After I ripped her body apart."

Maddie struggled, crying at the disturbing revelation.

Kieran shook her and pinned her back to the wall, forcing her to look into his terrifying eyes. "So you see, Madeline, if I have no reservations about butchering my own mother, I will certainly not think twice on killing you and everyone you know. Do you understand me? Give me Aidan, and I'll spare you. I have too much riding on this town. I'll make my own future here—one without the Aristans in it. Now, where is he?!"

Maddie saw a syringe on the steel table a few inches away from where they stood. She dared not eye it directly, or he would see her. Heaven help her, she was frightened. Whoever this guy was, he was disturbed and twisted, and now didn't put anything past him.

Whether she told him or not, he would kill her, if only to hurt Aidan. She was sure of it.

Maddie closed her eyes and willed every bit of courage she owned in the core of her. Gritting her teeth, she reared her knee up and tucked it into Kieran's crotch. As he released his grip, Maddie grabbed the syringe and stabbed him in the neck.

"You bitch!" He gripped the needle in one hand and his groin in the other.

Maddie ran towards the exit frantically, only to run into Kieran as he grabbed her once again. She was frozen in horror as she found herself staring into bright yellow eyes. Her voice was caught in her throat as he growled low. His face dark and stubbled. He looked more of a feral beast than a man.

And it chilled her to the bone.

"I've had enough of this cat and mouse shit!" he growled.

"What are you!?" she cried.

When he smiled this time, she screeched at the sight of his teeth lengthening into fanged canines, like some creature from a horror film.

This couldn't be happening.

"I'm exactly like Aidan." His voice was now unrecognizable, almost otherworldly. "Shall I show you?"

Maddie screamed as Kieran's arms that grasped her started to cover in fur, his muscles swelling and popping around her.

"I like to play with my food a little, so I'll even give you a head start, princess!" He loosened his grip, laughing demonically.

Maddie didn't think twice. She pushed past him and ran out the back door exit. With only a sliver of sunshine to her back, she ran out past the brushes with all the speed her frightened heart would muster. Her home was not that far past the hiking trails, if she could just get there. *Get to Aidan, then I'll be safe!* She didn't look back, just ran down the trail, panting as fear and the will to survive fueled every hastened step.

She gasped for breath as she heard brushes rustling not too far behind her, moving, catching up with an inhuman speed. Her side aching, she paused only to pick up a piece of branch that nearly tripped her. She quickly broke the length off with her foot and, despite the exhaustion, continued running.

The running kept coming. Faster, louder. The snaps of branches and twigs behind her told her he was gaining on her as the dusk set in, washing the forest in mild darkness.

Maddie screamed as strong arms grabbed her in the dark, nearly lifting her off the ground. Blinded by fear, she swung the stick, and the figure ducked her desperate attack.

"Maddie! It's me!"

It took Maddie a moment to realize it was Aidan's lilting voice in her ear. Aidan's arms around her.

He smoothed the hair from her face so she could see him. "Look, it's me, baby. Are you okay?"

Maddie's body shook from both the cold and the fear as her mind tried to register he was really there. "Aidan?"

She saw his handsome, dirty face turned to stone as she was suddenly whipped around behind him, protectively. Losing her balance from the swift maneuver, she fell against the tree. There she saw a shadowed, growling creature charge towards Aidan.

"Run, Maddie!" Aidan yelled. "You can make it! Don't look back!"

Maddie was frozen. She wanted to move, but she couldn't believe her eyes when she looked into Aidan's as he turned around. His eyes were bright, like the color of pure honey.

And his voice...

It sounded like...

"I'm exactly like Aidan."

Maddie covered her mouth as she realized what she was looking at. "Oh my God!"

She shrieked as the creature pummeled into Aidan, knocking him back. Aidan quickly recovered, grabbing the creature, slinging him against a tree.

Kieran slammed against the tree, his body racked against it. Despite the pain, he managed a laugh, deep and dark. "Glad you could join us, Lukos! I was just about to partake in a little midnight delight!"

Aidan kicked him. "You won't fucking touch her!" His anger made him careless as Kieran slapped his claws across Aidan's chest and knocked him to the ground.

Kieran pinned him down, snarling. "Aren't interested? That's fine. I brought some guests!"

Aidan brought his elbow fiercely up against Kieran's leg, knocking him over to allow Aidan to get to his feet.

Maddie shivered as growls and howls echoed behind fast until all she saw were shadows running up to Aidan, attacking. The men were so fast, one hitting Aidan as he charged forth. With every blow, she felt her heart wither as Aidan's face became dark and bloody.

Aidan gritted his teeth in rage and kicked the Thesian in front of him. He howled as he was knocked back a few feet from Maddie, who cringed as he landed. The blond shook it off and recovered, wiping the blood from his whiskered face. He charged forward to join with Kieran and the other Thesian.

Something silver caught her eye as the Thesian got up from the ground. As she reached for the cold steel in the leaves, gripping it tight, she closed her eyes, wishing for strength to do what she had to. She had only this chance.

"Give it up, Kieran." Aidan spit crimson as he heaved a breath. "There's a lot of people wanting to see your head on a spit. And as Alpha, I second the motion, you worthless piece of shit." He coughed up a laugh.

"I bet." Kieran scowled. "You're so into duty and following orders, Aidan. You made Papa so proud. Mother dearest, too. How else could a motherless bastard with no past win someone over, right? But they chose the wrong son."

Aidan gave a dark smile. "If my memory serves me right, the 'wrong' son kicked your ass all over the Selenium Circle. You could barely recover and weren't even fit to be the pack's Beta."

Kieran pulled out his blade and brought it up to Aidan's face. "And I owe you for that as well, you bastard...wait, I think I took that issue out with Ninon." He chuckled. "Ah yes, poor Ninon."

Aidan's eyes flashed red. "Don't you dare say her name, you shit!"

Kieran gripped his blade tight in his hand. "Well, join her."

"No!"

A shot rang out in the darkness, and in the faint moonlight, she saw the blond Thesian grip his side. Howling, he slumped to the ground. Aidan, Kieran, and the other Thesian stood still as they saw a very pale, very frightened Maddie holding the Glock pistol the blond had dropped on the ground. The smell of gunpowder wafted in the night air. Her hand shook, but maintained a decent balance for a woman who had barely touched a gun. And was surrounded by ShadowShifters. Three of them.

"Shit!" Brody breathed as he watched his brother slump down to the ground, dead.

Kieran growled low in his throat, casting a chiding look to the living Thesian, Brody. "You dumb shit! You leave a nightshade weapon lying around?!"

Brody's eyes widened. "It was Dante's! Not mine!"

"Let him go! Now!" She spoke through her teeth, hiding the fact that her heart was beating out of her chest. She moved the gun in an arc between all three of them, as Aidan was in the crossfire.

Aidan stood just as still as the others. He knew his poor Maddie was frightened beyond belief, and though it seemed she was trying to help, one quick move and Maddie could shoot him as well.

"Tell your courtesha to put the gun down, Lukos, if she knows what's good for her." Kieran's firm voice became more human as he slowly morphed back into human skin.

Aidan stared at Maddie, his eyes now a bright green. They were stoic. "Shoot, Maddie."

"If you shoot, courtesha, you'll risk hitting him. Is that what you what?" Kieran grinned.

"Don't listen to him, Maddie. Shoot!"

Maddie's breathing quickened as the tension rose. "Aidan..."

Please help me do this right.

Kieran held his arms up higher "Or do you wish him dead like the rest of us howling monsters?!"

Aidan, with a fierce growl, took the opportunity to push back against the Thesian and use the leverage to kick Kieran, putting distance between them. All of them breaking away, Maddie fired the pistol at Brody, hitting him several times in his abdomen. Her eyes watched his shirt turn red as blood seemed to erupt from his body with each devastating blast of the gun. Aidan moved away from him, ducking down, as Kieran disappeared into the dark woods fleeing from the shots Maddie was unleashing in every direction.

With tears running down her eyes, she kept squeezing until the barrel retracted finally in a click. Her body went cold and shaky, horribly unstable.

Aidan slowly same over to her, his steps poised and careful. "Maddie."

She still looked out to the woods, still aiming the gun out into the darkness.

"It's okay. You can put the gun down, Maddie. They're gone." He cautiously moved to her side and slid down beside her against the tree, watching her frightened, pale face in the moonlight.

She was hyperventilating.

His heart ached for her. He never wanted his world to touch her, and the violence that came with it. Unlike him, who had lived his whole life fighting and killing, Maddie was an innocent human who knew nothing of that life. It wasn't his intention to sully her sweet soul with his way of life. To be hunted and to fear him. She probably didn't right now, but Aidan knew she would hate him. They always did, sooner or later. It was not what he wanted, but maybe how it needed to be.

Her voice skipped between breaths. "Are you...are you alright?" She still didn't look at him, even as his arm circled behind her and began reaching for the pistol in her shaking hands.

"I'm fine, xerhmon. Give me the gun. It's alright." He crooned to her repeatedly until Maddie loosened her grip and he lifted the pistol away. He pushed the barrel back and threw it on the ground so he could hold her, rocking her gently. "It's okay, Maddie. I've got you, sweets."

Maddie burst into tears, unable to hold back the fear and confusion a moment longer. She gripped him tight, pressing her body against him as tears spilled down her cheeks. "Would you please tell me what's happening? Am I going insane?! What did I just see?" She sobbed against his battered, bloody t-shirt. "I don't understand!"

Aidan held her gently, kissing her forehead. "C'mon. Let's get you somewhere safe."

Maddie was lost to reason as she started to fade in and out of consciousness. He mumbled something in that strange, sensual language of his, the words distant, almost an echo. All she felt was Aidan pick her up, brushing his lips over her face.

He was so warm, so comforting that she sighed against him.

Yet when she looked up at Aidan, she saw a sadness in the jades of his eyes as it all faded to sweet darkness.

25

HAVEN

Maddie slowly opened her eyes to find herself staring up at a white ceiling. Wearily, her eyes glanced around to find herself in someone's bedroom. Rising up too quickly, she hissed as her head ached and made her woozy. The faint yellow light came from a beautiful antique wooden lamp. Resting on her elbows, she scanned the rest of the room and was in awe. She laid on a four poster bed. Beautiful framed portraits were on the golden walls. She shifted herself to let her feet hit the floor as she sat up on the enormous bed. The mahogany chest and vanity were empty on top, but no less antique and beautiful. It seemed as if no one lived in the room. It was just elegant and beautiful, but still warm. Not impersonal like a hotel room.

She looked around and realized no one else was here.

Then she saw Aidan's black jacket lying over the chair by the window.

"Aidan?" she whispered.

She looked down at the small scratches on her arm and hands from running through bushes. Then, all the twisted events came rushing back to her.

A faint click of the door made her jump back on the bed, as it slowly opened to reveal Aidan with a tray in his hand.

He made a slight jump himself, surprised to see her up already. "Maddie, it's okay. It's just me. I brought you something."

Maddie couldn't stop herself from shivering as she saw him there, her memory confusing and scaring her. Aidan's heart sank to smell the fear of his sweet Maddie. It was, ironically, his biggest fear: for Maddie to reject and fear what he was. He slowly sat the tray down on the floor, afraid to scare her any more with sudden moves. He locked eyes with her and kept his hands out, as if she was robbing him.

"Where are we?" Maddie took a deep breath in order to calm herself. Aidan stood before her, defenseless and quiet.

"We're outside the town by a few miles. An old bed and breakfast near the east end. The owner is a couple who left for the weekend. It's quiet and safe here for you."

"Safe..." Maddie pulled the pillow to her body defensively. "From whom, Aidan? Who were those men out in the woods?"

Aidan looked away. What would be more crazy than telling her the truth?

"Were they even men at all?" Maddie looked at him, curious and demanding of a truth he was afraid to give her. "I can't believe I'm saying this, but...they weren't human to me. Aidan, please tell me."

"I can't. The less you know, the better."

"That's bullshit, and you know it!" Tears ran down her face, and Aidan couldn't help but take a few steps to her. She tensed at his movements, and he paused in his tracks. "What the hell is going on? Are you really a bounty hunter? Who are you?"

"God, Maddie. Please don't be afraid of me." He pleaded to her. "Despite the things you saw, I could never hurt you. Ever. I need you to trust me on that."

The tone in his voice was so painful, so sincere, that it seared Maddie's, heart. He stood there so vulnerable, his beautiful green eyes searching. As he stood there, all she saw was the man who had helped when no one would. The man who held her and laughed respectively at her horrible jokes. The man she was hopelessly, unfathomably falling in love with. The truth couldn't be that horrible...could it?

"Please tell me the truth, Aidan. After all of this, everything between us--don't you think I deserve a little of it?" She said quietly.

Aidan lowered himself to the floor, sitting Indian-style on the beautiful Persian rug. It was an extremely submissive gesture that even Maddie realized was hard for a man like him to do. He sat still, looking up at her, all the time wanting to reach for her and hold her. A part of him demanded to get up and hold her and protect her, but he realized that this was absolutely necessary to gain her trust again. He hated the fear and confusion he brought to her. All he wanted was to hold her and tell her she was safe. But first, he had to finally tell her everything. "What would you like to know, xerhmon?"

"What 'xerhmon' really means, to start."

"I didn't lie about what it meant, Maddie." His face was solemn, uneasy. "It is an endearment. The direct translation is 'my lovely'...and no, it isn't Czech or anything like that, I'm afraid. It's Aristan."

Maddie looked at him puzzled. "Aristan?"

"There are two species of us creatures, Maddie. There are Aristans, and there are Thesians—each named after the goddess that created us. Both structured us with the essence of the wolf. Our kind are called ShadowShifters."

Maddie sunk back, trying to digest what Aidan was saying. "Like werewolves?"

"The term is quite inaccurate, since we change to different stages of a wolf, but for argument's sake..."

She stared at his eyes again and as beguiling as they were, something told her he was telling her the truth. No matter how crazy it sounded, jt was the only thing that could explain what she saw in the woods.

"You're not human?" Her voice was small as his explanation tried to work its way into her.

"Not completely."

Her face softened as she looked at his handsome, extremely vulnerable features. "You look human."

Aidan sighed, still sitting a distance from her. "I don't always look this way, Maddie. *We* don't always look this way. But our survival depends on this skin. It is a look we prefer, since we were created from humans and it allows us to dwell in your world, but we are more than that. The gravitational pull of the moon gives us power to transform when we see fit. As an Aristan, I'm able to transform at will. Our rivals, called Thesians, aren't so lucky with that gift."

Maddie thought back to remember that all the men except one fought as human in the woods. They must have been the Thesian werewolves attacking. The other, who was the leader...

"I'm exactly like Aidan."

...must have been an Aristan, since both were able to change.

Maddie shrugged hopelessly. "Why are they after you?"

Aidan shook his head."They aren't. I'm after them. Kieran is a killer, Maddie. I was sent here to retrieve him so he could face the injustices he committed against my pack. Now, he's threatening to hurt them again, and I can't let that happen. He knows I'm a risk, so he tried to get to me through you."

Maddie scooted closer to the edge of the bed, still holding the red pillow to her. "What did he do?"

Aidan's breath caught in his chest as the question left him aching. "He ransacked our pack's community, and he murdered my mother."

Maddie gasped against the pillow as what he said hit her. His eyes were far-away, close to melancholy as he mentioned the loss of his mother. Seeing him so haunted pulled at her soul for him. "Oh, Aidan. I'm so sorry." She slowly walked over to him, lowering herself to the floor in front of him. Amazed and struggling to put it all together, she couldn't help herself as she took her hands and ran them down his face. Her Aidan was flesh and bone beneath her fingers. He was real. How could this man be a werewolf?

In awe, Maddie let her fingertip linger on his cheek as he closed his eyes to her touch, savoring the feel of her, fearful it may be the last. "You feel human to me."

You've made me this way, Aidan thought to himself.

"I wish I could lie to you Maddie, but the truth is that what you saw out there is very true. Believe me, it wasn't my intention to get you involved in any of this." Aidan's voice dripped with sympathy, straining against the wave of emotions he began feeling with her so close to him. So much, he couldn't help leaning into her touch like a tamed animal desiring more affection from her. He was just thankful she didn't flinch or move away from him then. She just continued to look at him with those gorgeous almond-shaped eyes and stroked his face, still in awe that he appeared so human.

"I know you didn't mean for any of this. Guess this was the mystery you were keeping me from." She gave him a small smile, trying to lighten the air, but found it was really for her comfort. "And before, I thought you were just a fugitive from the law. Can't say I saw this coming."

He met her eyes levelly. "You saved my life out there." His eyebrows dipped. "Thank you."

"No, I didn't." She shook her head. "You could've beaten them. I know you could. I just couldn't stand to be there and see them hurt you." Her other hand gripped her chest. The weight of the situation on her heart was tortuous. Besides, why were they even scared? There weren't any silver bullets in the gun, were there?"

"No," He got up and walked over to where his jacket lay. He pulled out the Glock and emptied the barren clip. "But there may as well have been." He walked back over to her and squatted next to her. "Nightshade nectar is poisonous to ShadowShifters - both species. I don't know why, but once it mixes with our blood, we die. There's no remedy we've found to counter it. Thesians prefer to lace their weapons with the plant to make ordinary weapons absolutely lethal. These are the type of weapons Kieran is going to use to wipe out my pack." He pulled out another clip from his back pocket and loaded the gun.

Maddie's eyes widened. "Is this yours?"

Aidan shook his head. "No. I did, however, procure a clip for you. For Aristans, the last resort is always these weapons. Many of our packs don't even know how to make them." He handed it to her slowly. "The safety's on."

Baffled that he trusted her with such a dangerous weapon, she gawked at him. "Why are you giving this to me?"

"You need to protect yourself, Maddie. By now, everyone associated with Kieran knows that you are the one helping me. And he will hurt anyone close to me—believe me, it's happened before. I want you to house up here until morning, and then head out of town. Away from here. I don't care where, and it's probably best I don't know."

Maddie held the heavy pistol in her hands, immediately not wanting it anymore. She didn't want it anywhere near Aidan. She lowered it to the floor. "But what about you?"

"I can manage. I'll be fine." Aidan smiled in spite of himself at her sincere words. "You have such a big heart, Maddie. Good people don't live long around me, so I need you to get away from here. I would lose my shit if anything happened to you."

It reached him deeper than she could ever imagine that she wanted to help him. This woman could very well be the end of him. Before he could help himself, he leaned in and claimed her lips, his hand lightly cupping her face. His body roared to life as he felt Maddie kiss him back, her soft lips opening as she wrapped her arms behind his neck. She dug her fingers into his dark hair, pressing herself to him.

Pulling back, Aidan stared into her eyes. He felt so bare with her like this. And it scared the shit outta him. He shouldn't be with her now. It would only make it harder to leave. And he had to leave.

"I'm sorry. I better leave you to rest."

As he got up, she leapt up and grabbed his hand. "Where are you going?"

"I need to leave. Stay here and rest, then go as soon as it's dawn, you understand?"

Maddie frowned at him. He was running, and she didn't want him to run. She didn't know what she wanted, but she knew she didn't want that. "I don't want to rest. You're gonna just leave me here? Help me understand, Aidan. Please, I want to help you. I've always just wanted to help you."

Aidan cursed her stubbornness. "I don't want your help." He reached for the door, but Maddie put her hand over his.

She narrowed her eyes at him. "What are you afraid of? Is it me?"

Aidan's body tensed with an uneasiness he hadn't felt in ages. He felt exposed and confused. Here she was challenging him, and Aidan didn't know what to make of it. How could she want him there after all this? "I'm not afraid of anything. I'm not supposed to be with you, Maddie. I--" He was pinned by her eyes as she looked deep into him.

Maddie's heart began to sink against the tide of Aidan's standoff behavior. "Tell me, what is it you don't want me to know?"

"Maddie, this will not help. Let it go. I'll leave here soon."

Finally, she forced out her statement in frustration. "I don't want you to leave, dammit!"

Aidan's eyes darkened in attempt to intimidate her. "Stop this!"

Maddie didn't flinch. Her fear was trampled down by her hatred of being scared. Aidan wasn't getting rid of her this easily. He owed her the whole truth, and she owed him her life. "No! You stop pushing me away!" She started to pace, finally getting Aidan's full attention as he watched her every move. "Why do you do this? Why can't you just trust me? 'Cause I trust you! Why can't you understand that whether you tell me or not, I'm in danger? So you should tell me. Please!" Her emotions bounced around in her head and were making her crazy. She had seen so much, felt so much, and yet she craved more answers.

To protect you.

She shoved him. He didn't budge, but he grabbed her hands and pulled her abruptly to him. When he met her eyes, he knew exactly what to do. The moon was at its fullest, his strength now intense and peaking.

He had no idea if a blood connection would work on a human, but if she was truly his mate, they would share a bond. A strong alignment of their psyche to which he could tap in to show her his life. He was told that few Aristans had the power to pull it off with other ShadowShifters, regardless of mates, but he had to try. This was the best way to show her without having to tell her. He never once attempted or needed to perform it--until now. Aidan did trust her, more than she would ever realize. But a part of him was concerned what consequences lie ahead for showing her his history. She had not seen him kill before. Would she just think him an animal? Her fear would be justified, and at least he would get her away from him before she was harmed.

"Do you trust me, Maddie?"

Without hesitation, she nodded. "I trust you, Aidan. I do."

He calmed himself. "Close your eyes."

She paused for a moment. Was he going to change? Then, she shut her eyes and found herself still staring at Aidan's eyes. It was as if they were burned into her clear as day.

"Aidan?" she asked, confused.

Aidan tried to focus all his strength and energy on trying to open his mind to Maddie, needing her blood to connect her to him so he could show her his past. "I'm here. You'll have to relax. Now, I have no idea if this will work. But if it does, you'll know."

He pulled her closer. Goddess, he needed to clear his head, but it was no easy task with her in his arms. With his strength in full force, the primal side of him wanted her again. The connection opened far too many doors—some which needed to stay closed. But he had to get her to relax if this had a chance to work.

He leaned in and claimed her lips gently.

Maddie sighed against him as the tenderness of his kiss swept over her. He was divine, as if he were taking her in. Unable to help herself, she gave in to his tenderness, darting her tongue into his mouth. And when he arms wrapped completely around her, she swore she felt butterflies in her stomach.

Her initiative had him reeling. So much for taming himself. He felt the giddy anxiousness she felt as their connection began to lock. He found it hard to leave her lips, but he had to move fast before he lost his nerve to hurt her. Holding her hand, he pulled away from her lips and bit down on the soft flesh between her thumb and index finger. Maddie gave a soft whimper as she felt his teeth sink into her hand. Her body began to feel heat as he lingered there.

Her eyes closed, she saw history upon history of Aidan's life. As a boy, being hunted, tortured, beaten and cast aside into the wilderness. Cold and alone. His bouts of starvation leading to confusion and rage. So much fighting, and bloodshed. Smiling faces wanting nothing more than to hurt him. Then, a beautiful woman who wore the little compass Aidan gave her to wear. Ninon—the only mother he'd ever known—only to be slaughtered at the hands of Kieran.

Her poor Aidan had never known real peace. Her eyes watered as she felt the waves of torment and sadness of Aidan losing everything he'd ever known. A feeling of loneliness a hundred fold. How so many feared him, even as he defended them. His mother, his sister. He treasured his adopted family as his own. Then she saw his appearance at Riko's—those deep jade eyes staring at her with admiration and caution, ready to protect a woman he didn't even know. The way he looked at her...as if there was nothing more precious to claim as his own--all washed down with sadness.

Maddie couldn't take it anymore. She wailed and pushed him off. "Stop! Stop this!"

Aidan reached for her and pulled her back into the comfort

of his arms. "Come here." He stroked her hair as she sobbed. "I'm so sorry. This was the best way I could think of to tell you everything through my eyes, Maddie." He held her tight and sighed.

Maddie clenched him tight. "Why did they do those things to you?"

Aidan shook his head, a feeling of shame washing over him. "I didn't know there were two breeds of us. I didn't even know where I came from. I was ignorant and trusted people I should not have. Being Aristan, I'm lucky they didn't kill me."

"I'm so sorry, Aidan." Maddie looked up at him. Those eyes of hers were glossy and hurt. He gently wiped them away with his thumb. He wanted to fall into her at that moment. She was why he couldn't stay away. He wanted to protect her—but he had to let that go. They had no place for each other.

"I've done my share of fighting, Maddie. I've hurt and fought for the sake of my people. When it all comes down to it, it's true I'm just an animal. I've done many things I'm not proud of, and my past always haunts me." He led her away from the door and sat her on the bed. As she sat, he took a look at her hand. Aidan went to the bathroom and grabbed the first-aid kit.

It was then she comprehended the red bite marks on her hand. She started. "You...am I gonna—"

Aidan kneeled down and opened the kit. He began to pull items out. "No, Maddie," he interjected. "I didn't turn you. To show you my past, I had to share your life force. ShadowShifter blood isn't infectious. You're either born one or not."

She sighed, calming down at his explanation. "No silver bullets?"

"Not per se. The term comes from how the nightshade lacing tends to make the bullets shinier than normal, turning ordinary gray steel color into a more luminous silver shade. The term took a literal meaning somehow. I suppose to protect the truth of how to really kill us."

Maddie eyed him. "No vampires?"

"Someone watches a lot of Netflix." He gave a slight smirk, grabbing the disinfectant and gauze to clean her up.

Maddie shrugged, thinking that her curiosity wasn't that far-fetched if her boyfriend turned out to be a werewolf. "Well...they have movies about werewolves. They weren't too off point with that, apparently."

"I suppose not." He dabbed the swab on her puncture wound, pausing as she hissed. "I'm sorry. The soreness will be clear before morning. I promise." He blew on the bite mark before wrapping it up.

"Well, thanks for not giving me a hickey." she mused. "Greta would have a field day if you did." She offered him a smile.

Aidan, to his own chagrin, returned the smile, till tending to her. "How do you do that?"

She asked him, wide eyed. "Do what?"

"Manage to make something light out of a situation like this? You kinda did it when I first met you." He thought back to that night where he saw her stomp out of the bar, claiming she wasn't anybody's courtesha. Then promptly called him a Neanderthal...then finally offered a lollipop in her clinic. This was the first human he'd ever gotten close to, but he was sure most humans would not have reacted the way she'd handled the situation.

She shrugged. "I don't know. I guess I always have, in retrospect. My mother and grandmother often embraced the strange and unusual. Perhaps I'm more like them than I thought."

Maddie felt so safe with him, even now with the truth of him still fresh in her mind. How could he claim to be so evil and cruel when he done nothing but help her? "What are you going to do about Kieran?"

Aidan sighed. "I'm going after him. He thinks this is a game. Thesians are not the most trusted allies to have, and the weapons he has have to be destroyed before they mobilize to my pack. He gets off on mayhem, but I have to end him here, before he hunts down my people."

His face was so close as he tightened the bandage, his fingers gentle on her flesh. Aidan froze as Maddie caught his face with both her soft hands, letting her thumbs rub against his cheekbones. "Why aren't you supposed to be with me?"

There was such a long silence, she thought he was not going to answer her

26

THE BETTER TO SEE YOU

Aidan sighed at Maddie's question. This had become so complicated. Everything pointed to Maddie being his ideal mate, but when had a ShadowShifter ever found a mate in a human? "There are a number of reasons. You are not some courtesha, Maddie. You're not some human woman of casual sex. Thesians use human females that way, but I don't. In fact, Aristans are forbidden to have relationships with humans. Being with you can put you in more danger with all ShadowShifters. Thesians, because you associate with an Aristan—and Aristans, because you are an exposure risk to them."

She didn't want to ask, but it flowed out her mouth anyway. "Will they kill me?"

The ominous look in his green eyes told her the truth before he could speak.

His bright eyes were serious."You know I won't let anyone touch you. But the Azans will come and "clean" up the messes. That's what they do...that's what *we* do."

Maddie swallowed as he understood what he just said. "Are you?—"

He put his hand over hers. "I'm their leader, Maddie. Not only am I my pack's Alpha, I'm also the general of that Azanesti Order, and I know them better than any force on earth. Highly trained, fierce riders of the night. I won't let anything happen to you, but until I'm gone, you'll always be in danger with them and the Thesians."

Maddie shivered beneath his hand. She didn't fear for herself, as she knew greater danger must lie ahead for Aidan if he was caught with her. "What will happen to you? Will they punish you for being with me?"

Aidan shook his head. "You shouldn't worry about that, Maddie."

Worry watered in her eyes. "Of course I'm worried! Will they strip you of your leadership?"

Aidan sighed. It should be the least of his worries, but because it took him so long to be trusted, it was worse than death. The humiliation of falling from Alpha to the scapegoat omega wolf was painful, physically and mentally. Everyone who looked up to you suddenly thought of you as the fleas on their fur. A menace. An embarrassment. It wasn't like he ever suffered that way before; he just thought maybe that was all over. The laws were made long before he existed, he was sure. To break them and survive was to be above the law. And he taught his Order as well as he was taught: no one was above the law. To break it was humiliation and death.

He pulled back. "It doesn't matter. I'm just an animal, Maddie. My fate is of no significance, really."

Her heart sank at his words. She wanted to weep at how he dismissed himself. Aidan didn't deserve that. He was warm and protective and made her laugh when her heart wanted to break. He was the leader they deserved and a hell of a lot more. She knew he was a born leader, strong and protective. Maddie placed her hand over his heart, where she remembered his tattoo to be. She knew then the extent of his duties. The symbol over his heart, his leadership to protect his people, was what drove him. It was what owned him. A jealous pang rocked through her as she realized she desperately wanted what was beneath her fingers. The fiercely beating heart of someone she knew she would never be able to have. It wasn't fair.

"You're no animal, Aidan. You are more human than anyone I've ever known. You are still Aidan to me. I'm looking at you right now, and that's all I can see."

His heart raced as the words she spoke cut through him, his body feeling that same magnetic pull he had when he first wanted her.

Aidan, you are a selfish bastard. Let her go.

"Maddie..." He was breathing her in now, his senses primal and calling for her. His wolf heart called for its mate. "I can't ..."

Maddie leaned in to kiss him, her soft lips caressing his in such a tortuous way, she feared she'd weep from it. "Just be with me now, Aidan. I know who you are." She whispered against his face, her voice soothing and yet bewitching. "I just want you with me. Stay with me," she commanded. "Stay with me and love me." She kissed him softly, raining them all over his face.

Maddie wrapped her arms around his neck as she chanted. "I want you with me, Aidan. Stay with me."

Aidan couldn't take it any longer. He wanted to be with her too, and the mere thought of leaving her ripped at his soul. She filled a void in him he thought would never be appeased. His lips closed in on hers with a sigh as she shuddered against him. A tear ran down her cheek, finally shedding all the resistance she had for falling in love with him. The mere taste of him, the feel of his arms around her, was enough to sustain her for a thousand lifetimes. The inevitable pain of being without him fell with every tear, but at least she had him now.

He pushed himself up, in turn pushing her back against the bed. Careful of her wound, Aidan pulled back to let his free hand skim the soft olive skin of her stomach, down to the hem of her skirt. She moaned as his hand continued to push up her skirt ever so gently to touch the sensitive flesh of her inner thighs. Maddie opened her legs wide in invitation.

She gently took his hand and guided it up to her hips, where he slid her panties down her legs slowly. As he slipped them off, he kissed her hungrily, probing her mouth, wanting to taste her fully. She tugged at his shirt as he pulled it over his head. Her hands roamed across his tawny skin of his back as he ran his tongue down the sensitive flesh in the valley of her breasts.

Aidan breathed her in. Dear Goddess, how he loved her scent. It was warm. Compelling. Erotic. And when combined with her broken moans and cries of pleasure, she was irresistible. Eager to feel more of her warmth, he trailed a hand down between her legs. Her soft skin and his fevered rough hand were a sexually enticing duo for Maddie. Never had she imagined a touch so powerful could be so gentle with her.

"You feel so good." He murmured against her skin. She felt like home.

Her body hot, she arched her back as he sank two fingers inside her. Her cries came in rhythm with his determined strokes. Frantically, she reached for him, pressing wet kisses against the hollow of his throat.

Aidan claimed her lips again as he stroked her. He pulled away with a growl to look into her soft, delicate eyes misty with desire. There were so many reasons he should not be with her, more reasons that were dangerous and heartbreaking. But his armor was completely shed with Maddie. Non-existent. And all he wanted now was her, as much as she'd allow him to have. But he was greedy. He wanted all of her, including her heart.

Aidan withdrew his fingers and slid her skirt from her body, letting it pool to the floor as Maddie sat up and rolled him on his back, so she straddled him naked. Seeing her posed like that over him in all her glory was almost enough to make him come. She slid off of him down to his feet and took off each boot. Aidan undid his fly as she tugged his jeans from his body. Aidan watched in awe as Maddie climbed back on top of him like some sleek, seductive cat. She cupped him gently and sighed against his erection as her other hand began to stroke him.

Aidan couldn't breathe as Maddie took him into her mouth. A moan tore through him as she swirled her tongue over his tip, caressing him more than he ever thought possible. Maddie moaned at the taste of him. Never had she attempted this before with anyone; she never imagined it could be so wonderful. The pleasure in his eyes that racked him was truly unimaginable. She'd never wanted to please someone as much as Aidan. Over and over she teased him with her relentless assault.

"Maddie...please...not yet." Aidan pleaded, his eyes closed tightly. "I don't want to come yet."

Pulling away from him, she smiled teasingly. "Losing your resolve, general?"

Aidan leaned back with a gorgeous half-smile. "Which always seems to be the case with you, xerhmon." His voice was raspy, aching for breath. He didn't think she'd ever know how true that statement was to him. How would he ever be able to deny this woman anything?

Maddie straddled him and guided him into her body, the sensation of him sliding into her inch by full inch making her quiver. They both moaned in unison at their bodies joining. Her hand lingered between them for a moment, feeling him drive into her until she intertwined her fingers with his as she rode him with a steady, sensual rhythm that was purely driving Aidan to the brink of madness. He arched his back to drive himself deeper into her as Maddie bit her lip to quell her moans. It was all she could do not to cry out. This man filled her with such a wicked desire for him, all she could do was savor the heat and power of him as she rocked feverishly against him.

Aidan began to tense as he felt his feral side clawing to the forefront. He was used to fighting it, but something told him this time it was different. Struggling to swallow it back down, it racked him and threatened to tear him to pieces. The only relief he could have was to let a little of himself go. If not, his own body would teach him a whole new meaning of torture that would make his past history seem like an amusement ride, and he may not come back from his feral state for moons to come.

No!

The heady scent of Maddie and their lovemaking ripped through him with heightened senses. He shut his eyes tight, knowing they were changing, and felt a sharp pain in his stomach. Dear Goddess, not now!

Maddie felt his tension and gave a concerned look, "Aidan?"

Through clenched teeth, he spoke without opening his eyes. "We have to stop!"

She stopped moving and scowled. "Why? What is it?"

He squeezed her hands and breathed harshly. Each breath getting hung up on the next as if he suffered hypothermia. "I'm changing. Something's triggered...Part of me wants out, and I can't fight it any longer."

Maddie gave him an earnest stare. "Then why are you?" She leaned down and kissed his brow tenderly. "Open your eyes for me, Aidan."

"No! I don't trust it. I don't want to hurt you." The fear in his voice shook her. Nothing meant more than her safety. "Please, Maddie, just let me up."

She pulled her hand from his and smoothed his face, which beaded with sweat. Her heart ached for him. How long had he been ashamed and afraid of himself with others? Aidan had no business feeling such a way. There was nothing alarming in him. Nothing evil. She saw how wolves and humans alike had treated him in his past, and she wanted blood for it. No one deserved that much suffering.

Despite his stubbornness, she knew that in truth he only wanted to be loved. And he was in luck, because she craved him like nothing she'd ever known. Wanted to make him believe that he was worthy of being loved, just as he made her believe people could appreciate and welcome kindness.

"I know you're not going to hurt me, Aidan, and I'm no longer afraid now that I know the truth." She whispered as she steadied herself on his hips gently. "Open your eyes, Aidan. Let me see you."

She felt a tremor go through him as he slowly opened to reveal stark amber eyes. They were as piercing as they were beautiful. She'd never seen anything like it. The panic in them slowly receded as her hand caressed him. His mouth relaxed as she trailed her hand down his face, revealing his lengthened canines. Her Aidan was just as handsome as he'd always been.

Yes, she knew exactly who he was. The man that had stolen her heart.

She leaned down and gently kissed his lips. "I see you."

He expected her to leap from him or scream in horror, yet she was still with him, joined, smiling at him. It was enough to make him weep. Instead, he pulled her face back down to him so he could kiss her blindly. She moaned into his mouth as her tongue brushed against his fangs.

It was remarkable, having this man beneath her, surrendering himself to her needs. Their bare flesh intertwined with no more secrets between them. It was then she knew that she would fight for him. She refused to see him hurt or punished over her. One way or another, she would help him.

And when he pulled himself up to meet her stroke for stroke, she thought she'd perish from it.

No, nothing felt like this. Their bodies so close they melted into each other. Their rhythm unified as Maddie's body arched in a powerful orgasm so intense, she dug her nails into him. Aidan hissed at the exquisite mixture of pain and pleasure. She held on to him, feeling his muscles ripple beneath her hands as a deep, heated sensation flowed through her body.

He suckled her breast as he thrust deeper into her, wanting desperately to be as close to the woman he would soon have to let go. She made him want as no other person had ever made him want. To desire a life with her, loving and treasuring someone who would forever return that love. How long had he imagined having someone to give a damn about him, who wasn't ripped away from him?

Tell her.

He shook the thought away as he heard her panting escalate, nearing another climax.

Tell her. Instead, he nipped her ear softly. It was all he could do not to whisper to her all he felt for her. How much he loved her, and began to feel torn apart by his duties and his destiny.

It's useless. You weren't created for love or affection. Just be thankful she allows you to hold her even while she knows you're leaving her.

She cried out his name as another orgasm ripped through her, and this time Aidan, with an intense groan, joined her. Physically and emotionally spent, he fell back, bringing her down on his chest.

Aidan looked around, confused and riddled with feelings he didn't understand. Even if he wanted to leave, his body wouldn't allow it. Maddie was just as strong and brave as any she-wolf out there. Though frightened and far outside her comfort zone, she risked her life for him. He would do the exact same for her. "Do you have any regrets, Maddie?" He glanced down to see her toying with the sleek hairs on his chest.

"Only that I should have asked you to let go before. That was amazing." She looked up to see his eyes back to his enchanting greens, and grinned. Her face exhausted, yet exhilarated, she winked at him. "You're quite the proper lover when you're angry, Aidan. I look forward to many nights annoying you in order to drive the best sex out of you."

Aidan laughed at her contagious, and often ill-placed, humor. "As stubborn as you are, you probably won't have to try very hard." He kissed her hair and watched her tired eyes until they settled back down to sleep. Holding her, he intertwined his hand with hers and brought it up to his lips to kiss. He couldn't describe what he felt for her, but it was dangerous and magnetic. She lit something inside him that intensified his love for his people and the fight in him that wanted to keep her. He couldn't keep both, but he couldn't let neither go. Despite it, he never felt so alive and ready to rip at anything that threaten either of the things he held dear.

Aidan slowly opened his eyes to find Maddie still asleep in his arms. Her hand splayed out against his heart, her fingertips on his tattoo. He softly moved the dark brown curls away from her sleepy face and smiled. His arms were wrapped around her delicate, naked body. Bare skin, with no more secrets to keep from her. This is what it was like to be human. To be wanted. It was more precious than he ever imagined. Softly kissing Maddie's forehead, he couldn't help but give a gentle laugh against her skin. The irony of his life was darkly hilarious. A random, abandoned Aristan ShadowShifter managed to become Alpha of a pack from a family that wasn't blood; then found a human mate, of all things. Everything about his life seemed unconventional. Perhaps it was better that way.

It was the wee hours of the morning; the sun hadn't even peaked over the hills yet, but Aidan couldn't really sleep. He had been a fool. He had only tucked all the anger away to fulfill his duties. Now, that anger weighed him down like bricks. Stone after stone stacking on him until he simply couldn't see any further. For that, he was jealous of Leigh, which exercised her demons every time she had a chance. Though she preferred to when no one was looking. With vengeance in his heart, he made reckless decisions, like not asking Cameron for help. He needed to let go of all the pain he harbored to gain the strength to protect those counting on him. Time was drawing near where it was do or die, and Aidan believed himself a doer.

Slipping away from Maddie, he moved to the chair and dressed himself, all the while finding himself smiling at the gentle woman lying naked, peacefully in the bed. He grabbed his cell phone and texted Cameron his address of the B&B. He really could use his Beta to help him figure this out, and the crazy Celt is usually all too willing to jump into the fray. He texted him he was safe and had 'an ally' with him before heading out to find the highest point to pay homage to the Goddess Arista before they met to plan this out.

27

WITH TEETH

S tanding at the edge of the hill, overlooking the majestic view of the night, Aidan tensed his wolf body as he prepared to do what he denied himself before. Looking up at the sky, the stars waiting for dawn, he stared up at the moon. The silver glow of brightness owned the night sky, a symbol of this people and the Goddess Arista who created them.

Aidan wasn't much for praying. Though he respected the Goddess, he wasn't much of a spiritual individual till now. It wasn't for him as much as it was for his people, his family. Maddie. The foreign sting of tears threatened his eyes.

"Goddess Arista, I'm not much for such adoring words for homage. I only want to pay you tribute and respect. I'm so angry. Vengeance is written in my veins, but I just ask for your wisdom tonight. Wisdom to help me make the right decisions for everyone depending on me. You see, I fight for them. Not for me." He looked down. "Never for me. The blood I shed will not be for vengeance, but justice."

Pulling from deep within him the images of his life, Aidan howled to the heavens. Howled to warn others he was near, howled to release his past, and howled to remember the only woman he knew as a mother. Howled to become the Alpha his people needed and the man Maddie could love. They were the ones in his life who truly cared, and he would fight for them.

He drew so far within himself, his body was unable to stay in wolf form. And when his strong howl turned into a fierce human yell, he knew he was ready. As the sun peeked from the horizon in pinks and purples, he realized he had work to do.

"And I will finish it." He whispered to himself.

The ambiance of the early grays of morning started to twist and change as the sun stretched to rise. Brody stood heaving and panting, thrilled the moon was full, despite watching it slowly fade in the midst of the sunlight as it crept along the horizon, lighting the exterior of the little Bed & Breakfast. There were so many of them. Kieran had enlisted scouts to sniff around the area, anxious to track down Aidan. Riko's warehouse was busy as they set up to mobilize, but once a scout came back after picking up an Aristan scent, Kieran refused to get the Thesians moving until he settled the score with his 'brother.' Brody sighed. Another bout of this shit and they still have to tackle the Aristan's pack for the rest of the cash.

"Tamar said he tracked them here, but I'm not smelling anything now but humans and deer musk. Maybe they left during the night."

Kieran smiled with a tiny scoff. "Oh, ye of little faith. Maybe they have...then again, maybe not. Either way, isn't it just fun to be sure? If anything, we can flush the fuckers out."

"Kieran, the men are anxious. We should be focusing on mobilizing our pack for the raid. Everyone's been working all night."

Kieran grabbed the Brody by his collar. "We will leave when

Aidan's nuts are in a fucking vice! And I can't have him riding around jeopardizing our plan, so we're going to fucking deal with him now, before he gets wise and starts figuring shit out! Understand?" His rabid, bright eyes stared into Brody along with a low growl before finally shoving Brody away. Kieran took a deep breath, relaxing his muscles as he lit a cigarette. "Don't ruin this for me; it's not every day I get to kill my enemies." He stared at the large house in front of them. It was quiet and quaint. Barely dawn, he sighed as he imagined this would be a beautiful day. The end of a moon cycle.

"Ah, the beauty of the countryside. Welcome to all." He stretched his back, reveling at the cracking of his bones as he felt the glorious energy radiate in them. "I hope everyone in there are already bright-eyed and bushy tailed, or else this would just be far too easy."

He took a long drag from his cigarette and turned to the large Thesians who stood behind him, panting, with truly sinister grins on their shaggy faces. Two held red canisters in their muscular arms.

Kieran ran his tongue over his lower canines as he blew out smoke. His eyes bright with twisted joy.

"Burn it."

As the early sun started to peek through the curtains and onto her naked skin, Maddie heard the bedroom door creak open and slowly shut. Feeling the void in the sheets next to her earlier, she knew it had to be Aidan coming back into the room. She smiled as she stretched her body against his pillow. "Where have you b-"

A hand suddenly covered her mouth in the shadows and pulled her back. In horror, Maddie pulled her elbow back and, with all her force, dug it into whoever held her. The stranger behind her grunted but held her still as Maddie tried to reach behind her to claw at their face. Her voice was muffled but loud against the salty hand that tried to silence her. She'd be damned if she goes down without a fight.

In less than a blink, Maddie was pushed on her back and was startled to see a young blond woman giving her a fierce, quelling look through her stark amber eyes. Those familiar eyes that belonged to her Aidan.

"Calm down. I'm not here to hurt you!" she whispered. She looked towards the window, then turned to face Maddie. A long blond tendril of hair fell against Maddie's neck as the beautiful blonde stared back at her, hand still over her mouth. "But you must be quiet, or they'll hear us."

Maddie's breathing slowed to a normal pace as the woman removed her hands from her. There was something strangely familiar about her. Though she looked nothing like Aidan, there was something in her eyes that were eerily the same. It was then she remembered he mentioned a sister.

Maddie stuttered as she stared up at those eyes. "Are you Leigh?"

Leigh scooted from her as if she was as freaked out as Maddie was from the outburst. Her long blond hair was pulled into a tight braid down her back, and her large amber eyes appeared to suit her. Dressed in a black tank top and dark jeans, she reminded Maddie of some lone assassin. Her ultra-feminine face was sculpted and plush with youthful radiance. Despite her youthful beauty, it was apparently clear to Maddie that Leigh obviously had a deadly force to her, just like Aidan.

"That's right. I'm Aidan's sister." She stretched herself to one side, wincing at the area Maddie had struck her with her elbow. Leigh had a slight look of annoyance she immediately shook away. When Cam told her Aidan had an 'ally' here to protect, she did not expect a little human woman. Aidan's scent was all over her, and it was obvious they knew each other. If Aidan trusted her, and he rarely trusted anyone, then she had Leigh's protection, human or not.

"I'm sorry," Maddie said, pulling the sheet closer to her, hiding her nudity. "I thought you were a Thesian. I'm Maddie."

"Yeah, I got that. Though from how you hit I would've figured you a she-wolf." She gave her a small smile, which came across more awkward than friendly. Leigh sighed to herself. *How the hell do you talk to a live human who knows exactly what you are?* "Where's Aidan?" She stood up, looking around. "I heard him calling, I thought."

Maddie shook her head. "I don't know, I thought he went downstairs or something. What's going on? Is he okay?"

Leigh slinked away to the window and slowly peeked past the curtains. She pulled away with a curse. If they only got to Aidan's location just a bit sooner... "Dammit, Aidan. If my brother ever had an uncanny gift that kept on giving, it would be his ability to perpetually get himself and everyone else in a shit show."

Maddie watched her actions with concern. "Such as?"

Leigh walked over to the door and leaned against it, listening. Then cut her eyes to Maddie, wrapped in a sheet.

"Meaning that if you don't get dressed and out of here in...I don't know...less than three minutes, we're gonna be roasted in here like a barbeque." She tossed Maddie's clothes to her from the floor next to her. "Now hurry. We haven't much time."

Maddie leaped from the bed and scrambled to put on her clothes in record time. Panic etched her face as she wiggled into her skirt. Part of her felt missing as she kept worrying about Aidan. Where was he?

Putting on her shoes, she looked up at Leigh, who was peeping through the sliver of window between the curtains. "I can't leave Aidan, Leigh. What if he's hurt somewhere?" She pulled the pistol Aidan gave her from the nightstand, checked the safety and packed it behind her timidly. All she could do was chant to herself not to panic, and not to shoot the good guys.

But how will I know who're the good guys?

Leigh shook her head. "They wouldn't be here trying to torch the place if they had him. He's okay. Trust me, my brother isn't so easily taken." She gave her a knowing look as her eyes shifted from the bed to Maddie, then cleared her throat. "Guess you, uh, already know that."

Maddie couldn't stop the heat flushing her cheeks as her mouth gaped open in embarrassment. As if hitting Aidan's sister wasn't enough, now she had to add post-coitus to the mix...

As if Leigh could read her thoughts, she quickly sobered. "I'm sorry. I didn't mean to pry. I'm just glad he found someone who gave more than two shits about him. He's a stubborn, brooding Alpha, but he deserves the world."

Maddie tensed as Leigh suddenly went stiff, sniffing the air, and the room rumbled with her growl.

"Shit." Leigh hissed.

Maddie looked to her as she pulled on her shirt. "What?"

Leigh grabbed her arm and pulled her towards the bedroom door. "We gotta move!" A Molotov cocktail catapulted into the bedroom, engulfing the curtains in flames and punctuating her command. "Come on!" Leigh led her out of the room and headed down the stairs. The beautiful house was lit in an orange blaze as the other windows were spread with flames from the cocktails. The rails creaked as they ran down where Leigh was surprised by a beaten body at the base of the stairs. Maddie stopped cold behind her as Leigh sniffed the air and growled low in her throat.

"Get back, Maddie!" No sooner had Leigh uttered those words, a brawny, blond man leapt from the doorway and grabbed her. His face twisted in anger, barely human as he snarled and threw her on the stairs. She bared her teeth to him and brought her knees up to her chest, getting leverage to push him away. Maddie thought to pull the gun, but they were so close, she feared she'd accidently hit Leigh. Instead, Maddie grabbed the table by the banister and slammed it against the wall until she held a leg of it in her hand.

The Thesian yelled as Leigh bit into his arm. Without hesitation, Maddie ran down the stairs and, with all her might, pummeled the wooden piece across his head. Growling, he pulled back, and Leigh kicked him away, throwing him against the bookshelves. Flipping to her feet, Leigh ran up to him and kneed him in the groin. She connected both elbows directly to his spine. As he bent his head down in agony, Leigh snapped his neck, letting him slink to the floor. Exhaling forcibly through her nostrils, Leigh looked up at Maddie with respect. Some 'little' human.

"Thank you."

"My pleasure." Maddie ran down behind her as she headed out the back way past the kitchen, her makeshift club tight in her hand. Leigh looked to her, remembering the weapon she had earlier.

"Is that a nightshade weapon behind you?"

Maddie nodded. She cringed as she heard the howling outside.

"Then I suggest you engage it. We're going for it outside, and I don't know how many we're up against. The Thesians can change, but they are less likely to. Let me go first. Stay close to me and keep moving."

Maddie reached behind her and pulled the pistol, holding it in her hand. "I don't know what the hell I'm doing, Leigh." Her eyes were full of worry, feeling lost, suspended in a world she didn't understand. She was afraid, but she didn't want to share that with a woman who could grind her into bread.

Leigh nodded. "I think you do, Maddie. I like the fire in you. You'll be fine." She moved behind her and fashioned her hands over Maddie's. "First, gun class 101." She slid the rack forward to show Maddie how to chamber the round. "New clip, so you chamber for first round. Then keep your trigger finger straight until you're ready to fire, okay? Use both hands, like this." Leigh formed Maddie's hand around the gun to show her how to fire it. "You can do this. And I have your back." Leigh looked out the window, giving Maddie a cue that it was soon time to make a run for it.

Aidan was heading back when he paused to the war-cry howling in the direction of the bed & breakfast. The downwind caught burned wood and his heart raced. An Aristan called him, and all the signals couldn't be good, as he'd left Maddie alone. Instantly, he morphed to wolf form, running with intense speed to get back to her. The closer he got, the more he began to panic. Scents of blood, gasoline, and Thesians began to alarm him, and he bared his teeth in reaction. *Goddess Arista, help anyone who dared touch her.*

"I'm coming, Maddie!"

CHASE

L eigh jerked open the back door and rushed a raven-haired
Thesian, pushing him back far enough for Maddie to
escape. "Run, Maddie!" The Thesian backhanded Leigh, and she
staggered backward a few steps before regaining her balance.

"Let me help you!" Before Maddie could aim her gun, a large,
white wolf leapt onto the Thesian, sinking its teeth into his jugu-
lar. The Thesian growled until the sickening chomping sound of
the wolf's jaw on his throat finally silenced him. Maddie backed
away towards the bike behind her, not knowing if she should
stand down or shoot.

Leigh fell back as the wolf took another Thesian down forcefully. Maddie cringed as the man's neck cracked and the wolf
backed away, his sharp blue eyes staring at her.

"Dammit, Cam. Where's Aidan?" Leigh backed up and threw a
bag at the wolf's feet from the bike and grabbed Maddie.

The large, white wolf-like creature stretched into a tall, tawny
man with piercing electric-blue eyes and white blond hair. His
body was just as lean as Aidan's, but he had a long tattoo that
curved from his left bicep down around his heart, where she saw
the same tattoo Aidan had over his own. From the deep ripples of
his abs down to the entire length of him, bare for all the world to

see, he was gorgeous. The only thing missing was the same spark of giddiness and fire as she always had when she saw Aidan. And the fact that his nude body standing before her made Maddie not just a little uneasy, given their incredibly violent environment.

"He's on his way. I just called for him." Cameron looked at Maddie as if she'd appeared out of nowhere. He inhaled the air around her and grinned. "Well, that sneaky son of a bitch finally got laid! Nice," Cameron said out loud. "It's about damn time." Before Maddie could open her mouth to protest his implications and crudeness, he propelled her back her over to Leigh.

"There're too many of them here! Kittycat, just get the hell outta here with her!"

"Stop calling me that! Are you going to put some clothes on or what?" Leigh frowned, watching her guard but also finding Cameron's body a bit of a distraction.

Cameron looked down at himself, as if he was trying to find something wrong on what he was wearing--or not wearing, for that matter. He bounced his eyebrows up and down comically. "I'm Celt, baby. This *is* my military uniform."

Two blond Thesians came from the side, one with a gun aimed at Cameron. Before the gun cocked, both Thesian half-wolves were grabbed and pulled back to the edge of the house, screaming. A moment later, Maddie's heart lit up as Aidan came around the corner with his lethal gait. He was barely clothed, with his shirt bloody and torn. Maddie ran to him, covering herself with him. Aidan, thankful to see her safe, crushed her to him. He gently smoothed her hair back and kissed her head.

He pulled back to look into her eyes. "You alright?"

Unable to stop the tears, she simply nodded, finding it impossible to form real words.

Aidan didn't want this life for her. Just being with him put her in so much danger, and she didn't deserve it. "Come on You can't stay here, xerhmon. It's too dangerous." He looked around and lead her quickly towards Leigh and Cameron. "There's an Aristan haven on the other side of Bridgepoint called Greenwood's. Get hold of Devin, alright, and say you're with me! You and Leigh need to get outta here, now!"

Leigh got on Cameron's bike and helped Maddie on. Aidan frowned. "Since when did you learn how to ride, sis?"

He watched them exchange knowing glances. *Ugh, seriously?* "I thought I told you to stop indulging her...Or letting her boss you around." Either situation was plausible at this point.

She rolled her eyes, gave a helmet to Maddie and fastened one on her head. "Dammit, why does it matter? I'm here to save your ass!"

He pointed to Cameron, scowling, "And you, you albino nightmare, are putting her on bikes when you were supposed to keep an eye on her!"

"That's what I'm doing now!" Cameron yelled, his voice deeper as he teetered on the edge of a change. "Look, she's got helmets. See?"

Aidan looked back to his sister. "And my ass doesn't need saving."

Then, a horde of half-wolf, half-man Thesian beasts, came along the side of the house, charging towards them while Kieran stood to the flank watching. Leigh sighed and gave Aidan a terse slap on the shoulder. "Great. I'm glad you feel that way, big brother. We're getting the fuck outta here."

Cameron and Aidan cursed as they turned to witness the mass of enemies, easily outnumbering them 10 to 1.

Aidan waved Leigh away, urging them to leave quickly. "Go, Leigh! Take Maddie and get the hell outta here now! Continue heading out of town to Greenwood's! Don't stop! Don't trust anyone till you get there!"

"What about you?" cried Maddie.

His brows dipped in uncertainty. "We'll meet up with you. Don't worry about us." Aidan crashed his lips to Maddie's in a gripping kiss, tasting the salty sweetness of her lips, hoping it wouldn't be the last. "I'll find you, okay? Don't trust anyone, and don't look back! I will come for you!"

Nodding, she wrapped her hands around Leigh as the Ducati engine roared away from him, jetting past the crowd of danger, heading out to the highway.

Cameron slapped Aidan on the back. "Sooo, Maddie, huh? She's cute."

Aidan growled, keeping his eyes on the slew of wolves charging for them. "Don't lose a nut, Cam."

Aidan flung a Thesian over him, watching him yelp and slam against the ground in a loud thud. While Cameron's body staggered between the change, he pounced on one Thesian, pulling him into a headlock until he cracked his skull and snapped his neck. More and more seem to come around the corner of the blazing bed & breakfast, targeting him and his second-in-command. It was as they'd feared: Kieran had a healthy supply of Thesian ShadowShifters to fight for him. The more they eliminated now, the smaller his army could get.

"Kieran!" Aidan called out. Looking past the haze and smoke, he saw Kieran standing in the distance. His demented grin could be faintly seen past the smoke, watching the tirade of Thesians attack. "You cowardly son of a bitch! I'm right here!"

His body aching, Aidan stood ready to battle every single one of them to get to Kieran. *I will tear every single one apart if I must. Every. Single. One.*

Cameron stood next to him, stretching his bloody body for attack. It was a while since he got to go weapons hot in an all-out scrap. The raging animal within him would definitely be appeased now. "Well, let's get cracking!" Cameron yelled as he began to charge.

Suddenly, the fire-engulfed house gave a loud crackle like thunder, as the bed & breakfast exploded into deadly, flying shrapnel across the slew of ShadowShifters, including Cameron and Aidan. Bodies flew from the proximity as the heat and flames blasted a wave of destruction indiscriminately. The lawn was scattered with burning, flailing men and beasts alike as debris fell down over the area in black, thick smoke.

Watching the disaster unfold with marvel, Kieran roared to the sky and laughed, clapping while Brody cringed and ducked from the debris. "Beautiful! Fucking beautiful!" He looked down at Brody and smiled. "You see? Problem eliminated. Now, we can proceed to lay out my old pack and secure our finances."

Brody frowned, somewhat appalled that Kieran didn't seem to give two shits that his Thesian brothers had just died. "Someone escaped, I saw them through the haze. One got away on a bike."

Kieran growled, his teeth piercing his lips. "What! Why'd the fuck you mutts let them get away! They could call for help!" He shoved Brody out of the way, running to the truck they came in.

Brody growled. "Where are you going, Kieran?"

"To rectify the situation! I can't trust anyone to do this right!" He looked back. "And you, go back and tell Riko and the rest of the colorless to ship out!" Kieran passed by his scout, Tamar and shoulder checked him on his way to the truck. He grabbed a pistol from behind the confused Thesian outcast and loaded it. "C'mon, we're going hunting!"

Brody watched as Kieran and Tamar sped off in the truck and shook his head. This was not working out as he expected. Kieran was a loose cannon, who wasn't owning his promises. His temper made him reckless, and as he watched the smoke, fire and charred bodies of his brothers, just to kill one Alpha Aristan, Brody began to ask himself hard questions as he headed out to Riko's warehouse.

Leigh ground herself to the road as she zipped between cars and trucks on the highway, as Maddie gripped her for dear life. Kieran was hot on their heels, swerving into cars, literally plowing into them to get to them. Maddie held on to Leigh tight as they whipped around curves that normal humans couldn't possibly make. As bullets dodged them, Maddie couldn't help but screech as they narrowly missed an oncoming truck. Leigh leaned her body to accommodate the shift in weight.

This wasn't looking good. Kieran had begun gaining on them and was far too close, and the road too dangerous for Maddie. If Kieran managed to run them off the road, Leigh would survive, but Maddie being human wouldn't stand a chance. She had to get Maddie away from all this. She cursed herself as she realized their only chance. Risky definitely wasn't the word for it, but she had to get help, and that required amplifying out to find an Aristan ally. They had to be out there somewhere. But amplifying required focus, something she barely had, going 75 mph with a human in tow.

I promised Aidan I would protect her.

Taking a deep breath that gripped from her entire body, she shut the world out for what seemed like eternity.

"*My name is Leigh Bloodlocke of the Bloodlocke clan. I need help. I must get my passenger to a safe Aristan haven. Please, if there are any Aristans in the area, please, please help us!*"

"Leigh!" screamed Maddie, as Leigh opened her eyes to dodge another car.

Kieran reloaded his weapon. "Zippy little bitch, isn't she?" He leaned over the edge. "Run her down, she's honing for help."

Tamar looked confused. "What?"

"She just fucking amplified for Aristan help, you Thesian mutt, weren't you paying attention? Now finish this!"

Leigh kept her eyes peeled on the highway until a Ford pickup truck cut off Kieran's truck and timed a run to get on the opposite side of the road. Leigh sighed gently as a group of Aristan teenagers pulled up beside them, two in the cab and two in the truck bed. Thank Arista for wayward youth. Making eye contact with one of them, she nodded a farewell.

Maddie stared at the truck full of kids and didn't know what to do. Who were they?

"Leigh! What's going on!?"

Suddenly, Leigh dodged another car and gripped hard to pull them back on the highway. It was now or never.

"Maddie, listen to me. We have to move fast, okay? I can't take you to the haven. Kieran will follow us there. I can't shake him! These boys are going to take you there!"

"No!," she replied through the intercom. "What about you! I can't leave you!"

"Maddie, you have to! Go to the haven and ask them for help, or the pack is done for, you hear me? Don't take no for an answer! You got some fire in you, Maddie the human. Use it."

Something in Leigh's voice made Maddie uneasy. As if this was the last time they would ever see each other. "Leigh!"

The truck swerved out to dodge an oncoming car, and then the boys stood ready as they got back on the road. Both in the bed positioned themselves to grab her as they waited for Leigh to bring the bike closer.

Kieran saw Leigh's move and started firing. "Damn it!" Looking at the car blocking them, Kieran forced the Thesian driver out the moving truck. If he could ram the car in front of him with enough force, it would domino onto Leigh, and it would be all over for them both. He immediately slacked off some speed.

As Leigh inched over towards the truck, her gut feeling told her she had just one shot at this.

"Take her now!" Making her way over, the boys grabbed Maddie and lifted her into the truck just as the car in front of her pegged her wheel and threw her from the bike. Both Leigh and the bike flew up and crashed off the highway.

"Leigh!" Maddie cried out as the boys pulled her down on the truck bed, protecting her. "Nooooo! No! Stop!" Maddie clawed at them, but still, the boys held her back, trying to console her. The accident caused a continued pile up behind them with two other cars, including Kieran's truck, as it rolled off the road.

Maddie fought them off her as she tried to gather the horror of what just happened. "Please, please, we must go back to help her!"

The dark haired teenage boy shook his head, his eyes bright

amber. "We can't. She gave us strict orders to protect you and take you to Greenwood. No matter what happened to her. No matter what."

Maddie's eyes watered at the revelation. Why was this all happening? She felt weak and tired, wanting to collapse to the floor of the truck bed. Yet she stood, tears running down her face.

Another taller Aristan boy reached into his pocket and handed her a crinkled diner napkin. "Sorry, it's all I have."

Maddie nodded and wiped her eyes. "Thank you...uh?"

He snapped himself to attention. "Alexei, ma'am."

She smiled in spite of herself. He reminded her of Aidan. She was saved by little teenage boys that looked no older than sixteen or seventeen years old. "Thank you, Alexei. Where's this Greenwood?"

"It's an Aristan Haven on the outside of Bridgepoint. We're to get you there ASAP." Alexei kicked the inside of the bed getting the attention of the teen driver. "So let's get a move on it, Grandpa!"

The young driver yelled out the back window. "I'm trying! You want me to do get a speeding ticket? I can't get grounded again!"

"Whatever, Mama's Boy!", the other teen said with a scoff.

Alexei shook his head. "Excuse Jeff here, he thinks he's more human than Aristan."

"Shut up!" The driver yelled out the back window. "Show off."

Maddie ignored their bickering as she looked out into the darkness, gripping Aidan's medallion tightly to her chest. Part of her was so lost without knowing if Aidan, and even Leigh, were okay. She bit back her tears as she gathered the last bit of courage she had left to do what she had to do to help Aidan and the Aristans at all cost, praying that the B&B wouldn't be the last time she'd see Aidan's face.

Aidan felt his body began to drag against the ground when he came to with a start.

"Take it easy, Azan," Cameron warned. "Just take some breaths."

Aidan tried to take a breath but found himself coughing up old smoke and fumes from the blast. Points of his ribs ached as he coughed. Why couldn't those broken ribs heal while he was out?

Opening his eyes, he saw Cameron facing him. Wearing what appeared to be some poor Thesian's clothing, he looked in even worse shape than Aidan, with a bloodied jaw and a few nasty gashes on his arms and face. It wasn't uncommon for Cameron to behave rather invincible on the battlefield. Considering his comrade's checkered and rather mystic past, it was one eccentric quality he admired in the resilient Celt.

"You alright?"

Cameron looked around the ash and soot covered bodies of Thesians, either stunned, unconscious, or just plain dead. "Better than the rest of them. How about you?"

Aidan slowly rose to his feet. No sooner had he got his bearings than both tensed as they heard a gun cock behind them.

"Don't you fucking move a muscle! I have a mind to blow both your heads off right now, you psycho werewolf weirdo bastards!"

Aidan and Cameron slowly turned around to find themselves greeted with a 12-gauge shotgun, aimed by a very pale, very twitchy, very pissed off Sheriff.

29

WAX & WANE

Maddie tensed as the boys drove up to a little bar lined with bikes outside. As they pulled up to the bar parking lot, the boys lifted her out of the truck. "Thank you for helping me." She gently kissed Alexei's cheek, which held the smallest hint of peach fuzz. "Thanks for saving my life." Alexei's cheeks mottled red, and he smiled. "You're welcome, ma'am."

When she saw they didn't follow her to the door, she turned around. "Aren't you coming with me?"

The teen in the passenger side shook his head. "Can't. We're not allowed."

Maddie frowned."Why not?"

"We're underage and not allowed to hang with the Azans," Alexei explained. "But they will help you. They're a cool bunch of guys."

Maddie nodded nervously. She had certainly hoped so.

"Miss?"

Maddie turned to the boys, her eyes red. "Yes?"

He gently shrugged."We may look human, but our kind is quite strong. It'd take more than a motor wreck to kill us. I'm sure your friend will be fine. We'll head back to look for her on our way home."

Maddie smiled as the driver gave her hope that somewhere Leigh was alive. Her brows furrowed in gratitude of the young Aristan boys. "Thank you for helping me." She waved at them, hoping they would find Leigh alive and safe.

As they drove off, Maddie turned and faced the entrance of the haven. She remembered all too well what happened the last time she went into one. She could only hope the Aristans were more understanding and willing to help. Too many lives were at stake, and so much was counting on this. Aidan needed this.

Walking in, she immediately noticed the atmosphere was quite different to Riko's bar. Though it was no less short of beautiful people, it was still no less intimidating. Even more so, since she was fully aware of who these patrons truly were. They weren't just bikers hanging at a bar. They were something far more fascinating and terrifying. She was the only human in Greenwood's, which seemed more like a nice sports bar than a dive like Riko's.

As if they'd read her mind, a tall, dark-eyed blonde got up from his table a few feet away from where she stood, glaring at her. He was broad shouldered in his half-zipped rider's jacket, and had a deadly swagger that tempted her to run for the door. The look in his eyes suggested he'd like to crush her throat. *But I can't run. I won't take no for an answer.* She stood fast as he approached her before she could finish another thought.

He gave her a once over and his frown intensified. He held up his hand. "This is a private, members only establishment."

He towered over her, his eyes a dark, otherworldly ebony, as if the universe was hidden in them. His voice was thickly laden with the familiar lilt that was peppered in Aidan's voice.

Meeting his eyes, Maddie stood straight. "What is needed to become a member? I'm looking to speak to someone here."

The Aristan scoffed. "That is quite impossible for you, in any case. You're not welcome. Please leave."

He began to turn away until Maddie replied. "Even if I have an important message to give to you. A life or death situation?"

His body stiffened at her remark, as if he took it for a challenge. "Right. An important message for me?"

"Not just you." Maddie frowned, shaking her head. "For all the other Aristans."

As if she'd said some swear or blasphemous words, the Aristan growled at her and grabbed her wrists, trying to restrain her. "Who are you? What the hell do you know about Aristans!?

Gripping her so tight, she bit back a screech of pain. "A pack is in trouble nearby, and I'm asking for your help! Let go of me, damn you, I'm on your side! I need to speak to Devin! Devin Greenwood!"

He shook his head. "I smell spy all over you. Who sent you here?" His face crinkled in fury as he shook her. "Answer me, or I'll split you in two!"

Maddie helplessly pulled against him. "The Bloodlockes!"

With her shout, she grabbed the attention of the whole bar, each of them glaring at her. Some even baring their teeth at her, growling. It became clear to her that she may not make it out of there alive, let alone deliver the message to Devin.

The Aristan shook her. "You're lying." He looked to the others in the bar as the music stopped. "She's here to set us up! Probably some Thesian courtesha!"

Maddie frowned and writhed in his restraint."Please! Listen to me! Someone I care about is going to die without your help. Some of your people will die; please believe me! I need to speak with Devin. I want to help!"

His black eyes turned amber as he pulled her inches to his twisted face. His harsh, metallic breath washed over her face. "I am going to show you what happens to humans who threaten our pack!"

Suddenly, his man handling on her stopped, as a low growl was heard from the second floor stairway. In fact, everyone in the whole damn bar froze and stared at the darkness in the corridor.

"Is that any way to treat one of my guests?" The low female voice broke through the bar's silence. "That will be all Winter. Let her go so she can speak." The voice was feminine yet still animalistic in its determination. It made Maddie's muscles tighten at the fear of who it was. They hadn't been too welcoming so far.

Winter looked down at Maddie, then to the darkness of the stairway. "But Devin, she's –"

"You know I'm not in the habit of repeating myself, but I'll do it just this once. I said fucking release her, before I gnaw your arm off."

Winter cursed under his breath as he released his grip on Maddie. She backed away from him, afraid that he'd grab her again.

As her eyes flashed an otherworldly silver, Devin stepped out of the darkness from the balcony Walking, she focused in on Maddie, her look curious. She had flaming red hair in a strange razor hair cut with dark amber eyes. Her red and white biker suit clung to her body. Maddie was spellbound for a moment, as all the men froze at her word. Relief washed over her as she realized she had indeed found Devin. She was so beautiful, but erupted with a dangerous, rebellious aura as she slowly walked down the stairs toward Maddie.

"Let her speak. No one should silence someone's call for help in here. This bar is a haven." Devin stood less than a foot from her and smiled. "I take it that you must already know who and what I am, so please tell me why you're here." Devin looked around the bar, then back to Maddie. "You seem like a smart girl, so I won't bother patronizing you with warnings or threats that you probably already anticipated coming in here."

Maddie took a minute to comprehend if she was delivering a warning by saying that. "I mean you no harm."

Devin nodded. "Okay. You're human, but I think I can trust that. And I can tell you're no courtesha. At least," She glanced back at the men. "Female intuition says so." Devin looked into Maddie's eyes and cocked her head, pondering her presence until her eyes lit up. "You're in love with one of our own." She smiled in fascination over that revelation. She recognized the scent of the

Alpha Aidan that was light on her skin, along with soot and wood. "You must be the human mate he was talking about and agonizing over."

Maddie's eyes widened at the term, 'mate.' "Yes, my name is Maddie Ardelle. He needs your help, or he's gonna die, and many others. I'm here to ask for your help!"

Devin's smile faded. "What is it you need?"

Maddie bit back her tears that watered at the base of her eyes. "Thesians are preparing for war with Aidan's pack, and they are aiming to completely wipe them out. Everyone. For money! They are working with an Aristan, who's been helping them."

"An Aristan? Impossible!" Winter scoffed.

"Shut up, Winter!" Devin growled at him. He silenced immediately. "Let the grownups speak for a second." She looked back at Maddie, and her face softened.

"Thesians have been trying to end us for nearly three millennia. They will always be game to attack. Where are the Azans for his pack? He's a general, so I know he has an order at his calling."

"They are spread out all over. By the time they all return, it will be too late! They are already en route to track down the pack in Tarrytown. We need more fighters, more people to give them a fighting chance." Her eyes closed and Aidan's face flashed in her mind. He was sacrificing everything for his people, and she was hell bent on helping any way she could. "They attacked us on the other end of town." A tear ran down her cheek. "Devin, I don't even know if Aidan is alive. But if he is, he shouldn't be alone in this. His sister risked her life to bring me here, so I'll be damned if I leave empty handed. Your people need your help. Please."

Devin sighed. It had been a while since a good guilt trip washed over her. But this little human standing in front of her was just as potent as a nun right now. She was there, afraid, confused, but still fighting for the one she loved. It was inspiring really, and Devin herself was quite pleased Aidan had taken her advice and shared what he was. It seemed to have worked out for the brooding Alpha, apparently, or else she wouldn't be there advocating for him. Her pack was weary from fighting, but this was important. An Aristan traitor trying to lay waste to a pack with Thesian muscle seemed like the stuff of nightmares.

Winter frowned. "What if this is all a trick?"

Maddie shook her head. "Would you be willing to chance it?" She looked around, meeting the faces of the men and women in the bar. They were all cautious, angry, maybe even worried. "Look, I don't claim to know anything about your world. I only know a handful of things. That there are Thesians willing to kill you. Many are under the leadership of an Aristan who has killed his people before. The Thesians are all armed with nightshade tainted weapons. And they know all the secrets of your race from working with an Aristan." She looked around again and saw more anger, fury. Good, she wanted them mad. "You tell me. Are these odds worth ignoring?"

The Azans started to look at each other at the newfound information. Devin looked back at her team and smiled at Maddie. She nodded. "They are not worth ignoring in the least."

Maddie took a sigh of relief as Devin shook her hand. "Thank you."

Devin cut her eyes to her pack. "Winter, Teck and Sable." The large men stepped forward. "Load up our gear and wake up the others. Tonight...we ride."

Thrown from the bike, Leigh tried to stretch her body out. She growled in agony as the slightest movement felt like a hammer to her bones. She'd really screwed herself up this time. Her healing wasn't going as fast as she'd hoped for. *Note to self, don't do that again.*

At least Maddie was safe. The boys would get her to Devin

Greenwood and hopefully talk some sense into that pack. That was all that mattered in the end.

"You think you're so fucking smart, don't you?"

Leigh slowly opened her eyes to see a hazy figure of Kieran with another Thesian goon.

Staggering to get up, she leaned over and spit out some blood. She scoffed. "Outsmarted you, didn't I? Brother." She said his title as if she were spitting again. "We all should have known you would amount to shit. Look at you! Just look at who you hang with."

Leigh wiped the blood from her eyes. Disgust hung on every word. "Mom always said, tell me who you hang with and I'll tell you who you are."

Kieran grinned. "Well, thanks to me we won't be hearing any of Mom's annoying life philosophy. So you're welcome, sis."

That triggered ferocity in Leigh so abrupt, Kieran stepped back as her battered body lunged at him with a violent growl. Her eyes changed, and her canines surged forward. Tamar aptly grabbed each wrist restraining her. She writhed against him, but her body was in no shape to fight, despite her will.

"You're a bastard, Kieran. Rest assured, Mom should have eaten you! The only son she ever had was Aidan!"

Kieran reared back and slapped her. He frowned as he watched her head whip all the way to the left with the force. What kinda goddess would give him such a bitch of a sister? "You are a traitor, Leigh. You turned your back on your own blood for some...some rogue wolf! He ripped our clan apart, and you run beside him?"

Leigh sneered. "The only one I see killing loved ones and tearing clans apart is you."

Kieran grabbed her face. "I'm taking what's mine! Don't you fucking get it?! And if Aristans choose to stand in the way, then I shall cut them down just like any adversary! I'm a Bloodlocke!"

"Spoken like a true Thesian, O' brother of mine." Leigh spat her blood on him.

He reared to strike her again, but he paused. "That mouth of yours never fails to keep you in trouble, Leigh. It always has. As much as you'd like to be martyred for your crusade, I won't kill you." He got closer to her ear. "No, I'm gonna let you watch as fire, teeth, and nightshade lay waste to that fucked up pack of yours. I want you to see the people you love get grinded like meat." He stepped back and smiled. "And when it's all over and done, I'm gonna rip you apart and leave you for the scavengers."

Leigh gritted her teeth at the thought as he and the Thesians laughed. "Aidan is going to kill you, and I'm going to watch!"

Kieran turned back towards the truck. "Take her and shut her up! She's coming with us. Tie her and please, for the love of Arista, fucking gag her with some wormwood oil. She won't be able to amplify if she's stoned."

Tamar forced Leigh forward to head to the truck. "Aren't we going after the Courtesha? We gotta stop her before ---"

Kieran shook his head. "You gotta think more offensively, Tamar. There's not much assistance she could dig up here anyway. And even if she did, by the time they gather it'll be too late anyway. C'mon, it's time I visit my old stomping grounds for a reunion."

Aidan and Cameron stood motionless as Sheriff McTiernan stood before them, pointing a gun at the both of them.

"I want you assholes to pack up and get out of this county, or there's gonna be two more bodies on this ground."

Cameron growled. *"What's with Barney Fife? I don't like guns pointed at me, Aidan. I have a mind to make him fucking eat it."*

Aidan took a deep breath to respond to Cameron via whispering. *"Calm it, wolf, we don't know what that shotgun is loaded with."*

"Oh, I know what it's loaded with. The same stuff ole Barney here is full of. Bullshit!"

Aidan shook his head, darting his eyes to Cameron. *"Cam, let me reason with him first."*

Cameron scoffed. "Reason? Hell, I can run over there and snap his neck before he even squeezes that trigger."

Aidan sighed as Sheriff McTiernan moved closer, hearing Cameron's threat. "What the hell? Did you threaten me you son of a bitch?!"

"Oh shit, I said that part out loud didn't I?"

Aidan's internal voice got deeper at Cameron's slip up.*"Yes, you did, asshole! You want him to gun us down? I said let me talk to him!"*

Cameron stood there, eyeballing the pudgy waste of space with a shotgun. *"He's got one minute to lower that shotgun, or I'll tear him apart like a paper doll..."*

Aidan held up his hands in defense. "My friend's just talking crazy, okay. He's not gonna do anything, alright? And I'm not gonna do anything. We're just gonna talk. Now, I know how all this may look, but we're not the bad guys tearing up your town. But we know who is."

McTiernan lowered his gun a bit. "You're that Addington guy, right? You were with Miss Ardelle."

Cameron arched an intrigued brow. *"Addington?"*

"Long story." Aidan nodded staring at the gun. "Yes."

McTiernan frowned. "I've got people missing all over in my town. I've got bikers all over creation! Bar brawls. Blown up B&Bs. Then, I've got some creepy fang-toothed asshole who threatened me to keep quiet about my own town. Some wolfman motherfucker like...like you."

Aidan and Cameron looked at each other.

"Cam, you can't kill him. I think the wolf he met was Kieran. We need him. He may be even able to help us."

"Sheriff. Was he a wolf or something? Like a werewolf?," he asked.

McTiernan nodded his head violently. Panic knotted his stomach. "Yeah, like some of these dead creatures down here on the ground. What the hell is going on? This doesn't make any sense. Werewolves aren't real." He gestured to some of the Thesians who laid dead, crossed between a man and a wolf. "Yet, here they are." It wasn't uncommon for Thesians and Aristans alike to die in battle appearing that way. Both halves exposed at the end of life. I guess to humans they were werewolves and the stuff of horror books.

"Sheriff, look, we've been tracking him. His name is Kieran and he's very dangerous, okay? Listen to me. He did all this and we're here to stop him! You have to let us go."

McTiernan shook his head, raising the gun again. He didn't know who to trust. They all looked like monsters to him. Someone had to account for all this craziness. No one would believe what he was looking at, but it was true. "I don't think so, buddies. Look, I don't know who or what you are, but I'll soon as blow a hole in the both of you and simply omit this crazy werewolf shit outta my report than let you things go running about, killing up people!"

Cameron sneered. "What makes you so sure putting a bullet in us will stop us?"

Aidan's eyes widened. "Cameron!"

"He's not gonna understand reason, Aidan. Time for my tactic."

"We don't kill humans, Cameron."

Cameron sneered. *"Well, do something, because time is running out and I'm tired of standing here like some dumbass chimp waiting for Barney to prove his manhood!"* Growling, he advanced forward.

McTiernan staggered back and fired, but missed his chance, finding himself immediately thrown to the ground and pinned on his back by an angry Cameron with electric blue eyes.

"Sweet Jesus! Don't kill me!," he pleaded. Down on the ground only a few feet from the dead was too much of an omen to him.

Baring his lupine fangs to the Sheriff, Cameron pressed more weight on McTiernan's chest. "We're not going to kill you, though I'd be lying if the thought hadn't crossed my mind, Barney."

Aidan grabbed the shotgun and tapped Cameron on his back. "Take it easy. Let me speak to him." He stared down at the Sheriff, who was almost pale with fear. He couldn't imagine the things running through his mind. When he had awaken that day, he likely didn't expect to come face to face with the stuff of human nightmares. The day was beginning to fade to dusk, and he knew Kieran would wait till the cover of night to attack.

He walked closer to him. "Sheriff, now that we have your attention, I need you to listen to me. The one who did all of this. The one who's tearing up your town is a murderer. He killed his own mother. *My* mother. Turned against his own people." Aidan sighed. "He doesn't have any regard for anyone past his own desires. He'll hurt us or humans alike. We're here to bring him to justice. That is why we're here - before he succeeds in hurting our people again."

Cameron gently released his hold across the Sheriff's chest, allowing him to speak.

"And the human bystanders?" McTiernan asked as he listened to the sincerity in Aidan's voice.

Aidan shook his head. "We don't want to hurt any humans. We just want peace. We don't hurt humans, Sheriff McTiernan." He thought of Maddie's face and his chest ached. "I'm actually quite fond of one of them. I couldn't ever harm her."

McTiernan grimaced, slowly pulling himself up on his elbows. "Y-You're talking about Doc Ardelle, aren't you? The one you were with the other night at Miss Linda's?"

Aidan began to walk up to him, his eyes changing from green to amber. "Yes. She's in danger. We all are and need your help, Sheriff. This could all end tonight. My loved ones will be safe, and you'll have your town back." He squatted down so they were at mutual eye level. "You have to trust us. And it would be wise not to try and harm us again. We want the same thing you do." He presented the shotgun back to him. "Now, will you help us?"

McTiernan stared at Aidan for a long pause, then sighed. This was fucking bananas. But seeing was believing and as he sat there on a charred lawn surrounded by dead creatures he couldn't explain and the two pairs of yellow eyes staring at him, he could either run or fight. One really much of a choice as he watched Aidan and Cameron. He wiped his sweaty brow with his arm before Aidan helped him up to his feet. Quietly, he accepted the gun from Aidan. "I feel crazy even acknowledging this, but... I'm in. What do you furry bastards need from me?"

30

ALLIANCES

Kieran jumped out of the truck as Tamar backed it into Riko's warehouse. The slew of Thesians and even a few Aristans peppered the opening of the warehouse. It smelled like a kennel with wet animal fur, and the humid air put a sheen of sweat on all the human-skin ShadowShifters in there. Most were loading up the box truck with weapons, grenades and body bags for the eradication of the Bloodlocke pack. He stood and grinned at the sight. Everything was gravy. He had the numbers, he had the weapons, and with the colorless wanting money to support themselves, he totally had the motivation from them. This was it. This was what he was born to do. He was an Alpha, and it was high time he had the opportunity to show his leadership. He needed to no family. They betrayed him and chose a disgusting, pack-less, motherless parasite. So they reaped what they sowed. All Aidan could do was watch as his people were cut down, including his bitch of a sister.

Brody came over to him from the box truck. "Did you take care of the problem?"

Kieran smiled. "Of course I did. Even collected a parting gift." He turned and looked to Tamar, who pulled Leigh out of the back cab of the truck. Her feet and hands were bound with silver chains and her mouth gagged with a torn t-shirt.

Brody frowned as he smelled the wormwood oil. "Who is she?"

Kieran watched as Tamar dragged her up to him. Her feet couldn't quite find their balance, and she barely held her head up. Kieran reached back and struck her face back and forth to try and wake her. The smacking sound of the impact echoed in the warehouse. "My sister. Isn't she charming?"

"What are we going to do with her?" Brody cut his eyes both to Tamar and Kieran.

"She's coming with us. I need her to watch our assault. It's how we bond." Kieran grabbed her face, squeezing her cheeks between his fingers to force her to look at him. All she did was mumble something in the Aristan language. He shrugged. "She's a little doped up right now, but trust me, it's for the best. She is a Bloodlocke, after all."

Brody's frowned deepened. "We don't have time to deal with hostages! What the hell is going on, Kieran? This isn't a game!"

Kieran growled. "Oh, I'm aware of that, Brody. Relax." He turned to Tamar. "Load her up in the weapons truck. She's not gonna be so eager to play around in there if she happens to sober up." He tugged at Leigh's long blonde hair. "See ya later, sis."

Leigh jumped at him and surprised Tamar, who almost let her go while Kieran took a quick step back.

"Shit, wolf! You sure you got her?" Kieran scowled at a nervous Tamar as he tightened his grip on Leigh. "Please don't shit your pants, okay? She can barely count right now. Just add a little more oil and dump her in the back. It's not that hard, I promise!"

"Sorry, Kieran," Tamar muttered as he pushed her forward, heading to the truck.

When Tamar was out of earshot, Kieran turned his attention to Brody. "Don't ever question me again. Do you understand?"

Brody stepped up to Kieran. "This is going to shit, Kieran. This isn't a playground for you to see who's got the biggest dick. These loners on counting on you to lead, and I've tried to sit back on this..."

Kieran leaned his ear forward with a grin. "But?..." He prompted Brody to continue.

"But you are doing a shit job, Aristan!" Brody's eyes blazed with anger. "You're treating these men like disposable toy soldiers, and these are my brothers. I'm not going to stand by and let you lead them to turmoil, all for you to get revenge on your pack for not making you king of the fucking forest!"

Kieran bared his teeth and shoved Brody. "Mmm. I smell a challenge!" He began to walk around Brody. "What? You think you're the one who has what it takes to lead them, Brody boy? Hmm?"

The pissing contest started to get the attention of some of the ShadowShifters nearby. Others ignored it, desensitized to the all too common display of colorless ShadowShifters struggling for leadership.

Brody's body started to pop and build mass, all the while his bright amber eyes trained on Kieran as he circled him like prey. "Maybe we don't need a leader." Brody lunged for Kieran, who rolled out of the way.

When Kieran got back to his feet, his hair grew shaggy, and his animal eyes flashed bright at Brody. He waved both hands, daring Brody to come at him. "C'mon then. Let's see if you're right!"

Brody, fuming, charged at Kieran, spearing him with his head into his gut. As they fell back, Kieran kneed Brody in the face. Again, and again, until Brody rebounded by slamming his muscular fist into Kieran's chest. Feeling his ribs break, Kieran spit up blood, tasting the raw metallic flavor in his mouth. They found themselves encircled by a crowd of loner ShadowShifters watching and clamoring for no one in particular. Kieran straddled Brody and began to pummel his face with blows, each one more brutal than the next, until Brody's face was barely recognizable.

When all he could hear was the wheezing breath of his challenger, Kieran stopped and glared at him.

"You aren't fit to lead anything, Brody. You're an idealist without ideas." He looked around at the crowd. As much as he would have liked to kill him, in the eyes of the lemmings, they were all brothers. You didn't kill brothers...apparently. He looked back down at Brody, taking his hand to wipe the blood off Brody's beaten face. With fierce eyes, Kieran took his bloodstained hand and smeared it across his cheek. A sign that Brody was now an omega wolf in their pack.

He scoffed. "You're pathetic." Kieran rose to his feet and eyed the crowd. "We don't have time for scrabbles! We need to take what's ours and build ourselves a future!"

The group started to nod, and mumbling from the crowd confirmed agreement.

Kieran rolled his neck, cracking this bones and straightening his body. "Now, are we going to stand around here and chew ourselves up? Or are we going to head to Tarrytown like the soldiers we are and show them that true brotherhood is a fucking fearful thing?" He grinned as his rhetorical question was greeted with howls and yelling from the group. "Good. Now let's roll out!" Tamar stepped forward, and Kieran patted his back. "You're my new second, Tamar."

Tamar gave a smirk and nodded. "Thank you."

"Don't thank me. You've earned it. We're taking the weapons truck, so you drive."

"Yes, Kieran." Tamar looked down at Brody, who was struggling to move. "What about him?"

Kieran turned and sighed. "He'll live. You go on and get the truck ready. I'll take care of him." He watched as Tamar and the others got ready to mobilize. Some jumped on their bikes, others in pickup trucks ready to head to Tarrytown. He leaned over Brody and smiled. "You see what I did there, Brody? Togetherness. Unity. Look at how all of them rallied around and got to business. And here you were, trying to put a big ass wedge between all of it." Brody groaned as Kieran viciously kicked him in the ribs. He curled his body up, panting as Kieran squatted down next to him. "I expected more from you. Thesians weren't meant to lead, you know that. You fuckers can barely get out of your own way. Your goddess made you as an afterthought. A revenge fuck. That's all. You should be lucky I gave you the time of day to find some honor, some glory. But you wanted to be king."

Brody coughed and sucked in air. His eyes were barely open as both were swollen. "You're... going to lead them to ruin. It's funny, you know. This is the first time I will need to pray to our beloved Goddess Thesia to let an Aristan win."

Kieran smiled. "Well, flattery will get you nowhere, omega. It's too late to wish me luck."

Brody opened his bloodshot eyes wider. "I wasn't talking about *you*."

Fury erupted in Kieran's eyes, and he grabbed Brody's throat. "You traitorous mongrel!" Kieran grabbed his knife on his hip and put it to Brody's face. "I don't have time for torture, Brody boy. Even I can be gracious. I'll let you die with dignity instead of being omega. He lightly nicked Brody's side with the blade and backed away, sheathing his knife. Brody's strained body began to writhe as the poison started to course through him. Kieran shook his head. "That nightshade is a hell of a toxin. Sweet dreams, Brody boy." Kieran saluted him as Tamar came around with the truck. Leaping into the passenger side, Kieran banged the truck door, ready to roll out.

Maddie kept dialing her phone to reach Aidan when her text went unanswered, but it went straight to voicemail. A sigh of frustration hit her as she was cut off from him, and tension started to lock up her body. She just wanted to know that he was okay. Maddie leaned against wall quietly, watching the Aristans come in on their bikes and load up gear, weapons onto their bikes. She tried not to stare, but there was something graceful about their movements. Everything was coordinated and calculated. Even as they walked together, they seemed to move in little formations, like migrating doves. She didn't expect something like this when she thought of werewolves. But since she'd met Aidan, her mind had been blown about a lot of things.

Aidan... His green eyes popped into her head.

Maddie didn't know what to make of her being referred to as his mate. She had no idea what that really entailed, and upon knowing how the Aristans feel about humans in their world, part of her worried what would happen to Aidan if he paraded her as such. He was sacrificing so much; the thought of him being disgraced threatened to make her cry. The reality was that she didn't have a place in his world. Hearing that thought in her mind made her whimper out a cry at the horrible truth. Fearing attention from such strong creatures, Maddie quickly wiped her tears. She gave a soft, superficial smile as a couple of Aristans walked past her. None were rude to her since Devin talked to them, but they didn't go out of their way to talk to her either.

Devin walked from out the thicket and headed towards Maddie. She had her phone in her hand, but when she got closer to Maddie, she slipped it into her pocket. Devin looked up with amber eyes. "I tried to text Aidan that we have you, but no response. I called him too. No dice."

Maddie nodded. "Yeah, I know. Me too." She rang her hands as her nerves racked her, unaware that Devin was watching her.

Devin sighed. "I amplified for more assistance, but I don't know how close he is to pick it up. But our communication predates phones, so I hope so."

She wasn't too keen on consoling human chicks, or chicks in general. But she knew a worried mate when she saw one. Worry could lead to panic, and panic led to stupidity. Reason enough to try and console her. She gently picked up Maddie's chin. "Hey, he's fine, Maddie. That Alpha wolf is too fucking stubborn to die, trust me. And you said he has a friend with him, right?"

Maddie nodded.

"Well, that's even more reassuring. He's got someone to watch his back."

Devin gently let go of her chin and Maddie exhaled some of her tension. "You're probably right." She looked up at Devin with furrowed brows. "You must think I'm so stupid, right? He's strong enough to break someone in half, and I'm here shaking for him like a leaf on a tree." Maddie gave a nervous chuckle and tried to look anywhere but Devin's face, whose expression was very hard to read all of a sudden. What was it with these creatures and their poker faces?

Devin crossed her arms and stared at Maddie. "You're not stupid, Maddie. You're in love. There's nothing stupid about having concern for the wellbeing of your mate. I can probably imagine that Aidan is losing his shit thinking about you right now." She smiled as Maddie's watery eyes brightened.

"I don't know how all this stuff works, Devin. How to be someone's mate."

Devin scoffed. "Could've fooled me, human." She paused as Winter came by and handed her a leather bag with her gear. She slapped his shoulder. "Thanks, Winter." He walked past Maddie with a grunt, barely acknowledging her existence. Devin rolled her eyes and looked back to Maddie with apologetic eyes for her beta's behavior. "He's really cuddly when you get to know him...I think."

Both Maddie and Devin looked at him brooding next to his bike and laughed. They both knew that was bullshit.

"Maddie, being a mate is different for everyone, so no one has it all figured out. Just know that you are doing exactly as you should. You're here. You're ready to fight for your mate and his people." Devin paused as the reality of what she was going to say really impressed her. "I've known stronger she-wolves to be far lesser mates."

Taken aback by Devin's encouraging words, Maddie felt her body relax and smiled. "Thanks, Devin. Very kind of you to say."

"Well, don't get all sappy on me. I can't let the boys see me soft. Appearances, you understand." Devin winked at her. Perhaps consoling chicks wasn't as bad as she thought.

As they loaded up behind the bar, Maddie couldn't help but let her curiosity get the best of her. As Devin hid several blades in her boots, she saw many tattoos. One that stood out, in particular, was the edge of the same type of tattoo that Aidan and his friend Cameron had around the curvature of her breast. Hers was slightly different but had the same elements: a braided rope pattern encircling a paw print insignia.

"You're Azan?"

Devin looked up and gave a slow smile. "Of course. How else would I be able to handle this powder keg of a group? Especially Winters over there. You see how charming he is."

Maddie shook her head, embarrassed she sounded so amazed. "I'm sorry. It wasn't my intention to sound so sexist." She really wasn't surprised. The way all of them looked to her and obeyed her commands, only a badass would be able to do such a thing. Devin may be all smiles, but Maddie wasn't a fool. She was sure the Aristan woman could kick some serious ass.

Devin shrugged and straightened her body to full height. "Oh, you weren't. It wasn't easy to say the very least, but nothing in our world ever is. It takes a lot of respect to earn the love and loyalty of your order. Male or female. My clan where I was born was killed off many years ago, and I had to learn that I simply couldn't live by the old rules. If I was to survive, I would have to change those rules. In my youth, when others saw me, they saw a dainty little bitch – weak, and needing someone to come to my rescue."

Maddie scoffed. "And how do they see you after meeting you now?"

Devin grinned. "A fucking beast. I'll eat your young if you're not careful."

As sweet as Devin seemed to her, Maddie didn't put anything past her. She could only imagine the physical and mental games that had to be played to win over a league of edgy werewolves, like the ones in her bar.

Howling in the distance interrupted them. Maddie tensed a bit until Devin placed a reassuring pat on her shoulder.

"It's alright, Maddie. They are with us. You're safe."

Maddie looked around. "Where are they?"

"You'll see them in a moment." Devin looked up at the moon then to Maddie. "You said you don't know much about our world?"

Maddie nodded, still afraid of the consequences of revealing what she knew to them. However, Aidan knew Devin, and she knew he would never intentionally put her in any danger. "Correct."

"Well, prepare to see a lot more, sweetheart. There's gonna be a more weird shit from here on out." Devin squeezed Maddie's shoulder. "But whatever you see, Maddie, is for your eyes only. Our very lives and existence depends on it. Humans knowing of our world could be the end of us all."

As she said that, Maddie froze as a slew of huge wolf-like creatures ran out into the clearing. They were fast and agile with thick pelts of silver, white, grey and even red. All of their eyes were bright and reflective in the night. She saw them but still, couldn't believe her eyes. At least thirty of them stood before her next to Devin - the beautiful and frightening Aristan wolves. As scary as they were, she knew somehow she was the safest woman on the planet right now. They waited, panting and growling for Devin to tell them the next move. It was a formidable display of power that left Maddie in awe.

Devin jumped onto the loading dock, standing before everyone. "We ride out to Tarrytown, brothers. Thesians are planning an unwarranted attack on an Aristan pack, and we simply can't turn a blind eye to it. We don't know how many, could be hundreds. I've amplified for all of you to help us, so thank you for coming forth. The Thesians may be armed with nightshade weapons. If that scares you, you better sit this one out and stay the hell outta our way, cause we're going to show them who owns the fucking night!"

Devin's Azan Order howled and beat their chest at her words. Their wild eyes amber and their canines gritted in their mouths.

Devin nodded. "This one can get messy, so leave nothing to chance. It's time to kill or be killed, ladies and gentlemen."

All the wolves started to growl, along with the human-skin Aristans waiting on their bikes.

Feeling the energy of her pack, Devin howled to the moon before leaping down to the ground. "Let's ride out!"

With that command, the Azans revved their bikes, and the wolves took formation behind them. Maddie had never seen such an amazing display.

"Maddie, you can ride with me." Devin put her helmet on, then handed one to Maddie. "I need to get you a weapon. If you don't have teeth and claws, you ride armed." She started to hand her side arm to Maddie when she shook her head.

"I have one, actually. Thanks." Maddie pulled her weapon from behind her and showed it to Devin. "I could use more ammo, though. It's a Glock 23... and, uh, untainted rounds is fine." She looked at the pistol, then back at Devin, who stared at her with an arched brow and a slacked jaw.

Devin put her weapon back into her holster, still a bit surprised. "Well, excuse the fuck outta me." She grinned, amused that Maddie was quite an interesting human, indeed. Aidan had done well. Devin reached into her bag and pulled out a cartridge. "Here, uh, 40 caliber black rounds. Be careful with them."

Maddie took the cartridge and jammed it in her back pocket, then carefully secured her pistol between her back and her jeans, which Devin had graciously loaned her to wear. She looked back to Devin and gave a sheepish grin. "Uh, thanks."

Devin smiled. "No, thank you. That was incredible. After this, I might even start liking girls again."

Maddie exploded with laughter. Probably one of the most interesting compliments she'd ever received. "Thanks, Devin...I think."

"You're welcome. Just remind me never to piss you off." Devin zipped up her jacket, letting it mold to her curves. "Never saw your Azan mate lead his order?"

Maddie shook her head, "No." Then she blinked as she got on the bike with Devin. "Wait a minute. How did you know he was Azan?"

"I knew as soon as I met him. You have a very serious mate, Maddie. Aidan is all business, especially when it comes to you." Maddie held onto Devin as she tucked her hair into her helmet.

Maddie smiled. "Yeah, I'm getting that. Always the protector."

Devin laughed. "Sounds ridiculously Aristan to me. Maddie, when we choose a mate, we choose them for life. We'd do anything for them, even sacrifice our lives for them. There's no greater bond than family, and when we choose a mate, they are part of that family. Aristans don't choose just anyone to be their mate."

Maddie's heart ached. Aidan lived in such a dangerous world, but there was nothing more she wanted than to be with him in it. But despite what they wanted, would Aristan's pack allow it? She settled herself behind Devin and looked out to the forest. "How will we get there with this brigade? We'll cause quite a stir, I imagine."

"No worries, we have our ways." Devin turned her headlights on and off, signaling it was go time. "The riders will take the highway while the furs flank through the forest on each side. If anyone tries to approach us, we'll curve in and swallow them into the night.

31

CHILDREN OF ARISTA

Riko's warehouse just outside Iris was not very secretive, and it was a good thing. Some local residents were calling in with noise complaints that were routed to the Sheriff while they were on route. Aidan's adrenaline was pumping like crazy, eager to put a stop to this madness before it further spiraled out of control. His body clammy with sensory overload, all he could think of where all the unknowns. He had no idea what they would find at Riko's warehouse. He had texted Leigh and hadn't heard from her yet. He was going insane wondering if she and Maddie were okay. When his phone bleeped that familiar tone of no battery power, Aidan growled.

"No, no, no, no... Fuck!" He threw the phone down in frustration. Aidan leaned against the car door. His body felt painfully conflicted. He was ripped apart and wanted to break out of the car and find Maddie. His wolf half demanded to know if his mate was safe, and it was hard to quell the beast within him. Aidan's imagination started to go to a very dark place, and forced his animal heart to wrench and hurt, begging to see her. What if she and Leigh were killed? What if Kieran had Maddie right now, torturing her for answers? He promised to protect her and he just kept screwing up. The sharp pain in the back of his head threw him back and rocked his body. The warm sensation started to crack his bones, feeling his body grow in size. He felt as if he was tearing in two. "Let me out! Now!" He barked, with an almost disembodied voice.

The Sheriff drove frantically, obviously startled at Aidan's reactions. "What's going on?" He briefly turned to Cameron in the back seat. "Hey, what the hell is wrong with him?"

Cameron quickly shifted to the side directly behind Aidan and reached his arms around to hold him, pinning his back to the seat. "Shit! Just keep driving!" He used all his strength to hold onto Aidan, without cutting off his air supply, which was a lot harder than it probably looked. "He's alright. He just wants his mate. Sometimes it triggers a change in us, that's all."

Sheriff's eyes were wide and freaked out. "That's all? What the fuck? He's gonna rip this car apart if you don't put a rein on him!"

Cameron continued to hold Aidan as he growled and shifted in his seat. "Aidan, you have to calm the hell down. He's right, you're gonna tear this car apart if you don't. I'm sure Maddie is fine, so you have to get a grip, man."

Aidan heard his friend's voice through the haze of his own mind as the change desperately wanted to claim him. Cam was right, he needed to calm himself, but it wasn't easy when there was so much at stake. Maddie was out there somewhere without his protection. If he knew she'd got to Devin's, then he could at least breathe. Aidan swallowed a breath and writhed as he tried to function through the pain. Pushing it down, he started to pant.

Cameron eased up on his grip. "That's it, man. Push it down. Save that shit for later, cause we're gonna need it."

Finally, Cameron completely released him, allowing Aidan to curve his body forward as the change slowly receded. Refusing a reactionary change gave pain a new meaning, but one that neither Aidan nor Cameron were unfamiliar with. His bones felt like someone was scraping them with razors, his skin hot to the touch, along with the nauseous feeling one got after being kicked in the balls. Despite the agony, it didn't hold a candle to Aidan's worry over Maddie.

Cameron sighed and stretched his arms. He had never seen Aidan in a position of lost control. Granted, he was well aware of the stories of how Tiberius and Ninon found him, and the long rehab to control his rage and hunger. But by the time Cameron had found his way into the Bloodlocke pack, Aidan was already seen as a well put together Aristan. He has had an unmistakable edge that only other misfits could've picked up, but was still cool and collected.

Now, he began to understand why Aidan was so standoffish about taking a mate. He was afraid of being attached. It was that attachment that made him vulnerable.

"I know something we're also gonna need." Aidan paused and turned to McTiernan. "We need explosives, Sheriff. Those weapons in that warehouse have to be destroyed.

"What kinda weapons?" He asked as he turned the corner. They rode ghost, without headlights, as they approached the area near the warehouse. "Do I need to call this in? Exactly how many of these sons of bitches are in there?"

"You can't alert the authorities, not now. The fewer humans know about this, the better."

"Well, I don't have any explosives, son. I'm a Sheriff, not SWAT. I don't have access to that kinda artillery.

As they pulled up to the warehouse, Aidan instantly noticed the unmistakable scent of Thesian blood. The lights were dim on the outside, and there wasn't anyone keeping guard or moving outside.

"Turn off your lights and park right here. I don't want them to catch scent of us before we have a chance to see what's going on in there." Aidan ordered the Sheriff. McTiernan obeyed and slowed to a stop right before the tree line.

As Aidan, Cameron and the Sheriff got closer, they noticed the large tire track prints in the soft dirt outside the garage door. Cameron ran his hand across the dip, feeling the imprint, and watched it go out towards the road. "This wasn't too long ago, Aidan."

"Shit!" Aidan hissed. He ran up to the big, tin door and shoved it open, noticing it wasn't locked. He saw the musty warehouse with scattered crates, a couple of cars and bikes. Cameron and the Sheriff walked in behind him, surveying the surroundings for enemies. "We're too late. The fuckers already left!"

A sickening feeling washed over Aidan. They had to get moving to catch them up. Looking around, he signaled to Cameron, who met his eyes.

"We gotta get moving."

The Sheriff continued to walk through the warehouse, armed with his shotgun, ready to put down anything that was alive and wasn't them. As he slowly moved past a stack of crates, a hand grabbed his leg.

"Ahh!" McTiernan jumped back and raised his gun at the body on the floor. "We got a live one!"

Aidan and Cameron quickly ran up to where the Sheriff was standing. Aidan stopped and looked down at a beaten, bloody Thesian lying on the floor. Big, red blisters covered his arms and hands. His eyes were nearly swollen shut, and his lips were slightly parted, exposing bloodstained teeth. Death rode across his face, but the sound of short, shallow breaths told Aidan he wasn't dead yet.

Cameron recognized those blisters, and a chill ran over him. "He's not healing, Aidan." He gently put his hand on McTiernan's shotgun, forcing him to lower it.

Aidan looked down at the dying Thesian, knowing the evitable for him. "I know. Nightshade poisoning."

Brody finally spoke with a hoarse voice. "It was that bastard, Kieran...," Brody paused, wincing in pain. "...he left to kill your pack. He's got your sister."

Cameron frowned. "Leigh?"

Brody nodded. "He has her in the weapons truck."

Aidan's eyes widened. "Was she alone? Did Kieran have a human woman too?"

Brody shook his head. "No."

Aidan wasn't sure if that was a good thing or not, but wanted to believe that somehow Maddie got to safety despite Leigh being captured. He had to hold on to the belief that she was okay, or it would be impossible for him to focus.

Aidan squatted down next to Brody, seeing death eclipsing the Thesian's eyes. "How many fighters are with him?"

Brody began to grit his teeth as a shockwave of pain racked his body. His hands balled into tight fists, he tried to focus on speaking while he had a voice left. He was so cold as he awaited the moment Thesia would take his soul into her halls of Eoncé, those gilded halls in the upper Selene Palace. The halls where he'd find peace, love and eternal honor for serving his goddess. "About 150 colorless... they are taking..the back roads to Tarrytown."

Sheriff McTiernan scowled. "Probably taking Route 126. The back roads could shave about half an hour's time off getting there. We've gotta move."

Aidan looked up at McTiernan and nodded before staring back at Brody. "Thank you." He put his hand on his blade, still looking at his swollen eyes. Brody was writhing in pain, his body slowly shutting down at an agonizing pace. "I can quickly end this for you, brother."

Brody scoffed as blood oozed out the side of his mouth. "Brothers... we are not." He weakly laid his hand over Aidan's as he held his blade. "Save your blade...for brother..."

Then he was silent. A slow, final breath exhaled from his dark lips as he lay lifeless. Though there was not much remorse for the fallen Thesian, Aidan was grateful for the information he had elected to share.

Aidan stood up and looked at Cameron and the Sheriff. "That shit that killed him is on every weapon in Kieran's arsenal. Now, you've seen what it does. We can't let any of that shit get to Tarrytown."

"You're goddamn right it's not getting there," Cameron replied, shaking his head at the corpse on the ground. He couldn't imagine Leigh or any of the pack dying in such a horrifying way. His anxiety already escalating, he was ready to stop Kieran and find Leigh at all costs.

"Open some of these crates, see what we can use. Go!" Aidan ran into the office while Cameron and the Sheriff split up and started opening up the crates. In the office, papers littered the floor, and the old computer was busted. As he sifted through the papers on the desk, he found nothing of importance.

Cameron smashed open a crate with his fists, and, in seeing the contents tumble out, he whistled.

Both Aidan and the Sheriff ran up to him. Cameron held a grenade in his hand. "Looks like we've found some shit that can go ka-blooey, after all."

Aidan allowed a corner of his lips to curve. "Good. Grab a bag. I'm going to amplify for Devin outside. "

As Aidan turned to exit the warehouse, Cameron grabbed his shoulder. "Wait a minute. We can't use this while Leigh's on that truck."

Aidan looked back at him with calm, amber eyes. "Of course not. Which is why we're gonna get her off first." Cameron's puzzled eyes demanded an explanation that he wasn't ready to give, so he just continued. "If we destroy weapons, we all have a fighting chance. Now, when you're done, meet me outside. I have a plan."

Maddie held on to Devin as they zipped through the highway. She felt like she was the only one who could see the yellow eyes in the dark of the night. Like stars appearing after staring into the black sky long enough. The Aristans were out there, chasing the ghosts in the night. Ready to attack as they moved through the terrain on either side of them. Her thoughts trailed to Aidan and she wondered how he looked in his wolf skin. Would he trust her enough to let her see? Would his people even allow her to be with ever again? All she knew is that she missed him and couldn't stop worrying.

Suddenly, Devin and the others on the road slowed down and shifted onto a country road. Concerned about the reason, Maddie tried to yell to Devin. "Why are we stopping?" Devin didn't respond. Finally, she pulled to a stop and the others on their bikes circled around her and paused. Devin took off her helmet, which prompted Maddie to take off hers. "Devin, what's wrong? Why did we stop?"

Devin smiled. "It's alright. We were amplified to make a stop here. Just a pit stop."

Maddie grimaced. "Amplified? By whom?"

She paused as two men on bikes, followed by a Sheriff's department cruiser, came burrowing down the other end of the dirt road. Skidding to a stop a few feet from Devin's bike, a familiar face turned off his engine, engaged his kickstand and smiled as her eyes illuminated as he walked towards her like a ghost.

She could barely focus as her watery eyes blurred her vision. Dropping her helmet to the ground, words jumbled in her mouth as she tried to scramble off the bike. "Aidan?"

Before she could make any leeway to get up, Aidan grabbed her, pulling her off Devin's bike and hoisting her up against his chest. Her legs wrapped around him instinctively as she hugged him tight.

"Maddie, he breathed against her. He couldn't describe the feeling of holding her again. Seeing her face and hearing her voice. She'd probably never truly understand.

He smelled her hair and smiled. When Devin responded back with news that Maddie was with her and on the move, Aidan couldn't believe the amount of relief in his heart. He cast his eyes to Devin, who sat back on her bike, grinning and shaking her head. "Thank you," he quietly mouthed to her, grateful that Maddie was safe. "Devin was telling me you're quite the wrangler. I told her you had experience, though."

Laughing, Maddie pulled back, her tiny hands on his scruffy face, and planted a huge kiss on his lips. "I was so scared something had happened to you!"

Aidan slowly released her legs and lowered her so she could stand. "I'm sorry, xerhmon. I'm alright. I just happy you're safe."

Maddie shook her head, wiping tears from her face. "Leigh risked her life for me. Her bike crashed trying to get me to safety. Aidan, I didn't want to leave her--"

"Leigh survived, Maddie," Aidan interjected. "But Kieran's taken her with him to Tarrytown. I have to get to her."

Cameron walked up into the circle, just as Devin got off her bike. She eyed the Celt, looking him up and down with crossed arms. She stared at his nearly white blonde hair and electric blue eyes and smiled. "You must be the Celt. Aidan's second-in-command?"

Cameron slowly nodded his head with a smirk. "That would be me. You must be the notorious Devin Greenwood." He extended his hand for a shake and Devin unraveled her folded arms to accept.

The Sheriff stared at Devin and frowned. "I know you. You're the one who set up that bar outside of town."

Devin whipped her head to meet his eyes. Her expression less than pleased. "What the hell is he doing here!?"

Before Aidan could say anything, Devin leaped over her bike and ran over to Sheriff McTiernan. She pounced on him, slamming him against the hood of the cruiser.

"Jesus Christ!," McTiernan yelled in horror as he stared into Devin's furious yellow eyes. A low, threatening growl rumbled in her throat, and her canines were extended, nearly drooling.

"I'm going to fucking eat your face, lawman!" She tightened the grip on his collar, pulling him closer to her twisted face.

Aidan put his arm across McTiernan's body, glaring at Devin. "Devin, now's not the time for this. He's been helping us. He's a friend. Let him go."

Devin shook her head. "We don't need him! He's been giving me shit since the day I arrived in this area! Following me, tracking my bar inspections." She leaned into him. "You even tried to get my liquor license revoked!"

"I was only doing my job, lady!" McTiernan choked out. "I knew something was strange about you and your crew. Just never imagined...this."

Aidan pushed the Sheriff down, forcing Devin to release him. "I said, let him go. Your fight isn't with him tonight, Devin. He's a friend of the Bloodlocke pack. Release him now."

She heard the warning in his voice, and a simpler Devin would've told him to fuck off. But this wasn't the time. Devin exhaled a fierce breath and finally released him, causing the Sheriff to slam back against the hood of the car. She jumped down off him and glared at Aidan. "Save Maddie, I'm not a fan of the company you keep. Just do yourself a favor and keep him away from me if you value his life."

"Fair enough." Aidan looked at McTiernan. "And you. It would be wise to keep your distance from her and her pack."

McTiernan scrambled off the car and picked up his hat off the ground. "You don't have to tell me twice." He fashioned the hat on his head and picked up his shotgun. Looking at Aidan, he gave a quick nod of respect. "Thank you."

"You're welcome." Aidan cleared his throat. "Alright, now that, um, everyone's been properly acquainted, let's go over the plan. We don't have much time, so listen up." Aidan opened the map and laid it on the hood of the car. "Kieran and his crew are moving 150 strong, but they are going caravan style. Several SUVs or pickup trucks, probably on 126 highway. That's several trucks, so it's gonna be easy to spot. The weapons are in a separate truck. Either a van or a box truck, something generic and inconspicuous. My sister Leigh is with them in that weapons truck. I need a couple of guys to come with us as we catch up to them. We go after the weapons truck, alright? I'm going to first open it and get Leigh out, and then blow that fucking thing off this planet.

Devin looked at Aidan. "What about us?"

He pointed at the map. "I need you and the rest of your pack to take the turnpike southwest till you hit the Androscoggin River. If you ditch the bikes and go on foot from there, you can follow the river south past Auburn and get there at the same time, if not cut them off. The pack's community is right where the river crooks east. They are waiting for you." Aidan nodded to Devin. "You got it?"

Devin smiled. "Fuckin' A. Good to know you're not just another pretty face." She turned and trained her eyes on Winter. "You, Sable and Griswold go with Aidan. I got the rest." She walked towards her bike when Winter grabbed her arm.

"Devin, who's gonna watch your back if I'm not there? This already isn't our fight, and you're trying to go at it alone?" His gravelly voice and light green eyes were loaded with uncharacteristic concern.

She scoffed and jerked her arm free. Her voice was a low volume tailored to his proximity. "I'm the furthest thing from alone. Look at all of them. They are all our brothers. Just like the ones we're going to help out in Tarrytown. Make no mistake, Winter, this *is* our fight. It's us against them, and I don't know about you, but I'm tired of riding the fucking pine when I'm built to be in the game. Now, do as I say and watch your ass!" She hit her fist on his chest, before walking away to face the rest of the pack. "Alright! You know the score, so let's get moving!" Devin hopped on her bike, as did the others. They howled and jeered, revving their engines before Devin rode away, her crew of Aristan ShadowShifters following behind her.

Onyx walked through the community as the pack gathered up weapons, boarded up bungalows and anything else in between. He was sure that everyone saw a calm and collected Aristan when they raised their chin to him in respect. But in reality, his patience was slipping into oblivion. His dark eyes looked at his phone, almost willing it to ring with the news of Aidan or Cameron. Anyone. Yet, there was nothing. The pack made a decision to stay and fight, and although he understood the majority's sentiment, he tried his best to help them understand that there were a long list of unknowns. No one knew how many were coming for them. If they were overtaken by numbers, it would mean the end for all of them.

After explaining the death of Bastien and that it was all tied to the attack, they were ready to move forward and protect their home. As he walked by burnt bungalows and charred trees from the previous attack, he understood the decision very well. No more would they be bullied and pushed from their home. It was time to show them what true unity was, and how dangerous it could be.

His thoughts trailed off as his phone finally rang. Quickly, Onyx opened his phone and answered it. "Hello?" He sighed. "Aidan, it's sure good to hear your voice."

Aidan smiled. "Same to you. Look, Kieran is coming your way with about 150 ShadowShifters."

Onyx frowned. "150? Armed? We barely have 70 of us healthy and ready to fight, and that's with the Azans who've finally returned."

Aidan continued his pace while he continued. "Yeah, I know. Cam and I will disrupt their weapons. At least without the night-shade arsenal, we can even the odds, despite the large number. I'm also sending an ally there to contribute to the manpower, so be vigilant. They are Aristans coming to help us. The Alpha's name is Devin Greenwood."

Onyx nodded as he walked. "Okay. I'll update the pack. We'll be ready."

"Good."

"And Aidan..."

"Yeah," Aidan replied.

"Be careful out there. Come back to your pack. We need you."

Aidan looked at the group of Aristans with him and nodded to himself. "By Arista's hands, I'll be there." With that, he hung up.

Maddie stood quiet, even as she watched the ShadowShifters in wolf skin run off into the night, the forest their cover from the eyes of the human world in which they lived. Aidan came up behind her and rested his chin on the top of her head.

"Welcome to my world, xerhmon," he said quietly. His voice sounded more of an apology than a true welcome, and it made Maddie turn around. His eyes matched his tone as they were heavy with remorse.

"I'm okay, Aidan. Truly." She tried to touch his face, but he grabbed it instead, preventing her from completing the gesture. "What's wrong?"

"I want you to stay safe, Maddie. I can't focus, wondering if you're protected, and where I'm going, I can't protect you."

"Aidan, I--"

"You need to go with Sheriff McTiernan and head back to Bridgepoint."

Maddie stepped back as if he'd slapped her. "What? No, I'm not!"

Aidan sighed. "Maddie..."

"You can't just send me back, Aidan. I want to help you! Let me do this, please!"

Aidan saw the pain in her eyes, but his logic was unrelenting. She was lucky to be alive. The bike crash could've killed her. She could've died at the B&B if it weren't for Leigh. All that was waiting for her was death if she followed him, and he couldn't bear it. He thought about how he had felt earlier when he didn't know if she were alive or dead, and how his mind began to unravel. If that happened again, he could get them killed. Aidan felt a stab of emotion hit behind his eyes and tried his best to bite it back. The idea of losing Maddie was reason enough, even if it meant her hating him.

He gently grabbed her shoulders. "No! You cannot come with us! This isn't your fight, Maddie! You're human, and you're fragile, and if I lost you I wouldn't know what to do, alright?" He gently shook her, watching tears stream down her face, both of their hearts breaking at the same time.

"You can't just shut me out like this," Maddie's voice cracked as she stared into his eyes. "Just leaving me here."

Aidan released her and sighed. "I'm doing it because..." His voice trailed off. *Because I love you, Maddie,* he voiced in his head. But if he told her, then she would never let him leave. He needed her far away from him. "... it's dangerous, xerhmon." He hugged her and kissed her head.

Maddie held onto him tight. Her heart wringing with sorrow and fear. What if he didn't come back? What if he met his death and she never got to tell him how she felt? The words itching at the back of her throat, her hands tightened into fists on his shirt as she held them back. No sooner than he'd welcomed her into his world, she was booted out. Because he had a duty to protect his people now. They were the ones that needed him now that she was safe. Telling him how she felt wouldn't be fair to him. She didn't want to force him to choose. "Please be safe, Aidan."

Aidan pulled away and wiped her tears. "I will." He gave a soft smile to her before turning to Cameron and Devin's men. "Alright, let's go. Cameron, you got the bag of goodies?"

Cameron nodded as he got on his bike. "Hell yeah."

"Good." He turned to McTiernan. "Take care of Maddie. You both get back up to Bridgepoint and lay low. There could still be some of Kieran's boys hanging up there doing spy work. Watch yourselves." He shook his hand. "Thank you for your help, Sheriff."

McTiernan grasped Aidan's hand and gave a weak smile. "You sure you're gonna be alright?"

"Yeah. We've got the numbers and a plan. We gotta go get to it, that's all." Aidan got on his bike and started the engine. He cast a look to Maddie, who stood with folded arms. The angst in her face was unmistakable, and the last thing he saw before he and the others rode away.

She stood there, watching the tail lights fade into the distance of the country road until the Sheriff gently tapped her shoulder.

"C'mon, Doc Ardelle. Let's get you home."

Maddie walked to the cruiser with him and got in. She plopped down in the seat, anger, confusion, and helplessness haunting her as the Sheriff drove them away. Away from the world she needed to be a part of.

32

ECLIPSE

As Sheriff McTiernan continued down the highway, he noticed that Maddie hadn't said a word. For the past two miles, she sat with folded arms, looking out her passenger side window. Her cheeks had streaks where her tears had carved a river down her face. He probably had a million questions for her. Main one being how she'd manage to get tangled up in this crazy mess of half animal creatures. He remembered how Aidan talked about her, and couldn't help but feel a sense of curiosity on how such a mild-mannered town veterinarian met him. He didn't know quite how to absorb all that was happening around him, and if his mind was spinning, ready to implode, he was sure that hers was probably fast approaching such a meltdown.

"You alright?"

Maddie didn't turn her head. "No, I'm not, Sheriff."

McTiernan nodded. "Guess that was a fair answer."

Maddie wiped her face, still facing the window. "It's an honest answer. Not a fair one."

She watched the black silhouettes of tall tree figures moving so fast they blurred into one, monstrous dark mural of the night. Beyond it was backdrop of the silver moon, shining bright against the deep black foreground of blurry trees. Maddie imagined Aidan somewhere out there, fighting, and wanted to crawl inside herself. Her body shook with the intensity of her anger and it sucker punched her worry for him. Her throat was dry and muscles tense with the need to explode. *I know why he did it, but that doesn't make me feel great that he did it.* Aidan wanted to protect her and, as much as she loved him for it, Maddie had frankly never felt so abandoned. They were a team. At least, she wanted to think so. What if he was in trouble and no one could get to him?

I love him.

She tilted her head begrudgingly against the cool window. Why didn't she just say it? She groaned to herself. "I made the right choice, didn't I? He needs to focus on protecting his pack." She mumbled to herself, but it was louder and more coherent than she thought.

He turned to her, briefly. "What did you say?"

Finally, Maddie turned to face him. *Fuck this. If Devin was right, it's kinda my pack too.* "We need to turn back."

He immediately shook his head. "What? Hell no! We just got you outta harm's way, and the kinda mess that's brewing there, we don't have a part in! We are going back to Bridgepoint to get you safe."

Maddie frowned. "We can't just turn tail and run from this! People are going to get slaughtered! You're gonna just leave?"

McTiernan sighed. "Now, I don't know who they are, but they are definitely outside my jurisdiction, Doc! Have you seen those things attack?"

"Yes!"

"Good! Well, then you know that you and me and probably half the goddamn world is ill-equipped to tango with a bunch of creatures like that! And I'm sure as hell not gonna put an innocent bystander such as yourself into that kinda danger! That Aidan guy was right to do what he did." McTiernan briefly lifted his

Sheriff's hat to let a little air in against his thin, curly hair. "I know you don't like it, but it is what it is."

Seething, Maddie bit her lip. She hated that saying because the rough translation always seemed like 'tough shit.' "We shouldn't be running away, Sheriff. There were times Aidan could've turned a blind eye to the shit that happened to me in Bridgepoint. But he didn't." Maddie thought about the first time she met him. Angry and cocky, ready to take on a whole bar just to protect her--a human he didn't even know. "I owe him my life. I can't just walk away back to my little apartment and pretend everything will be fine, cause it won't!"

McTiernan shook his head. "Aidan seems like a pretty decent...man. But like I said, we don't belong there, and even he knew that. So I'm sorry, Doc." He saw the bright lights of a gas station and breathed a sigh of relief. "Ah, sweet nicotine!" He started to turn in the parking lot. "Now, I'm gonna grab some cigarettes real quick and--"

"No! They're gonna die, and it's my fault!" Maddie started to hyperventilate, her breathing erratic and forceful as she grabbed her chest with watery eyes. "Oh God, oh God! I can't breathe!"

McTiernan's eyes grew wide as he watched Maddie in his peripheral gasp for air. He frantically pulled into a spot, afraid that she was going into shock or something. "Just take it easy, Doc, alright? Just breathe!"

As soon as they pulled in, Maddie flung the door open and dropped to her knees. "I-can't, I-can't breathe! Help me!" Her body heaved over, one hand gripping the grimy pavement, the other gripping her chest.

Without turning off the engine, McTiernan ejected himself from the cruiser and rushed around the car to her side. "Doc? Doc? Relax, it's gonna be alright!" His voice sounded softer in efforts to soothe. However, the urgency within it couldn't remain hidden. "Just breathe, I think you're having a panic attack."

With frightened eyes, Maddie looked up at him. Her voice choked up between breaths. "P-paper. B-bag...breathe!"

McTiernan frantically nodded, then turned to the store entrance and the clerk inside bagging up someone's items. "Okay! Just calm down! I'll be back!" The Sheriff started to run to the door of the convenience store to fetch a paper bag, leaving Maddie on the ground. Maddie watched McTiernan get to the door and quickly shot up. She jumped into the passenger side, closed the door, then scooted across to the driver's side and quickly closed that one, too. The fake hyperventilating had already jacked up her heart rate and senses, but the amount of adrenaline pumping through her as she shifted the cruiser into reverse was almost unfathomable.

As McTiernan harassed the store clerk for a paper bag, he paused as the screeching sound of tires interrupted him. He turned to see his cruiser burn out of the parking space.

"Shit!" McTiernan ran out of the convenience store in full force. His determination was heroic, but fruitless, as Maddie shifted again and pinned the pedal off onto the highway. "Dammit, Doc! What the hell are you doing? Stop! Stop!" McTiernan threw his hat, furious and defeated.

Maddie looked in the rearview mirror as she sped off down the highway. Her knuckles were white as she gripped the steering wheel, her fingernails digging into the pliable leather of the wheel cover. "Oh shit! Oh shit! Oh shit!" she chanted in the void of the cruiser. "I...I just stole a fucking cop car! Maddie, what the fuck are you doing?" She swallowed hard and tried not to think about the fact that she'd just committed a felony, but she couldn't help but unleash some emotion. A strange metamorphosis began, her panic turning into shock, then slowly into exhilarating laughter. Finally, it ebbed into a raw determination as she saw the mile marker towards Highway 126.

Riding two abroad, Aidan and Cameron sped through the night with Griswold, Sable, and Winter, tightening the formation behind them. When the red tail lights began to come into view, Aidan's eyes zeroed in on a box truck hauling ass down the small, empty highway. The instant he saw it, he knew it had to be

Kieran. There were no other Thesians riding with him, which led him to believe that they must have gone ahead of him. Aidan gripped the handles and accelerated, silently praying to Arista that Devin and her crew was able to catch up to them. Onyx was a seasoned fighter, but he was also a much older wolf that was out of the battle game for many moons. He would need the force of Devin along with the Azans to protect those who were there but could not fight, like the elders and the children. Aidan glanced to Cameron riding beside him.

"He's unprotected," Aidan whispered as he rode.

Cameron nodded. "Yeah, I know. Intelligence never was his forte. The others must have ridden on."

"Yeah, I think so, too. I need to get Leigh outta there. Keep the goodie bag with you until I give the word."

Cameron reduced speed a bit. "You got it. Griswold and I will watch your rear."

Aidan nodded. "Good. Sable...Winter. I'm gonna need a distraction to get to Leigh. I need his eyes on somewhere else other than me, at least till I get onboard. I won't be able to if he spots me and starts fishtailing. You got that?"

Sable pulled up close to him. "No problem."

Pulling up to the sides, Sable and Winter moved up in front of the truck, keeping Tamar and Kieran occupied with what was in front of them. Kieran shook his head. "Fucking Aristans. Can't fault us for perseverance. But it's fucking annoying!" He punctuated the sentence with flicking his cigarette out the window. "Mow them down now!"

Tamar sped up, trying to close the distance between him and the two Aristan riders in front.

Aidan sped up directly behind the truck, inching closer and closer to the handle and ramp. He couldn't miss, or he would never be able to catch up to them again without his bike. He shifted his gear and flattened his body against the bike, getting to as much steady speed at possible. It was now or never. Aidan felt that sweet warmth coursing through his veins and, with superhuman prowess, leaped forward off the bike and landed on the ramp. Clutching the door handle, Aidan leaned in as he watched his bike swerve to the side and skid up the highway. Cameron and Griswold swerved out of the way as they caught up to him.

Tamar looked in his rearview mirror. "What the hell was that?"

Kieran peered into his side mirror and saw the bike, along with Griswold and Cameron following behind them. "We're being boxed! Get moving, asshole!"

Aidan broke the lock on the door and raised it just enough to roll in. Hearing the muffled, grunting noise in the darkness, his eyes adjusted to see a tied and gagged Leigh leaning against the crate of weapons. Her eyes were tired and her restricted movements dragging. He rushed to her. "Leigh? Leigh, are you hurt?" He pulled off the dirty cloth gag and smelled the familiar, spicy scent of wormwood oil. He tossed the gag away and untied her hands, hearing her mutter something in Aristan. "Leigh, I need you to focus! We gotta go, sis. C'mon!" He shook her until she finally focused on his face.

Leigh's eyes were wide and slowly turning amber as she stared at her brother, the bitter taste of the wormwood drug still on her bloodied tongue. His stupid face was a sight for sore eyes. "Inisi polaga dolgo, branakos?"

Aidan smoothed her hair back, seeing the relief in her eyes. Her beautiful blonde hair stained red with her blood. "Seriously? I've been rounding up a cavalry to get you. That's where I've been, you little ungrateful brat. He held her tight, squeezing her. "Don't make me come after you again."

"I can't make any promises." She retorted, as smug as her hazy mind would allow her.

Aidan scoffed. "Spoken like a Bloodlocke. Ninon would be proud. Now, let's get out of here."

He helped her up, just as the box truck swerved to the left, shifting them against the crates. Seemed like the secret was out that he was on board, by the swerving of the driver. And it was only a matter of time until it got too risky for her to jump. "C'mon Leigh! We gotta move!"

"Arrrgggh!"Leigh felt the fog in her head and couldn't shake the buzzing effects of the wormwood. If she couldn't fire at all cylinders, she would be an even bigger liability, and this wasn't the time to be weak. In desperation, she tried to focus on the change, in hope that it would allow her mind to heal as much as her body. The fire in her bones forced her to grow a foot taller, and the electric pulses within her begged to be released to the night. Leigh dropped on all fours and heaved, focusing on the moon until she felt the beginnings of the drug fog lifting.

Opening the door of the truck all the way, Aidan looked to Cameron. "Toss me the bag!" Cameron got in close, tossing in the bag of grenades to Aidan.

"What's that?" Leigh asked, trying to straighten her body.

"A way to destroy all these weapons," Aidan replied. He slung the bag over his shoulder. "I need you and Cameron to catch up to the rest of the kill squad that is heading straight for Tarrytown. The destruction of these weapons will help even the odds, but we still need numbers."

Leigh nodded in agreement; even her own compliance amazed her. "Okay, brother. What are you going to do about Kieran?"

Aidan's eyes lit with an intensity Leigh had never really seen before. "I think you know what I'm going to do. But I need you to get outta here!"

When they saw Leigh finally standing, Cameron and Griswold took it as a signal to flank the sides of the vehicle, as Aidan and Leigh climbed onto top of the truck. Cameron pulled up on the side, ducking traffic and swerves as Kieran and Tamar tried to wipe them out. He finally looked up at Leigh. "Hurry up, kittycat!"

Leigh focused her sights on Cameron and the bike, until finally she jumped off and landed behind him. The force of the landing swerved the bike, but Cameron veered off and gained control quickly.

"You two get the hell outta here and head to the community!" Aidan balanced his body on the top until he saw Kieran pull himself out of the cab of the truck from the window.

Kieran watched Cameron ride ahead with Leigh in tow, flipping him off as they sped past Winter and Sable. Griswold caught up, and all rode away. "You sneaky bitch!" He finally cast his yellow eyes at his lifelong rival, Aidan, and it felt like time itself slowed down for the both of them. So much rage and emotion bubbled between them. Betrayal. Deceit. Jealousy. Reckoning. Standing atop the speeding truck, where they felt like they were the only beings on the planet right now.

Aidan's body grew tight and incredibly controlled, as if they were standing still. Justice and vengeance were hungry to seduce him tonight. Who would win, he dared not ask."You have to stand accountable, Kieran, for what you've done. It's over!"

Kieran stretched and popped his body, letting his footwork atop the truck display his agility. "I should've known it was a matter of time before you stuck your fucking nose where it doesn't belong! Now, I'm gonna see to it you suffer every minute of your short life, Aidan!" He charged towards Aidan with such fury, he envisioned knocking Aidan's head clean off his body. He finally made contact and drilled Aidan to the truck top. Grappling, Aidan used his strength to push enough distance between them to connect a brutal hook to Kieran's face. And another.

Kieran tasted the sweet metallic flavor of his blood and smiled. "I find it amusing you're so bent on justice for a mother that wasn't even yours!"

Kieran hit Aidan with a left hook, forcing his face all the way to the right. "You have no mother. No one wanted you!" A right hook to the face. "You're a parasite!" Another left hook punch to Aidan, until Kieran yelped as Aidan gripped his hair and pulled him down. He butted his head against him and threw Kieran off him.

Aidan rebounded to his feet, and in a heartbeat kicked Kieran across the face, watching blood erupt from his mouth. The wind whipped around them as they grappled. "You whine like a bitch, Kieran." Grabbing his shirt, Aidan then kneed him in the stomach. "Very unbecoming of a supposed leader of the free and colorless." Kieran tried to block, but Aidan was far too fast and punched him so hard, his head bounced against the truck with a thud. Aidan reached for the bag strapped to him when Kieran swept his legs. Aidan crashed onto the truck top, but quickly rolled away from Kieran's foot as he stomped a dent into the steel truck.

"I'll show you a leader you could never be, Aidan!" Kieran's body trembled and shook, panting as his body started to double in size. Hair grew longer on his face and arms as his Aristan body met a perfect unison of wolf and man. It was the stuff of nightmares in the human world, and it was the sweet torture of their kind. When the moon was the fullest, Aristans were able to change into various stages of metamorphosis. Aidan growled as he watched Kieran turn and charge at him, unwilling to back down from a fight. He took the bag and swung it at Kieran's half-beast face. The hit connected but Kieran rebounded quickly, pulling Aidan down and punching him. The second punch he threw was a miss, but smashed a hole through the hull of the truck, where the bag of grenades fell through.

Aidan began to change and, as he rolled to the side, the force of his body growing forced him off the side of the truck, gripping the edge to regain balance.

Kieran's massive body approached the edge. His human face was barely recognizable, except for a semblance of an arrogant smirk. "You always was second best, Aidan." His otherworldly voice boomed. "You never could live up to the Bloodlocke name!"

Aidan had to get to those grenades. He looked up at Kieran. "Neither could you!" With all his strength, Aidan completed the change and pulled himself up. In full, swift force, Aidan tackled Kieran and pummeled him through the top of the truck. Both of them crashed down into the back of the truck as crates smashed around them.

Going blow for blow, they fought. Each punch, each kick, was a declaration of hate. As Kieran choked him, Aidan faintly heard the sound of sirens and began to reach for the bag of grenades. *Just a little more*, he told himself, as he struggled to clutch at least one of the explosives.

Kieran smiled. "Don't have much to say now, do you?" He turned his head at the cop car and sirens barreling down the dark highway towards them with sirens blaring. Recognizing the decal and colors, Kieran scoffed. "Friend of yours? That fucking Sheriff is going to get ripped apart! And as for you. I want you to look me in the eye and know that your death will be the first of many tonight from the Bloodlocke clan!"

Aidan roared, reared back and punched Kieran hard enough to hear the snap of his jaw. "You first...rogue." With that, he dropped the grenade between the rungs of the crates and leaped out the truck, landing on the hood of the cruiser.

"Gotcha!" Maddie yelled as she swerved a bit at the force of the catch. Aidan's body cracked the windshield and muddled her visibility, but she still managed to keep the car on the road.

Aidan glared at Kieran in the back of the truck and tossed the key from the pulled grenade back at him. "Keep the key, asshole!"

Aidan's face did a double take through the broken windshield as he recognized the driver. What the hell? "Fire in the hole!"

"Shit!" Maddie began easing off the gas, trying to put distance between them and the truck as it exploded. The heat from the blast radiated off the cruiser, and Maddie veered onto the shoulder, pulling to a stop as the box truck rolled on its side and skid to a slow halt.

Finally stopping since she fled the convenience store, Maddie put her head against the steering wheel and sighed. "I'm gonna need a tranquilizer." She jumped as Aidan tapped on the windshield. "I'm alive...barely." Maddie crashed her head back on the steering wheel until she heard and felt her car door open. Aidan pulled her out of the car. "What are you--"

She was silenced by his lips crashing against hers as Aidan pressed her against the side of the car. Embracing her tightly, he didn't really have the words for her. She was stubborn, reckless and completely amazing. She came back to help him at all costs, and it hit him terribly hard in the heart. He held her like she was life itself. His own angel who was much stronger than he ever imagined. "What am I gonna do with you, Maddie?"

Maddie gripped the cloth of his torn up shirt. "Just love me, because I love you, Aidan. I couldn't just leave. I couldn't. I'm in this with you."

Her words tore him apart. They stripped him down to his raw nature. The piece of him that longed to hear those words from her, and it made him feel invincible. He finally pulled back enough to look into her watery brown eyes. "Arista's hands, I love you too, Maddie." His thumbs rubbed the budding tears away. "You're amazing, xerhmon." He ran his lips against her cheek affection- ately. This woman did things to his soul that nothing could ever undo. "You're gonna have to tell me one day how you managed to steal a cop car."

"Yeah. Hopefully, it's not the day I'm wearing an orange jump- suit, talking to you behind glass." She gave a nervous chuckle.

He kissed her again. This time was quick as he looked at the remnants of the explosion.

Maddie squeezed his arm. "Is Kieran dead?"

"I'm going to find out." Aidan released her and tried to dodge around the superheated wreckage. He moved some debris around, but only bits of torn singed clothing remained. He cursed as hot metal burned his hands. He stopped as Maddie pulled the car up to the wreckage and got out bracing against the car door.

"Aidan! We can't stay here! Your people!"

He frowned at the debris before stepping away. He needed this closure, but she was right. The weapons were finally gone, but it's time to make the stand in Tarrytown. There wasn't a moment to lose. He turned and started for the car. "I know. We need to head up there. It's only a few miles up the road."

Maddie froze as he suggested a word she didn't expect. "We?"

Aidan smirked. "Yes, I think I know better than to try to send you away to safety. But you're driving, while I ride shotgun. No sirens. I don't want them to know we're coming."

With a nod, Maddie got into the cruiser and turned over the engine as Aidan slipped into the passenger's seat before she sped off down the highway. Now the urgency was meeting Devin and the others to show the colorless that no one terrorizes their pack.

33

RING OF FIRE

The night's darkness seemed to welcome the sly approaches of danger as Riko hushed the men to silence. The moonlight cast a soft blue tint across the tall, muscular bodies of Thesians and wayward Aristans that awaited the word of their leader to pounce on the quiet, unsuspecting community. But as they waited, ticks became tocks, and there was no sign of Kieran or the weapons. There was also no sign of Brody, who even being beaten, Riko expected to still show his face for battle. Everything they had worked for led to this moment. The colorless listened and respected him and Brody. They trusted them to keep their best interests at heart, despite them following a traitorous Aristan. When the guys told him Brody was not in the trucks with them, Riko assumed he was with Kieran. He grunted to himself. No one was dependable. *I should've known better.*

"Where the fuck is Kieran?" One of the Thesians whispered to Riko. Despite the low volume, his voice was terse with annoyance. "He's slighted us, I just know it! What the hell are we out here, standing like neutered assholes?"

"Shut up!" Riko replied, his eyes still watching the grounds. "We don't need him, or weak ass Brody."

"Like hell, we don't. That asshole had our weapons! What the fuck are we supposed to do now?"

Riko shook his head. Simple youngsters. "Our ancestors fought the Aristans for hundreds of years without our advanced weaponry."

"This is bullshit!"

A blond haired Thesian gave an arrogant smirk. Half of his face had an intricate tribal tattoo. "You can turn tail if you want, pussy, but I came here to take what's mine. With or without those shitty weapons!" He punctuated his haughty speech with a shove to the anxious Thesian, hungry to antagonize him.

A growl was his only response as the shoved Thesian's eyes trained on him, ready to teach him some manners. He bared his teeth, showing off his sharp canines as he started the circle the other Thesian.

Riko stepped between them and immediately broke them apart with a push to both of them. "I said shut up! You want to sound the alarm we're here?" Riko looked around and felt the tension mount between all of them. They were ready to tear something apart. Now whether that would be the Aristans or each other, that would be up to Riko's next move. He should've known not to trust a stupid Aristan with a chip on his shoulder. Brody was sadly right. The asshole only cared about his own gain. Now the brothers were tired, angry and needing support for all they had done for the cause. They were here for the money and reputation Kieran had promised them, so retreat was not going to be in their vocabulary. Something had to prove fruitful for them, or they would die trying.

"Screw this, Riko. We need to strike before they get wind of us." The blond Thesian whispered with his baritone voice. "We have the numbers, and I can still smell burnt wood in the air here. They barely recuperated. We can send a violent wave through this shitty excuse for an Aristan pack and lay waste to everyone without so much as a sweat!"

The other Thesian scoffed. "He's right. We haven't even seen a single Azan guard patrolling. It's like a candy store, Riko."

"You're right. Now's the time to move in." Riko tightened his grip on his bat, and turned to the panting and ravenous beasts in front of him. "We have the element of surprise, so use it! Two sets break into flanks on the left and right. Move towards the bungalows, and those with Molotov cocktails start to slash and burn. That will drive 'em out. Now, let's move!"

Under the cover of darkness, Riko and the others moved past the brushes, blending in with the night as they started to close in around the commune like locusts in a wheat field. From what Nornos and Brody told him before, fire was pretty effective in creating the confusion to scatter the Aristans. Most had been in their bungalows, unaware until it was too late for some of them. So eager to protect their spawn and elderly, Kieran and the boys had picked many off by the distraction alone.

Looking ahead, he and the others saw the town hall building with light in the windows. That was exactly what they were looking for. He knew they were somewhere and it was almost too good to be true to have most of them in one place. But then again, Aristans were known to parade around as one unit. They didn't have sense not to put all of their manpower in one group. Riko signaled to the group on the left flank to get ready to fire bomb the building.

Quietly, they moved through the community, which felt a little like a ghost town. The bungalows were silent, and no light shone in them. Riko began to wonder if many of them left the area, but as he focused on the town hall, he wasn't convinced all of them were gone. Probably holed up in there, praying to Arista for protection. Real cute. Riko remembered how smug the Aristan Alpha treated him, and was ready for a little payback. He wasn't keen on Kieran's ridiculous rivalry until the asshole came and screwed up his bar and smacked him around. It was time for some justice, with or without that lunatic.

Finally, one of the Thesians kicked down the door of a bungalow, splitting the wood apart to find nothing but smashed, abandoned belongings. He scoffed and continued on till they stood before the town hall. Riko frowned and tilted his head at the team leader at the left flank "Torch it!"

Several Thesians flung their combustible bottles with force through the town hall windows, watching them smash into a bloom of flames. Some of them chuckled at the growing flames, anticipating screaming to soon follow. But as they stood watching for a minute, they were denied amusement. There was no screaming. No movement. No flailing.

They turned to Riko, who looked equally stunned. "What the hell is going on?!"

His question was answered by the howling of wolves that seemed to come from all over. Growling, Riko frantically looked around until he saw the amber eyes of Aristans in wolf skin stalk from both the left and right flanks. A white wolf and all black wolf stood before them as the Thesians stood still and at the ready.

Riko growled as the white wolf's electric blue eyes narrowed to thin slits as he stepped forward. "What is this?"

Cameron, in his white wolf's skin, whispered to Riko in a low, dangerous tone. "*You're trespassing, Thesian. Your very breath right now insults us, and if you want a slightest chance of survival, I wouldn't move an inch more, or we will tear you to pieces. You and your wayward, colorless brothers.*"

As some of the colorless tried to back up, they were met with more wolves behind them, and warning shots of arrows at their heels. Cutting through the sea of heaving, muscle bound Aristan wolves were Devin and Winter. Both wielded a crossbow and a grin. "Ohhh, I just knew when I got outta bed this morning I'd get to use my toys on some naughty Thesian trash!" She cocked her head and smiled at Riko. "Hiya Reeks."

He scowled at her. "Devin, what the hell are you doing here? We had a truce, dammit!"

Winter shook his head. "That's right. 'Had' being the key word, shit for brains."

Devin nodded. "And that truce went bye bye as soon as I learned that you were in bed with some lunatic Aristan and ready to tear down this pack over his madness. It's a shame, really. I would've preferred peace. We could've been the first two Alphas to show the world we could co-exist." She loaded another arrow into her crossbow, and a gave a nonchalant shrug. "Oh well." Devin raised it to aim right at his head. "This arrow may have been dipped in nightshade... Maybe not. But make a move, and we'll certainly find out."

The fire continued to grow and started to trail around the community of bungalows. The flames hastily sprinting across the grass as it quickly began to encircle the Thesians in a blazing ring of fire with the Aristans inside.

Cameron sneered. "Now, it's much too late for you to leave. You're mine!" His internal voice continued on. "Azans!"

The Azans began to call to the moon and spread out behind in formation on the outer flanks. Some were still in their biker gear, while others were either nude or half-nude, ready to morph and tear the colorless limb from limb. They stood there, praying, waiting for the order from their beta leader to set them free on the enemy.

Tension among the confused colorless wolves threatened to hit a fever pitch as the horrible realization of an ambush set in. But some were not willing to go down easy.

"To hell with this! My brother burned alive in that B&B attack. I want blood!" The blonde Thesian roared, and immediately morphed into second stage change. Charging for Devin, the blonde Thesian triggered the others to attack. Dodging her arrow, he leaped to the plateau where she stood, only to meet the brutal force of her fist. Growling, Devin grew in size, ripping her suit as her sharp nails dug into the gruff flesh of his throat as he picked her up and threw her down below. With lightening speed, the Thesian warrior jumped down to land on top of her. Devin quickly rolled out of the way as he landed inches from her with an arrow through his throat. Devin looked up to see Winter giving her a nod as he dropped his empty crossbow, before grabbing another wolf to toss.

"Atenya!," Cameron yelled the Aristan battle cry for 'attack', and the Azans flooded into the fray. The ground rocked with the showdown of Aristans and Thesians. The only serenity was the light of the moon that shone upon them, quickly being drowned out by the orange flames that engulfed the territory once more.

Cameron and Onyx began ripping through the crowd as Thesians and colorless Aristans alike began to fight. The flames encircled them all now, forcing them to attack and defeat the other. Cameron tackled, clawed and mauled until his teeth was stained with the blood of his rivals. The dark metallic taste of blood dulled his tongue, and all he could think of was that the Thesians wanted them dead, and that wasn't going to happen without a fight.

Two of the Thesians wrestled Onyx to the ground as one savagely bit through his leg. He howled in pain as one bit danger-ously close to his throat. Leigh, in human skin, suddenly pounced on the biting Thesian and forced him off as he ran, trying to free her from him. This allowed Onyx to rebound and kill the other Thesian, breaking his neck with his teeth in two places before running off to attack another. His blood was red hot and lit with a fuel to fight and protect by any means necessary.

Leigh's hair flung about, holding on tightly as the Thesian wolf bucked and growled to get her off him. Building her strength, Leigh roared, and with all her might pulled him down to the dirt on top of her. The putrid scent of bloody, wet fur threatened to smother her as she continued to strangle him. In a heartbeat, she heard a thud and the wolf gave his death howl, relaxing his muscles against her. Pushing his massive body away, Devin assisted and pulled her blade out of the dead Thesian's head. She offered her hand, which Leigh grasped to pull herself up to her feet. She nodded in gratitude. "Thanks."

Devin wiped her blade and gave her a wink. "Anytime." Hearing a car engine coming close, Devin pushed Leigh back just as a sheriff's cruiser came crashing through the clearing and through the ring of fire, flinging Thesian bodies into the air as it came to a sudden halt.

Leigh smiled at the sight of the cruiser. "Aidan!"

"Well, I'll be damned. Took him long enough!" Devin added.

As Aidan leaped out, he grabbed a Thesian and threw him against a tree, crushing him. It was an all out war there, and no one was backing down yet.

He turned to Maddie. "You can't stay here! Get to high ground and watch your back!" Aidan turned back and slugged Riko, knocking him back several feet against another wolf. "Remember me, asshole. If you're smart, you'll stay down." Aidan warned as he charged against another Thesian rebel.

Maddie's eyes followed the chaos they'd just driven into. Humans, wolves, and half-beasts fought with fist, teeth and claw. The smell of blood and fire singed her nostrils and escalated her breathing. Some flung over the car, and some pushed against it, denting and degrading the integrity of poor Sheriff McTiernan's car. She had promised Aidan she would try to stay out of the main event if everything was going south, and try to protect only those who were vulnerable. Looking around at the massive, fighting creatures pummeling each other, she quickly realized the vulnerable were not here. Yep, it was time to get the hell outta there.

Riko pulled himself up and growled as he saw the little courtesha in the car. She was trouble everywhere he saw her. He wiped the blood from his lips and charged towards the car. Rage fueling him, Riko grabbed the car door to the back seat and ripped it off to get to Maddie.

"You little--"

His wide eyes focused on the 12 gauge shotgun aimed at him. The sound of the gun cocking and the blast was the last thing he heard before dropping to the ground, missing most of his face.

Panting, Maddie cocked it again, ready for any other surprises before she made a run for it. Maddie screamed as the car window behind her was smashed, glass flinging about. Strong hands pulled her and her shotgun through the window as a large wolf jumped in the backseat where she was moments ago. The large foot of her captor kicked the wolf in the face.

"Get your goddamn hands off me!" She hissed and struggled before she focused on Aidan's wide, green eyes glaring at her. He had a game face that could make any mortal cower. "Oh."

Aidan looked over her, watching her back, then arched an eyebrow as he cut his eyes back to her. "Baby, you're sexy as hell right now. But you're gonna give me a fucking heart attack if you don't get the hell outta here!" He ducked and pulled her close as a Molotov cocktail flew past them. He kissed her and nudged her between the path between two bungalows. "Head past the town hall building to the church! We keep the children and elderly there. Go now!"

Maddie didn't look back as she clenched the shotgun in her hands and ran past the flaming bungalows until the burning town hall was in front of her. Her chest was constricting as she heaved breaths, adrenaline her only fuel as she bulldozed through the thick, grassy field. But her panting breath wasn't without company. Quickly glancing behind, her eyes caught a giant grey and black wolf fast approaching, snarling as it trampled with gaining speed. As if a light switched on within her, Maddie went into hyperdrive and moved past the town hall. Panic shot through her bones as the sound of the snarling and panting got closer. Simple logic ran through her mind as a split second reaction was made.

Maddie stopped running, turned around and aimed the shotgun at the wolf charging toward her. The wolf made a leap forward, and in the moments where time seemed to slow to a halt, Maddie locked eyes with the furious beast before she pulled the trigger. A howl cried out into the field and Maddie screamed as the wolf collapsed, less than a foot from where she fell to the ground.

Scrambling away backwards, Maddie felt hands pull her up.

Her heart caught in her throat from the surprise. She sighed, seeing it was Leigh.

"Arista's hands, Maddie, are you alright?!" Leigh found her answer as she watched the giant Thesian rogue wolf take his last breath. He must've been six times Maddie's size and running like a freight train. "Holy shit!"

Maddie's body still trembled under the weight of the incident. "If I continued to run, he would've either caught up to me, or I would've led him to the children. I had no choice."

Leigh turned to her and grabbed her hand, pulling her to run with her. "C'mon, let's get to the church. It isn't safe out here!"

Aidan punched a colorless wolf and smashed his face down to the dirt. Backing up, he felt himself back into another person. Whipping his head around, Aidan saw his naked, white-haired beta, Cameron. The only white left on him was his hair as his nude body was streaked with blood; most likely someone else's.

"Hey! Just like old times, eh Aidan?" Cameron yelled as he held a massive Thesian in a headlock and squeezed his arms to crack his neck.

Aidan threw his opponent down and kicked him in the ribs. "I don't know what part of old times you're referring to, Cam. The part where we're knee-deep in Thesians, or the part where you tend to reminisce about old times with your balls out."

Cameron shrugged. "Both?"

Aidan looked around and saw the numbers of the colorless were waning. He saw his Azans scattered about and had an idea. He jumped onto a giant rock next to Cameron and whistled.

Suddenly, the second string of Azans came out of the woods behind him, standing at attention. His second string were his most seasoned soldiers. Every single one of them had fought and bled along with him as he'd climbed the ranks as their general.

"Azans!"

They all shouted in unison, "Ha-oot!"

"We end this tonight! This is the last time we will live in an aftermath of terror. Tonight, we will not allow another of ours to fall." Aidan's green eyes turned amber as his body grew in size. A dark sneer crept over his handsome face. "Crush them into the fire wall until they flee, die or burn!" He jumped down from the rock to lead them. "Sweep!"

They moved in a semi circle on the outer edge, shrinking the fight area. As they closed in, the first string Azans joined them and attacked with exponential force, destroying and fighting as they slowly crushed the colorless on top of each other against the wall of fire behind them. Yells and howls invaded the night as one by one the colorless either fell, ran or were engulfed in the flames. Tonight, these pyres would be for the ones who terrorized, not for the victims. By the light of Arista, Aidan vowed to make it known with blood and fire tonight.

The smoky air wafted through the commune as whatever remaining Thesians retreated into the darkness of the forest and river bank. The fallen were left behind, abandoned in the dirt spilled with blood and fur.

Aidan calmed his body, returning to his human skin. *Maddie*, he thought. He turned around to see her and Leigh walking with a child in her arms. Her brown eyes lighting up as she saw him, Maddie quickly handed the child to an elder. "Aidan!" Dropping her gun, she ran directly into his arms as Aidan crushed her against him, lifting her off the ground.

"Maddie...," he breathed her name against her damp curls. He closed his eyes and breathed in her scent. Beneath the soot, sweat and blood remained his beautiful mate. Courageous in spirit and holding true possession over his heart. "Are you okay?"

"Mmm hmm." She nodded. Her eyes watched as the Azans glared at them with puzzled and strange expressions. Her breathing quickened. She'd forgotten that the Aristans would not welcome an outsider. It was clear that Aidan, Leigh, and Cameron had no qualms, but that didn't mean she wasn't in any danger. What if they wouldn't allow her and Aidan to be together?

Maddie sighed against him until, out the corner of her eye, she saw a dark figure pointing something at them. The masculine figure stood erect with bright yellow eyes staring at them. At Aidan. In a blink of an eye, she recognized what the man was holding and quickly jumped against Aidan, shielding him as the night echoed a gunshot.

Pain sliced through her as they both fell to the ground, her body on top of him.

Aidan lifted his head to see an unconscious Maddie.

"Maddie? Maddie!" His hand touched her arm and felt the warm wetness of blood. It pooled out of her, and he frantically pulled her close. Horror washed over his eyes as he sat up and saw the bullet wound in her upper shoulder. "No, no, no, no, no! Maddie! Maddie!" His voice breaking, he leaned over her and shook her. Leigh ran to her side and laid her down to look at her. She immediately put pressure on the wound as her eyes glanced to Aidan, who was trembling. Shock and turmoil bubbled underneath his surface, and it was really hard not to change. He watched as his mate lay quiet on the ground, and all he could see was her blood.

Aidan, nearly blind with rage, turned to finally focus on the culprit. There before him stood a bloodied, battered Kieran. Part of his face was charred, as were most of his clothes, as an indicator that he had narrowly escaped the truck explosion. His hand with the gun was still extended out.

"Shit. That shot was meant for you. Not your whore." He shrugged. "Oh well, there's more where that came from." He pulled the trigger and froze as the familiar click of an empty chamber rang out. He racked the slide and pulled the trigger again. Nothing.

Kieran tossed the gun and laughed. "Whoops! You lucked out, Aidan, my boy. Perhaps dear old Mom was right about you after all. Arista certainly has her blessings on you." He began to clap. "Bully for you. Perhaps we share the same luck. Bet you weren't expecting me to show, right?" He coughed up some blood and wiped his drooling mouth. Kieran looked around at the aftermath. "A little late, yeah, I know. But, traffic was a killer."

Leigh scowled at him, "You will pay for what you've done."

Kieran scoffed. "Shut up, sis. I'm not the only offender, you know. Where's old Bastien? I bet he's harboring some secrets, hmm? Come out, come out old man! The gig is up!"

Leigh lifted her head. "He's dead."

Kieran's grin dissolved and stared at Leigh. "Bullshit."

"I should know. I executed him myself for treason. Of cavorting with you, you arrogant, loony piece of shit!"

Kieran gritted his teeth. "Mind your manners, sis. You don't wanna end up like mommy, do ya?"

Aidan slowly slid away from Maddie as Leigh and Onyx worked on her. His deep breaths did nothing to calm him. Nothing to appease the beast within him. The beast that wanted justice for all Kieran had done was fast approaching reckoning. And as the heavens held Arista, Aidan vowed there would be a reckoning. He continued to walk toward him, and Kieran chuckled maniacally.

"What? You're pissed because I put down your little human bitch? Don't worry, cause you're gonna join her!"

Aidan's steps grew in determination as his stone face zeroed in on Kieran. His body leaped forward and, with superhuman strength, reared back and punched. "Ninon was right. You were the only one in the pack who never belonged. You were more a threat and a stranger than there ever could have been. Isn't it ironic? The one who fought so hard to be Alpha to the Aristans has become Omega to the Thesians."

Kieran growled. "I'm Omega to no one! They are my followers! You think those Thesian mutts know anything about victory and honor? Of taking what's rightfully yours? They were nothing until I showed them the way! Just like your clan is lost without me now!"

Aidan grinned with fanged teeth. "Don't worry. None of it will matter in a few minutes."

Kieran gritted his teeth, flinging everything he had at Aidan.

Meeting his eyes. "You took everything from me, you parentless bastard. All my dreams were ripped from me by a worthless rogue pup!"

The Aristans gathered, slowly forming a Selenium Circle. The same ritual that determined the next Alpha and sometimes the judgment of offenders. No one went in or out until a victor was declared.

Kieran swung and missed, flinging his beaten, tired body around, picking up momentum. Aidan viciously connected a hook to the face, and two to the midsection, hearing Kieran groan at the beating.

Finally, Kieran charged toward Aidan, who kicked him in the ribs and connected several jabs to his already bloodied face before collapsing to the ground.

Aidan stood over him, looking down at his rival-once-brother down in the dirt. He was pathetic, weak and violent. Worst of all, murderous of his own. There was no rehabilitation for their kind. No second chances. No mercy. His fury wanted to viciously rip him apart and make him suffer. He ached to exact that pain upon the murderer of his mother. But as he looked up to see everyone watching him, including Leigh and a barely conscious Maddie, Aidan knew he had to do this right. With a nod from Leigh, Aidan looked back down to Kieran and proceeded to judge him.

"Kieran Bloodlocke, for the horrendous crimes of murder, siege, mayhem and treason, I as Alpha of the Bloodlocke clan, sentence you to death."

"You treasure this, Alpha. After all, it's in your blood, rogue wolf." Kieran choked out before the snap of his neck silenced him forever.

A fierce wave of relief coursed through him as Aidan howled to the moon. Others joined him.

Aidan ran to Maddie, whose eyes were slightly open. "Maddie, baby. Just stay calm, you're gonna be okay." He looked up to Onyx for confirmation, but his brows furrowed with concern.

"It's a nightshade bullet, Aidan. Lucky for you, it lodged in her shoulder. If it would have struck you or went through her, it would've been over for you. But it's lodged in there deep and there are fragments. Our kind can't pull it out. She needs a hospital or she's gonna bleed out."

He gently lifted her head. Pools of water formed under his eyes as he stared at her. She'd saved his life again. Despite what was right, his emotions got the best of him. "What the hell are you trying to do out here, Maddie? Huh? Give me a heart attack?"

Maddie's eyes opened a bit more, pain clearly visible in her glossy pupils. "Something like that."

Aidan bit back tears and smoothed her brown curls back from her face. This wasn't the life he meant for her. She deserved better, and whether or not she found it a problem, she clearly didn't understand how much Aidan wanted to see her happy in a normal life. "Didn't I tell you I would lose my shit if anything ever happened to you?"

Maddie's face was pale and her voice raspy. "And did I ever tell you that I would lose my shit if anything ever happened to you, Aidan?" She reached up and touched his face, trailing her finger down the path of his tear. Her heart ached as she never would've expected to see him cry for her. Pain throbbed through her, but she held no regrets. Despite the crazy logic in her head, she had a much better chance surviving a gunshot from a nightshade bullet than Aidan. As she felt a chill creep up her body, Maddie hoped the logic rang true.

Aidan started to pick her up. "I'm taking her to the hospital now!" He hoisted her up and into his arms when an old brown pickup truck hastily rolled in through the once gated entrance. Everyone on edge, the night filled with growls of warning from the tired Aristans until a familiar face stumbled out from the truck. Aidan took a breath.

"What the hell are you doing here, McTiernan?"

The Sheriff threw up his arms as he was greeted with lots of yellow eyes and ferocious growls. He likened the feeling to walking into a lion's den. "After dear old Doc stole my car, I had to bully the cashier to give me his keys. I came to check on you and the Doc." His eyes cut to the woman bleeding in Aidan's arms and recognized a bleeding, half-conscious Maddie Ardelle. "Shit, Doc. What happened?"

"She's shot and she needs to get to the hospital fast. We can't help her here!"

McTiernan nodded. "C'mon. We'll take her now! He hopped back in the driver's side and leaned over to open the passenger side.

Aidan quickly moved to the passenger side and gently sat Maddie upright. "It's gonna be okay, xerhmon. I'm coming with you."

Maddie opened her eyes and put her hand against Aidan's chest. "You can't, Aidan."

"What the hell do you mean? Watch me."

Maddie shook her head. It was then she finally understood his love for her. So much that he was willing to leave his duties behind to tend to her. But he was made for this. Whether he knew it or not, Aidan was the leader his people needed. He was the friend and brother Leigh and Cameron needed. He was the man she needed. Flattering as it felt, she couldn't allow him to focus on her when the greater picture mattered the most.

"You're needed here, Aidan." She cut her eyes to the group of Aristans watching. They had just been through hell. "I'll be fine, but they need you right now and I can't deny them that."

Aidan's green eyes dropped. "Maddie..."

"You can't deny them that. Not for me. I can't have you do that." She felt the sting behind her eyes but prayed the tears wouldn't materialize. She squeezed his hand and gave a tired smile. "You put the pieces back together, Aidan. That's what you do. That's what you're good at."

Aidan leaned in and kissed her lips. His people needed to find a new territory and rebuild. There were losses and terror and betrayals and they had to heal from it all. They needed their Alpha to do what was best for the pack. As painful as Maddie's words were to him, she was right. He had to put the pieces back together.

Maddie pulled the pendant chain off and handed it to him. "You can always bring it to me to hold for you again." *I hope, just like your heart.*

Aidan clenched the pendant in his hand, flecks of her blood staining the beautiful medallion. His eyes locked on hers and, as if they said all they'd wanted to say, Aidan closed the door to the truck as the Sheriff backed up and finally drove off. He stood silent as the truck drove off with the bravest, most beautiful soul he'd ever met...leaving him behind.

THE THIRD TOWN

A idan stood outside the boarded up town hall building, waiting for Onyx and the others to finish their discussion. Soon, it would be his turn to discuss the future of the pack, along with choosing a new place to call home.

In the aftermath of the battle, Aidan was thankful that Cameron was at his side to help with the organizing of the pack. There were times where his thoughts would trail off and all he could think of was Maddie. McTiernan kept in contact with him, and though he assured she was doing fine, it just wasn't enough. Aidan missed her voice and longed to hear it again. But she didn't call him, and when he called, she didn't answer.

She took a bullet for you. She probably came to her senses and decided this wasn't the life she wanted.

Aidan clenched his fists, as his thoughts once again raced with the musings of the woman who'd snuck into his heart. There were days where he found himself naked and alone in the woods, as if his animal half went out in the wild, determined to go to her. At some point, exhaustion would take over, leaving him to awaken, disoriented and crestfallen. The wild beast within him was desperate to be with its mate, and lately, that part of him seemed to have the most sense. *I hated and loved that you made me stay, Maddie. I'm not gonna stop till I find a way back to you.*

"You're gonna be okay?" Devin's voice broke his concentration and he looked up at her fire engine red hair blowing in her face. The scars and wounds on her appeared to have all healed, revealing smooth, olive skin as she flung her biker jacket over her shoulder. "You seem preoccupied with something." She waited a beat before speaking again. "Or someone."

Aidan cleared his throat, pushing his body off the sidewalk rail. He faced her with a quiet, polite smile. "My brain never shuts off. I'm sure you can relate to the feeling, Alpha."

Devin scoffed. "Oh please. I can't lose sleep over my wayward pack of guys. They'd laugh in my face if I told them I secretly worried about them." She quickly looked around, making sure no one but Aidan heard her say those words.

"I saw you talking to Onyx earlier. Did he convince you to merge with us?" Aidan already knew the answer to it, but it was more of a way to pry on what they were conversing about.

Devin smiled and shook her head. "I think you know better than that. Merging is only acceptable when a pack has no viable choice for an Alpha, or one is willing to concede or mate to the other to unite the two into one."

Aidan nodded.

"Well, no offense, Bloodlocke, but our packs have strong, relentless Alpha leaders. So strong, that I know that neither is willing to concede to the other. And your heart, as fighting and celebrated as it is, belongs to another."

Devin watched as Aidan's eyes dipped in sadness at the mention of Maddie. "How is she?"

"Still in Bridgepoint. She's healing and back at her practice. She's also not speaking to me."

"Well, go to her."

"She told me to stay and take care of my pack." Aidan sighed. "What if I go to her and she decided that this life is not for her? She's worked so hard to rebuild her life. To build her own practice and sense of self. I can't just roll up to her, ask her to run away with me and come live in our commune. It isn't fair to her - and not to mention dangerous." He still had to own up to having not one, but two humans involved with the recent battle. Onyx and the others hadn't brought it up yet, but he knew it was probably the area of discussion going on in the charred town hall as Devin and he spoke.

Devin gave a small shrug with empathetic eyes. "Then let her go."

"I wish it were that simple."

Devin crossed her arms. "I get that. Let me ask you something, Aidan, and I want you to tell me the truth."

Aidan raked his fingers through his hair. "Okay, ask me."

With eyes trained on him, Devin asked. "What if being with your mate meant walking away from your pack? Would you still choose her?"

"Yes."

She arched an eyebrow. "But you'd still be unsatisfied, right?

Aidan nodded truthfully. "Yes."

Devin inclined her head to him. "Why?"

"Because I love Maddie just as much as I love my people. They are family and I want Maddie to be a part of this family. The group of people who took me in when I should've been abandoned. The selfless woman who saved me. I need both. 'cause I'd be lost without either one. When the Bloodlockes' pack found me, I had no identity. I had no family. Just an angry, hollow shell that was tired of being betrayed and alone. I was just a kid, I know, but I had a terrible, violent past. I could've been like Kieran. I'm sure that is what those like Bastien expected. But I wasn't, because of the family that found me. It wasn't till I met Maddie that I realized I was deserving of their love. That I just may be deserving of hers." He chortled at his confession, realizing what it really meant. "I'm a greedy asshole, alright. I thought I had everything I needed until I met her."

A smirk grew on Devin's face. "No, you're not greedy, Aidan.

You just want what everyone wants. That's not greed, that's normal." She cast her eyes to the town hall doors as they began to open. Devin looked back at Aidan and winked. "So go and live the best of both worlds."

Onyx stepped through the doors and nodded to them both. "Aidan, we're ready for you. Hello, Devin. Are you coming in?"

Devin shook her head. "Nah. It's time me and my crew head out. We have a lot to do and we're losing daylight." Devin extended her right hand to Aidan. "I'll see you around, Alpha. Think about what I said."

Winter, Griswold and the others pulled up their bikes and sat in idle in front of the town hall, apparently awaiting word from Devin.

Aidan gave her a soft smile as he shook her hand. "This pack is in your debt for supporting us, Devin. I appreciate everything you've done for us."

"Hmm. I'll keep that in mind. One day, I may come to collect."

With that, Devin clicked her tongue, slipped on her jacket, then simultaneously put on her shades and straddled her bike.

Cameron walked past her and lightly lifted his chin with respect. Devin grinned deviously and started her bike, riding off with a slew of others trailing behind her.

As Aidan entered the town hall, Cameron followed behind him. "You're late, beta."

Cameron gave a sloppy, mocking salute. "Yeah, well, I lost my clock in the fire."

"You know, that excuse is not going to work *all* the time."

Cameron grinned. "Lately, it has."

Aidan and Cameron stood side by side as Onyx closed the doors, closing all the pack inside. Aidan watched as Onyx pulled up a chair and sat next to the only other elder left: Vega. Aidan turned to see his Azans come in behind him. Their faces were all familiar, quiet and very stoic. He'd taught them well, as he had no idea if they loved him or hated him right now. Perhaps it was just as well until everything was sorted out.

Onyx and Vega both rose from their seats and stared at Aidan. Onyx stepped forward. "Alright, we have a lot to go over, so let's get started. After Tiberius died, it was his wish that the council maintain the operations of the pack until his sons were ready to fight in the Selenium Circle. Once an Alpha was chosen, the council would dissolve." He turned to look to Vega then back to Aidan. "Today, we are going to honor that request."

Aidan furrowed his brows.

Onyx smiled. "You and your beta have shown amazing leadership, protecting our pack. You are resourceful, strong, and above all, loyal to your people. The elders have no reason not to entrust this pack, your family, into your very capable hands."

With an air of calm, Aidan replied. "Thank you, Elders." He glanced at the smiling faces of the pack and sighed. "I would like to address the issue of the Aristan law and my human allies who have assisted us when we needed it most."

Vega raised his eyebrow. "Oh?"

"It's important that I'm forthcoming and honest on this situation if you and the others are going to trust me with pack decisions."

Onyx nodded. "Go on."

"The law states that Aristans are not to reveal ourselves to human, nor fraternize."

Vega nodded. "Yes, that is the law. It is older than all of us and designed to protect our people and humans alike."

Aidan put his hands behind his back. "This is true, and clearly I have broken this law. I have revealed our true nature to Madeline Ardelle and the Sheriff of Bridgepoint. They have sworn to keep it secret, and I trust them. I ask that whatever punish I must face, that I alone face it and not them. Please, spare them, as they made sacrifices to help me."

The town hall rumbled with incoherent chatter, until Onyx raised his hand. "Aidan. We were there when the woman Maddie came to fight alongside us."

Leigh stood up. "I was there when she killed a Thesian to protect the children."

Onyx smiled. "And I was there when she saved your life, Lukos. Lucky for you, Vega and I are no longer in the business of enforcing old laws, but even if we did, we would not harm Maddie or the Sheriff. They have earned their place as an ally to the Aristans, so we seek no punishment."

Though Aidan's face held a stern expression, tension lessened from his body at those words. All he wanted as Maddie to be safe and to live her life. "Thank you."

Vega smiled. "It is as your father Tiberius said long ago: Laws without compassion are like a blade without its sheath."

"Eventually, it erodes away the precision, till only dullness remain," Aidan added.

He glanced at Leigh, who was smiling ear to ear with approval. She couldn't remember how many times she'd heard those words from her mother and father. And to finally see them in action and Aidan standing as the pack's true Alpha, Leigh couldn't help but look upwards hoping that her mother and father were just as proud as she. Aidan gave her a soft smile before turning to face the whole of the pack.

"The first order of business is that we decide on our new territory. I know that many of you have expressed that though Tarrytown has been this pack's home of many years, the recent attacks have left us with dark memories of terror and loss." His gaze dropped to the floor for a moment. "I, for one, understand this feeling." He looked back to the crowd. "But whatever we do, we will do as a unit. Together to rebuild and start a new life where we can continue to grow our future."

His words were met with claps and howling.

"I advise we find a new territory and build a new commune. This location has been exposed not once, but twice to our enemies. Many of our structures are too damaged to mend. We would have to demolish everything just to rebuild again. In a new place, we can make it as we see fit. All in favor?"

A resounding shout of agreement from the pack welcomed him.

Aidan crossed his arms. "Very well. The Azans had done scouting before the fray began. The three locations will be up for vote by this afternoon." His thoughts cut short as he felt Cameron's hand on his shoulder. Aidan turned to him long enough to grab the slip of paper from his hand. As he read the three locations, he shot his eyes to Cameron. "This can't be right."

Cameron nodded. "Yes it is. All three are viable locations for us. Devin suggested one and I seconded the vote, as well as all the Azans and the Elders. It's legit."

Aidan stared at his friend with confused admiration. His fingers traced over the letters of the location name as if he couldn't believe it to be real. Why would Devin propose such a thing? To even be a viable option, her pack would have to leave the area and find a new territory. It didn't make any sense.

"So go and live the best of both worlds." Aidan remembered her words.

He looked at Onyx, who stood quiet. A hint of complacency in his smirk. "We don't need to wait till later to vote. I suggest we do it right here, right now, Alpha. I think we are ready." He motioned to the pack. "Am I right?"

Clapping and shouting served as a response to his question.

Aidan took a deep breath and began to read aloud. "Option one. All in favor for Lincoln territory? Step up and use your voice."

Despite the light mumbling, there was no one who voted for that territory.

"Option two. All in favor for selecting the Portage Lake territory… step up and use your voice."

Nothing but crickets. Aidan scowled, wondering if people were really understanding what they were supposed to be doing. "No one would like to move to Portage Lake area?" His eyes widened as he saw scattered members of the pack actually shake their heads. "Okay, no votes for this option." Aidan kept staring at last territory name on the paper. His throat drying, he cleared it quickly and looked up at the pack. His family and friends that he would give his life for. He offered them the last option. "Option three. All those in favor for selecting the Bridgepoint territory for our new commune...step up and--"

His voice was drowned out by boisterous howling, clapping and cheering. The Azans and Cameron next to him were just as loud with their approval. Onyx, Vega and Leigh were all smiles, clapping as well their vote to move the pack to Maddie's home.

Cameron slapped Aidan's back and leaned into his ear. "Sounds like a unanimous decision from your people, Alpha."

Onyx stepped forward. "We have chosen the Bridgepoint territory. We'll rally together tomorrow to start organizing the move, including purchasing the land. Alpha, let us know what we can do for you in your absence while you purchase the property."

Flabbergasted, Aidan simply smiled. "Thank you, Onyx."

"The pleasure's mine, Aidan. It always has been."

As they exited the town hall, Leigh playfully punched Aidan in the kidney, forcing him to turn into her embrace. She squeezed him so tight, like she was hugging more than just him. "Look at you, bro! All grown up and stuff. Mom and Dad would've been so proud." She stepped back and smiled.

Such a rare thing to see from his sister, but when Leigh did it, she looked the very image of Ninon. Happiness glowed on her face and it warmed his heart to see it after all that had happened. "Thank you, sis. I was going to say the same thing about you. I couldn't have been gifted with more a kinder, stronger sister."

Cameron rolled his eyes. "I'm sure if you'd just prayed to Arista, she probably would've gifted you a better one." He erupted with laughter till he received a punch in the side; a bit harder than she'd given Aidan. "Ow! Kittycat! Relax!"

"Arrggh! Stop calling me that!" She shrieked as she punched him again.

Aidan got in between them like a parent between two children. "I still don't understand how this happened. How will we do this? Why would Devin--"

Cameron shrugged. "It was her idea. She talked with Onyx and they negotiated a deal. She'll have a new larger and sanctioned territory to own for her pack, so we could take over Bridgepoint." He sobered from his playfulness and continued. "The pack is well aware of the impact of Maddie, Aidan, and how you feel about her. This would be the first time we would have human allies to help us...the first time we welcome a human mate."

Aidan's body tensed at those words. "And that doesn't freak you out?"

"Hell no. We're a younger generation, Aidan. It's time we break into a few firsts. You know you always have my support. Besides, I like her. She's strong, kind, and must love the hell outta you for taking a bullet. She's a keeper, Aidan. We could all see that."

Aidan couldn't help but smile, hugging his friend before running off the steps to Cameron's bike. Cameron frowned. "Hey! What are you doing?"

Aidan slipped on his shades and turned on the engine. "You know exactly what I'm doing."

Cameron gave a nervous chuckle. "Uh, okay! But do you have to do it with my bike?"

"Yep! Mine's totaled. Let Leigh drive you around!"

Before Cameron could retort, Aidan grounded the tires into the lot, spinning its wheels until he finally sped off with the evening sun on his back.

MYLAIGH

THREE WEEKS LATER...

Maddie felt like a zombie all day. She thought about closing early a few times, but figured the work would serve as a distraction. Nothing really helped. She kept convincing herself that it was for the best. Aidan was needed with his people. He'd found a home, and love and respect. She couldn't have him barter that for her. She of all people know how important it was to find a place to belong--a place that was yours. His pack looked up to him and trusted him. She knew they needed him to make things better for them. It was the gracious thing to do.

But why did it hurt so bad?

Greta was out on vacation, so during her leave, things were extra lonely. Who knew she would miss Greta's unstoppable optimism and tasteless sex jokes? She walked over to the window and saw the bar that was once Riko's boarded up with a 'For Lease' sign. The town was pretty quiet nowadays. Maddie didn't venture out very much after the attack on Tarrytown, but every so often, she would hear a motorcycle and get a bit on edge. She rubbed her arm as it sat in the blue sling from the doctors. The wound's pain had subsided with some fantastically effective pain meds, and these days just itched like crazy. She finally had an interesting war story to tell at those dreaded dinners with her landlord, Ms. Lamont, but who the hell would even believe her?

Hi, I'm Madeline Ardelle. I'm a veterinarian who used to be a nice girl. I also stole a police car, got shot and shagged a sexy werewolf named Aidan...and yes, if I could do it all over again, I would.

The town was slowly going back to normal. Actually, the Sheriff did so much cover up for her and the ShadowShifters, she teased that he should've worked for the Nixon administration. Even going so far as taking her to a hospital in Iris instead of Bridgepoint, where there were too many familiar faces. Though he did get to chew her out for leaving him stranded all the way to the hospital, he didn't press charges. McTiernan made it clear it was best for both of them to forget it ever happened. *Ha, easier said than done.* On most days since she had been discharged from the hospital, he would come by and check on her, but since he came yesterday, she wasn't expecting him today.

She didn't have nightmares, but Maddie was with memories of Aidan in the night. She had missed him terribly, and her heart cracked just a little more every time she ignored his calls. Maddie had to, or else she would've never be able to let him go. Every day in the hospital, she would wake, hoping to see him standing there. The flash of his bold, green eyes. His gorgeous smile and laughter that made everything feel like it was going to be okay. How he held her, squeezing her hips as if to mold her against him like clay. The touch of his skin. She groaned to herself. She'd give anything just to rub her fingers against the scruffiness of his face. *Ugh, I'm just torturing myself.*

Finally deciding to close up, she grabbed her bag when she heard the purr of a motorcycle engine. It made her heart stop as she saw the headlights turn off through the windows. Suspecting Thesians who may have come "collecting" for her as she'd played a part in the events, she reached behind the counter and grabbed her baseball bat, ready to bust anyone's face in who wasn't friendly. No one was gonna scare her away from her home.

Maddie took a deep breath, opened the door and rushed outside with her bat aimed and ready. "Who's out here?"

Before she could blink, a force grabbed the bat and whipped her around to face the stranger who embraced her. Protesting, she stopped mid-gripe as she saw a familiar face.

"Shhhhhh." Aidan coaxed in his deep whisper. Her intimidating game face softened as she recognized him, and he fell in love with her all over again. Her quiet badassery was an insane turn-on. "You've gotten pretty handy with that thing." He stared into her bright brown eyes that he missed so much. He was tired of feeling the pang in his heart when he thought of her name or her sweet face.

A storm of emotions bombarded Maddie in seeing him again. Most she couldn't comprehend. "Aidan..." Towering over her, he leaned in and claimed her lips. She moaned at the taste of him and how rich she craved it. Maddie shuddered against him as if this was the first time he'd ever touched her. It had been too long, much too long without him. His hands squeezed her hips ever so gently and pulled her closer to him. Her body didn't want to pull away, but her emotions had her needing to know his reason for coming into her life again. She'd worked so hard to try and let him go and that journey was painful. Ignoring his calls made her cry so much, she had to wear shades to work for a week to hide her swollen eyes. They couldn't keep doing this to each other. Maddie pulled her hands back gently. "What are you doing here?"

Aidan pushed a tendril of hair away from her face. "I've missed you, xerhmon. It's been a hard couple of weeks."

Maddie's eyes stung. They were definitely rough for her, too. At one point, she entertained the idea of just packing up and leaving Bridgepoint altogether. Everything was a reminder of the man she couldn't have, and she missed him terribly. *Let him go. He will always need to protect his pack and there will be no room for you. Not long-term.* Her heart sank at her mind's negativity. "So, you decided to stop by and say hello?" She folded her arms defensively. "You shouldn't be here."

Aidan stepped back, dejected. "Do you want me to leave?"

"That's not what I meant." She plopped down on the steps of the clinic in defeat. "You should be with your people, Aidan. I understand that now. When I forced you to stay, it was because as much as I like to call you Superman, you can't be at two places at once. I know you wanted to be with me, but your people needed you more. I can't stand to see you in this tug of war. It isn't fair to you, so I made a choice. Please don't make this harder by popping back into my life, Aidan."

Aidan sat down next to her. His hand connected with hers as it rested on her lap. He glanced at her wounded arm in the blue medical sling and a knot formed in his stomach. He'd never wanted to see her hurt, and it tore him up inside when he couldn't see her. Now, the anguish on her face made it clear to him why it pained her to see him now. She'd never wanted him to leave---she didn't put up a fight because she thought he needed to be with his pack. She wanted to see him happy. It was why he loved her so much it hurt. "Maddie...look at me."

She turned and faced him with wells in her glossy eyes.

"I know why you made that choice, but I want you to know that I'm here because I love you and I want you with me." His breath caught as she squeezed his hand. "Everything you are, how you fought for my people and for me. The way you love and care for others - even when they don't deserve it. I love all of you, Madeline Ardelle." Aidan tried to keep his composure, but couldn't help his voice from cracking. He owed her this honesty, and there was no room for bullshit. He couldn't imagine a life without her a part of it. The sheer thought of it was inconceivable. "I've never met anyone like you and all I want is to belong to you. I don't care what I have to do to make that happen, xerhmon. All I know is that I want you."

Maddie looked up at him smiling, as he wiped her tears away."I love you too, Aidan. I was so afraid to conflict you. To make you have to choose between me and your pack. I never want to do that to you."

Aidan gently kissed and nipped her fingers as he pulled her close. "I know. Which is why I'm here."

Maddie grimaced. "What are you talking about?"

Aidan stood up and looked out from the steps. "Well, the pack voted on finding a new place to build our new lives. A place that would allow us to live peacefully, happy and unsuspecting." He turned to her. "A place where their Lukos could finally be close to his beloved mate and keep a watchful eye on her."

Maddie sat quiet, her eyes widened at his words. "What are you saying?"

Aidan smiled and helped her stand. "I think you know what I'm saying. The pack is moving just outside of Bridgepoint, so I'm staying here." His hand smoothed her curls back from her gentle, awestricken face.

Tears gathered in her eyes and Maddie smiled. "Aidan, I..."

"Did you really think I would let you get away from me again?" He pulled her into his arms, his bright eyes staring into hers with that glorious intensity she'd grown to love. "I told you. You are amazing. I would be a fool to not have you in my life. You're everything I could ever want in a mate. In our tongue, we call them a *mylaigh*. A companion that loves unconditionally. That will fight for them till their very last breath. That will be there for their other half, no matter what." His hand brushed against her face, letting his thumb rub her trembling bottom lip. He reached down and put Ninon's necklace in her hand. "I want to be your mylaigh, Maddie. If you would accept me, I promise to live out my days loving and protecting you. Everything I have will be yours," Aidan lifted her hand with the necklace and put it to his chest. "Including my heart."

Maddie sniffed back tears and stared up at him. Who was this beautiful man? This creature that came out of the darkness one day to sneak into her life and turn it upside-down? All his flaws, his worry, his kindnesses--it made him perfect to her. His world was rough and dangerous, but so was the world in general. But that wasn't what frighten her. It was facing it without Aidan at her side. Maddie leaned in and kissed him deeply, putting her whole soul into it.

Trying to steady his composure, he softly broke away from her lips. "Sooo, was that a yes?"

Maddie laughed, feeling her face reddened at her bold behavior. "I'm sorry. I've really missed you, Aidan." She cleared her throat and locked eyes with the man who made her believe in love again. "Aidan, I love you and I accept you as my loving mylaigh. Forever and always."

A brilliant smile grew across his face as he scooped her up into his arms. Leaning his head against hers, with their eyes closed, he felt a bond between them that Arista herself couldn't break. She was his. His mylaigh. Come hell or high water, he would love and protect her at all costs. "I love you, Maddie." He gently claimed her lips as he felt her cool hand rest on his scruffy cheek.

Her big brown eyes sparkled as she smiled at him. "I love you too Aidan. *All of you.*"

EPILOGUE

A Year Later...

Maddie ducked her head out between the double doors of her clinic in the commune and smiled. "Alexei, you're up next."

Alexei frowned and shook his head. "Actually, I'm good. I'm just visiting." He instantly felt a smack at the back of his head from his friend, Edward. "Ow! *Asshole*."

Edward laughed. "Just get it over with, wuss. You train every day by sparing and getting kicked in the face. You can't get a shot?"

Maddie chuckled. She didn't remember Edward so brave either when it was his turn. "Edward, I don't need your assistance." Smiling at Alexei, she motioned to him. "Come on. It'll be quick. I promise." She winked at him, trying to be as comforting as possible. Since she started spending a percentage of her time attending patients at the commune clinic, she'd learned some fascinating things about her husband's people. For one, none of them liked getting shots. It would be funny if she didn't have to constantly figure out new ways to stick them and comfort the biggest of babies. Onyx avoided her for a week after their encounter. *Everybody's got their something, I guess.*

Finally, Alexei stood up and sauntered past the double doors into the examination room. Maddie closed the doors and crossed her arms at her chest. "Okay, Alexei. What'll be? Human skin or wolf's skin?"

Alexei groaned. He hopped on top of the examination table. "Are you gonna have to take my temperature?"

Maddie nodded her head.

He cringed. "Human skin!"

She smiled and put the infrared thermometer to his ear to get a reading. "103.5. Very good." She turned and pulled fluid out of a vial into a syringe. As the needle filled, Alexei took a deep breath.

"Doc Ardelle. Is this really necessary? I mean, the wound's healed just fine. Our kind regenerates."

Maddie nodded. "Yep, you do, but as you get older, the process takes longer. Antibiotics help boost your system, so your gashes and gaping wounds don't stay gaping wounds all day long, for your high school friends to wonder about." She squeezed out some excess fluid and looked at him. "Okay, this is gonna sound weird coming from me, but I promise, the older you get, the words will sound more enticing."

Alexei sat quietly, not watching her, but the needle.

She shrugged. "Drop your pants, please."

Begrudgingly, Alexei's mortified face focused on the floor as he hopped down. This was way different than being naked out in the woods running with friends. This was the legendary Doctor Maddie. The one he and his friends had had the honor to save a while back. This wasn't some teenage Instagram fan; this chick was badass. Alexei always thought Doctor Maddie was not only badass, but the perfect example of what an awesome mate should really be. Human or Aristan. He knew it was years from now, but if he ever chose a mate, it would be someone like the Doctor.

His face flushed. Alexei unbuckled his pants, turned around to place on hand on the table, while letting the other drop his pants to his ankles.

Maddie took a cotton ball with alcohol and swabbed a little area on his cheek. "Now, take a deep breath. It's just a little prick." She finally gently punctured his skin and injected him when the door burst open.

Maddie and Alexei jumped at the intrusion, and their eyes focused on Aidan as he peeked inside. He trained his eyes on a shocked Alexei, who was scrambling to pull his pants up. Aidan growled. "What the hell is going on in here?" He pointed to Alexei. "What the hell do you think you're doing to my wife?!"

Maddie folded her arms. "Aidan!"

"Shit sir, I'm just getting a shot, that's all! I would never, ever..."

Aidan's frowned deepened. "Oh, so you think she's *ugly*?"

Alexei's eyes widened in shock. *WTF!* "No sir!"

Aidan shook his head, trying his best not to laugh."You better get the hell outta here before I lose my shit, kid!"

Alexei didn't hesitate. Finally fastening his pants, he ran past him and continued out the door. Maddie ducked out and yelled for him to come back behind Aidan's laughter. "Alexei! He's only kidding! Come back! I'm so sorry!"

She turned around to see Aidan keeled over, laughing till his heart's content at the joke he'd played on the young Alexei. Maddie smiled and gave a disapproving headshake. She pushed him, but that didn't stop his laughter. "That poor boy. He was just afraid of needles. Now I'll be lucky if I ever get him in this clinic again, you big bully."

Aidan finally sobered. "I'm sorry, baby. He's wound tight and reminds me of me." That was truer than he'd liked to admit, but nonetheless quite accurate. Since he'd had a chance to get to know the Aristans from the nearby towns, his world had opened up to a bigger network of ShadowShifters. Alexei's family belonged to a pack in Vermont, but ever since the visiting boy and his friends found himself saving Maddie one night, he'd continued to visit Bridgepoint, sparring with the pups of the pack. Just like he was as a young wolf, Alexei wanted to prove himself. But first, the boy had to learn how to relax. So, he'd decided to take a page out of Cam's book and screw with young wolf every chance he got. Aidan shrugged. "I just wanted play Cameron for once. You see his face?"

Maddie threw the syringe away and pulled off her gloves. "Cameron doesn't need any clones, thank you very much."

Aidan walked up to her and curved his arm around her waist, pulling her against him. "You do have a point. I don't think the world could handle another Cam."

"*And* I expect you to be a better role model for the younger troop. You may as well get some practice in while you can."

Aidan paused and arched an eyebrow. "While I can?"

A gentle, but knowing smile grew on Maddie's face as she took his other hand and led it to her stomach.

Aidan's eyes darted to her stomach to her eyes and his jaw went slack. "You mean..."

Maddie slowly nodded. "Uh huh. Confirmed with the doctor Wednesday. I didn't know when to tell you, but seeing as that it has shut you up, I guess this was as good a time as any." She paused as Aidan stood there looking at her. Not being able to read him, she suddenly felt exposed. "Please say something."

Then, as brilliant as ever, Aidan laughed and pulled her closer, into a kiss. Joy filled his heart and it was hard to imagine being any happier than he was right then holding her. Maddie had given him so much and the thought of them having a child together amazed and frightened him like the grandest of roller coasters. Arista help him, he was going to be a father. At that moment, he silently made peace with himself and vowed to be a father that Tiberius and Ninon would be proud of. As he inhaled the heady ginger scent of her curls, Maddie held onto him and giggled against his face. It was all she could do to express her happiness that Aidan was thrilled to be a father. Though Onyx had told her that hybrids had existed in the past, he said it was extremely rare. Leave it up to her and Aidan to beat the odds. This child was going to special, but no one would know how and in what way. They just had to wait. As long as he or she was healthy, Maddie didn't care.

Aidan pulled back to look fully at his mylaigh, his *mate*. There wasn't a strong enough word in neither the English language nor in Aristan that summed up what he felt for her. But the bond was as powerful as any force of nature he'd known. He felt it when she smiled at him, touched him or even said his name. She *was* love. Her very existence. Feeling his heart was about to explode, he kissed her again and released her with a sigh. "You're going to be a phenomenal mother, just like you are a phenomenal wife."

Steadying herself from the last kiss, he planted on her, she ran her fingers along the scruffy curve of his face, knowing he belonged to her. "That's good. I want you to keep saying that as the months pass by and my tummy continues to get enormous."

Aidan kissed her forehead. "I'll keep saying it till my last breath, xerhmon. Forever and always."

Tall, Dark & Deadly

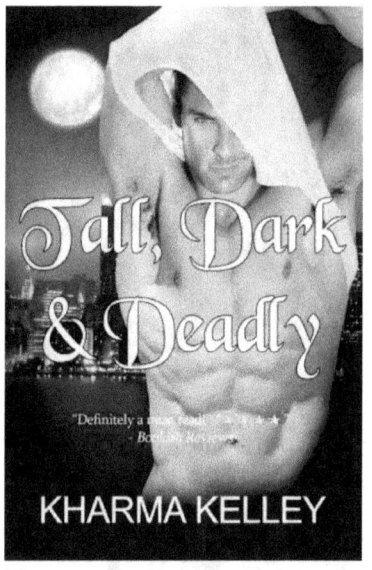

Available Now!

Chloe Hunter can't seem to stay out of trouble. Incarcerated by The Bureau after running amok for a century with a gang of vampyres, grifting and terrorizing humanity, she's ready to make up for her dark and naughty past. Luckily, when The Bureau would rather see her at the end of a wooden stake, in comes her new straight-laced boss, Ethan Raines who's got other plans. An enigmatic vampyre who finds her hybrid blood and sexy street prowess too irresistible to pass up, Ethan requests The Bureau to release her into his custody.

Her debt to society is to punish other supernaturals who break the law and cut them down. When Chloe's old gang involves her in a plot to unlock a mysterious box of woe, she's forced to make some hard choices that threaten to betray the trust of the man who's given her a second chance at life and love.

The Dead of Night

Coming in 2021!

After the fallout of the town of Bridgepoint, Devin is chosen as Alpha over a wider territory of New England and moves to New Hampshire to establish a new Haviscasi. It doesn't take long to realize that not only humans but fellow Aristans are turning up murdered in an strange, ritualistic fashion.

Devin's pack presence suddenly attracts the attention of the local authorities, along with the tenacious detective, Kaden Greene. A cop who